BEHIND SUNSET

BEHIND SUNSET

DAVID GORDON

THE MYSTERIOUS PRESS
NEW YORK

BEHIND SUNSET

Mysterious Press
An Imprint of Penzler Publishers
58 Warren Street
New York, N.Y. 10007

First edition

Interior design by Maria Fernandez

Library of Congress Control Number: 2024949875

ISBN: 978-1-61316-653-6
eBook ISBN: 978-1-61316-654-3

10 9 8 7 6 5 4 3 2 1

Printed in the United States of America
Distributed by W. W. Norton & Company

To William and to all my friends and family in LA.

BEHIND SUNSET

PART I

1

Pornography was making Elliot sad.

When he'd first taken a job as associate editor at *Raunchy* magazine, he'd expected a certain underworld glamour, at least, a little noirish romance perhaps, and for sure, a lot more money. After all, despite being strictly legal, he was dwelling in the realm of what the cops on TV still sometimes called vice, and if vice didn't pay, then what hope was there? So far, he'd barely left the office. Soon enough, adventure and desire would come knocking, followed swiftly by danger and fear, but for now they were nowhere on his morning to-do list. Today there was only one unsolved mystery open on his desk: What was there left to say about a naked woman?

He lifted his eye from the loupe and sat back from the light box, where the sleeve of colored slides glowed like a stained glass window illuminating the stations of the pornographic passion play: clothed, half clothed, naked; touching herself here and there; standing, sitting, splitting. He picked up the smudged photocopies of the model's ID and signed release: Leontynka Smejkol, citizen of the Czech Republic. She looked pale and glum in her passport photo, bundled in a scarf, a depressed sister to the prancing, eager fawn in the slides, sprawled and squeezed into a dozen contorted forms on the cheap bedroom furniture Elliot recognized from other sets by the same photographer, slathered with makeup, hair piled and permed, dressed in black plastic hip boots and gloves, and smiling like Miss America.

But no all-American gal would give so much for so little. According to the model release, she had received two hundred dollars, which a top stripper could earn dancing on a single lap. Since the collapse of the Soviet Union, it was mostly Eastern Europe and Russia that fed porn's insatiable hunger for new bodies. Was poor Leontynka being exploited? Of course. But this was also no doubt the most money she'd ever made, probably for the easiest, least degrading work.

So what was Elliot's excuse? He was a highly educated, twenty-five-year-old American pissing away his prime for $6.9230 an hour after taxes if you figured on a ten-hour day. Unlike his employer, he didn't deduct for lunch. He reasoned anytime his job required him to be where he wouldn't otherwise choose, it was work. He also, therefore, included his driving time to and from the office, as well as the five-block walk he made twice daily to the closest free, legal street parking.

For Elliot, work was war. Or rather, since it was all too obvious who'd won this class war, work was a kind of POW camp. You did what you had to do to survive, jumped and saluted, laughed at the commandant's jokes and pledged allegiance, but in your heart you remained an enemy and you kept up the struggle with what few weapons remained at your disposal: complaining, loafing, petty theft. Every illicitly licked stamp or pilfered pen was a tiny raise, each afternoon crossword session in the men's room stall a triumph of the human spirit.

That said, his piss-poor attitude had an upside, efficiency-wise. It made him a demon for deadlines: he'd rather slit his wrists than spend his off-hours worrying about the unwritten copy sitting on his desk. He reserved that personal time for thinking about how he wasn't getting paid enough. He'd become a kind of porn magician, glancing at each photo just long enough to improvise a backstory for the inane action, pulling aliases out of a name-your-baby book, and churning out the copy as fast as his fingers could type, often in a single draft:

> "I have always fantasized about feeling two dudes in my butt at one time," big dreamer Donna declares. "Everyone laughed and said it was impossible. But I wasn't going to let negative thinking hold me back and ruin my Christmas!"
>
> "I'm a romantic at heart," lovesick Leslie sighs. "That's why I shave my quim. Every morning I think, this could be the day I meet my prince."

Elliot sat back with a sigh and flexed his tired wrists. Could he get workman's comp for porn-related carpal tunnel? The saddest part was that this was by far the best-paying job that he had ever held and the one that made the best use of the master's in English and Comp. Lit. that he'd ruined his credit struggling to pay for. It was, frankly, the only time he'd been published anywhere or that anyone had ever paid him to write. If he'd sold his soul, then what was truly obscene was the price. The wages of sin were, as it turned out, disappointingly low. Such was the labor of lust.

His duties at *Raunchy* were several, and included editing, journalism, and fiction writing, often all at the same time. Under an assortment of pseudonyms, he would write an article on, say, "How to Spot a Nympho," fill it with expert medical quotes and statistics drawn from his own aching head ("A nympho will sleep with anyone, a slut will sleep with anyone but you"), write the cover lines hyping it, then edit and respond to the letters attacking it, in one case promising an irate reader that he would fire himself. He also wrote his own letters, scorching confessions of debauchery attributed to some Suzanne or Collie or Jill, then answered the mail the girls received from eager suitors, mostly men in uniform—soldiers, sailors, convicts, and the occasional janitor. But the heart of his work, the lifeblood of the magazine, was the girl copy. These little soliloquies that accompanied the photos, the fake names and ridiculous personalities he invented each month, were, he was told, why men bought the magazine. Elliot found it hard to believe. Text seemed entirely superfluous, and he was sure you could reprint the phone book next to an open crotch shot and sell just as many copies, but the mail proved him wrong. If Elliot said that a moonfaced blonde diddling herself in a VW Microbus was a "flower child" who adored Jerry Garcia and longed to spread "free love," some old freak wrote in claiming to be a dead ringer for the bearded fat man. If he had a single mom with three kids and fake pointy nails call herself a hungry cougar, a whole frat house volunteered to be her prey. It seemed that they weren't buying sex after all; they were buying desire, the chance to fantasize, and Elliot's overheated brain was the sweatshop that provided the dreams.

There was something oddly poignant about these letters. They were protestations of faith, gestures of hope that, against all evidence to the contrary, there existed some enchanted valley somewhere full of women whose highest aspiration was to get down and dirty with them. After all, utopia is where the desires of others somehow exactly match your own, and in this way porn, like the romance novels these men's wives and sisters and moms might be reading (when they weren't peeking at *Raunchy* too), was a species of fantasy. Or perhaps sci-fi. They seemed happy just to know the promised land existed and that he, their surrogate, was reigning in it as a prince of the realm. "You have the best job in the world," a typical fan letter ran. "I wish I could be a *Raunchy* editer."

Even more astounding to Elliot than the men slathering over the make-believe women, were the scores of eager, real-life women begging for a chance to become make-believe. Each issue contained amateur photos sent in by ordinary women in polyester lingerie with framed portraits of the kids visible on the wall in the background, posed on waterbeds with whiskey bottle collections on the shelves or proudly displayed atop a bright red Camaro. Elliot spent many hours with his nose inches from these Polaroids and blurry snapshots, reading the questionnaires the contestants filled out and spotting, through his magnifying glass, the objects in their homes and trailers, the Jesus posters and World's Best Mom mugs, the self-help books and Marilyn Manson CDs. Many were strippers from Lubbock or Cincinnati or Myrtle Beach, hoping for an "as-seen-in-*Raunchy*" boost to their résumés, and some were hopelessly reckless party girls headed straight for rehab or prison—like Deenie, an eighteen-year-old dropout captured butt naked on the kitchen table with a homemade tattoo on her leg that read *Beer* in a first-grader's slanted scrawl—but most were regular folks: secretaries, dental hygienists, waitresses, and warehouse workers with husbands and kids. Maybe, if you spent all day separating chicken parts or answering 411 calls, spreading your legs for the world felt like freedom and empowerment. The most popular fantasies were lesbianism, being the star of a gang bang, or having sex in the rain, and the number one hobby was writing poetry. That had once been Elliot's hobby too.

Of course, these were Elliot's relatively normal readers. Every morning's mail delivered smeared, scrawled, misspelled pleas and provocations from the insane, the perverse, and the moronic.

> Dear *Raunchy*, I am a virgin (45 y.o.) who loves to masturbate outdoors. I am very excited that there are girls like Brittany in your June issue who like to have sex in cars, buses, elevators, and playgrounds. I would definitely subscribe to your fine magazine but my mother wouldn't allow it.

> Dear *Raunchy*, as a natural, pure Aryan racialist I was disgusted by that race-traitor Chrissy *(Chrissy, Buck, and Leroy: 2 Black, 2 Strong, 2 Long)*. That slut deserves to die of AIDS. And so do you for printing it you Jew bastard.

> Dear *Raunchy*, Thank you for the hot, hot three-way with Chrissy. She's almost as hot as my wife. Do you know if those two studs could do her? She and me would both really appreciate it.

> To the Editor, Jesus tries to break into my house every night. He can make himself small to crawl in the drain or huge to crush me in his giant hand. Insane Catholic cannibal eat the flesh and drink the blood of God. My doctor said if I wrote you any more letters he would put me away. Can you help protect my rights to free speech and religion?

> Dear Editor Sir, I am wrongly incarcerated for a crime I did not commit. Can you help me get a new lawyer and send some free magazines?

> Dear *Raunchy* Editor, Why don't you show more Dutch girls with very large bottoms and blond bobs?

Elliot slouched forward, face in his hands. There was no end to this parade of human folly. Like Miss Lonelyhearts, driven mad by his desperate readers' ceaseless pleas for answers where there were none, Elliot had nothing but lies with which to comfort his yearning flock. Weird as they were, at times their desires seemed no more ridiculous than his own: a job he liked and someone who liked him.

The door popped open, catching Elliot in this slump of despair, spiritually naked in his shirt and tie. It was the mail room clerk, a slightly younger soul in a slightly worse tie and mismatched shirt, his face still bursting with acne, his sweaty fingers staining the mail in his cart.

"Hey . . ." he mumbled, dumping yet another stack on his desk along with a copy of the new issue, hot off the press. "Cool issue."

"Thanks."

Elliot picked it up. November 1994. The cover lines blabbed about a feast all Americans will be thankful for, breast and leg lovers both, along with extra gravy and plenty of stuffing, but the real treat was stills from a scandalous home video featuring Eddie Hex, a washed-up metal drummer who'd built a career around hard partying, light Satanism, and heavy Brit schlock rock, and his wife, Sindy Lou, a bikini model who starred in a show about cops patrolling LA's beaches disguised as bikini models. Apparently there were no bikinis or cops on their yacht, just lots of drugs and champagne.

Ahoy, Mateys! Elliot's copy blared. *It's yacht rock around the cock with buoyant beach babe Sindy and drummer hubby Hex, who shows off his stick work on this cooze and booze cruise!*

The response from the lower regions of the media world had been uproarious, with the tabloid press, afternoon trash chat shows, and late night comics gleefully jumping into the warm water. Flipping through, even Elliot had to grin. His phone rang and he picked up.

"Gross," he said.

"You're dead, mate," a smoky British throat gargled. The accent was extra-thick working-class English, the scratchy, boozy timbre pure scotch. "I'll rip your bollocks off and feed 'em to me bulldog, you fookin' tosser."

Alarmed, Elliot asked, "Who's speaking please?" his voice cracking, which alarmed him even more. The voice cackled and hung up. Great. The first death threat of the day. At least it woke him up, adrenaline coursing through him like no espresso ever could. His hands shook. He sat down and used his tie to dry the sweat that beaded on his forehead, despite the frigid AC. You'd think you'd get used to it, but he never did. All he'd really done was answer an anonymous email offering the tape, then exchange a copy for a first payment with some messenger on a motorbike who never even removed his helmet.

Breathing deep, Elliot checked his watch: 11:31. One more photo set before lunch. Sipping lukewarm coffee, he reached for the next folder on his pile, the immediate, urgent, right-now pile, that is. The bodies were stacked everywhere in his small office. The teetering towers of folders reached past his head, organized into Girl, Girl/Girl, Girl/Boy, and Other. He'd tried, at first, to create substacks based on hair color, costume, and so forth, but it quickly became clear that was impossible, like trying to sort snowflakes in a blizzard.

This folder, however, was special. It contained next month's cover girl, a spot still personally chosen by the boss and founder each month, in this case January. (Not that January was really next month. Since newsstand shoppers tended to buy whatever seemed newest, porn magazines had started competing to be earlier. By this point, the January issue would come out in early December, which meant it had to be in production well before that.)

Elliot could see what his boss had seen in Miss January. Yes, she was lithe and lovely with auburn hair tumbling over narrow shoulders to a snowy bosom, a lucky combination of youth and genes. But that was true of thousands of LA women—everyone here had been the cutest girl or boy in high school. One thing about Hollywood: even a nebbish like Elliot could go to dinner and be waited on by the King and Queen of the Prom. What was extraordinary about this model was her ordinariness. With her wide grin and sparkly blue eyes, she looked . . . nice. This was the sad truth at the heart of Elliot's business: research showed, over and over, that whatever *Raunchy*'s readers thought they wanted—bigger, harder, softer, wetter, weirder, badder—what they instinctively responded to, what made them stop and hand over money, was a sweet smile and kind gaze that seemed to be just for you. It was rarer than it seemed. After all, how many of us really live next to the girl next door?

And this girl—what was her name again? Egad. Crystal Waters!—Crystal had that homemade goodness coming out of her ears. Or eyes. Or something. Honestly, it troubled Elliot a little. He realized, as he crouched over his light box again, staring into the loupe, that he was pressing down hard enough to leave a ring on his cheek, as if instead of staring at a two-inch colored slide, he'd been peering into a microscope, studying some exotic life-form, or better yet, into a telescope, gazing up at the heavens. In other words, he was daydreaming, which was something he could only afford to do at night. Yet, he found himself feeling—not turned on or amused, shocked or tickled—but touched. She seemed real, even familiar somehow. Was it possible they'd used her before? He flipped through the sheets of slides, searching for the paperwork that accompanied each set, which would give him her real name and location. But there was nothing. He checked his desk, the floor. Nope.

This was unheard of. Existing as they did one small step inside the law, perpetually prepped for a raid or a lawsuit, they were absolutely scrupulous about such matters. Elliot was trying to decide what to do about this, and trying to think of a way not to have to do anything, when right on cue, his phone buzzed. This time Elliot jumped, as if his fight-or-flight response had been triggered, but since neither was possible he just sort of ejected from his desk chair for a second, then cleared his throat and lowered his voice to a laconic baritone:

"Hello?"

"Hey, it's me." It was Margie, the art director and his real-life girl next door, calling from her own office down the hall. "You sound weird. Do you have strep again? It's from the AC. I told you to bring a scarf to work."

"No." He breathed a sigh of relief and sat back into his seat. "Just deep in creative thought."

"Well then, you better wake up," she said. "The Ear Guy is here."

2

Margery Chow, dimpled and bespectacled, with an Alice band on her long black hair and an angora sweater protecting her shoulders from the AC, was a recent art school graduate who got up early to paint and play with her cat, dressed in vintage clothes she hunted in the thrift shops of Venice, and was a fan of B (and B minus) movies, underground comics, and the bad, old Hollywood.

"Hey, Margie," Elliot said, and then, as he came around the corner of her desk and saw her screen: "Good Lord."

Her high-end monitor was filled with a high-rez blowup of a delicate pink orifice, elegantly curved and coiled like the inside of a seashell, bristling with fine gray-black hairs. This was one opening into the human body that no *Raunchy* reader had ever drooled over. Yet. In the chair beside her, where Elliot usually sat on his visits, a bald man in a suit and tie was carefully shifting back and forth, gazing at the glowing screen through his eyeglasses, then removing them and peering down through a magnifying glass at several more gorgeously colored prints on the desk, marking them with a red grease pen and muttering to himself. Elliot glanced enquiringly at Margie, who shrugged back. This was The Ear Guy. Apparently, each person's ears are as unique as fingerprints, and much easier to obtain through a telephoto lens. The pair in question belonged to a hard-right congressman, one of the loudest railing against the sinfulness of rappers, porn merchants, video gamers, and Hollywood stars, all dwelling in the Sodom and Gomorrah of New York and LA, which happened to also be the only two places Elliot had ever lived.

Elliot reached for the folder, which contained stills from the video from which the giant ear shots had been blown up. The original tape showed said congressman, a thin, dour, gray-haired man in a blue suit, parking outside a motel in the afternoon, then walking to a door accompanied by a handsome, much younger man in a sleeveless T-shirt and tight jeans, sporting an outdated '70s look of full, frizzy hair carved into a round bush and a handlebar mustache along with dark shades. They entered the room together and shut the door that bore the number 23. The next scene, shot through a window apparently, showed the interior of room 23. In a setting even dingier and less romantic than one of Elliot's photo sets, the congressman embraced his pal, they disrobed—the second man was tan, lean, and beautiful, a head taller and a couple of decades younger than the congressman, with a tattoo of what looked like a winged skull between his shoulder blades—and then the public servant knelt in close consultation with a favorite body part. Not the ear.

Raunchy had bought the show and now they were trying to ensure that, if they ran these highlights and got sued, they could prove, legally, what was quite obvious to the naked and illegal eye: when he wasn't excoriating sinners, the congressman gave great head. Elliot sat and waited, watching the ear expert, who made his living testifying in trials, usually for the prosecution. The expert's own ears lacked lobes while being a bit oversized and floppy. Was that a source of secret inner sadness? Was he a kind of fetishist? And why, really, did a close-up of one fleshy portal elicit so much more madness than another?

Elliot recalled the night, a couple of months before, when he'd sat here sharing a very different view. There'd been a little party in the conference room; it was Karen from HR's birthday, chocolate cake and sparkling wine. Feeling a little bubbly, and looking a little rosé, Margie had sidled up to him. "I can't believe the Eddie Hex and Sindy Lou tape's right upstairs."

"I know, but what good does it do us sitting in the vault?" Elliot asked.

Margie shrugged coyly. "Might be someone happened to figure out the combo."

"What? How?"

Margie demurred, explaining that she trusted his "integrity" but not his "maturity," which sort of made sense when he thought about it, so he fetched more cake and wine while she snuck upstairs and got the tape.

They sat side by side at the monitor, laughing as the two long-haired celebrities cavorted naked on a yacht that cruised in pilotless circles. Neither had tan lines, but he had far more wrinkles. They laughed hardest when the famous blonde knelt before the graying rock star and, aiming the camera at his own manhood, he was heard to mutter "Awesome." It was also revealed that neither of them could roll a joint—apparently assistants usually took care of that. Margie and Elliot laughed and cheered. Then, as the couple got down to business, bumping and thrusting and moaning and groaning, an uncomfortable silence descended. Elliot almost thought he saw Margie blushing, but who could be sure in the dark? Besides, they were both completely desensitized at this point, weren't they? And he was sure he'd heard her use the term "girlfriend" more than once in a specific sort of way. Perhaps her cheeks were merely aglow with alcohol and sugar. Still her sidelong glances and heavy breathing seemed undeniable. Moving one centimeter at a time, he tried for a kiss, sort of, if you can imagine a snail making a pass at a butterfly. But as he leaned in, the chair swung abruptly on its spring and his champagne dashed forward, swamping the cake and rushing into the VCR's maw, threatening the precious tape.

"Oh my God!" Margie had cried, leaping to her feet and hitting EJECT. It was okay, just a little damp, but from then on his Margie policy had been strictly hands off. He did try and get the combination again. She had stroked her chin thoughtfully. "Let's just say that you see it, but you never really notice it."

"I don't get it. Give me a hint."

She laughed at him. "That is the hint, dummy. The clue's right there in your face. Speaking of which, you've got chocolate on your chin."

❖

The Ear Guy looked up from the magnifying glass. "It's him," he said, and put back on his own glasses.

"You're sure?" Margie asked. "You'd testify to it? A hundred percent?"

He nodded. "I identified sixteen points of comparison. That is 99.9 percent likely."

"Thanks, Doctor," she said, shaking his hand. He stood and gathered his gear. "Send us your invoice." As he left, she swiveled to Elliot, who took his chair. "Looks like we're in business. Now we just need to call the lawyers and tell them our asses are covered."

"Better tell security too. And the mail room." Elliot passed her the file with the photos of Crystal Waters. "And while we are covering asses, why doesn't she have any ID?"

Margery raised her eyebrows toward heaven. "Word comes straight from on high. Apparently Miss Crystal's real identity is a secret. But you'd better check."

"Shit. He's not in is he?"

Margery shrugged. "I haven't smelled cigars."

"I wish you could just peek in the vault for me."

She tapped her keyboard and a fuzzy pink crevice more familiar to their readers appeared on her screen. "Not this time my friend."

❖

Elliot left the elevator on the building's top floor, known colloquially as the Vatican Suite. The gleaming reception hall was done up with wood paneling, tasteful antique furniture, and Tiffany lamps, all presided over by a gigantic oil portrait of Elliot's boss, Victor, and Sarah, his deceased wife, standing happily beside her husband at their tenth wedding anniversary party, back when he could stand. She'd been gone for five years. Elliot crossed a gorgeously patterned carpet, longer than his driveway, to the mahogany desk of the receptionist, Miriam, who sat before the vault.

With her kohl-lined eyes camera ready, and her impossibly curvaceous proportions sheathed in a pinstripe suit, wide lapels revealing cleavage like the San Andreas fault, Miriam was the only employee who actually looked like a porn star, though she had been hired originally as a nurse. Rumor had it she was one of Vic's overseas relatives, receiving her medical training under fire in Chechnya or Afghanistan. She eyed him like a small animal she might not bother to kill, until he was directly before her, then spoke in her mysterious accent.

"Jes?"

"Hi, Miriam." He tried smiling, "It's me, Elliot from, uh, downstairs."

She exhaled impatiently. "I know who you are," she admitted, then looked down at the large bound calendar before her. "I don't see any appointment."

"No, no . . ." Elliot assured her. The last thing he wanted was to go through those double doors to Vic's palatial office. "I just wanted to tell you that the congressman's ear checked out. So I need to make the second half of that payment."

Miriam nodded and began entering it in her ledger. Elliot cleared his throat.

"Also, I had a question. The January cover girl. I was told her ID and release are up here. I wanted to check. I know how careful Vic is about legalities." Her nostrils trembled in annoyance and she narrowed her eyes at him. "If you don't mind," he added, trying to look sweet. "Please." Then, with a sigh of impatience, she stood and turned to the infamous vault.

The vault was not quite a vault. It was a large safe, the modern kind with a keypad, about the size of a closet, set in the wall behind Miriam's desk. In it sat copies of two separate forms of ID and a model release for each and every person to appear in the magazine—proof of age and consent, ready and waiting for the FBI to storm in, in which case they still had to get by Miriam's icy glare. The safe also contained the scandalous secret photos, videos, documents—dirt or gold depending on your view—that *Raunchy* bought and sometimes published. But that was only the tip of the red-hot iceberg. There were the goodies Vic bought and did not print too: celebrities, CEOs, judges, and ministers all caught with their pants or panties down. Some said the reason the great powers never really went after Vic was due to the embarrassment of riches in this vault.

Now Miriam fingered the keypad and swung back the door, giving Elliot a fine view of her stocking tops but blocking the inside of Aladdin's cave. Elliot meanwhile scanned the room, looking for the combo. He imagined it written on the chair where Miriam sat, like a hen guarding her eggs. She rummaged a bit, then shut the vault and re-perched on her seat, handing Elliot an envelope of cash.

"No," she said, severely, making a note in her ledger. "The girl is not inside there."

Fuck, Elliot thought. "Thank you!" Elliot said, and nodding and smiling, he backed into the elevator, glancing at the clock on the wall. One minute to twelve. At least it was lunch.

Elliot locked his office door. He took off his tie, being careful to pull it over his head without undoing the knot. He couldn't tie it himself, and since this was the only one he owned, he got one of his housemates to do it for him, then simply pulled it on and off each day. It was badly creased and developing a tendency to veer off to the left like an unruly vine, but Elliot wasn't about to spend any money on new clothes. Next, he took off his shirt and sat down, stripped to the waist, to unwrap the sandwich he'd brought. Despite having to dress in business attire at this job, he was still a hopeless slob when eating and he cut down on dry cleaning costs by having lunch alfresco.

He was wiping the mustard off his chest when the phone rang and he reluctantly lifted the receiver. "Elliot Gross?" he asked, as if not entirely sure.

"Y'all like the videeeo?" a deep Southern voice twanged out, sweet as syrup and obviously, ludicrously false. "Ready to contribute to the good congressman's election fund?"

"Yes," Elliot said. The original call offering the tape had been from an equally preposterous Russian, KGB-style voice. "We're ready."

"Fine and dandy. Meet by the garbage in ten."

"Okay, but how will I know . . ."

"Pink polish." The connection broke.

Elliot dressed and took the elevator. He was dying for a cigarette and by the time the elevator touched down he had the filter clamped between his teeth and the lighter out. The flame was going before he hit the door, and the second his shoes touched cement, he ignited. He sucked in deeply and held the smoke awhile, nestling it in his chest, before letting it out in a long, cleansing stream. The nicotine passed into his lungs, through his blood, and rose to coat his brain. That was it. Although he would take a hundred drags in the next half hour, he had already experienced the only pleasure this habit would bring him. It wasn't even a cigarette that he wanted. He just wanted to not want one for a while.

Elliot walked rapidly, exiting through the rear of the building. Out front, where the six-foot-tall *Raunchy* logo stood proudly under American and Californian flags, tourists were busy taking photos. Occasionally someone flashed their goodies for the cameras, and a couple of times security had to chase off a naked wannabe, but mostly they lined up and snapped each other exactly as if they were in Disneyland posing with Mickey. Elliot headed toward the alley where the trash was collected. A loud honk shook him from behind. He turned to see a midnight-blue Lexus at the curb. The tinted passenger window lowered, just a few inches, and a slender hand waved out, the long nails painted a shining pink. Elliot put the envelope in the hand and it withdrew, window rising. The car sped away, drawing honks as it rolled a stop sign and joined the traffic's flow.

Heading back to the trash cans, he lit another cigarette. This was where he came to smoke and think deep thoughts. For instance: How old did a man have to be before he could officially declare himself a failure, and did he need to have a specific goal he'd fallen short of achieving in order to do so? When could you gracefully drop the idea that you had the potential to be something other than yourself?

Then he saw the kids. They were young, maybe eleven or twelve, and running full out, but also laughing hysterically. "Get back here, you little shits!" a voice boomed behind them. "Think you can ruin my goddamn car!"

Curious, Elliot poked his head out of the alley and saw a buff guy in designer jeans, tight T-shirt, and expensive shades pounding down the pavement. He'd bailed from a white Mercedes that was at the curb, door open, with a telltale streak of yolk across the hood. The two boys had egged him and now he was out for blood. The kids were fast, and no doubt their hearts were surging with terror, but they were also laughing with such total abandon that they wobbled on their skinny legs, losing ground. They couldn't help it. They were overcome with joy. Elliot took a step out, purposely looking the wrong way, and collided with the Mercedes driver, taking his momentum on the shoulder like a linebacker. He was knocked back as the guy stumbled into him, glasses flying.

"Hey! Out of the way!" the guy yelled as they both fell back against the wall.

"Jeez," Elliot said, playing dumb as the kids disappeared around the corner. "Sorry, but you came out of nowhere, man." He got up and offered a hand. Mercedes shook it off and stood, gazing longingly. "You okay?" Elliot asked, looking concerned.

"Yeah, forget it," Mercedes grumbled, picking up his glasses. He stalked back to the car and roared off.

As he watched, Elliot's own childhood rushed back to him, the grand adventures and petty crimes he had not thought of in years, he and his first crush, Christine Smith, of the long blonde hair and small white teeth, bombing a passing bus with snowballs. A well-placed shot had sent the bus into a drift, and when the enraged driver jumped out with the same immortal cry—*you little shits!*—they'd fled down alleys and through a basement window to hide and share the smooshed M&M's from her pocket. And that was where he'd had his first kiss, bestowed by the angelic Christine. Her lips tasted like melting chocolate. And since every debt to heaven must be paid, he'd faced judgment that very night, coming home hours late without the scarf his mother had knitted, the mother who'd been desperate, about to call the cops, terrified that he'd had an asthma attack and fainted from the cold air, and who'd made the now-cold soup, salted with tears.

His father had raged biblically, waving a spoon as his sister watched, thrilled by the drama and happy not to be the star of the show. "If I had a mother, and she made me soup, I would never be late," he declared, broth running down his wrist to the warped and faded numbers tattooed on his arm. "But in the camp we had dirty water with maybe one half of a rotten potato. And I never saw my mother again."

By now Elliot's own tears were flowing, not to mention snot from his defrosting nose, and he could feel his chest tightening, as if the snow crystals were within. He sneezed.

"See, I knew it," his mother said, pleased now that she was proved right. She handed him a tissue. "God bless you."

His father laughed, dunking bread. "There is no God. Stop crying and eat your soup."

3

Elliot returned to his office whistling a merry tune, but his good cheer flatlined when he saw the blinking button on his phone, and it curdled into fear once he pressed it. There was a message from Miriam: Vic wanted a meeting. At his house. Elliot shuddered. Ever since he'd been hired, his contact with the publisher and editor in chief of *Raunchy* had consisted of nothing but an endless stream of criticism and reproof, so that the mere sound of his master's voicemail, or more often the sight of his red marker on his copy, made Elliot cringe and yelp.

Victor Kingman, who had started out selling dirty playing cards on the subway in Brooklyn, now owned the entire office building where Elliot toiled as well as the *Raunchy* family of publications. He also owned a shelfful of mainstream magazines purchased with the cash flow from his filthy hidden spring, a fact of which the readers of *You*, and *Now*, and *Pleasant Gardens* were blissfully ignorant. He was a paunchy man in late middle age, one of those strong old guys whose gut looks like a sack of cement. His thinning gray hair was slicked back in corrugated streaks above a perfectly tanned and shaved face. His heavy facial bone structure and the meaty bags of his jowls gave his head the appearance of a creased and battered helmet from which sharp black eyes glared like slits in his skull. He wore custom shirts open at the neck, with a platinum watch the size of a clock radio on one wrist and a gold bicycle chain on the other. Diamonds wrapped the stubby, construction-worker fingers. In most respects he was no different from the other self-made men Elliot had worked for, except he was the first to occupy a gold-plated wheelchair and sport a diamond and ruby oval pendant, big as a serving platter, strung on a gold chain that gleamed like fire in the bushy gray wilderness of his chest hair.

It was these two items that had riveted Elliot's attention when he was first interviewed in that glass office overlooking Beverly Hills. Vic sat in his mobile throne like a Bond villain. He'd been shot by a white supremacist for publishing photos of white women with Black men. He'd also fought, and won, numerous obscenity trials, libel suits, and civil trials against everyone from preachers to Scientologists to the federal government. He insisted on sending complimentary copies of *Raunchy* to every member of Congress every month, despite their furious attempts to cancel. Along with being a smut peddler, and proud of it, he was a libertarian-anarchist whack job and provocateur who just happened to be worth a hundred million dollars. Half gangster, half zealot, all hedonist, he loved to fight most of all and kept his bodyguards and his lawyers by his side. It was, Elliot came to think, like working on a pirate ship, floating just off the coast of America.

Also present that day was Moishe, the overgrown Russian killer in the gray three-piece suit who was introduced as Vic's associate when Elliot arrived and whose handshake had made him want to drop to his knees and confess. Elliot felt him sitting there on the couch, just outside his peripheral vision, but well within range of snapping his neck off like a beer cap. He flinched every time Moishe laughed or grunted at Vic's monologue, like a thuggish Ed McMahon.

"I'm in the pussy business, pure and simple," Vic was saying. "I've known them all. White, Black, brown, and yellow. I like them shaved clean and smooth or hairy and wrinkled as my grandfather's ass crack when he snuck off the boat from Odessa. I like them sweet or sour, fresh and powdered, or dripping wet and ripe. All sizes. I love them deep and wide as a subway tunnel through which a dozen children have been born, or tight as the keyhole on a virgin's red leather diary in which she scribbles all her innocent young dreams." He grabbed his pendant and held it out as though bestowing a blessing. The light caught the diamonds and glared in Elliot's eyes. He reflexively raised a hand, as if to ward off the magic. "That's why I commissioned this from my own design. It's a great big vagina. And I'm proud to wear it, since that's what made me rich. And, Elliot, if you don't love and worship all these pussies as much as I do, without bias of any kind, then I'm afraid there's no place for you here at *Raunchy*."

Moishe grunted his approval of this and Elliot realized, from Vic's sudden silence and angry stare, that he was expected to say something.

"Oh, yes, sir. I do. I mean the love part. I can't say I've known as many vaginas as you, but . . ."

"Fair enough. We'll give you a shot," Vic said, lighting a gigantic cigar with a gold table lighter. "Karen from HR will show you your office and teach you how to use the voicemail."

After that, Elliot learned to avoid face-to-face chats with the boss, aside from sudden, frightening encounters in the elevator. Vic never greeted him by name or even acknowledged him, answering Elliot's stuttered good mornings or good afternoons with a vaguely annoyed stare. Even these meetings were soon curtailed by Elliot's growing sensitivity to Vic's cologne and cigar smoke. The building was, of course, now nonsmoking, but who was going to tell the landlord that? So, at the slightest whiff coming around a corner, Elliot would duck out of sight or run down the corridor, warning the other serfs, who scattered.

On the other hand, his written and voicemail communication was constant and warmly abusive. Vic, it turned out, was the most pedantically exacting and infuriatingly expert editor Elliot had ever seen. Every piece of copy he turned in came back, often just minutes later, crawling with red ink, blistered with queries and obscure proofreading symbols.

"*Come* is a verb meaning to arrive, or more colloquially, to experience orgasm. When describing ejaculate, the correct spelling is *cum*."

"Don't use *pussy* twice in one piece. It's a quim, a quiff, a snizz, a snatch, or a slice! Don't be lazy!"

The phrase "I wish I was licking you now" triggered a lengthy lesson on the proper use of the subjunctive mood.

Elliot was both impressed and depressed by the realization that he was woefully underqualified even for a job he'd thought beneath him. He'd slaved over his last batch of copy, desperately seeking the approval of a man he didn't even want to work for, the Harold Ross of porn, and as he exited the building, he swallowed a surge of fear along with his smoke, steeling himself to face not just dismissal or broken fingers, but a diatribe on English style and usage.

This time Elliot went out the front.

"Excuse me, sir?"

A clean-cut young fellow in a short sleeve button up, the kind of plaid shorts that looked pressed, and loafers accosted him. His blond hair was side parted and his pale face was already red with sun. He held out a camera.

"Could you take our picture?" He pointed at two other clean-cut types, standing in front of the *Raunchy* sign, eagerly waving.

"Uh, sure," Elliot said, reluctantly.

"Can I ask? Do you work here?"

Elliot nodded, taking the camera and searching for the trigger.

"Oh man, that is so cool. As what?"

"Senior associate editor," he admitted.

"He's an editor!" Blondie yelled at his chums. "Senior associate!"

They cheered, thumbs up, as he focused, and then said cheese, grinning big as he shot.

❖

Vic lived in the hills behind Sunset, a ridge that ran above the boulevard all through town, the green and blue canyons that sheltered the rich, while also letting them gaze down on the rest of us, sweating in the glare. Those winding switchback roads, shaded grottoes, and angular outcrops contained multitudes, hiding everything from Marlon Brando's reclusive compound to the site of the Manson murders. The Hills were uptown, the penthouse floors of the hierarchy, to which you self-promoted after you made your killing down in the flatlands.

Elliot wound his way north, through Beverly Hills and West Hollywood, west on Sunset, where he was stuck behind a Rolls Royce convertible. The driver, a shriveled man who looked to be in his eighties, like a walnut in a tracksuit and shades, stopped to pick up a blonde Amazon in her twenties wearing pink plastic short-shorts and matching platforms. Finally, the light changed and, gunning the engine on his feeble old car, he climbed up into the Hills. Now he had to be careful and follow the directions Miriam had left on his voicemail. The roads looped and swerved in curlicues, and street signs were fewer, or hidden by high shrubs and hanging branches. Immediately, the temperature dropped—a sure sign of luxury.

Vic's villa was like a clean, modern version of Don Ciccio's place in *Godfather II*. Elliot paused at a gate in the pink plaster wall, announced himself to the squawking speaker, then proceeded up the winding drive, past flower beds, grapevines on trellises, and cypresses nodding in the breeze. At the top he entered a courtyard with a burbling fountain at the center, clustered outbuildings, and rising above it all, the house, several whitewashed stories fitted with terraces and towers and drenched in a pink-and-purple foam of bougainvillea.

A bodybuilder in a white T-shirt and shorts, tight enough to show off various bulges, and dark wraparound shades, waved him down and guided him to a line of ordinary dusty cars parked safely away from the sleek Bentley and gigantic Humvee limo that slept in the open garage.

"Hi, how are you?" Elliot said as he got out.

"This way," the muscleman said, and turned.

"I'm fine, too," Elliot muttered as he followed the broad back. "Thanks for asking."

They walked a cobblestone path around the house, past rosebushes and under a blooming archway, emerging at the back, where a kind of sunken grotto opened up, complete with fake ruined pillars, pissing cherubs, armless Venuses, and priapic satyrs. Imperial purple-and-gold lounges and pink umbrellas were arrayed around a sapphire pool, in the center of which a nude woman floated on a heart-shaped red raft. Elliot goggled. The model, looking at nothing from behind her mirrored shades, was like a statue herself, perfectly still. Sunlight bounced around her. Elliot squinted, trying to confirm she was real.

"Hey, buddy!" A voice from heaven boomed. He looked up. From a terrace, a bearded photographer was behind a tripod, aiming a telescopic lens. He waved Elliot away. "You're casting a shadow."

"Sorry!" he yelled, then to the floating mirage: "Sorry, miss . . ." She didn't stir. Elliot realized his escort was already at a door.

"This way," he said, holding it open and beckoning Elliot in, though the glare of the sun made the interior nothing but a dark hole.

"There he is. There's the little motherfucker," Vic shouted as Elliot stepped through the door into Vic's study. He waved him in, cigar in the air, as Moishe, gently but firmly, steered him to a spot beside Vic's wheelchair. Most of the senior editorial staff were there already, grinning hard and perched on the couch or upholstered chairs. They were of the same general type as Elliot, awkward young men from Princeton and Cornell, still visibly stunned at how life had tricked them. The one old-timer present was Myron, the cartoon editor. A '70s throwback, bald in front but with the remnants of his once proud Afro still defiantly rising up around back, he had broken teeth and shaky shoe-leather hands, but, with a nip from his flask, he was still the only one able to draw the magazine's bandit-eyed mascot, Raunchy

Raccoon. They all turned to Elliot. No doubt Vic was going to make an example of him, perhaps by having Moishe hang him off a balcony while he conjugated the verb *to fuck*.

"Some of you," Vic boomed, waving a xeroxed sheet, "may remember this, if you read it and weren't too busy sniffing Wite-Out that I paid for."

It was a memo Vic had issued the week before, decrying the inferior quality of the "figurative" language the staff had been using to describe the human anatomy of late. Too many tired twats and ding-dongs. Too many clichéd boobs and balls. Vic had demanded that everyone coin new terms, promising a handsome reward for the best brainstorms.

"Now, I've called you all here because I'm happy to announce that at least one of you mutts can think a little." He snatched up another sheet of paper and handed it to Elliot. "Read that. Loudly."

Elliot looked at the page. It was his own submission, drawn from a four-page spread featuring a model he'd dubbed Triple D Danielle and titled "Wham Bam, Thank You Mams." He read haltingly. "Perhaps, we can call her breasts money bags or milk maidens. And for male ejaculate," he added, pronouncing the *ate*, "why not, gonad goo or nut butter?"

"Gonad goo," Vic roared, slapping Elliot on the back. Moishe barked out his approval. "Milk maidens," he shouted at his employees who burst into dutiful applause, smiling and congratulating Elliot, who blushed, looking down in shame to avoid the scorn in their eyes.

Clown, *ass-licker*, they were thinking, he knew, because he was thinking it himself. They were right to hate him.

"It was for that reason that I had him write the cover lines for our latest investigative exposé, which will be released to the press Monday and rushed into the next issue. Moishe?"

Moishe held up a mock-up of the December issue, designed by Margie, featuring the usual bikini-clad elf sitting on a randy Santa's lap, and the red and green "Hoes Hoes Hoes!" but now with the blazing headlines: "Inside this Issue: See Congress's Not-So-Proud (But Stiff)

Member! Horny Hypocrisy on Capitol Hill! Secret Meeting with Committee Head!"

Vic chuckled richly as he read the lines aloud, puffing smoke like a demon. Miriam came in, balancing a tray with flutes of champagne. "It's moments like this that make it all worth it," he said, reflectively, raising a toast. "All the work. All the sacrifice." His minions nodded in humble agreement. "We should all be proud of ourselves for doing our patriotic duty. We are on the front line, protecting free speech, free thought, and a nation of free individuals. Even if they put you in jail, or in a wheelchair."

The smiling young faces stopped nodding, looking a little sick. Only Moishe grunted his assent, and Myron said, "Hell, yes," raising a fist. "Truth to motherfucking power!"

"But this time, it's Elliot in the spotlight," Vic announced, "and from Victor goes the spoils." He opened a desk drawer, and Elliot felt the disgust in the room shift to envy. What would it be? A check, a raise, a Rolex? Surely, a man who once dropped a million dollars playing blackjack in Vegas would crown his new favorite with gold. Victor pulled out a gift box and everyone looked on as Elliot unwrapped it. The box contained a black satin bomber jacket with the *Raunchy* logo emblazoned in bright pink across the back and the title EDITOR embroidered in red over the breast. His own name was inside, stitched under the label. Vic raised a jeweled finger. "Now I want to see you wearing this gorgeous jacket, especially when you are representing us out in public."

"Wow. Thanks, Vic. I love it," Elliot managed, trying to keep his smile gripped in place as Moishe helped him into it like a puppet. Once again, his coworkers launched into applause, but louder now and full of the sincerest joy. They admired the jacket and demanded that he turn around to show it off while they clapped with glee. The merriment ceased only when Vic grew bored. "Okay, drink up. One glass each. We've got work to do." He pointed at Elliot, who was about to bolt.

"Except you. Hang around for a second."

Elliot nodded in surrender and slid back into his seat. Vic blew a smoke ring and then watched it dissipate, like a falling halo in the air.

"Elliot," he asked thoughtfully. "Have you ever been in love?"

"Love?" Elliot was startled, as if this were a trick question, as Moishe and Miriam both stared, awaiting his answer. As a matter of fact, he himself had often wondered the same thing. His relationship with his college girlfriend, which he had assumed would be a lifetime together in a room full of books, had melted away when she'd gone into a PhD program in Minnesota, and he, at loose ends, had made a series of poor choices that ended at this meeting with Vic. Her letters—once passionate paeans to Shakespeare and Shelley, grew cooler as she moved on to Barthes and Butler, then harsher with Foucault, and finally, after an inscrutable note on Derrida—had stopped completely.

"I think so," Elliot said. "Once."

"Twice for me," Vic said. "First my wife, of course, my soulmate. When I lost her, I lost my soul and I thought, that's it. My heart is closed for business. And for years it was. Till I discovered Crystal Waters."

Elliot stared, thinking of an actual bubbling spring at a fancy resort.

"Our January cover girl."

"Oh right, yes . . . the one . . . Miriam and I were just discussing . . ."

"She came into my life like the wind. And she left like a summer rainstorm. No . . ." He stopped and pointed his cigar at Elliot. "She came like a storm, full of lightning and floods, and left mysterious as a summer wind."

"I see."

"That's why I picked you to write her copy." He rubbed his cigar between his fingers. "You've got a feel for the language."

"I do? Well, thanks, but . . ."

"It's not just about sex."

"No. I didn't . . ."

"I want to make her a star. Girl of the decade. With your help."

"First of all," Elliot chose his words carefully, "let me say I'm honored. And touched. But you know . . . according to Miriam"—he gestured just slightly at her, as if afraid she'd bite—"we don't have ID or anything. Even a real name."

"I don't know her real name." Vic shrugged his massive shoulders. "She'd never tell me anything about her past. And I was afraid to ask. I didn't want her to slip away. And sure enough, she vanished without a trace." He pointed his burning cigar again. "That's why I need you to find her."

"Me? What about your lawyer?"

"He's on the case. I got a PI firm, too, checking the usual channels, but let's face it. People in our world won't talk to a lawyer or a detective. They will talk to a reporter from *Raunchy* though, wearing that official jacket. You can do it. I see how you handled that congressman thing. And with what you learn, you can write her the best damn girl copy any porn mag ever printed. Next to the best damn girl."

"Yes, sir. I'm on it," Elliot said, trying to sound like he meant it.

"One more thing." Vic tapped a thumb-sized ash into a cut glass tray that glittered in the light. "There's a certain item, a highly sensitive videotape that she might, or might not, have in her possession."

"She stole it?"

Vic waved that away in a scribble of smoke. "No, no, nothing like that. The copy I bought is safe in the vault. But it's possible she got her hands on the original and is thinking about doing something foolish with it."

"Selling it?" Elliot asked. "Publishing it elsewhere?"

"Maybe." Vic shrugged, lifting his hands and then dropping them. "Though I hope to God I'm wrong." He thumped the golden arms of his chair. "You know I'm in this chair for what I published, and I've never regretted it."

"Yes, sir."

"But that tape, it's different. It can never be seen. Handle it like nitro, understand? Don't look at it. Don't even touch it. Just call the bomb squad right here." He gestured at Moishe who gave him a solemn nod. "Got it?"

"Um . . ."

"You're the only one we can trust with this." Elliot tried to think of someone else as Vic looked him in the eye. "That's why you're my senior associate editor."

Sighing deeply, Elliot nodded. Vic reached out a hand and grabbed his knee. "Find her for me, son."

"Yes, sir. I'll try my best."

"I know you will." Vic sat back and took a big puff. "Meantime, I think you might be ready to tackle a full feature. Next month's lead story."

"Really?" Elliot brightened. "I mean, thank you," he said, and a spark of hope rose in his mind. Maybe he'd get to travel somewhere or tackle a free speech issue that didn't make him blush. As if on cue, Moishe hoisted a large carton onto the desk and removed a box illustrated with a nude photo of a blonde, blue-eyed woman. He yanked out a hank of fake blond hair attached to an emaciated plastic face decorated with painted-on blue eyes and a red hole of a mouth, like a shrunken head with bad makeup.

"The new sex dolls are in," Vic explained "And the *Raunchy*-licensed sex toys. I want you to take all these home over the weekend, fuck them, rate them, and give me 2,500 words for the special Valentine's Day issue."

❖

Elliot had looked forward to spending this weekend like he spent every other. He rushed to the video and convenience stores to stock up on movies, sweets, and cigarettes, then stopped at the Thai place that he ate at every night when he wasn't eating at a taco stand.

It was night when he finally got home, to a house on a quiet street: three bedrooms, hardwood floors, and a fireplace, all shaded by palms and citrus trees. (Elliot had thought they were limes till they turned yellow and became lemons.) It was a nice old house, he reflected as he pulled into the driveway and through to the backyard, tapping his remote control garage door opener. Unfortunately, he didn't live in it. He lived in the garage. The door rolled up like a curtain to reveal the stage of his squalid drama, ablaze in the headlights: a futon, a TV, a cardboard carton with a lamp on top. He unloaded his noodles, his smokes, his Cokes and candy, his videotapes and his dolls, and weighed down with all the ingredients for a weekend of wanton pleasure, stepped into his boudoir and hit the button to lower his metal wall.

He paid $450 a month for the garage, which theoretically included use of the bathroom and kitchen in the house, although his housemates, Feather, Area, and Sequoia, made it clear he was only tolerated, not welcome. Feather, the willowy blonde from Texas. Area, the vaguely foreign beauty with caramel skin and soft coal eyes. Sequoia, the second-generation hippie, whose idea of bohemian life was to jump on the Concorde at a moment's notice or take yoga at the same place as Madonna while everyone else was at work. None of them worked. They were always bumming cash from Elliot and yet they drove new SUVs, wore designer clothes, traveled, and ate out. Elliot suspected family money. He suspected escort service outcalls or strip clubs in the Valley. But the truth, he surmised, was that they were just too pretty to need money and too busy to work. They were no slackers. They never bummed around like him. They were up at dawn for Pilates and personal training. They rushed from massage to pedicure, from Al-Anon meeting to acupuncture. Porsches and Land Cruisers came and swept them away, limos brought them home. Their phones and pagers and answering machines never stopped beeping and yelling and vibrating. They were aspiring actress/models who, besides the occasional soap opera walk-on or dandruff commercial, never acted or modeled. But to think they were desperate or failures in the sense that Elliot was a desperate failure would be to miss the whole point. Aspiring actress/model was a type all its own, a lifestyle, and even if they didn't appear on sitcoms, they were still appearing in the sitcom that was their charmed life.

Elliot lived on the same lot as this life, close enough to smell it occasionally on the warm breeze, but separated from it by a yard full of their dogs' shit. They all had dogs, of course. Big ones. In the morning the pack chased him to his car, stamping his white shirt with muddy paws. At night, as he staggered in slippered feet to use the kitchen or shower, he stepped among their piles like a commando in a minefield, always forgetting what time the sprinklers were set to go off and explode under his robe.

Still, it was only right that Elliot live in the garage. In a city with few basements or attics, the garage was the appropriate place to house the deformed stepchild or ne'er-do-well half brother. Also LA was, famously, a city of cars, of freeways and parking lots more than buildings and people. Elliot had a driver's license when he moved here, but he'd never driven more than three or four times a year. He couldn't even pump gas, much less change a tire or open the hood. LA, however, was designed as a drive-through, and Elliot learned to live behind the wheel. The best thing would be to not even have a bed or chair in his garage, but merely hit his electronic door opener, roll in, park, and reach for his TV remote. It was as if the landscape only snapped into place and made sense when you sat in a moving vehicle and saw it revolve around you. Where were you, standing on the corner of such and such in LA? Nowhere. And walking to the closest store, a gas station, of course, for smokes, he saw no one but a cat. LA was warmer, cheaper, and more polite than New York but the coldest city Elliot had ever known.

4

Elliot slept in for as long as he could ignore the ringing phone. Each time it cried, at eight, eight thirty, nine, and ten, he came to life for a moment, considered facing reality, then rolled over and buried himself again. But by ten thirty he had no choice; he had to use the bathroom, which proved he was alive. Rather than activate his rolling metal wall, he grabbed his robe and opened a more discreet wooden side door, inset with a panel of dusty glass. He sneaked to the main house and back with coffee, then killed a couple of cigarettes while he considered his carton of loot and the shameful jacket, which had been tossed in a corner, the phone wailing like a neglected infant all the while. Finally, he picked it up.

"Hola?"

"Good morning. Is this the residence of Mr. Elliot Gross?"

"No comprendo, señor," Elliot sang out. "No hablo inglés."

"This is Mr. Crown from National Credit Corp calling regarding your outstanding debt. Defaulting on student loans is a serious thing and—"

"Lo siento, señor. Hasta luego." He hung up. Immediately, it began to ring again. He fetched a bicycle pump that was rusting in the pile of debris beside his garage and set to work inflating the plastic girls. He picked up the phone, cradling it on his shoulder while filling polyurethane buttocks with air.

"Joe's Pizza. Sal speaking."

"Elliot Gross, please."

"Hold on." He lowered his voice and put on a ridiculous accent. "Joe here, what's amattah for you?"

"This is Mr. Crown from—"

"Yeah, Mr. Brown, youse gonna order pizza pie or no?"

"Elliot," the voice on the phone said, "avoiding me isn't going to help."

"Okay, you call back when youa hungry."

He hung up the phone and tossed the pump aside. Hands on hips, he surveyed his domain and commanded that the orgy begin. It was shaping up to be quite a party. There was Lola, a pudgy pink temptress with puckered seams and pointed breasts that could take your eye out if you weren't careful. There was Tabatha, a brown girl with identical bright-red rubber rings for mouth, vagina, and anus and a shocking Afro that seemed made of cellophane. There was Lola Plus, Lola's big sister, with the same dead yellow hair and blue doll's eyes but with a separately inflatable bosom that the dirty-minded playboy could fill with warm water, milk, or scotch. There was Desiree, a saucy French number, with red hair and bush and an electric cord running out of her tush. The cord attached to a handheld control switch on one end and to what the box copy called a "vibrating orgasmic egg" on the other. This was a pleasure center hidden in Desiree's womb that would provide a lifelike shaking when you made love to her. Finally, there was Big Joe, a handsome brute with sandy hair and beard who sported a foot-long unit, impressive despite its tendency to jut off at an acute angle to the right. Although clearly all man, Joe did have a ring just like Lola's mouth attached to his behind, suggesting he was open to exploration.

At first Elliot just tossed his guests in a big pile on the futon, but the similarity to a heap of corpses was a turnoff so he arranged them around the room in cocktail party poses. Then he dug back into his treasure chest and pulled out the rest of his toys. Along with the usual glow-in-the-dark dildos and flavored ointments, there were state-of-the-art, deluxe items like the Starfuckers. These were *Raunchy*-licensed products, life-size, flesh-toned plastic models of genitalia, cast from the real models who appeared in the magazine. Apparently, pretending you were molesting the hacked-up body part of your favorite porn star wasn't just for serial killers anymore, though the toys actually just blew up into shapeless blobs of harmless plastic, suitable for teaching kids to swim.

Scariest of all, however, was the SuperStud line of sexual appliances. These were strap-on monsters, length and girth enhancers, and electric vibrating shaft-rings, equipped with belts and switches and jutting black rubber knobs. They came with ball stimulators, three-speed clitoral activators, and double-pronged attachments. Elliot imagined the experience to be like sticking your penis in a blender. What was he supposed to write about these things? *Battle-ready space-gladiator gear for the heroic pervert! A crotch-borne chainsaw you rip-start with a cord! The brave new age of Onan is here, and only the strong will survive!* Or should he warn readers about the risk of electrocution? *Use* Raunchy *Gear with caution—it's not a toy, it's a tool!*

There was a knock on the door.

"One minute!"

Elliot jumped up and looked around at the dolls and body parts everywhere. There was another knock.

"Just a minute. I'm coming."

He grabbed the dolls and began stuffing them into the wardrobe, but they wouldn't fit. Arms and legs kept popping out. He pulled the plug on Desiree and began jumping up and down on her chest, trying to squeeze the air out.

"Hold on. I'll be right there!"

Outside, two sturdy old ladies in hats and dresses were waiting, armed with a Bible and a handful of Jehovah's Witnesses pamphlets. Curiously, one pressed her head against the dirty glass of the door. She peeked in and saw a wild, unshaven man, wearing only boxers beneath his flying robe, stomping on a nude woman and kicking her carcass under a blanket.

"Oh, Jesus," she moaned, leaning back, fighting not to faint.

"What is it?" her friend asked, looking in. She saw parts of several bodies sticking out from the wardrobe. Elliot had Tabatha and Desiree in there and was grappling with Lola Plus.

"Lord help us." She turned and began running.

"Hold on. I'll be right with you," Elliot called, but when he opened the door, no one was there. Catching his breath, he looked over his garage. All the love dolls were hidden either in the wardrobe or under blankets and coats, forming odd piles around the room. Who had knocked? The mailman? Or had one of his roomies stopped by to ask him to kill a bug?

He went into the house but no one seemed to be looking for him, so he grabbed more coffee and came back out to his den, then lit a smoke and sat down on a box to gather his thoughts. It had been hard work assembling his playland and, as he unveiled his plastic playmates, he realized that, right up until this moment, he had avoided thinking about what he was actually going to do with these things. What did Vic think? That he would really have sex with them? Not even he could stand such abject humiliation. But then again, some men did, apparently, and paid for the chance. How could they be any worse off than he was? It was a sad and wondrous place, this world of men. The creatures born of men's desire stared back in agreement, fixing him with hungry eyes.

The phone rang again and Elliot snatched it up impatiently. "City morgue," he barked. "You kill 'em we chill 'em."

"What?" His mother shouted. "Who is this? What have you done with my son?"

"It's me, Ma. I was just kidding. It's a joke. I'm working."

"What kind of person jokes about that? I thought you were dead."

"Did you say you're working at the morgue?" This was his father, who had picked up the other extension in the bedroom, while his mother stood by the yellow kitchen wall phone.

"Why would he do that?" his mom asked. "He has a master's degree."

"Hey, it's a city job. Better than that fakakta magazine."

"Do you two want to finish this conversation privately?" Elliot interrupted. "Or is there a reason you called?"

"We called to see if you're all right, smart guy," his father said.

"You usually call every weekend," his mother added.

"Well it's Saturday morning," Elliot said. "The weekend has barely started. And I'm busy. Not at the morgue, I'm . . ." He looked at his inflatable guests. "Doing some journalism."

There was another rap on the door and he headed over, phone tucked under his chin. "Hang on, someone's here," he said, and cracked it open to find two cops pointing guns at him, with several more spread out behind them.

"Hold it."

"Freeze."

"Hey, what's going on?" Elliot asked.

"What do you mean?" his mother answered. "We told you it's the weekend."

"Put your hands in the air."

"Get on the ground. Face down."

Elliot tried to raise his hands with the phone in one and his cigarette in the other.

"Drop the phone, dirtbag. Drop it now and hit the fucking deck."

He dropped the phone and two cops charged him and pulled him out the door, pinning him on the ground. One, a hunk with biceps the size of Elliot's thighs, drove his knee into his back while the other, a mustachioed lunk, cuffed him. They ground his face in the grass. It smelled like shit.

"Hello? Hello? Operator, I've been cut off," his father's voice demanded from the fallen phone as more cops rushed into his garage. One of them hung it up.

Then an unmarked Impala pulled up with a squeal, and a sturdy Latina in an electric-blue pantsuit hopped out of the driver's side, hand on her hip holster. From the passenger's side, a tall, thin Black man in a tan summer suit eased out and followed at his leisure, setting a straw fedora atop his head. The heads of neighbors appeared over the fences on both sides.

"Detective Santos, Homicide," the woman declared to everyone. "This is Sergeant Anderson." She looked back to see where he was. He nodded, taking in the scene while she strode up to where Elliot was being held down by the two cops.

"Are these your dogs, ladies?" she asked his roommates. Feather, Area, and Sequoia had come out, holding coffee mugs, to see what was up. The dogs ran around barking. "Please call them off and then step inside for your own protection. This is a police action."

"Bunky, come!"

"Here, Leroy!"

"Here, Blue!"

The dogs ignored them and careened around happily, running in and out of his garage. The cops yanked Elliot up and dragged him to the rear steps of the house.

"Hey, not so rough," he complained. "What is this about?"

Santos peered at him. "We have a report of a possible multiple 187 in progress."

"What? I didn't see anything."

While the detectives guarded him, the other cops swarmed all over his garage, guns drawn, ducking around corners for cover and waving each other forward like on TV.

A dog ran out with a plastic vagina in his mouth.

"What the hell's that?" Santos asked.

Elliot shrugged.

"Blue!" Sequoia called. "Come show Mommy what you've got."

The dog ran over and dropped his treasure in front of them. It was chewed and drenched in slobber, but still clearly recognizable.

"Jesus, Elliot, that's so gross," Feather said.

"It's not mine," Elliot explained. "I need it for work."

Santos snorted. "What work?"

The garage door began to rise, and everyone gathered to look. The cops had tossed his place and now Tabatha, Desiree, both Lolas, and Joe were all sprawled wantonly about. Desiree was half-deflated and Lola Plus's hair had come off. The cops were poking around the sex toys with their batons. Sergeant Anderson strode over, careful to sidestep the dog poop, and pulled on a glove.

"Looks like we solved this case." He chuckled. "Typical lovers' quarrel. This must be the murder weapon." He held a Supercock gingerly in his gloved hands. Everyone laughed appreciatively, the neighbors conversing among themselves in a mix of languages. Mustache kicked a doll into the air and Biceps tapped it back like a beach ball, but Santos eyed him with fury.

"Quite a party you got going on, huh? Aren't you a little old to be playing with dolls?"

"All right," Anderson said. "Cut him loose. No law against being disgusting . . . yet."

The two uniforms yanked him to his feet and uncuffed him, giving him a shove.

"Have a nice day, ladies," Santos said to the girls who were standing with their dogs. The other cops tipped their hats.

"Thank you, detective. You too," they chirped as the police left. Area and Sequoia turned away from Elliot and went back into the house. Feather handed Elliot his mangled vagina.

"Thanks," Elliot said, staring at his feet. She turned and went inside.

Anderson shook his head. "I suggest you take a good long look at your life, son. Or at least buy some curtains."

"Yes, sir," Elliot said, eyes down. "Sorry."

Anderson clapped him on the back. "Forget about it, kid." He winked. "It's Koreatown." And chuckling to himself, he got back in his car. The second the door shut, softly, Santos backed out with a shriek. Now watched only by a few remaining neighbors, Elliot made his way around the dog shit back into his garage. The door came down behind him.

5

Elliot's first mistake on Monday morning was coming into work. Not that he had a choice, but he picked the wrong entrance. Following the public announcement of the congressman's private oral testimony, and the carefully planned "leak" of a teaser photo, protestors had already begun to gather, just as Vic hoped. By the time the issue came out, there would be a media feeding frenzy. For now, it was mainly just religious nuts waving crosses or signs, condemning them to hell, though there was a bearded guy dressed as Jesus in a ratty robe and sandals. A couple of local TV stations were covering it—suave, overdressed reporters in heavy makeup posed before the small crowd, who barked and shook their fists obligingly.

As Elliot walked by, trying to circumvent the circus, a photographer leaned from a minivan and aimed a long lens. Instinctively, he flinched and looked away as the camera fired.

❖

The next mistake was checking his voicemail. Again, not much choice, but the litany of death threats, hellfire, and political tirades made it hard to enjoy his corn muffin. Not even the devil's home team was backing him: Eddie Hex had decried *Raunchy* to the press for soiling the sanctity of his marriage. And then there was Vic checking on

Crystal, who seemed to smile mockingly at him from the photos spread on his desk. Unable to face her, he fled down the hall to Margie.

"Ugh," he said as he walked up behind her. There was Crystal again, eyeing him from Margie's monitor as she polished up her image for the cover. She seemed to silently reproach him. *Find me!*

"Ugh you too," Margie answered, not looking up. "Take a look at this." Margie swung her mouse over Crystal's body, poised beneath the *Raunchy* logo. "If we crop her here, she looks odd. But if we leave this full frame, we get the nip slip right at the bottom." To mail out copies of the magazine with a nipple visible on the cover was a federal offense, one not even Vic's ace lawyer could beat. As for why a glimpse of a nipple was so taboo, when all humans had seen or suckled one at some point, and most had at least two of their own, was a question beyond their pay grade.

"Can you make her hair longer?" Elliot suggested, leaning over Margie's shoulder and touching her breast—Crystal's, not Margie's. Her luxuriant red waves fell just below the shoulders. "Make it more Botticellian and we can cheat the nip. Shame to crop her boobs and waste all the money she spent on them."

Margie laughed. "That's what I like about you, Ellie. Cultured yet crass." She tapped the screen with her nail. "But where are my cover lines?" The spot where the title went just said *TK* over and over—*to kum* in the obscure term printers still used to ply their ancient craft. Elliot sighed.

"I know. I know. I'm stuck."

"Stuck? That's not like you."

"I don't know what to do. I got a nudge from Vic this morning too." He winced at the memory.

"Angry?"

"Worse. Excited. It scared me more than the death threats."

Margie shrugged. "It's your own fault for making him like you."

"I miss the days when he didn't know my name. Called me Billy."

She patted his shoulder. "Poor Billy. Maybe get some advice? Ask a fellow writer to share their insight and experience?" He thought of his peers, the crew who'd been jeering at him at the meeting. Most lasted a few months at most. They hid in their offices, hoping not to get fired, emerging only to run home, blinking at the light, coffee and ketchup on their shirts and ties. The poor shmucks hadn't even figured out the topless lunch trick.

"Let's face it," Elliot told Margie. "They're a bunch of losers. By definition. If they had any insight would they be working here?"

"Ask Myron?"

"Myron! Ask him what, how to beat a urine test?"

Margie shrugged. "You might be surprised. He's been here since forever. He's an OG. A survivor! With all that experience, he's got to have some wisdom."

Elliot wondered. Yes, it followed that experience taught us something, but was it something Elliot really wanted to know?

Myron's office, down at the end of the corridor, was the only one on their floor that had been personalized. It looked how Elliot imagined a '70s dorm room looked: you brushed through a beaded curtain as you entered, carefully, since the inside of the heavily pockmarked door held a dartboard that still showed Reagan's face. There were old rock posters on the walls and a batik cloth over the couch. Jazz murmured soothingly all day, from a turntable, of course. Where Elliot had stacks of photo sets, Myron had cartoons: pinned to the walls, piled on the desk, stacked shoulder-high along the floor. As editor of one of the few national outlets that still bought cartoons and hired illustrators, Myron wielded his own godlike power over a sad, tiny realm, a king of trolls.

Elliot found him way back in his recliner, watching a cheerleader porn video on fast-forward. It was an old trick—the movies were far too insipid to really watch, and you only got fifty bucks to review one—so they zoomed right through, gleaning the general idea.

"What? I'm busy! Oh it's you . . ." Myron hit PAUSE, freezing the bodies in midbounce, and retrieved his beer from where it was hidden behind the chair. "What's up, kid? Building on fire?"

"Nope."

"Course not, then you wouldn't look so glum."

"It's the January cover girl, Crystal Waters. I need advice. Vic has me looking for her and I'm completely lost."

"Hey kid, welcome to my world." He cackled. He hit a button on his recliner so that it slowly raised him to his feet. "Check this out. I drew it in a blackout and now I can't think of a caption." He went around to his desk and showed Elliot a drawing: Raunchy Raccoon was grinning at the viewer while pissing into a punch bowl, while a bunch of portly guys in suits held drinks. A banner on the wall read CONGRESSIONAL FUNDRAISER.

Elliot thought it over. "How about . . . 'Now that's what I call Goldwater Republicans!'"

"Hey! That's funny!" He grabbed the drawing back and jotted down the note. "That's probably what I was thinking before I passed out."

"I'm sure."

He finished his beer and reached into a small fridge. "Thirsty?" he asked.

"No thanks. I'll stick to coffee."

"Well that's your first mistake right there, rookie," he said as he cracked open a fresh beer and it foamed onto his lap. "Fuck," he muttered, blotting it with a drawing from an aspiring cartoonist. "Rule number one," he said, lifting his beer to Elliot. "No one can do this job sober for long. You've got to drink." He quaffed, as if to prove his point, then sat back with a sigh. "It's better if you're stoned too. But that damned fire alarm keeps going off. They threatened to fine me! In Cali! If I wanted Big Brother telling me when and where I can do a doobie, I'd move to Moscow, comrade."

It crossed Elliot's mind that marijuana was still illegal the last time he checked, even in the Republic of California, but he let it go. Myron was on a roll.

"Not that this place is much fun anymore anyway," he went on. "Not since Sarah died. That changed everything." He sighed. "What a lady."

Sarah Kingman had been a stripper in Vic's club back on Forty-Second Street. Then a top model in his magazine. And soon his partner in life and crime, co-running the magazine and cohosting the drug-fueled feasts and orgies that legend had it still stained the walls of the offices and the pool of the mansion. But that was before Vic got shot. And before Sarah, the love of his life, fell in the first wave of the AIDS epidemic, snuffed out like a Roman candle before anyone even knew what it was.

He lifted his glass to a picture on the wall of Sarah, dressed in stockings, a corset, and pearls. "Pure class. That's who I went to when my juices got blocked. She'd get you writing, believe me. Now this girl, what's-her-name, Miss January . . ."

"Crystal."

"She's pretty, sure. But she's a blank. Empty. Just like her name. She needs character. Charisma. Personality. Even tragedy. Because that's what porn is my friend. It is the agony and the ecstasy. And if you don't know that, you haven't been keeping your eyes open. You're a reporter. Work your sources. Put your nose to the ground. You need the taste of her in your mouth. Her smell in your nose. Know what I mean? Like John Donne. Or Shakespeare's Dark Lady sonnets."

"Hey, easy. It's just girl copy."

"Just?" Myron shrugged. "Perhaps that's why you're lost." He guzzled. "Still, maybe you're right. The world's changing. Porn used to be about sex and revolt against square society. Freedom. Now it's just capitalism. Product. There was a time when you had to go to a theater to see a dirty movie, or a strip club, a peep show. Some kind of reality with the fantasy. But now it's all about videotapes. Soon, they say, with this internet thing, you'll be able to just push a button."

Myron finished the beer and tossed the bottle into the trash, where it shattered. "What the fuck were we talking about again?" he asked. "You had a question?"

"Never mind," Elliot said. "Thanks."

"Yeah," Myron said, reaching into his fridge. "You're welcome."

❖

Elliot was more ambivalent than ever about the wisdom of Myron, but he wanted to survive the January issue, so after lunch, he went to see Farah Foxxx, the closest thing he had to a source. She lived in one of those typical West Hollywood setups, two stories of apartments surrounding a pool and patio area, with parking underneath, a metal security gate, and a few old palm trees nodding sadly over it all. Every so often a coconut fell in the pool. Farah was also to be found poolside, basting herself in coconut oil and cocoa butter, though as she was fond of saying, "Black don't crack." Her desultory flirtations with Elliot were strictly business—she admitted he was too old for her—but she was a porn legend after all and had to play the part. She'd made a string of hits in the '70s and '80s, then cannily shifted into MILF territory, billing herself as a panther who preyed on younger men. Her premier appearance in *Raunchy*, with a hirsute white partner named King Dong, had been one of the reasons that Vic got shot and she got notorious. Now she worked the nostalgia angle, signing old video boxes and magazines at conventions and making private appearances at fiftieth birthday celebrations or bachelor parties for third marriages. She'd been a little affronted when, after proposing her "Porn Star Advice Column," Elliot was sent to tell her that the title would be "Dear Slut."

"Hmph . . ." She'd sat back, crossing her legs and trying to appear indignant, which was quite a trick since she'd been sunbathing nude when Elliot arrived. She pulled on her see-through top and shook out her long glossy hair. "How much does it pay again?"

"Four hundred a month."

She laughed and reached for her cigarette case, one of those old-fashioned ones that held a pack and had a little pocket for the lighter. She lit a Kool 100. "Why not? I've always flown my freak flag proudly."

Since then he'd duly stopped by once a month, with a handful of the letters sent in by readers, seeking tips on everything from anal sex—"Lube, lube, and more lube"—to increasing the size of one's ejaculation through protein shakes—"That's all myth. Drink plenty of water. Or pineapple juice. Even if there's not a bigger load, it will be sweeter!"—and the perennial favorite, convincing your wife to have a threesome. "Tell her how hot she'd look with another woman. Don't join in unless invited. And most important of all, fellas, take it from Farah—always, always cum on your own wife!"

Elliot looked forward to their visits, when he'd sit back and nibble the snacks she put out—salted peanuts mixed with M&M's, cubed cheese, and salami on Ritz crackers—while he recorded her free associations, then went back and wrote them up, more or less. This time, since she claimed to know everyone in the biz, Elliot ventured an off-the-record question.

"Hey, do you know anything about this new girl, Crystal Waters?"

Farah laughed her throaty laugh. "Do I know her? Honey, I'm the one who introduced her to Vic."

"Oh yeah?"

She reached for a cigarette. Elliot lit it. "Sure. She was working a strip club out by the airport. Wild Side West? Nice, but you know, second tier. A lot of out-of-town businessmen from Asia and tech nerds from the Valley. Dental conventions. I bought a lap dance from her and she knew who I was, asked about taking it to the next level. She was already saving for tits. But I told her, it takes more than a couple of fresh melons these days. Still I could see she had something. So I schooled her a little, you know, gave her a makeover, set her up with Vic. I was the one who gave her the red hair!"

"It wasn't natural?"

"Boy, please." She flipped her long straight locks. "About as natural as mine. But I said, hey, this is the big leagues. Big-boobed blondes are a dime a dozen. You need to stand out. With that fair skin and red hair. Wow." She tapped her ashes, leaning forward conspiratorially. "I even tipped her off about her bush."

"How so?"

Farah shrugged. "I said, girl, when you get your shot with the man, let that hair grow out awhile and get Orlando, that's the stylist, to dye it red also. It was super eye-catching. Like a flame!" She snapped her fingers. "Vic's a '70s dude, after all. Those old salty dogs can't get enough hair pie. Same with Myron. He ain't happy unless he's picking hair from that gap in his teeth."

She offered a plate of canapés. Elliot frowned and shook his head. She shrugged and took one, sliding the morsel off with her lips. "It worked like a charm," she went on. "Farah knows men. Old Vic fell to his knees like he was seeing the burning bush!" She laughed, head back, exulting. "Not literally, I mean. You know . . ." She lowered her voice. "He's dead below the waist."

Elliot nodded.

"I heard he just got a pump," she added, confidingly. "I wonder how that works exactly."

"I'd rather not think about it," Elliot said.

Farah shrugged. "We all gotta eat." She drew on her cigarette. "Thing is, as per usual, I was too smart for my own good. Vic went and fell in love."

"With Crystal Waters?"

Farah pursed her lips. "Even paid for her to go to Dr. K."

"Dr. K?"

"You never heard of Dr. K? The Beverly Hills miracle worker? Oh honey. Every rich housewife, ex-wife, or mistress goes there, sometimes for matching noses. I can't say his name. Something Jewish." She shrugged. "Or Polish. Or whateverish. Anyway, next thing I knew, she's the queen of the castle up there on that hill. And now Farah can't get her calls returned." She shook her head. "I used to do threesomes with Vic's wife Sarah! We were like family."

"Do you know where she is now?" Elliot asked, hopefully.

"Not with Vic?" she asked, intrigued.

"She's gone. Maybe you know her real name?"

She laughed. "Honey, I don't even remember my own real name." She put her cigarette down and chose another bite, nibbling it thoughtfully. "You know, I got some old photo sets of her somewhere, artistic nudes she took for her portfolio, back when she was just a regular old nobody. Probably got a name and contact on there. Or return address. Though I would need to be compensated for all that time, digging in my dusty boxes instead of out by the pool."

"Definitely," Elliot said, a little too eager, surprising himself. "I mean, anything that you can do would be greatly appreciated."

Farah licked the toothpick. "I'll call you in a few days." She sat up and straightened her see-through blouse, shook out her hair. "My pool boy's about to stop by," she added with a wink. "Girl's got to get her filter cleaned regularly."

"I'll leave you to it." Elliot stood.

"Wait," she called. She pointed a long curved talon. "Don't forget your jacket."

"Right." He sighed and pulled it on. She nodded her approval.

"Satin. Nice. Vic must really like you."

❖

As he pulled away, Elliot noticed a car parked across the street from Farah's—a midnight-blue Lexus with a slender pink-tipped hand flicking cigarette ash out the window. He flashed on the car and manicured hand he'd handed the money to. Was it possible? There were a lot of fancy cars and painted nails in Hollywood. And even if it was, so what? Still, he drove around the block out of curiosity, but the Lexus was gone.

6

Elliot watched, pen in hand, as the girls rose into the air, like squabs held high by a waiter. They revolved on a giant lazy Susan while stage fog pumped around them. Writhing together, the six kissed and tickled, giggled and nipped. A blonde nymph pulled off a friend's panties and snapped them at another girl in play. The crowd of men watched in silence and stillness, breathing hard, as the stage descended and the team moved into the audience, hopping onto tables and chairs. One girl, a tiny sprite, opened a cute pink case and began unpacking dildos—big, bigger, huge—as if playing tea party with four stunned businessmen, each more than double her age. They stared in awe, struck dumb as if by a miracle.

Elliot wrote *miracle*, and closed his notebook.

"Yo, that dumbshit's taking notes." A dude in a Lakers jacket and hat elbowed his identically costumed friend and pointed at Elliot.

"I'll give him lessons," his buddy quipped. They laughed and high-fived each other. Then he saw Elliot stand and walk by. "Yo," he told his comrade in a new tone of respect. "Check the jacket, dude."

"*Raunchy* rules!" they yelled at him. "Editor! All right!" Elliot waved shyly, as a couple of pros in bikinis appeared and began talking to them, smiling, stroking, each holding a wad of folded cash. They led the two men off by the hand.

Poor bastards, Elliot thought. Those girls will eat them alive. Nothing left but empty wallets and sticky underwear. Still, this was perhaps the only place on earth where his jacket was a status enhancer. He'd flashed his *Raunchy* business card to get into Wild Side West for free, explaining, only half a lie, that he was doing research, maybe asking a few questions for a "possible piece," but it had worked a little too well. He was shown right to a ringside seat and, within minutes, the whisper network spread as one by one the girls started coming by for their "interviews," all assuming he was there to make them famous.

"It's about freedom," Sally, who danced under the name Dusty, explained. "This is how I choose to express my creativity. I put a lot of work into my dances. I select my own costumes and music." Now, her music for the dance Elliot saw was Madonna and the costume was a leopard-print bra and panties and some kitty ears and no one there would have paid a dime for her creativity if it hadn't expressed itself in the form of a naked handstand, but still. "It's my choice. No man controls me."

Dusty/Sally had a point. She was seizing control of the ultimate means of production, her own body, and exposing the ultimate capitalist reality, a world where everything, especially sex, was magically converted into money. The dancers bragged to him about their college degrees and stock portfolios. They demonstrated the mesmeric control they wielded over men. They raked in thousands a night. In cash. They were nude entrepreneurs. So who was exploiting whom? Maybe everyone.

But where, Elliot asked the mirrored walls and grimy floors, was the love? Love can't stand too much ugly truth, and as he spoke to the girls, yearning briefly for each, Elliot couldn't stop seeing how they were working him. He knew that believing a stripper liked you when she smiled was like thinking a cash register liked you when it dinged. Of course, they were no worse than anyone else, morally superior, even, since they were honest. But that very honesty made Elliot hopeless. It killed the last chance for human warmth by exposing it to the cold, clear light of the real.

❖

"It's okay to touch me," she said into his ear. Introducing herself as Tina, the dark-haired girl in the glow-in-the-dark pink string bikini had simply climbed into Elliot's lap instead of sitting beside him. Her arms were folded around his neck and her body shifted back and forth, lapping against him like a gentle wave against a dock post. "This is fun," she said. "Let me show you around."

She led him by the hand through some curtains to a small movie theater and eased him into a seat. A porn film was showing on the screen, a close-up of a pink piston engine. He plucked a twenty from his pocket and handed it to her. He'd drawn fifty bucks tip money from petty cash under Miriam's withering glance.

"Thank you so much," she murmured.

"Thank you. I was wondering . . . maybe you know a friend of mine . . . Crystal?"

She pushed the bikini straps off her shoulders and let her breasts fall softly into her hands.

"Who?" she asked, as straddling him, she pulled his face forward, nose between her breasts. Elliot sat motionless, feeling both aroused and ridiculous. He inhaled and smelled her skin, perfume and powder and an undernote of sweat.

"Crymsmf . . ." he mumbled.

"Do you like that?" she asked.

"Mm-hmm," Elliot said, nodding between her breasts. Her fingers twisted through his hair and traced the rims of his burning ears.

"So, you're the guy from *Raunchy*."

"Mmf."

"All the girls are talking about you. You're a real player aren't you?"

"Nnn-nnn." He shook his head.

She leaned back, freeing Elliot's head. He took a breath while the sweat dried on his blushing face. "I'm just here, you know, interviewing the girls, doing a little bit of research for um . . ." Her crotch was in his face now. "A possible piece."

"Will you help me get my bottoms off, Mr. *Raunchy*? They're all wet."

Elliot pulled the bikini down over her hip bones. She wriggled loose and draped her legs over the back of the seat, floating just millimeters from his face. What was expected of him now? A kiss? A whisper? He wasn't familiar with the done thing in these places. He felt the strange urge to tell a secret. She slid back down into his lap, pulling her bikini bottom up, and raised his folded twenty in her small hand.

"I like doing research with you. Do you have any more of these?"

"Not really. Like I said, I'm here for a possible . . ."

Elliot trailed off. She was already up and leading him back into the main room, where the music was too loud to speak. Her eyes darted around, seeking richer targets.

Another dancer, Lisa, a tattooed Bettie Page, complained about the middle-aged executive who just handed her a twenty and presented his penis. When she explained nicely that she wasn't about to do that and asked him to put it away, he looked at her forlornly, still proffering his humble offering, and asked, "Why not?"

"Like a four-year-old," she laughed. She had a four-year-old son herself, she explained, telling the story to Elliot, recrossing her naked legs as he struggled to keep his eyes on hers, so she wouldn't think he was a sucker like that chump.

It was, in fact, the four-year-old, rather than the raging beast, that these women brought out in men. They clustered together by the snack bar, grown men giggling like schoolgirls, a dumb pack of bison around the water hole, big and dumb and slow, ready to be picked off. No wonder women despised men. Elliot despised himself, but at the same time, any reflexive rant about male domination seemed ridiculous. These men had no power now, at least not over themselves.

Lisa grabbed Elliot by the hand.

"Come on. Maraya's dancing next. She's awesome."

In the next room a blonde girl was prancing around to Led Zeppelin, leaping across the stage and churning her arms in a breaststroke.

"Take something off," a computer nerd bellowed.

She dropped her sheer gown. This was the girl who'd described herself as a performance artist and choreographer earlier. She'd studied gender theory in her MFA course and concluded that "dancing is one of the most liberating things a woman can do." Now she did a somersault and landed in a wobbly split. The men cheered. She waved a scarf around. Elliot felt kind of bad for her. But then again, he was a no-talent would-be artist himself, and no one was throwing money at him. The best he could manage was, as the moron said, taking notes.

Next, Maraya came out. Her body was hairless, like the others, her crotch smooth as the inside of a seashell, and her breasts small and high and unenhanced. She wore thigh-high boots with dagger heels, a cape, and a devil mask, a triangular red face with a slash mouth and sprouting horns. AC/DC roared over the sound system. She stalked the stage, thighs twitching. She fell on her back and scissored her legs. She turned over and pumped her buttocks at five thousand rpm. She spread her legs and tasted herself, uncoiling a long tongue through her mask and staring straight at Elliot. He put a five on the stage, trying to smile politely, but her red-nailed fingers drew his eyes from the cloven place betweeen her thighs up to the devil's grin.

> "For my sister and me, stripping is the yellow brick road to freedom. We're from a blue-collar background. For us, having a nice home, nice car, dental insurance, it's like a dream."

> "I didn't really know my dad. He took off and then showed up like ten years later wanting to be buddies. Asshole. My mother's boyfriend was a cop who used to slap her. So am I fucked up about men? Sure, so what? I'm no victim. I was a waitress. Who sat in my section? Men. I cut hair. Who came to me? Men. My looks are always what gets me my money, at least now I'm getting what it's worth. And it's worth a lot."

"It's definitely hard on relationships, dancing. The nice guys want you to quit. And the guys who don't care are creeps. It's like the old joke. What does a stripper do with her asshole before she goes to work? Drops him off at band practice."

"Some girl had a box cutter. She went straight for my face because I used a song she wanted to use. That's what they do, they try to put you out of work."

"After work, I have to wash my breasts off in the sink, because of all the greasy hands and sweat from all the men."

"Crystal Waters? Isn't she the gang bang queen? I hear she's doing a shoot tomorrow. They were looking for fluffers but that's not my thing. I'm a trained dancer, doing research for a performance piece I'm working on."

"I think she came in here once, and took a booth, with some manager guy, I forget his name and that white rapper kid, Dejavu? He has that song, 'Let's Get Pimpin'.' They ordered champagne, threw money around, so she must be doing good."

"At work, I try to love each person I come into contact with. I try to give them compassion, which is what I think they're here for, whether they know it or not. I give them the physical touching that everyone needs, even animals. I see a lot of women who need affection and they're going out with guys just to get it. I'm getting paid to get it. I used to have low self-esteem, but there's nothing like getting paid a hundred dollars an hour by a cute sexy guy to make out. I pray before I go to work that somebody like that will come in."

❖

"Excuse me, sir. Can you come with us?"

This last statement was made not by a dancer perched on his knee but by a looming bouncer whose hand fell heavily on Elliot's shoulder. He did not bother to write it in his notebook.

"Uh. Sure? Where? Why?"

The naiad he'd been interviewing slipped back into the frothy current as a second bouncer reached out and took his notebook. "Please just come with us, sir. The manager wants a word."

The manager turned out to be as wide as the bouncers were tall, filling one side of a booth in the bar, with a cheese-and-meat platter and a wedding-sized shrimp cocktail on the table before him. A similar heap of oyster shells were stacked on melting ice, having already been emptied. While the bouncers stood Elliot at the table, the manager slurped the final oyster, then reached for his notebook with a surprisingly slender, manicured hand and delicately turned the pages. "Help yourself to a nibble, please," he murmured to Elliot, who demurred.

Looking up from the notebook, and taking a long white cigarette from a pack, the manager said, "Please tell Vic that while we are always eager to cooperate with a legendary publication like *Raunchy*, truly one of the pillars of our industry, we host a lot of VIP clients . . ." He waved a lighter, as if casting for examples. "Athletes, celebrities . . . even congressmen." He flicked the lighter and held the flame not to his cigarette but to Elliot's notebook. "And we have to insure their privacy, by whatever means necessary." As the paper flared up and then blackened, he held it by a curling corner and then dropped the smoking mess in the oyster shells, where it hissed in the ice. Then he lit his smoke. "Understood?"

Elliot smiled big. "Absolutely."

"Excellent." The manager nodded at the bouncers. "Please make sure this gentleman gets to his car safely."

Elliot tried to exit with some dignity, though it was a bit awkward with one of the bouncers holding each of his arms gently but firmly, as if they were ward nurses and he'd had a stroke. The girls had all moved on. The dudes in the Lakers gear spotted him again.

"Fuck yeah, *Raunchy*!" they yelled. "You rule, dude!"

He gave a little wave but the bouncers sped up, lifting him slightly as they proceeded, making his legs dance as if he were a marionette treading the air. "Night, fellas," he called as they pushed him out the door, whereupon they gave him a hard shove and he stumbled to his knees.

"Hey," he said. "You call that safely?"

They said nothing, merely gazing down with a contempt that matched the respect he'd received just an hour before. Customers coming and going in the parking lot watched with interest, including a crew piling out of a white minivan. In the dark they could have been the tourists from the office. Then again, so could any of the guys now watching his disgrace in their interchangeable uniforms of shorts and ball caps.

"Nothing to see here, gentlemen," the bouncers called. "Come on in, show's about to start." As they waved the dudes along, Elliot stood and dusted off his pants. And then, across the quiet parking lot, he saw a figure, a rider on a motorcycle, only a dark outline in the shadows, but seeming to stare his way behind a helmet. Suddenly, he did actually feel safer with the bouncers watching as he walked to his car and pulled out, one eye on the rearview. The biker revved up and the cyclops eye of the headlight came alive, causing Elliot to hold both his breath and steering wheel a bit tighter. Should he drive to the police station? He had no idea where that was, or what he'd say as he ran in for sanctuary. Vic was probably just spooking him, with his paranoid tale of a forbidden tape. Then again, he was the one in the wheelchair. Elliot drove faster, as the white spot hung in his mirror. But then, as he merged onto the freeway, the light grew larger, the engine louder, and the biker blew past him, disappearing into the red constellation of taillights ahead.

7

Elliot came to the Valley. The cigarette smoking between his lips, the heat waves cooking off the hood of his car, the sun poisoning prickling up his left arm—everything seemed on the verge of bursting into flame. Sun flashed brilliantly in the dirt on his windshield, blinding him like a handful of crushed glass. Dust crept up his nose and down his throat. It was always ten degrees hotter out here than in the city, and when he rolled down the window he sneezed twelve times in a row, as though allergic to something in the atmosphere, perhaps the same fallout that had killed all the trees, and burned away the clouds, and left only wide, unpeopled streets where nothing stirred under a sky of ungodly blue.

This was the Valley, a vast land hidden behind the Hollywood Hills, over which Elliot climbed and then descended. Here was a sky without weather, without depth, hard as a skull, bright as a needle, unnatural and unreal, a switch with two settings, night and day, and every day the same day, under a murderous sun that, if you dared glance at it directly, appeared to be a white hole in space.

He parked behind a line of cars at the end of a long driveway. He gathered his tape recorder, sunglasses, notebook, and cigarettes, and then, reluctantly, donned his jacket once again, before hiking up to the house and following the bundled power cords through the unfurnished rooms. It was like a stage set of a mansion, huge and elaborate but built of only the shoddiest, most temporary materials, by the worst artisans with the least care: concrete poured into the mold of a crumbling chateau, hollow columns, fiberglass stonework, and granite counters already chipping to reveal they were just veneers. Handed off between actors and singers as they passed through the spotlight on their way to oblivion, it was rented out betweentimes for low-end film shoots, commercials, rock videos, and of course, porn.

Two naked men were chatting in the kitchen, snacking on chips and hummus. One was tall and bony, wearing only black dress socks and tassel loafers. His penis poked its pink nose from a thick black thatch like a mouse sniffing the breeze from its lair. The other, squatter man had his back to Elliot. He was both bald and hairy, the growth beginning at the nape of his neck and spreading to his shoulders, then deepening into a carpet as it marched toward the dense and fertile valley of his buttocks. The tall man made a joke and the hairy guy's buttocks shook with laughter, rippling on the bone. Elliot moved on quickly. He passed another naked man in the hallway, bending over to tie his shoe. Elliot kept staring straight ahead, moving fast and pretending he saw nothing, as if walking through a haunted house on a dare. Then he found the backyard. He'd never seen this many naked bodies in one place before. Almost all were male, drinking beer and snapping photos of one another. Many had brought video box covers and magazines, souvenirs they wanted autographed. One held a bouquet of roses. Elliot found his eyes drawn, not, as he'd feared, to the genitals, but to the ludicrous footwear, the knee-high athletic socks and Nike sneakers and hiking boots.

Tentatively, Elliot approached the troops with his tape recorder. He was unsure of how to strike up a conversation with a naked man, but when they learned whom he worked for they gathered around, asking questions and laughing at his jokes. Two-hundred-pound men, ten years his senior, smiled and giggled shyly like tween girls meeting a pop star. There was a warm spirit of fellowship in the air. Some had flown in from across the country, or driven over together from work, making an adventure of it, as if seeing a beloved heroine being honored. God bless her, they said. God bless *Raunchy*, and God bless America.

"Hey, buddy."

A bearded man, clothed as it happens in a ball cap, safari jacket, and jeans, took Elliot by the elbow. "Leave your clothes in the house, buddy. Don't worry about your wallet. There's security."

"Oh, no." Elliot urgently corrected him. "I'm a reporter." He pointed over his shoulder at his own back. "I'm here from *Raunchy*."

An expensive white smile appeared in the black beard. "I'm Buck Harder, the director. Also husband and manager. " They shook hands. "Nice jacket."

"Thanks. You too."

"Let me introduce you to our star."

Elliot spotted the lady of the hour, posing for pregame publicity shots. Dressed only in high heels, she was held in the air by four fans, spread lengthwise as if on a chaise lounge. Then she squatted and grabbed two by the balls, smiling for the camera.

Meanwhile the crew, easily identified by their clothes, were busy setting up video cameras around the raised mattress where the main event would take place. Men began to line up and the fluffers, a pudgy, multipierced, and tattooed Asian girl and a crack-thin blondie with enormous scarred implants, got to work, livening up the crowd. Pushing his way ahead, Buck led Elliot over to where his wife was lying on the mattress and smoking a cigarette. She was not Crystal Waters.

"Hi," Elliot said. Once again, he found himself talking to someone while ignoring the fact that she was naked. He'd become an expert at keeping his eyes unwaveringly locked on theirs. "I'm Elliot from *Raunchy*. Can you spell your name for me, just for the record?"

"Hi," she said, smiling, and held out her hand. She had tattoos of serpents running up her arms and legs. "I'm Krystal Kanyons, with two *K*s and two *y*s." She squeezed his hand. "Will you be joining in the party today?"

Elliot smiled big and took his hand back. “Well, I’m working, you know.”

“So am I.”

“Business before pleasure right?” Then, realizing he couldn’t just leave, he added, “I was wondering if I could ask you a few questions, for a possible piece?”

“Sure. Fire away.”

Elliot kneeled on the edge of the mattress and opened his notebook. Krystal propped herself up on one elbow, casually stroking herself with her painted nails.

“I am not a whore. I’m a dirty, nasty slut and I want credit for it,” she told him, pointing accusingly. “I’m a feminist and I’m doing this for myself, not for anyone else. I’m not sexually fucked up. I have orgasms every day. I love sex. I love men. I used to be afraid of men, but now I understand them and I have the power. It’s like a spiritual act, you know? I’m not choosing, saying, like, you look good but you’re too fat or old or whatever. I’m saying we’re all beautiful, you know? We all deserve love in different ways. My husband understands that. He’s a feminist, too.”

❖

By four, the wind descended, lifting paper plates and napkins from the snack table and chasing them over the lawn. A plastic bag jumped and swam in the heat like a manta ray brushing the surface. A vanload of Japanese businessmen disembarked. They were on a worldwide sex tour and had already visited Bangkok, Amsterdam, and Las Vegas. After this they were off to Costa Rica for virgins. At their tour leader’s instruction, they promptly stripped down and lined up, smiling and nodding through the grumbles from the American men already in line. A brief argument ensued about their cameras. The director objected to video and Krystal, bleary and semicoherent, demanded extra money for still photos. Finally, they struck a bargain: no video and ten bucks for a photo with the star, propped up with a smiling tourist's head hugged to each breast. The other men laughed approvingly at this and the air of good-natured camaraderie was restored.

Next a fraternity from UCLA showed up, ten guys in two cars, dressed in team shirts and sports sunglasses held on with stretchy cords, hooting and carrying cases of beer. One overeager college boy, still halfway back on the line, lost control and squirted semen onto the next fellow's leg. There was a scuffle as the soiled victim shoved him and began to throw punches, knocking him down.

"Homo," yelled the angry naked man, clad only in Air Jordans and a Yankees hat. "He tried to slip it in from behind!" He kicked the crawling man in the butt. The fallen man's frat brothers came to his aid and a brawl began to develop. The security guards dove in and broke it up.

Meanwhile, beer cans and condoms piled up around Krystal, who was soldiering forward on all fours. The sun drenched everything in migraine colors, and men stumbled around blindly behind mirrored glasses. Leaves shook free from an avocado tree and flew. One slid all the way across the pool, trailing its shadow on the bottom. Stumbling away from the mattress, the men stripped off their condoms and went to piss on the avocado tree, then grabbed a fresh beer and got back in line. A crew member in gloves moved in to wipe Krystal down with a towel, and the makeup artist cleaned up her face. Her eyeliner was smeared, darkening her cheeks like a battered boxer's. Her lipstick bled out, blooming over her wounded mouth and chin, as if someone had been stuffing roses down her throat. Sweat glittered on her skin. Her body glowed. She raised her arms, lifting her head, like she had something to say.

"Lube," she called out plaintively. "Bring me the fucking lube."

By now Elliot was used to men in the crowd commenting on the jacket, but as he passed two big-bellied white whales in ball caps and boots he heard a shift in tone. "My cousin who works in the sheriff's office said it's a setup." "Ruined a good man." "Goddamn lefties and you know who controls the media." Elliot knew who. Him, and his kind.

They were talking, he realized, about the congressman. "Should've reloaded last time they shot him," one joshed to the other and they guffawed. "Hell, I'll give this one a running start. Use that jacket as a target."

Elliot began making his way to the exit, head down, still grinning and nodding at the random dudes who staggered drunkenly around. He glanced back to see one of the whales pointing him out to another guy in a mullet who had an American flag draped around his bare shoulders. They yelled something at him. Elliot picked up the pace.

As soon as he hit the driveway, he broke into a jog. But dozens more vehicles had arrived since he'd parked and his car was blocked in. In a kind of slow-motion panic, he began the elaborate business of pulling out, cranking the wheel all the way left, moving an inch, then putting it in reverse before cranking all the way right, and rolling back an inch, then repeating, again and again while the sweat poured down his back and over his chest. The car was like a pizza oven. He had just about squeezed out and was negotiating the elaborate seven-point turn he needed to point his nose back down the driveway when they appeared. The vigilantes.

It wasn't quite a lynch mob. They weren't waving pitchforks or even fists. And there were only four or five of them—the whales, the flag guy, and another fellow who was carrying a beer cooler. They had dressed, sort of, and now wore shorts and no shirts, or shirts and only briefs.

"Hey, boy, where you going? Party's just getting started!"

"Hey, pussy, stick to pussy and stop picking on good people."

"Hey, come have a beer."

Finally, he threw the car in drive and was about to release the brake, but whale number one, the big boy, blocked his way. He leaned over and mooned him. "Make me a star, *Raunchy*!" His pals hooted with joy.

Still trying to play it off, Elliot smiled and waved. "Gotta make deadline, guys! Have fun!"

"Get out of the damned car, boy, I want a word with you . . ." The whale yelled and, as his buddies gathered, he leaned menacingly on the hood of the car. And screamed.

Elliot's hood, which had been cooking in direct SoCal sun for several hours, must have been ready to roast beef. In any case, it seared the tender pink flesh of the whale's palms and he howled in pain, jumping back. His cohort rushed to his side. Elliot floored it and saw the injured bully shoving his hands in the beer cooler as he skidded past, fishtailing down the drive.

"Get him!" he heard the flag-wearer yell. "He burned Norris!"

They scampered into a white pickup, its profile higher than the surrounding cars. Several climbed into the bed. In his rearview, Elliot could see the front plate was a Confederate flag, which he took as a bad sign. He was just pulling onto the street, and figuring his chances of outgunning the pickup on the open road (low) and of there being actual guns ready to come out (high), when a biker appeared.

It was a big motorcycle, black, powerful, loud. The rider, too, was in black with a silver helmet and Mylar visor that gleamed like a shield in Elliot's eyes.

"Fuck," he shouted to himself. "Now what?"

But the bike didn't join the chase. It turned up the drive and quickly encountered the pickup, which had to slam on its brakes. The driver leaned on his horn. The biker stopped and, waving a gloved hand in acknowledgment, began backing up. Elliot turned onto the main road and didn't look back.

Was this the same bike from the strip club? Was it following him? He didn't know. It had been too dark. He knew only one thing for sure. He had to get the hell out of the Valley.

❖

He was badly rattled, but he was almost on empty. So he floored it for a few miles of freeway and then, when he felt safe and his pulse had slowed, he slowed, too, and pulled into a gas station. It was one of those high-modern dream stations, spotless and empty, with a dozen pumps on islands under gazebos (for the one day it might rain, or to keep the gas fumes from igniting in the sun?), and a low glass building stocked with a rainbow of cold sugared drinks, fountain sodas, five awful flavors of coffee, donuts, muffins, even hot dogs for the suicidal maniacs. With a grateful sigh, Elliot stuck his nozzle in and gave the clerk his card.

"Fill it up," he said and gathered some comfort treats—chips, a Snickers, a mega Coke with just enough ice. He was taking a long, soothing sip as he walked back to his car when someone shoved him, hard, from behind. "Hey," he yelled, or coughed, really, spitting out his straw and stumbling forward. The soda splattered, a brown stain across the pure concrete. Before he could even turn, hands grabbed him by the shirt and a white minivan squealed up. The door slid back and there was the blond tourist with the pressed shorts from the office, springing out with his pals.

"Surprise, asshole!" As they began to pull him toward the van, Elliot squirmed and struggled, not so much fighting as mounting a sort of passive resistance.

"What the hell do you want?" he shouted as they dragged him over the ground.

"What the hell do you think?" Blondie demanded. "Where'd you get the tape?"

"I didn't," Elliot said, trying to wriggle loose. "I don't even know where to look." His bag of chips burst underfoot, spraying crumbs. Blondie got his hands on Elliot's throat.

"Who sold it to you? Who?"

Elliot had no answer, but even if he did, he had no voice as he felt the grip tighten. He struggled but more hands and knees held him tight.

"Hey!" A new voice called from somewhere. "What's going on?"

Instantly, the hands released. Elliot rolled away, coughing and gagging as the clerk strode over. The boys backed off, getting into their minivan. Just then, another, identical white minivan pulled up, this one loaded with kids, who tumbled out, chased by a bearded dad and pregnant mom. "Caleb! Noel! Clarissa!"

Blondie gave Elliot a quick but vicious kick in the butt. "You're going to hell," he hissed as he jumped in the van. "Soon."

They rode off. Elliot climbed slowly to his feet.

"Here," the clerk said, holding out his hand. "You forgot your Snickers."

8

It was dark out by the time Elliot got home and the wind was picking up. Still freaked, he parked around the corner and snuck into his place through the backyard. He even took the unprecedented action of calling the office after hours. Miriam called him back promptly. Vic was indisposed, she said, but not to worry. Relax and they'd handle it on Monday.

So he lay low, cowering in his garage. He hit the deck at a sudden loud noise, like a kettledrum thumping in his yard. Or rather, since he was already lying on his futon, he just rolled off onto the floor, then peered out the window. A huge plastic garbage can had come bouncing down the driveway. The cans had all blown over, spilling their contents, and with a rueful chuckle at his own chickenheartedness, Elliot began chasing them through whirling tornadoes of garbage. He grabbed one and the wind caught it, filling it with air like a sail. He felt the can pulling against him, fighting to rush away with the spinning planet beneath his feet. Streetlights flapped like scarecrows. Trees bent. The razored clouds tore the moon to shreds. On the corner, the stop sign shook itself violently, as though having a fit, and the street echoed with its ringing. At last he managed to drag the cans back into place beside the shrubs. He weighed down their lids with decorative bricks from the neighbor's garden and surreptitiously kicked the trash into the gutter. Huddling back across the lawn, he noticed Area watching him from the door.

"Hey, Elliot, what're you up to tonight?"

Elliot shrugged. "I don't know. Not much."

"Cause we're all going to this party in the Hills and I wanted to see if maybe you felt like checking it out?" Elliot shrugged again. He was wary of their occasional invites. The last time he'd been the designated driver on a journey to Pasadena and they still owed him for gas.

"Maybe. Whose party?"

"This guy Joseph who's a talent manager—he handles that new rapper Dejavu. I hear he might perform."

Elliot remembered that name. Supposedly Crystal Waters had been in the strip club with him, tipping big and drinking champagne. Then again, another supposed clue had nearly led to death in the Valley.

"Why not?" he said with a sigh.

"Great. Eight o'clock." She smiled, like a flashbulb going off. "Oh, and it's a birthday party—so you should probably bring a gift since you don't know him." Elliot nodded. This was starting to sound less appealing.

"Just pick something up and then go ahead and make the card out from all of us," she added helpfully, as though making things easier for him. "Thanks." She shut the door. Elliot turned back to the wind.

Elliot scanned his garage for a suitable gift. There was hardly anything here he even wanted himself, but buying something was, of course, out of the question. If it had been for a woman he would have crept around the block and picked flowers from someone's yard. But what, from among his disposable possessions, was the most appropriate gift for a talent manager? Purple dildo or butt plug? Which sent the right message? Elliot considered giving him a book from the stacks against the wall, a "property" he believed talent managers called it. Then inspiration struck. His *Raunchy* jacket. He wiped the cobwebs from an old carton, packed the jacket, and wrapped the whole thing in tinfoil. He showered, shaved, and stanched the blood. Back in the garage, he dressed, smoked a cigarette while watching *Jeopardy!*, and went back up front, precisely at eight.

"We're almost ready," Area called out when he announced his presence. Two hours passed. Elliot watched the fires on TV. All day, helicopters had been dropping giant water balloons on the flames. Fire crews arrived from other states. As Elliot stared, enraptured, the fire became a weather system unto itself, sucking air into miniature tornadoes, lightening and darkening the night. Trees hit like match heads, blowing their lives out in sudden blooms, leaving only skeleton ladders and a range of broken teeth. Rocks split. Across black fields the orange fire flowed.

Elliot began to get drowsy. He was losing momentum, and just as he began to reconsider his plan for the evening, the girls entered, Feather in white, Sequoia in black, Area in jeans and a tiny T-shirt that exposed her pierced navel. He should have been used to it by now, but still the combined impact of their tripled attractiveness knocked the air from his lungs. They eyed him and his gift suspiciously.

"What did you get him?" Feather asked.

"A satin jacket."

"Real satin?"

"Of course."

The girls smiled. "You look great," Sequoia said. "Let's go."

They loaded into Sequoia's all-terrain assault vehicle and rolled into the Friday night traffic. In the back seat, Elliot stared out the window and let the warm wind flow over his face. He liked these blank spaces, in between here and there. Wherever he was headed, when he got there, he always felt a small urge to just keep driving.

They bounced up into Beachwood Canyon, and while Area and Feather fixed the makeup they had just spent the evening applying, Sequoia wrestled the gigantic cruiser around the narrow roads. She lurched through a hairpin turn, hit the curb, and took out half a hedge. The smaller the driver, the bigger the truck, seemed to be the rule in this town. Except they weren't called trucks now. They were sport utility vehicles, though it wasn't clear what sport exactly utilized them, unless you considered shopping or one-handed mobile phone driving athletic events. Sequoia shot past a stop sign and another car, screeching to a halt, honked and flashed its lights. Sequoia waved. "Thank you!"

They found the house, a bunker hung over a ravine, then backed woozily down the steep hill looking for parking, past packed BMWs and Porsches. Finally Sequoia edged someone's trash cans off a cliff and parked. Elliot hopped out. Waxed legs flashed as the girls clambered down from the cockpit. They had arrived.

They made their entrance, winding through sparsely peopled, sparsely furnished mid-century modern rooms to the crowded poolside where a bartender and DJ had set up shop. Trailing Charlie's Angels, Elliot knew he enjoyed a real advantage, a sudden spotlight that couldn't help but illuminate him. No one could ignore the stir his housemates' arrival created and this would make him momentarily interesting to both men and women. But the moment would quickly pass.

"Hey, ladies, thanks for coming." A muscled young white guy with gelled hair sauntered over. A blazingly white dress shirt clung to his tanned, popped torso and was carefully tucked half in, half out of his baggy jeans.

"Joe," the girls yelled. Each one kissed his cheek.

"Here," Feather said, waving at Elliot. "We got you something."

"Thanks," Joe said. "You didn't have to do that." He took the gift from Elliot.

"Hi," Elliot said. "I'm Elliot."

"Hey," Joe said, as if just noticing he was there, attached to the box. "How's it going? The food's over there. Help yourself." He turned to the girls and gestured in the opposite direction. "Come on, let's get you a drink."

As they headed off, Elliot nodded, a smile on his face, and walked deliberately to the table, where he pretended to inspect the empty trays. He ate a chip, and then, in case someone was watching, coolly lit a cigarette before turning to survey the scene. Most of the people there were in their twenties and thirties, the women cast from the same talent pool as his roommates, while the men dressed like construction workers in Dickies, Carhartt, and flannel but with tattoos and elaborate, tricky-looking facial hair. Elliot could barely shave without cutting his throat. The older, paunchy guys, all wearing sports coats over expensive T-shirts and jeans with cowboy boots or sneakers, were producers of something (music, TV, film) unless they were wearing baseball caps, which meant they were directors. The few older or overweight women present were, no doubt, powerful industry figures, casting directors or studio execs.

No one was actually famous, in the sense that Elliot knew who they were, but the scene was packed with the celebrity adjacent. Barbra Streisand's dog trainer was supposedly there and the patterned trim around the pool had been done by the guy who did all of Brad Pitt's tilework. A thin blonde girl gushed about how down-to-earth and friendly Cher was when she helped shampoo her hair and a boy bragged about playing basketball with George Clooney. In this way, they were all somehow part of Hollywood, which was a small neighborhood but a vast realm. At its center, like a secret power source, were the truly rich and famous, whom you could live your whole life here and never see. Then, radiating outward, were these circles of lesser characters, who revolved around the stars and encountered each other at trendy restaurants and nightclubs, gyms and health food stores. And far out, in the murky swamps, less admired than even Harrison Ford's electrician's assistant, were Elliot and his ilk. Nevertheless, he was still in showbiz, sort of; it was normal for him to see a porn starlet he'd interviewed at the car wash, or a record executive his housemate had dated at the dentist. Elliot might be way out in the cold, like Pluto, but he was still in the same orbit, and as the Star System rotated, their paths crossed and recrossed.

A white hipster in his twenties sidled up to Elliot. His face sported two thin spiraling sideburns and a long wisp of hair waving like kelp from his chin.

"Hey, bro," he called. "Got an extra smoke?"

"Uh, sure." Elliot held out his pack.

"Mind if I take two, for my girlfriend? Cool. Got a light?"

Elliot gave him a light.

"Thanks, bro." He sauntered back to an actress with low-slung pants, pierced belly, and baby T who glanced at Elliot and giggled. Elliot nodded and headed off quickly in the other direction, glaring importantly at his watch and acting like he just remembered something he had to do. It was vital to keep moving. A moving person was going somewhere, while one standing alone obviously had no place to be. But this strategy wore quickly in a confined space, and after circling the pool and pretending not to hear two more bros calling for cigarettes, he headed into the house. He blundered into a room where two girls were making out and left. He waited for the bathroom, which gave him a reason to stand still. Once inside, he washed his hands and face, then poked around in the medicine cabinet, taking a few of each pill. In the living room he found a half dozen people watching a time-coded screening copy of a soon-to-be-released blockbuster. Elliot leaned casually against the couch next to a model, a six-foot-tall Black girl with a buzzed head tottering on giraffe legs. She glanced at him and didn't leave, which was promising, so he kept on watching the movie. A tanker exploded in the middle of the ocean and, a dramatic pause later, world-famous action star Chet Hunter popped up in the wreckage, wearing only torn Levi's.

"Bobby? Bobby!" he cried, his face distraught, his hair calm.

After another moment of suspense, Bobby popped up. He turned out to be Julio Montez, a young Latino comedian who specialized in sidekick roles. The star dragged him to safety atop a piece of wood.

"Damn, Homie! Look at my suit," the sidekick sputtered, holding up his tattered clothes. "Next time, I'm driving!"

Chet chuckled. "No way, José. I'm not trusting you with my car."

The movie ended and everyone stood up. Elliot tried to mill around with the crowd, guessing whether the model had liked the movie. She seemed too French, he decided. Cynicism was more European.

"Well," he said to her, "I guess I just saved nine bucks." She stared at him blankly, and Elliot was about to ask if she spoke English as a guy who looked like a better dressed, slightly taller version of Elliot came up and put his arm around her.

"This is my husband, Peter," she said in a cool British accent. "He cowrote this film."

"Hey, man," Elliot said. "Great work."

"Thanks," Peter said, extending his hand. "What's your name?" Mrs. Peter eyed him murderously.

"Isaac," Elliot said. "Isaac Babel."

"Well, it's good to meet you, Isaac."

They walked away, glancing back as she whispered in his ear. Elliot noticed that the room was empty. He fled outside, but turned away when he saw the screenwriter. A guy with a waxed villain mustache blocked his path.

"Hey, bro! Got a smoke?"

He swerved again and, smiling and nodding convulsively, wandered not-so-nonchalantly past the food tables and out to the pool area, which was now completely packed. The birthday boy—Joe was it?—was standing on the small platform behind the DJ gear with a mic.

"Thanks everybody for coming out, I hope you enjoyed the eats and drinks, and now I know you're most definitely going to enjoy the tuneage because, without further adieus, I'd like to bring up my very special guest and brother from another motherfucker . . . Dejavu!" The crowd howled and hooted as a pale teenager leaped onstage, smooth and pretty in a white shirt, slacks, and shoes, with bleached hair and a heavy rope of gold around his neck. He wore shades, despite the darkness. The two men hugged deeply and the younger man took the mic.

"Yo! How's everybody in the house tonight? Y'all getting your party on? Damn there's a lot of cool pimps and fine hoes here tonight! Let me hear it from the bitches!" Huge cheers from the women. "Cool. Cool. I want to thank my brohemian Joe and wish this pimpster a very happy birthday, man."

Joe stuck his face to the mic. "Thanks, love you Day."

"And now," Dejavu went on, his voice rising, "Let's get pimpin', people!"

With another roar from the guests, the music rose and they began awkwardly hopping and grinding, a spectacle that made Elliot feel simultaneously disdainful and left out. And then he saw her, red head bobbing up in the crowd near the little stage, looking more or less like all the other girls in a cropped white top and low-cut jeans, hugging the birthday boy. There she was, the problem called Crystal. Elliot stared. What was the word for the opposite of an inspiration? A desperation? But now, as if by divine intervention, she'd appeared.

"Hey, Crystal!" he yelled, waving, but his voice was lost in the din. He started to move toward her, as if toward a mirage, weaving through the crowd and finding his way around the perimeter of the pool. Buffeted about, he lost sight of her and was craning for a view when he felt a hand on his shoulder.

"Oi, you Elliot?" croaked a foggy voice that was somehow familiar. "The bloke from *Raunchy*?" Relieved to meet or maybe make a friend, he turned, smiling and nodding.

"Yeah, that's . . . me?" He faltered. It was Eddie Hex. He had just a moment to take in the famous weathered visage—tan wrinkles and a matched set of purple eye bags, a leather vest and no shirt, dangling necklaces including a heavy cross, long dyed black hair, and was that eyeliner?—before a fist landed in his belly, forcing all the air from his body.

"That's for me wife!" the stringy rock star yelled, drawing looks from the crowd. "And this is for me, you wanker!"

Hex landed another blow, a nice one, right on the chin, and Elliot stumbled back into the pool, the sound of cheering muffled by the water.

This is actually kind of nice, he thought for a moment as he sank. Refreshing. Relaxing. And perhaps if he could have just remained there, on the bottom, he might have been able to rest in peace. But a moment later his head broke the surface and he saw the laughing, happy faces beaming down. There were his roommates, looking disappointed. There was Mrs. Peter, grinning. There were the bros, high-fiving Eddie Hex. The only upside was that the whole party was dancing now and focused on the stage, mostly ignoring him. Laughing and waving, he paddled to the steps and climbed out, dripping wet. Already a few nymphs were following his lead, stripping down to their undies and diving in, somehow looking far more graceful. He scanned the crowd for Crystal, but she was nowhere in sight, if she had even really been there. Maybe it had been a wish.

"Party on, bro!" a dude with a Vandyke yelled, clapping him on the back. Another guy with a goatee high-fived him. Nodding and grinning, he slopped across the deck and walked right into some shrubs, stumbling uphill to a small sheltered spot, and then squatted in the dirt, screened by greenery from the party below. He briefly entertained the thought of swallowing all the pills in his pocket, but he didn't want to be found dead by Joe's gardener. Even worse, it might not be enough to do the job, and he'd be caught, stumbling and drooling, by a couple looking for a place to copulate. Better to save the pills for an emergency. Elliot didn't truly consider himself suicidal. He wasn't about to do anything anytime soon. But on nights like this, knowing the pills were there gave him the strength to go on. It was like having your parachute packed and ready, knowing that if the moment came, you could pull your cord and bail. He reached into his pocket, as if to touch his lucky charm, and felt mush. The rainbow of pills had all melted into a brownish muck, like a watercolor set. With a sigh, he wiped his hand on his pants. He'd have to go on after all.

There was a sudden rustling in the trees around him and Elliot froze, holding his breath. An irrational fear surged through him. Did coyotes rip the faces off grown men? Had he heard that? What if it was a skunk? He strained his eyes, searching the darkness for another set of eyes staring back, for a gleaming fang or claw. Finally, a cat stepped out, meowing. Elliot smiled at himself.

"Here, kitty," he whispered. The cat rubbed against his leg, letting him pet it just once, before smoothing its fur with a paw and, suitably primped, heading down to the party. Elliot sat down, exhaling, finally releasing the whole thing, and took off his shoes. This was no big deal after all. He'd be laughing about it five years from now. He began wringing out his socks when he heard more rustling and then, just as he was expecting the cat's return, a stream of urine emerged from the bushes, splashing into his empty shoes.

"Hey!" he yelled.

The stream stopped abruptly. A face popped out. Handsome, smooth-shaven, with a mane of thick black hair. The sharp brown eyes took in the scene, and then he laughed, a loud, very familiar laugh. "Elliot?" he asked.

"Yes," Elliot admitted, somewhat reluctantly.

"It's me. Pedro. Pedro Plotkin."

"Pedro?" It was true he'd had a friend named Pedro, a best friend actually, but that had been a continent away and a lifetime ago. Elliot peered deeply at him, searching for that kid. His once chubby, sloppy, sweaty childhood pal was transformed—handsome, beautifully muscled, and smartly dressed in an open-necked black shirt and black pants, with an expensive diver's watch—but around the eyes, and in the smile, it was him. "Wow. How long has it been?"

Pedro squatted beside him. "Fifth grade. So like twelve years? Or fifteen?"

"Right. What are you doing here?"

Pedro shrugged. "Of course I'm here. Free drinks and a chance to see a lot of bougie white girls being called bitch and loving it? What could be better?" He patted Elliot's shoulder. "I didn't realize that was you who jumped in the pool. That was classic. Hope you peed while you were in there. They're all splashing in it now."

Elliot shrugged.

"Ha! You did, didn't you? That's my boy." He stood, brushing off his pants. "Well, speaking of pee, I better be getting back. They'll wonder what happened. I won't hug you, because . . ." He gestured at his own perfect looks. Elliot nodded. "But we should catch up. Got a card or something?"

"Um, here, sure . . ." Elliot reached into his pocket and pulled out his damp wallet. He peeled off one of his limp cards.

"*Raunchy*? Associate editor?" Pedro held it by a corner like evidence. "That's amazing. I always knew you'd make it big."

"Um, thanks," Elliot replied, crossing his bare feet. "Actually senior associate now. The new cards aren't ready."

"Pedro! Oh, Pedro!" a chorus of drunk voices sang out as they approached.

Pedro laughed. "Okay, better run, talk soon," Pedro said, fixing his collar. And he went.

Time passed until Elliot noticed that the music had stopped. He stood carefully, rubbing his cramped legs, and peeked through the shrubs. The party was over. The girls were probably looking for him. He headed through the bushes and was stepping down onto the patio when he heard laughter and splashing. He ducked behind the tables and peered around a corner. His three housemates, stripped down to bras and panties, were lounging in the hot tub with Joe, Bro Number One, and the screenwriter and his wife. The model/wife had her arm around Area and they giggled while her husband watched with a grin. Joe handed Sequoia a beer.

"Whatever happened to that roommate of yours?" he asked.

"I don't know. Maybe he went home with someone."

"Yeah, right," Joe said, and the group laughed. Bro lit a joint and handed it to Feather. She took a hit and coughed.

"Hey, don't waste the chronic, babe," he said, closing in to draw the smoke from her lips.

Elliot sat under the table. Now what? He considered calling a cab, but he didn't even know the name of the street he was on and he doubted the seven moist dollars in his pocket would get him home; so he was walking. But first things first. He went into the bathroom, and regarded himself. There were leaves in his hair and dirt on his hands and face. He washed up, and was drying off, when he noticed the toothbrush hanging innocently over the sink. He remembered Pedro and then, on an impulse, he grabbed it, held it over the bowl, unzipped, and drenched it. Glancing up at the mirror, Elliot was shocked by the smile on his face, the look of pure joy. He began to laugh, harder and harder, the laughter growing as he put the toothbrush back, washed his hands again, and left. Laughing his ass off, he walked downhill, toward Hollywood.

A few turns down the road, Elliot found himself on what could have been a country lane, if not for the glow and hum of a giant city just over the hill behind the trees. All cities, he supposed, had their sparse patches where nature broke through, but in LA they felt particularly strong, these sudden eruptions of the wilderness you thought had been successfully stamped out. Perhaps it was because LA was spread thinner. In New York, the only sign of true wildlife was the occasional hawk hunting pigeons in the canyons of Wall Street or those weird weed trees that sprang from cracks in the cement. Otherwise the main species left competing were rats, roaches, pigeons, and us. In LA, even the weather was a dormant but dangerous force of nature. While mostly nonexistent, mere painted backdrop, it threatened at all times to return with a vengeance, as earthquake, mudslide, wildfire, or some other horrible compound word (fireslide? mudquake?) and wipe man's vain scribble from the map.

Again, invisible creatures breathed in the undergrowth, raising the hair on the back of Elliot's neck. He could smell smoke faintly on the wind, the breath of far-off fires. Something stung his eye, and when he squinted at a lone streetlamp, he made out tiny particles fluttering down whitely like moths. Snow, he thought for an inane second, and held out his palm. A gray flake landed and he smudged it: ash, churned into tiny particles and drifting with the dew. In the morning all their cars would be covered.

He heard a car approaching. The engine separated itself from the general babble of traffic, clearing its throat, and headlights rose behind the trees. Elliot felt a wave of worry. He thought of the minivan gang and of Eddie Hex. He even imagined that Joe had somehow detected his pee and was hunting him down. He stepped into the bushes and crouched down as the headlights passed. It was a limo, nearly as wide as the road, and lit yellow from within like a swaying train carriage. Through the window he saw, or thought he saw, Crystal Waters and Dejavu, arms around each other and laughing. And there, across from them, facing back at Elliot as they passed, was Pedro. As the limo vanished around a bend, he tossed a cigarette butt out the window. Its embers scattered like stars, but fortunately they faded to black before they could ignite a conflagration.

Pedro knew Crystal? Perhaps if he called him and asked a favor of an old pal . . . but of course, he couldn't call; Pedro had taken his card but offered none. Still, the random encounter with his oldest friend had given him heart, though, if he was honest, Pedro had been trouble from the day they met.

It had all started with a poem. In general, Elliot was smart enough to hide the fact that he actually liked books from his fourth-grade classmates. But this time the teacher had given him an A, and as punishment, was making him read his effort aloud.

"O Winter Wind / Blowing so cold / Who knows if you / Are young or old?" he'd warbled out, and as his classmates dully applauded he could see the contempt in their eyes. Trying to trip him on the way back to his seat, Ronald Scuznik had hissed "dickbreath," and his sidekick, Terry O'Flynn, had muttered "lunger," his nickname ever since he was first excused from gym for chronic asthmatic bronchitis in first grade. He'd been on the bench, coughing, ever since.

So that day, at recess, he was dawdling by the fence as usual, when Ronald and O'Flynn left the dodgeball game to corner him. Terry declaimed, in an Irish lilt: "O Winter Wind / You smell like shit / Why don't you suck / Your mama's tit?" Everyone liked this poem much better, including Elliot, who laughed along, but that only enraged Ronald more. Elliot could still feel that punch, ringing in his head like a bell, and hear the happy cheers of the crowd. He was moving in for the kill, when a voice piped up.

"You better watch out. He's a lunger!" It was Pedro, the odd, goofy kid with the untucked shirt and messy hair who was often removed from class for being "hyper."

"It's contagious right?" Pedro asked him leadingly. "The disease you got?"

Finally, catching on, Elliot dug deep into his clogged tubes and hocked up a phlegm bomb, launching it onto the front of Ronald's shirt. Pandemonium ensued, as Ronald screamed and flailed and for the first time, the crowd was on Elliot's side, laughing *with* him, as they say, and *at* somebody else. But the sweetness was brief, as Ronald and Terry announced his execution for 3:00 P.M. sharp. Only Pedro, whose fault all this was, lingered by his side. He told Elliot to meet him right after school, and that was when he learned what his weird new pal was capable of. Pulling off one sneaker and sock, he slipped a piece of broken brick into his sock, then put the sneaker back on, and tucked the weird puppet in a pocket before they started to walk home. When the bullies approached, backed by an eager crowd, he yanked the sock out, wound up, and like David facing Goliath, bonked Ronald right in the face. He went down, yelping, with a bloody nose. But there were no cheers this time. Terry turned and ran. So did everyone else. Even Christine, the next time Elliot saw her, failed to congratulate him on finally winning a fight, sort of.

"How could you kiss me when you're infected?" she demanded. "What if I have your disease now?"

"No," he stammered. "It's not really like that."

She turned and biked away, golden hair streaming, the white pom-pom on her hat bouncing into the falling darkness.

9

Elliot spent a peaceful Sunday hiding out from both his unseen enemies and his roommates. Monday morning, he walked an extra block to sneak in the back entrance at work and avoid the protesters. So far so good. But just as he was feeling normal, standing at a urinal in the men's room, he caught a glimpse from the corner of his eye: there, in the handicapped stall, were wheels. Terror struck. What if it was Vic? Of course it was! There were no other employees in wheelchairs. He saw the wheels shift and frantically zipped himself up, then rushed to wash his hands, glancing over his shoulder in panic. *Come here*, he imagined the booming voice commanding. *Wipe my ass!* And then just as he was grabbing a paper towel and frantically drying, the stall door opened. Elliot froze like a rabbit in a gunsight, and heard himself whimper. Out came the janitor, with a mop, pushing along one of those wheeled buckets. He nodded at Elliot and began to clean the sinks. Elliot nodded back.

It must have been some kind of omen, because just as he was about to head down the hall to the art department, steal some coffee, and say hi to Margie, she came hustling out, away from her desk and the elevators.

"Red alert!" she called to him. "I smell smoke!" But instead of heading outside for safety, she darted into the shelter of the women's room. Elliot sniffed deeply. He too caught a faint whiff of cigar and took off running down the hall, scurrying back into his office.

There was Vic, dressed in a red satin robe and white slippers, pushed by Moishe and accompanied by Miriam, now in a nurse's outfit, white dress, white hose, and pumps, with a red cross on her cleavage, wheeling an IV drip that ran into his arm.

"Gross!" he yelled. "There you are." He waved his cigar and ash fell on Elliot's desk.

"Yikes!" Elliot yelped, jumping a foot in the air. "I mean, good morning, sir. Are you okay?"

"What the hell do you mean?"

"Um . . . medically."

"Oh. This is just antibiotics," he noted, glancing at his drip. "A little follow-up procedure. Where are we on Crystal?" he demanded. "Any leads?"

"Yes, definitely. I've got a lot of leads, well, several, though none have quite panned out yet, per se."

"I hear things got a little hairy out in the Valley."

"Hairy?" Elliot shuddered. "Yes, sir . . ."

"That's good news," Victor announced. "Means you're getting close." He waved his cigar dismissively. "Don't worry, they'd never kill you unless you had the tape. That's basic dollars and cents."

"That's good to know, I guess."

He reached out and grasped Elliot's arm. "I bared my heart to you, Gross." Moishe and Miriam glared from over his shoulders. "Don't let me down."

"No, sir." He squirmed like a worm on a hook.

Victor sighed. "But first things first, I've got an urgent assignment for you. A real plum. You're going to love this."

Elliot nodded. "Okay . . ." He rooted around for a pencil.

"Dr. Gary Kishkewicz."

"Right." Elliot tried to sound it out as he scribbled on his desk pad.

"He's a top-notch surgeon doing amazing things with pussies and dicks."

"Wonderful . . ." Elliot heard his voice crack and cleared his throat. "Sounds wonderful."

"I want you to head over and interview him, pronto. He's a game changer." Vic waved his cigar and sprinkled more ash like holy water. "Plus we owe him a big favor."

"Yes, sir. Is that with a *z*?"

Moishe slapped a business card on his desk. Beverly Hills address. Was this the mysterious Dr. K?

"Where's the jacket?" Vic asked then.

That paused him. "Sorry?"

"The jacket I gave you. You're not wearing it."

Elliot looked down at himself, as if surprised. "Well, it's been a bit warm, you know." Actually it was freezing in there.

"I want you to wear it when you go over there. Let Kishkewicz know we're serious."

Elliot began to sweat despite the icy AC. "Well, the thing of it is, sir. I didn't want to say this but, it was stolen."

"Stolen?" Vic sat forward. Moishe loomed as if the malefactor was under the desk. "By whom?"

"I wish I knew. I wore it to a party up in the Hills. This talent manager, he handles a rapper . . . Anyway, I took it off because, well, I ended up in the pool, haha! But when I went back it was gone. Terrible."

"Did you call the cops?"

"Cops? No. Do you think I should, for insurance maybe?"

"No. Never the call the cops for anything."

"Right."

Vic turned to Moishe. "I told you those were going to be a hot item. Soon people will be killing for them, like those leather eight ball jackets."

Moishe nodded in agreement. Elliot sighed with relief. Disaster averted.

"Exactly," he concurred. "I'm lucky to be alive."

"Which brings me to the other reason for my visit. We realize the stress you're under and brought you a little extra peace of mind. Miriam?"

With a curt nod, Miriam opened her white leather medical bag and pulled out a gun, a flat black automatic.

"There you go," Vic said, as Elliot stared. "Not as big as the Desert Eagle Moishe carries but easy to conceal. Don't worry, it's loaded. You do know how to use a gun, don't you?"

"Well . . ." Elliot lifted it carefully by the muzzle, with two fingers.

Vic shook his head. "And you're from Brooklyn?"

"Queens," Elliot said, laying the gun on his desk blotter.

"Still. Moishe can take you down in the basement, give you some pointers."

"No," he snapped. "I mean, thank you but no. I need to get right on this story."

"Good point. They're expecting you. Carry on." Vic waved his cigar and the procession wheeled around. "And remember, we are all counting on you."

Waving at their backs, Elliot sat down, exhausted, and breathed in Vic's exhaust. His tiny office stank of cigar smoke and the window didn't open. Thinking about his supposed leads, he checked the phone book for Pedro Plotkin. No listing. He called Farah and promised to expand "Dear Slut" if she came through. He looked around for a place to hide the gun, decided to take it home, then worried about having it in his car. Finally, he wrapped it in sheets from last month's *Raunchy*, tied it with rubber bands, and tucked it casually under his arm, planning to stash it in his trunk and just hope he didn't get pulled over. When the elevator opened, he was so focused on being casual, he got on without glancing at the lone passenger.

"Morning, mate."

"Oh fuck," Elliot jumped back and raised his arms protectively, fearing another blow. Then, remembering he was armed, he began unwrapping his parcel. "Stay back, I'm warning you. Hang on a minute." He'd tied it too tight.

“No worries. Just here picking up me dosh.” Hex patted his pocket.

“Dosh? That means money right? Like quids?” His gaze narrowed. “So it was you selling the tape all along?”

The rocker tapped his nose with a finger.

“But then why did you hit me?”

He shrugged. “Bit of theater innit? I thought you knew! Got to give the punters a show, outraged husband and all. Plus . . .” he leaned in. “The wife doesn’t know. So do us a favor? Keep shtum.”

Stepping into the sun together, they both slid on shades and popped cigarettes into their mouths. The protest had grown; there was now a group of nuns with signs and a couple of priests waving Bibles and sprinkling holy water on the building, gingerly, as if expecting blowback. Cop cars were parked by the curb with the officers keeping the entranceway clear.

Hex whipped out a gold lighter and gave Elliot a light, along with a gleaming, mostly gold smile. “No biz like showbiz, right?” Then he strode over to a big, black Harley parked by the curb. Elliot stared. Was it the same bike? He didn’t think so. But the white minivan parked at the corner made the hair on his neck stand up. He hugged his parcel tight.

“Hey,” he asked the former rock star, “could you do me a favor?”

Hex shrugged. “Why not? I owe you one.”

“See that minivan? Think you could, you know, intimidate them?”

Hex grinned, cigarette between his gold choppers. “That’s not a favor, mate. That’s a pleasure.”

He hopped on the bike and kick-started it, jumping up and down, grinding the throttle. With a roar that could be heard even over the chanting, he cruised majestically over to the minivan and stopped in front. Meanwhile, clutching his parcel more like a security blanket than a weapon, Elliot sidled up to the front passenger side, where Blondie hung out the window, scanning the building through his camera. Elliot grabbed the camera’s lens hard and twisted, yanking him by the strap.

“Surprise, asshole,” he said, voice low. “Nice to see you again.”

Blondie jerked back, turning to his pal in the driver's seat, but Hex was blocking them in, revving his engine and giving them the two-finger British "up-yours" sign. The cops were leaning against their car nearby, enjoying the carnival atmosphere. They were trapped. Elliot leaned in.

"Now tell me who the hell you are and why you want this tape, or I'll call those cops right now. You with another magazine? You trying to publish it?"

"Publish it?" Blondie was incredulous. "That tape already ruined my daddy's life."

"Your daddy?"

"Congressman O'Malley is my father. He was a great man and you just humiliated him in front of the whole world. I want the bastard who set him up. I want justice." He paused for breath, visibly distraught, and the driver patted his shoulder. "You know," he said, "he can't even show his face in church."

"Sorry," Elliot said. "But I really don't know. It was all anonymous. Does it even matter?"

Blondie shook his head. Tears trickled from his eyes. Hex was now making devil's signs, throwing up horns, and flicking his tongue at the protesters. The nuns scattered. A priest flicked some holy water at his bike, but backed off as he gunned it.

"You should go home," Elliot suggested. "You don't belong here."

"How can I?" he asked, eyes wide. "How can I face my mom?"

10

"When it comes to the penis, most focused on lengthening, usually by inserting a rod that stretched the skin, or an inflatable sack of some kind." Elliot nodded thoughtfully as Dr. Kishkewicz recalled his moment of inspiration. They were in the doctor's office, a pocket recorder on the desk between them. Kishkewicz leaned back in his chair, light skipping between the diamond studs that dotted his gold eyeglass frames, and weighed his place in medical history, while Elliot admired a leather-bound photo album full of his creations. "But I was the first to thicken."

Steeling himself, Elliot began to page through the book. It featured men in "before" and "after" poses, photographed from the neck down, holding their flaccid, mopey-looking genitals beside rulers and poking them through holes in a metal template that measured girth.

"So what I do here," the doctor explained, "is I go in under the skin and build up the penis with dermafill."

"What's dermafill?"

"It's derma that's harvested and treated."

"Harvested from where, the leg or something?"

"It's harvested from cadavers."

"What? This is dead people's skin?" Elliot lost his composure and gawked openly at the doctor. "Wow."

"It's common practice," the doctor said, a bit defensively, and grabbed the next album. "Let me show you my vaginas." He handed over another finely tooled leather volume: "before" and "after" shots of dozens of retrofitted and renovated bodies with the heads cropped out. Elliot was both impressed and appalled. He felt like a dazed witness trying to identify the victims of some freak disaster. *That's her, Inspector. Her head's gone, of course, but I'd know those killer abs anywhere.*

"It all started when I was doing a lot of mother-daughter liposuctions. And I noticed that there was a difference between the vaginas of the mother and daughter. Finally, I figured it out. Fat loss. That was the key factor. By adding fat I'm able to make the mother look like she used to look when she was young."

Until he moved to LA, Elliot had never even knowingly conversed with a woman who had breast implants and had relegated plastic surgery to the exotic realm of strippers and socialites. Here it was so common that women didn't even hide it, discussing collagen-enhanced lips or saline-engorged breasts in the same breath as acupuncture or the best preschool. But even by the eugenic standards of this town, Kishkewicz was no run-of-the-mill tit-and-nose man. What made Dr. K more than just another multimillionaire running a Beverly Hills body shop was his bizarre development of ever newer and crazier improvements on the human form: penis growing, labia plumping, vagina tightening.

"I've got a three-month waiting list, without advertising. It's like a club. At parties, the women will go into another room and show each other their anatomy."

"Amazing," Elliot said, and meant it.

"I can make a nipple," Kishkewicz boasted, "where there isn't any nipple. I build it up out of erectile tissue."

"So it gets erect?"

"It's always erect. I've done six so far. Six patients, so that's twelve nipples." *Six patients = twelve nipples,* Elliot scribbled in his spiral reporter's notebook. Dr. Kishkewicz was no perfect specimen himself.

With a flat forehead and low, bushy Neanderthal brow, a short, plump frame and wondrously thick, dark hair plugs that all stuck up into exactly the same game-show-host wave formation, there was something simian about his appearance, despite the white-on-white shirt with French cuffs and the Rolex. When he stood to pull another album down from a shelf, Elliot peeked at an invoice on the desk, reading it upside down: *breast aug: $10,000.* He felt woozy. The doctor had said the vaginal "puffer" job ran about two grand, and that on surgery days he scheduled back-to-back construction jobs from eight in the morning till late in the evening. Elliot realized that in one good day, Kishkewicz easily made more than he would in a year. Perhaps his sense of superiority should be reconsidered. Here he was interviewing the guy after all.

"I guess there's a lot of money potential in these new operations," he suggested to the doctor, prodding him to keep talking until the tape was full.

Kishkewicz shrugged disdainfully. "I guess, but I'm more interested in the creative side. That's the reason I keep my prices low. To me my operations are art. That's why I introduced my Celebrity Models." He flipped through the photo album. "See, this patient has a nose and thighs exactly like Betty Grable's." A murky Polaroid of a woman with two black eyes was pasted next to a glossy black and white of the pinup. "But this woman wanted Audrey Hepburn's nose and jawline. They like to mix and match, you know, Pam Anderson on top, Sharon Stone on the bottom."

"It's like sculpture for you then," Elliot said, forcing an expression of rapt concentration onto his face by drawing his brows together and looking Kishkewicz right in the eye, something only the truly bogus can pull off. "But of course you're more than just an artist. You're helping people."

"That's true," Kishkewicz admitted modestly. "I help make people into their best selves, I make the outside match the person they feel like they are on the inside."

Best being a subjective term, Elliot admitted, he did sort of have a point. So then what was Elliot's problem? After all, he knew a hundred people who had modified their bodies with ink or piercings. And what about feminization surgeries? Patients from all over the world flocked to Dr. K for breasts, which he offered at a discount. He sometimes performed them for free for mastectomy patients, who often took the opportunity to go up a few sizes. We owned our bodies or we didn't, Elliot supposed, and in the end it was nobody's business. Or rather it was somebody's—Dr. K, who was glancing at his diamond-studded watch.

"Misty should be here by now," he said and led Elliot into the waiting room, where a woman in her late thirties sat with a boy of nine or ten playing a handheld electronic game by her side. She hopped up and gave the doctor a kiss.

"Misty, this is Elliot. He's writing an article on me for *Raunchy*."

"Pleasure." She shook his hand.

"Misty's our best patient," the doctor said.

"He's worked on everything but my ears and my ankles," Misty announced, spreading her arms to show off the work. Her lips were full blooms. Her nose was narrowed and permanently pinched above the nostrils as though something always stank around her. The skin shone with a pink, inhuman cast, the result of a recent peel. Her breasts jumped up and wiggled as if desperate to escape her tight black workout suit. Her body seemed to curve into some forced perspective, dwindling down over surgically trimmed stomach, hips, and thighs to the vanishing points of her high heels.

Elliot tried for a charming smile. "Well, your ankles look great to me."

Misty peeked around her breasts to check them out. "They're okay."

"A bit thick," the doctor observed, as though about to reach for his pocketknife. Misty nodded.

"So," she said, "you wanted to talk about my cooch lift?"

"Ah, yes, definitely," Elliot said, glancing over to see if her son was taking this in, but he was staring blankly into his little beeping box and furiously working his thumbs.

"Let's go in the consulting room," Kishkewicz suggested, leading the way. "I want to see how that breast aug is coming along." Elliot hung back, but they waved him along, and he hesitantly followed them into a small room with an examining table, medicine cabinet, and scale. Misty immediately removed her top and bra. Her breasts remained exactly in place, like two angel food cakes in a baking dish. The doctor mauled them thoughtfully while Misty smiled at Elliot.

"Lay down on the table," Kishkewicz instructed. "I want to show him something." She lay down. "See how they flatten a little when she lays back," he asked, poking one. "It's more realistic."

"Yeah, that's really good."

"Go ahead and feel them," Kishkewicz said. To Misty he explained, "He's an expert."

"No, that's okay," Elliot said.

"It's all right," Misty assured him. "I think of you like a doctor." Elliot reached out one hand and gave her right breast a little squeeze.

"Come on," the doctor urged. "Is that how you feel a girl's breasts?"

Elliot took a breath and moved into a better position.

"Excuse me," he said to Misty. He took a breast in each palm and squished them in and out. They felt like they had bones in them.

"They feel great," he announced.

"Thank you," Misty said.

"Show him the labial," the doctor instructed.

Elliot stepped back nervously as Misty hopped down and peeled away her tights and G-string. It looked a lot like her mouth.

"Wow," he said again.

"I'd let you touch it," Misty said, "but I just got back together with my ex-husband and it was a Father's Day gift to him."

"Right, I understand."

"It's kind of, like, private."

"No problem. How does he like it?"

"Oh my God, he loves it. The only problem is it feels so good he complains he comes too fast."

"Tell him to call me," Kishkewicz advised.

"How does it feel for you?" Elliot asked.

"It's amazing. It's like having a double clitoris. Like when you wear tight pants and just walk around the market, it's like having a vibrator built right in. And I never worry about him cheating. It gives you that little edge over other women. No matter how beautiful they are, you know you have something they don't. It's like, there are vaginas and there are vaginas. And then there are vaginas!"

Elliot changed into scrubs, a blue cotton smock that tied up the back and matching pajama bottoms. He stood with his arms out while the scrub nurse tied the smock closed. The receptionist helped him slip blue booties the size of plastic sandwich bags over his shoes and fitted a shower cap onto his head. Although one woman was pink and the other brown, both had the same narrow noses, burst lips, and cantilevered Frank Lloyd Wright breasts as Misty. Outside, it was an ordinary day, but the blue fluorescent light and refrigerated air made him feel like he was in a space station, rotating through a vacuum with droid-women preparing him for a walk on the moon.

He followed the scrub nurse into the operating room. A tall blonde woman was laid out in a crucifixion pose with a blue cloth covering her face. She had a navel piercing that was bandaged now in white gauze and her belly rose and fell with the sighing respirator. The anesthesiologist cheerfully introduced himself. Fiftyish, with fading yellow hair and a blooming carnation of a nose, he reminded Elliot of a burned-out wedding band musician, a bit shaky but grateful for the gig.

Kishkewicz entered, dressed in an operating outfit just like Elliot's, except for magnifying lenses that snapped on over his glasses and made him look even more like a mad scientist, Dr. Strangerlove. He began drawing on the woman with a Magic Marker, talking the whole time about what parts he would cut out or build up, outlining choice sections of her thighs and belly like one of those charts in the butcher shop. He used a Polaroid to snap "before" photos. He made Elliot pose next to him in front of the woman and the scrub nurse took one of them together.

Elliot had met the patient, Lara, before she'd been prepped and had taped a pregame interview. She was having her breasts and vagina altered today, with a little lipo thrown in, a package deal that would minimize her time off from work and the gym.

"It's like, when the tires on your car wear out, you buy new tires," she told his tape recorder. "If you can improve yourself, to me it's a thumbs-up. What could go wrong with this?"

Elliot's mind teemed with things that could go wrong as the anesthesiologist announced they were ready and the scrub nurse wheeled the instrument tray to the table. Dr. Kishkewicz invited Elliot in for a closer look. In his article, Elliot planned to describe Lara as "a leggy blonde marketing executive in her midthirties," and to Elliot's untrained eye, her freshly shaved "anatomy," as the doctor called it, seemed just fine as it was.

"Yeah, everything's there, together," he agreed, fingering her with white-gloved hands like a connoisseur. "It just got a little skimpy through the years for her." He turned to blink at Elliot through his eye gear, irises floating crazily, big as fish in twin bowls. "She must be from German stock," he concluded. "Germans have the best anatomy of anybody."

First the doctor sliced into her nipple. Elliot gasped. He'd never seen one person stab another, even by request. One's immediate urge was to yank the blade away or run for help. Instead, Elliot braced himself against the wall and gritted his teeth, grateful for the mask. Other writers had covered wars, riots, fires, and floods. Now it was his turn to face reality and report back. This is what we are made of, the truth beneath the skin: fat and blood and, for some, a saline bag that jumped and jiggled in the nurse's gloved hands like clear Jell-O.

But he hadn't figured on the smell. As Dr. K took up something like a soldering iron and began separating fat from muscle, making room for the implant, smoke came out and the room filled with what he realized was the smell of roasting human breast, and that was all Elliot could report because he fainted, dropping back into the nurse's outspread arms.

11

Elliot woke up in a bed, under a sheet, in a dimly lit room, with an IV drip in his arm. Where was he? As reality snapped into focus and he remembered—Dr. K's House of Horrors—he felt a wave of panic. Were his body parts all the same? Did he have experimental genitals or a nipple on his forehead? The door opened and the receptionist stuck her head in.

"Hi there. You're awake."

"Yes, thanks. How long . . ."

"You've been out for a few hours."

"What?" He looked at his watch.

"Your BP dropped so the doctor had us push some fluids. It's just saline. Feeling better?" She removed the needle and wiped the entry point with a cotton swab.

"Yes! Fine!" He nodded eagerly and tried to get up but immediately felt woozy. The receptionist eased him back.

"Just rest," she said. "And keep your voice down. You have a roommate sleeping next door."

As she tiptoed back out, Elliot realized that the room was divided by hanging curtains that partly concealed another bed and IV. By leaning back and turning his head all the way left, he could see a sleeping profile. She was in her midthirties, blonde, and white, and oddly familiar. He knew her from somewhere. He slid to his bootied feet and tiptoed carefully over. Silently, he parted the curtain. Of course. She looked just like Vivian De Fay. At least she had from across a dim room. One of Kishkewicz's Celebrity Models line. Up close he could see the maker's hand: lips too plump, cheekbones a bit high, skin too tight where it had been pulled back around the eyes. And she was younger than the real movie star, whom Elliot had himself mooned over in his youth and whose face he knew intimately, not because he'd ever seen it in person but because he'd seen it projected ten feet high. Elliot had to admit, the creep did nice work.

Elliot felt creepy himself, staring at this sleeping woman, but she'd paid a lot to look like someone you couldn't help staring at. Now she lay, perhaps dreaming her own fantasy life behind those closed lids. Self-conscious, he was about to turn away when he noticed that the IV ran into her right arm, but the crook of her left arm was bruised, too, and he could make out a line of tiny healed scars, like little darns of paler skin over the tanner flesh. He leaned in close. Old punctures? Could this be due to multiple operations, or was she a drug user as well? A junkie?

Her eyes opened. Elliot gasped and stepped back. But she was still asleep or, anyway, absent. Her eyes were blank, the pupils tiny pinpricks of black in irises of an unreal blue. Opiates. Only her body was present with him in the room, while she was lost somewhere back beyond those blues.

There was a knock.

"Up and around?" It was the receptionist again and Elliot quickly turned his back on the sleeper.

"Yes. All better. Thanks."

"Great. The doctor suggested you get dressed and wait in his office. I'll make some coffee."

Elliot wanted coffee badly, but he needed smoke more. "Actually I'm going to nip out for a cigarette," he said.

The receptionist leaned in, whispering. "You can just pop into the rear stairwell, that's what I do."

So Elliot smoked on the back stairs, nodding to the other figures, some in scrubs, who were scattered over the landings, their smoke drifting up like a giant chimney. As he opened the door to return to the hall, he saw Dr. K himself, still in scrubs and his shower cap, waiting by the elevator. Elliot paused as the door slid back and a man emerged. He looked like a dad, round and ordinary, with slouchy shoulders and a fringe of graying hair, but in a gorgeous blue suit cut from cloth Elliot's father never so much as touched. The two men hugged.

"Thanks for coming the back way," the doctor said. "It's much more private."

"No problem. Sorry to put you out," the man said. "Is everything ready? I know I'm early."

"Yes, yes, you're going to be very happy I promise . . ."

He opened the door to the office and the receptionist and nurse both stood there, like ladies-in-waiting, murmuring as he passed by. A VIP patient, no doubt. Elliot frowned as he imagined what sort of high-end super-advanced work he was getting done. Penis transplant? Testicle lift? At least Elliot would not have to watch it. He paused a minute before going back in himself and ducking into the doctor's office.

While he waited, Elliot took a peek at the pile of files on the doctor's desk, hoping to find "before" and "after" photos of the woman in the recovery room. The stacks were not quite as high as Elliot's but still, he managed, while trying to rifle discreetly through, to spill the pile onto the floor. Shit. He scrambled to clean it up. He stuffed photos back in folders, trying to match the right parts. He reattached clips. Then he paused. He was fixated, fascinated by a picture, but not by anything that had been enhanced, reshaped, or reduced. He was caught by a freckle.

It wasn't a conscious connection at first, more a flicker of recognition. He'd spent so long studying the images, blown up on his screen, and miniaturized on his light box, scrutinizing her magnified skin, that this sprinkling of brown dots, the circular mole on her shoulder, the birthmark on her thigh: they had become like stars to the astronomer, or sky maps to the sailor, or even signs to the believer. This was Crystal Waters's file. He was certain. But when he flipped back to the front, he saw a different name, a real name obviously, but one familiar to Elliot from some deeply buried back file of his own. And the "before" face, in the washed-out Polaroid, with its greener eyes, rounder cheeks, blonder hair, and gappier grin, was more familiar too. He knew her. She was Christine Smith. His first crush. His first kiss. A girl he had not seen since, what was it? Fifth grade?

Elliot felt elated making the connection, a sense of a key turning in a lock, his inner Rubik's cube snapping into place. Something in him had spotted something about her. That explained the confusion and the obsession with a girl who had seemed more or less like all the others. But she wasn't the others, she was the first. What were the odds that, after all these years, she would turn up on his desk?

He was about to turn the page, hunt for an address or a number, when he heard a knock and saw the knob turn. He shut the folder, and just as the door opened and the doctor came in, holding lattes for himself and his new best pal, Elliot glimpsed a Post-it note stuck to the front of Crystal/Christine's file: *SHRED!*

Elliot practically skipped back to the office. He had cracked the case of Crystal Waters. He knew who she was and, just like that, he also knew who she would be on the January cover: The Girl Next Door. The Hometown Sweetheart. The First Kiss. That would be the theme of the girl copy, her extraordinary ordinariness. He would immortalize her in prose. Vic would reward him, and then, fate having crossed their stars, he would reveal himself, like Cyrano. Or she'd see his name on the masthead and remember the young poet she once knew.

He was almost eager to ride the elevator up, and even gave Miriam a nod and smile, as he followed the scent of cigar into Vic's throne room. His chair was parked behind the huge antique desk, something Louis XIV once signed guillotine orders from, while behind him the sunset view went so far west one could almost sense, through the glowing, gorgeous smog, a touch of ocean blue.

"Good evening, sir," he said as he entered. "Hello, Moishe," he added to the giant on the couch. Vic just grunted, cigar and coffee in his ringed hands, eyes on the *Wall Street Journal.* Undeterred, Elliot cleared his throat and went on:

"Don't worry. I know who Crystal is, not how to find her yet but close, and I've got a few ideas I think you're going to love. You're right, she really is the best girl we've had in ages. I understand now why she's so special . . ."

"Crystal?" Vic looked up at him, his huge face showing something like real surprise and with it, real vulnerability. Suddenly, he seemed weak, like an old man in a wheelchair.

"Yes, sir," Elliot pressed. "Her real name is Christine. Christine Smith and . . ."

Vic waved him off. "I don't want to know."

"But . . ."

Vic cut him off, rotating away to face the windows. Moishe, too, seemed to bow his mighty head in grief, like a loyal hound dog. Miriam entered, a nurse sensing distress.

"Her cover has been canceled," she explained in a low voice.

"No one told me," Elliot said. He appealed to Vic's back. "I didn't know."

Miriam guided him toward the door. "Moishe and I will come destroy all photos and notes regarding her and no further mention of that project will be allowed. And here is the new cover girl." She waved a folder and Moishe rose, herding him out from behind. Vic didn't move.

Back in his office, while they gathered the Crystal Waters slides, Elliot opened the file and held the transparencies of the new girl up to the light. As far as he could make out, she was a small blond Asian with huge fake boobs shot in a hospital bed, casts on both arms, then posing with a Black nurse with identical boobs, then joined by a white doctor, his hard-on sticking out of his lab coat. He even had one of those mirror things attached to his head.

"This is due tomorrow," Miriam snapped in her harshly accented English. "So no time to sit around pulling off your pud."

Moishe stared, too, cracking his knuckles one by one. Was he getting ready to strangle him for upsetting the king, or just pull off his pud?

"I will get right on it . . ." Elliot started, but she was already striding out the door, followed by Moishe, who shut it behind him. The message light on his phone was blinking furiously. He punched the button. It was Farah.

"Hey, hon, guess what? I found those frickin' photos. I had to go into my storage bin in the garage and there was this ginormous spider that I got Adolpho the pool boy to kill. But it was so worth it. These pictures are smoking hot and there is mucho info in the portfolio about our little Miss Crystal. So come by tomorrow. I've got to jump out of a seventieth birthday cake tonight. But your girl came through, baby, so you're gonna have to be very sweet to Farah."

With a sigh, he hit delete.

It was dark when Elliot got home, so he didn't notice the biker until he was already in the driveway. He was startled when his headlights caught the black machine lurking there, waiting, and he stomped on the brake. It was the same one he'd seen at the strip club and at the gang bang and, for a moment, he longed for the gun in his trunk. Then the rider's gloved hands removed the helmet and he saw Miriam shake out her long hair. He breathed. He opened his door and stepped out, smiling, he hoped, with something resembling pleasant surprise.

"What a pleasant surprise."

"Vic," she said, as if answering a question he had not asked. "He is not like other men."

"Yes," Elliot agreed, wondering where one would even start. "I have definitely noticed that about him."

"I know that to you, he seems so strong. A leader. Like a general or president."

Elliot nodded. "True."

She put a gloved fist to her heart. "But believe me, though he never shows it, he carries a deep sadness too. He lost so much. His wife. His legs."

Elliot shook his head. "I swear I didn't know you canceled the cover. Was there a memo?"

She put a finger on his chest.

"And also, you know, he has an extremely large heart . . ."

"Oh? Is that serious?"

". . . with a soft spot for you. So he has brought you a gift, to show he still cares." Then she actually smiled and waved toward the street, and he turned to see the limo pulling up. It was massive, something a Third World dictator might ride in for parades, and sitting on a raised suspension, so its headlights beamed right into Elliot's face. The passenger door opened and Moishe climbed out, waving him over, then opened the rear side door. A ramp descended. Blinded and confused, Elliot approached as Vic came rolling down.

"Hey, kid," he called.

"Hey, Vic," he said, hesitantly, "what's going on?" He hoped they didn't expect to be invited into the house. The limo's interior looked nicer. Elliot glimpsed a little den of buttoned leather, gleaming bottles, a glimmering TV.

"We've got a little surprise for you," Vic said. Grinning, he led him to the rear of the idling limo, which glowed like a furnace from the red taillights. A faint smell of baking fuel drifted from the throbbing exhaust pipe. "You're gonna love this. Show him, Moishe."

Moishe tapped on the roof and the driver popped the rear door. Joe the talent agent was in there, hog-tied and with duct tape over his mouth.

"That's the fucker who stole your jacket," Vic said, as Moishe rolled him face up with his slip-on loafer, so that Elliot could get a better look. "The little bastard even tried to say you gave it to him." He smiled. "We knew you'd want first crack at him."

Joe's eyes rolled wildly, trying to blink SOS for help. He groaned at Elliot, squirming around. Moishe reached into the limo and pulled out a bat. He handed it to Elliot. Both men looked at him expectantly. Joe writhed, screaming through his sealed mouth.

"Um," Elliot said, gingerly fingering the bat.

"Prop him up," Vic told Moshe. "Give him a good shot."

Moishe yanked Joe up, setting him carefully like a pin. He stepped clear.

"There you go, batter up." Vic said.

"Well, the thing is," Elliot said.

"Don't worry about getting blood on anything."

"No, it's not that. It's just."

"What?"

"Well," Elliot said. "The thing is, I guess maybe I kind of did give it to him."

"What?"

"I kind of did."

"You gave it away? The jacket I gave you?"

Elliot nodded. "Kind of."

Joe whimpered his thanks and tried to crawl to Elliot. Moishe pushed him back in and shut the door with a bang. He glared down at Elliot.

"Give me the bat," Vic told Elliot.

Elliot hesitated.

"Give me the bat."

He handed it over, and stepped back, bracing for flight. He fought the impulse to shut his eyes and cover his face with his hands. Vic sighed deeply, hefting the bat. "Well, obviously you're fired. I can't have somebody around I can't trust."

Elliot nodded eagerly. “Sure, sure, I understand. And let me say I’m deeply sorry.”

“But,” he continued. “I have a soft spot for you, I admit it.”

“Yes, I know you’ve got that large heart . . .”

“So I’m only going to let Moishe hit you once. You choose where.”

“Thanks, Vic. Thanks a lot.” He glanced at Moishe’s engorged, purple face. “Thanks, Moishe.”

Working his joystick, Vic rotated and drove back up the ramp into the limo, engine whining. Moishe closed in, forming a giant fist.

“Okay,” Elliot said, “I guess just hit me in the chin or no, the stomach, I think . . .”

Suddenly he was on the ground, doubled over, fighting to breathe. All his internal organs felt like they’d been driven up into his throat. He heard Moishe get in the limo and shut the door. As Elliot crawled, retching, on his knees, Vic lowered the window.

“Don’t forget,” he called. “I still need that girl copy on my desk by tomorrow.”

Elliot was too sick to lift his head, but he managed to wave faintly as the limo pulled away.

12

Elliot woke up sore. As he lay in bed, blinking at the dusty dimness of his garage, he found it hard to believe he really had nowhere to go, but the large purplish-yellow bruise on his stomach convinced him. So did the awful stiffness he felt trying to stand up. He pulled on his robe, tottered to the house for coffee and back, and then worked his way through a chain of cigarettes as, in a mournful daze, he composed his final girl copy for his final cover. He was wondering how he was supposed to turn it in, and dreading the idea of walking into the building, when Margie called. She'd heard the news and offered to stop by during lunch to pick up the copy and drop off his final check. That inspired him to at least take a shower and get dressed, and by then he felt well enough to eat a peanut butter and jelly sandwich. Moishe had not, it seemed, ruptured any vital organs, causing maximum pain with minimum damage. He was a true professional, as precise in his way as a surgeon.

Margie turned up as promised, in a white blouse, with a silk scarf over her hair. She had a hard time negotiating the lawn in her pencil skirt but one look at the chaos in his garage was enough for her to decline entry. She accepted a coffee and they sat in the backyard. Being a gentleman, he offered her the chair and took the milk crate. She gave him the envelope with his last paycheck and he handed over his copy, which he had printed out and trimmed, tearing off the sprocket strips and separating the perforated pages with only a few minor rips. She glanced over it.

"Slut . . . Interrupted." She laughed. "I like it." Elliot had concocted a ridiculous yarn about Chelsea, a young nympho, whose parents send her to a sex addiction clinic after she is injured in a road-head incident and unable to masturbate. Of course, she ends up having sex with the doctor and nurse.

"I was inspired by that creepy surgeon," he explained.

"I heard he designed a high-tech pneumatic penis pump for Vic and that's why we're doing a piece on him."

"I guess that's one good thing about getting fired. I have way too much of that kind of stuff lodged in my brain," Elliot said. "Imagine it rising from his chair." He hummed mechanically while lifting a robotic hand. "Now that's an image I will never get rid of."

Margie laughed. "I heard that's why Crystal Waters vanished. Vic wanted her to take the maiden voyage on his new robo-schlong and she balked."

"You think?"

Margie smiled and shrugged. "Who knows what lies in the dark regions of the heart?"

"You got that right." Elliot's thoughts drifted back to all he'd learned over the recent days, and how little he knew. "It's all a mystery to me."

She laughed. "That's for sure."

Elliot frowned at that and she patted his shoulder. "But you are a pro at making up stories based on the body's other regions. And that is a valuable skill. Somewhat."

"Is it? I haven't been getting a lot of offers."

She shrugged. "I have. There's this rich dude up in Seattle, Armond Laxo, who's financing an internet company up there. He's looking for people."

I laughed. "The internet? In Seattle? I didn't think anything could be a step down from *Raunchy*, but I admit, I was wrong."

She shrugged. "I'm not so sure. Anyway, thanks for the coffee. And the copy." She kissed his cheek and sauntered off, heels sinking into the lawn, waving her pages. "Stay in touch."

As it happened, he saw Crystal again that very day, or rather Christine, since that was who she officially was once more. It was at the car wash, where he had gone for a spot of lunch, now that he was a man of leisure, aka an unemployed bum in flip-flops. He was waiting for his tacos and browsing the rack of tabloids. That's when he saw Christine. She was blonde again and both eyes were her old green. She was deliriously happy, with a wide, white, celebrity smile, head back in joyous laughter. And she had her arm around her equally ecstatic fiancé, action movie superstar Chet Hunter. The two had just announced their engagement, although, according to the article that Elliot consumed under the fluorescent lights, "close friends" had known for months that the two were deeply in love. The wedding plans were top secret, of course, but sources indicated the couple were planning a private beach ceremony soon after Chet's eagerly awaited new movie, *Eliminator III—Hard Justice* came out. As for Christine's own line of work, she was discreetly if vaguely described as "an up-and-coming talent to watch." Maybe this, rather than the pump story, was the real reason her big porn premier had been scotched: either way, a better ride had come along and she had hopped on. There was no mention of any tape.

If Elliot had had anything better to do, would he still have called Farah? Probably not. He might not have even seen the tabloid, and the strange case of Christine would have faded away, one of life's many unsolved mysteries. He had plenty else to think about—his job, his future. But what he found himself thinking about was her, or them:

Christine, the girl he'd once known so well, and Crystal, the stranger he'd never managed to meet. And just maybe, he really had become a little bit of a real reporter, in spite of himself. He just couldn't let go, this close to cracking his biggest story.

So he called Farah. He left a message, and when she didn't reply in her usual prompt fashion, he became even more curious (had she heard he was fired? Was someone else ghosting his Dearest Slut?) and left another message, saying he planned to stop by for the photos of Crystal she'd promised and a friendly chat. When, by late afternoon, she still hadn't answered, he put on proper shoes, got in his car, and drove over.

A motorcycle messenger in black gear and a helmet was coming out as he went in. He was a little taken aback, but the biker politely held the door.

"Thanks," he said. The helmet nodded and moved on and Elliot smiled ruefully to himself as the biker mounted a bright red machine, one of those Italian rockets, and took off. Skirting the empty pool, Elliot crossed the courtyard to Farah's. He knocked on her metal grating and rang the bell, but then noticed the inner wooden door was ajar, so he stuck his head in.

"Farah!" he called in. "It's Elliot. Are you home?"

All at once the dog bolted by, slipping right past him.

"Shit," Elliot muttered, then yelled louder. "Farah! The dog got loose! Sorry!" Still there was nothing. He pushed open the door, calling, "Hey . . ." again as he entered.

Elliot noticed light coming from under the closed bathroom door and heard water running and thought, she's in the shower. He was wondering about the polite thing to do—sit and wait? Go chase the dog?—when he saw the pool of water on the floor. Like a tiny tide coming in, a thin fall of water flowed from under the bathroom door and spread, swift and silent, across the room.

"Farah!" he yelled now, splashing through the puddle, and pushed open the door.

Had Elliot ever seen a real dead body? In person, if that was the proper term? He'd seen hundreds, thousands, perhaps, real and contrived, in movies and photos and on TV, so many that he somehow thought he was used to it. He was not. Then there was the one wake he'd been to for an elderly Irish neighbor back in Queens, but she'd been so prepped and primped, covered with makeup like frosting, that she seemed more glamorous than ever in life, when she shuffled around in a housedress with a cigarette in her mouth.

Farah Foxxx was slumped dead in the tub, with a belt tight around her throat. Her eyes bulged grotesquely, like red Ping-Pong balls with brown centers. Her tongue lolled out, fat and gray. The leather cut deep into her bruised and swollen skin. Apparently, the overhead pipe from which the belt had hung had pulled loose. It jutted now from the broken ceiling and sprayed water over the body and the room. Horrified, he leaned closer, afraid to enter but unable to look away from this inert form that until just a little while ago had a soul in it, had been Farah. Now it was meat in a velour tracksuit with a note pinned to it in Farah's graceful script: *So sorry! I had to go!*

The dog ran back in, brushing past Elliot once more, scaring him shitless, and began to yelp at her dead mistress before leaning down to lap up some of the water with a little pink tongue. Elliot turned and fled.

He jumped in his car and took off, as if something was chasing him, then, just as abruptly, he pulled into a strip mall and parked, hands still gripping the wheel. When he caught his breath he got out and went to the phone booth next to the 7-Eleven. He called 911 and asked for an ambulance at Farah's address. He said someone needed assistance, which was, he decided, not totally a lie. She needed care, even if she was beyond help. When they asked his name, he hung up. Then he sat in his car for a little while longer before he drove back home.

❖

It was the next day that the police called. Elliot had gone into hiding—not from anyone who might be seeking him—but from shock and horror. All he could think to do was shut the door, lie down, and shut his eyes. But shutting his mind was harder. He ended up watching TV, then tossing all night, sleep stirred by nightmares that were just replays of what he'd seen—daymares, wake terrors—till finally he blanked out just as dawn was peeking through the cracks in the garage, and a rooster crowed from somewhere, like a mystical call from beyond, at which point he slept till noon and woke up groggy and dried out, as if from a hangover. Still he was alive and safe in his own bed, or on his own mattress. That was the main thing. The best course, he felt, was to say nothing to anyone, try to think nothing to himself, and eventually feel nothing either. Life went on, proved by the fact that, with no food for twelve hours, he was actually hungry, and he was deciding which dollar taco place he should go to—the one attached to the car wash or the one in the truck in the vacant lot—when the phone rang. He grimaced, assuming it was a collection agent, but remembering the debacle with his parents, he just cleared his throat and asked, "Hello?"

"Elliot Gross," a voice accused, rather than asked. "This is Detective Santos, LAPD."

"Yes, hi . . ." He immediately felt not only accused, but intensely guilty, seeing Farah again, her plaintive note of apology. "I'm sorry."

"Sorry?" Santos paused. "Is this a confession?"

"What? No! Just sorry I can't talk. I'm on my way to a lunch meeting."

"You'll have to reschedule," Santos said. "The sarge wants a meeting, down at the station. And he already had lunch."

❖

Santos met him at the desk, wearing a white suit with a red shirt, her badge clipped to her belt. She buzzed him in and led him sourly down a long dim hall. Anderson was waiting in a small, poorly lit room with a table and four chairs.

"Gross, thanks for coming by."

"Sure."

"Cop a squat," Santos said, and he gingerly sat, while she stood over him in a wide-legged stance, as if ready to tackle him. "He didn't give me any trouble," she admitted grudgingly.

"'Course not." Anderson smiled. He wore a tweed jacket, gray slacks, and white shirt and maroon tie. "I'm sure you want to cooperate, right, Elliot?"

"Right," Elliot said. "With what exactly?"

"Do you know a Joseph Sangiglio?" Anderson asked.

"Pal of yours?" Santos loomed over him.

"No. The name's not familiar."

Anderson reached into a paper bag and pulled out a plastic bag. It was sealed, stamped EVIDENCE in red, and appeared to contain his *Raunchy* jacket, now stained with dried blood. "What about this?" he asked, laying it on the table between them. "Does this look familiar?"

Elliot blinked, flashing back to the man in the trunk. Joe.

"It might look like one my boss, former boss, gave me. I mean, it's similar."

Anderson turned back the jacket to reveal where his name was stitched inside. "What about this?"

Elliot stared.

Santos loomed. "Is that similar? Except for the bullet holes?"

Elliot nodded.

"And yet," Anderson said, "you say you don't know Joseph Sangiglio, who was shot dead wearing it last night."

"I gave it to him," Elliot said. "But I didn't really know him. I just knew him as Joe. I only met him once, briefly, at a party."

"Where?"

Elliot shrugged. "In the Hills somewhere. I don't even know."

"But you gave him a fancy satin jacket," Santos said.

"It was his birthday. I had to give him something."

"That checks out," Anderson said. "Witnesses said it was a gift from his birthday party."

"His last birthday party," Santos noted.

"I guess he liked your gift though." Anderson tossed the jacket onto the table. "Because he wore it to a rap concert last night."

"Friends say he wore it ironically." Santos flicked quote fingers in the air.

"Nothing ironic about the drive-by though." Anderson sat back. "Looks like a gangster rap feud."

"East Coast, West Coast," Santos said. "Or Crips and Bloods."

"Now," Anderson stretched back, hands behind his head. "Did you say former boss? That would be Victor Kingman?"

"Yes. Actually, I left the job."

"Any special reason?"

Elliot thought again of the trunk, the bat, and of Moishe's fist. He shook his head. "Just, you know, not a good fit."

"I'd have to agree," Anderson said. "I think you're out of your depth. You're not a suspect in this case."

"Not at this time," Santos added.

"But you're bound to get in trouble sooner or later."

Santos aimed her fingers like a gun. "Could be you next time."

"What do you mean?" Elliot asked.

"Think, Gross." She pointed her finger pistol at her own temple. "What if you'd been wearing the jacket? Might have been one of those beefs like with the leather eight ball jackets."

Anderson shrugged. "You never know. People kill each other over sneakers these days."

"Happens all the time," Santos agreed, glancing under the table at Elliot's beat-up Converses. "Probably not those though."

"Point is, we see your type every day," Anderson said. "Folks move out here to make their dreams come true. City of angels, right? For most those dreams come to nothing."

Santos nodded. "For pretty much all of them."

Anderson waved it off. "So what? That's reality. They end up like you, regular schmoes just trying to get by."

"Hey . . ." Elliot started, then shrugged.

"No offense," Santos said. "That's showbiz. We can't all be stars."

Anderson sat forward. "But for some," he said, "the dream turns into a full-blown nightmare. Drug addicts. Sex freaks. Psychos and all kinds of crazy cults. What you see on the news is just the beginning."

"Who knows what goes on up in those hills?" Santos said.

Anderson laid his hands on the table. "Look, kid, I've been in LA my whole life."

"Same here," Santos said, "born and bred."

"This might be a warm sunny town, but the other side of Hollywood?" Anderson shook his head. "It can get mighty dark."

Santos nodded in agreement. "Nothing is more dangerous than broken dreams."

Anderson smiled at that. "Welcome to LA," he said. "Beware of falling angels."

"Remember." Santos leaned in, a finger on the jacket. "That's how the devil got his start."

PART II

13

It might have been tough to believe, but after his career in the skin trade came to a crashing halt, things somehow actually went downhill for Elliot. He started applying for jobs at magazines and newspapers, then moved on to adjunct teaching, then bookshops and offices, and finally hit bottom working a single rainy day as a pizza delivery guy, driving hopeless circles in the Hills, with the Thomas Guide map book on his lap—Skylark Circle, Skylark Crescent, Skylark Terrace—till the suavely scruffy fellow in the mid-century modern (a writer, Elliot felt sure) demanded his Special Hot and Crusty for free since Elliot had taken more than thirty minutes on his Rolex. Without a word, Elliot threw the Hot and Crusty all over his tasteful succulent garden, tossed his Hot and Crusty Hat in the driveway, and went home, of course getting lost on the way.

His steadiest employment came as an office temp, stapling things and stuffing envelopes. These jobs weren't so bad. A lot of places didn't have anything much for him to do and seemed mainly concerned that a chair not be empty while Mary or Bob was on vacation. As soon as he was comfortably ensconced behind the photos of Mary's kids or the metal golf sculpture labeled "Bob," they forgot all about him. Taking their messages, drinking from their BEST DAD mugs, he grew sort of fond of the person whose lumbar-support chair he was filling, almost protective, as if he were covering for the fact that maybe Mary didn't really do much all day either. In a month, Elliot worked for six of these companies and never once learned what they did except be a division of something else.

Staring out a window or at the empty day planner on his desk, Elliot was pretty content, except for two drawbacks: (1) He couldn't smoke. (2) He was actually getting poorer. The jobs paid so little that even working every hour offered and never taking lunch unless ordered to, he still couldn't break even. With no benefits or insurance or job security, a flat tire or a cold would ruin him.

Just when it looked like things couldn't get any worse, and he might have to accept the money his mother offered him each week and which would prove his father right, a sort of California miracle occurred. It was winter in LA, which felt to Elliot like an East Coast spring—rain, cool temperatures, fresh air. Eventually this would result in flash floods—when the LA "river," normally a damp concrete ditch mainly used for skateboarding, housing the homeless, and shooting car chase scenes for TV, suddenly dropped its quote marks and overran its banks—and then mudslides, when the earth, which Elliot had always considered a relatively solid substance, abruptly collapsed or melted away and ran down the hills. But for now it was a relief to feel something other than a blast of dry air when he stepped out into the world. He'd received a call from some employment agent—there were so many—telling him to report for a job interview with an outfit called LoveWorks, which in LA could be anything. So he put on his clean shirt, slid his tie over his head, and found the address, a small West Hollywood complex on a drab block above Sunset. He opened a ground floor door to find a small sharp woman with a tight black bun and big, black-framed glasses staring at him angrily from behind a desk, as if he had already annoyed her. Another woman, with a looser blonde bun and smaller, round glasses, like a softer, watered-down version, sat at another desk, typing. She stopped and looked up, too, sort of hopefully, as if he might bring good news.

"Yes?" Black Bun asked.

"Hi, I'm Elliot Gross, I was told to report . . ."

She immediately picked up her phone, hit a number, and barked, "Your appointment is here."

A voice boomed from someplace farther in back. "Send him in!"

She slammed down the phone and spoke through gritted teeth. "Go on back."

"Thank you!" Elliot chirped. He crossed to a closed door and gave a rap before pushing it open.

The small room was stacked floor to ceiling with shelves full of audiocassettes, all featuring a petite and pretty white woman with long brunette hair in a flowing white robe. There was also a poster of her that read LOVE WORKS! And beneath that, WISDOM AND HEALING WITH MELODY BRIGHT TONIGHT. A worktable held a row of tape machines, each containing four decks. There was one big desk, completely covered in heaps of paper. And sitting in a ruminative pose by the light from the one window, his elbow resting on a stack of unopened mail, was Elliot's childhood pal, Pedro Plotkin.

❖

The waitress brought Elliot's coffee and Pedro's cheeseburger, fries, and chocolate shake. Pleading starvation, Pedro had refused to answer any questions until Elliot followed him to a burger joint on Sunset patronized by streetwalkers on breaks with their pimps, whose fabulous rides were parked in front of the red-white-and-blue awning. He stirred cream into his scorched coffee and watched as Pedro took a bite of his double cheeseburger and began splashing ketchup on the fries.

"Remember those genius prank calls we used to make?" he finally asked, taking Elliot by surprise. Was this the interview?

"Um . . ."

"Back before Star 69," Pedro went on. "It was the golden age. Paging Dick Hertz at the airport. Or when we used three-way calling to connect the Chinese take-out place with the pizzeria?" He began to laugh, growing red-faced and choking out his words while still stuffing fries into his mouth. "Or what about egging those cars or dropping wet toilet paper out the window on people so they thought it was bird shit?" Elliot had to grin as Pedro slapped the table. "And that idea you had to use chocolate syrup?"

"My idea?" Elliot shook his head. "I give you full creative credit for that." As he recalled, Pedro was the demonic genius behind all their pranks and schemes, starting with that first visit to his family's home, after the fight. Their apartment was more luxurious than Elliot's, with a fireplace and a bar cart featuring crystal decanters full of liquor in autumnal shades, and two bathrooms, which seemed incredible, but there was also dog and cat hair everywhere, and the pet mynah bird flew around squawking, and the space under Pedro's bed, where the pet iguana hid, was stuffed with dirty laundry. There were no set mealtimes. Everyone just ate whenever they wanted, helping themselves from the fridge—cereal for dinner, Fudge Town cookies at 4:00 P.M. There was a scorch mark on Pedro's ceiling from a chemistry experiment gone wrong, and darts stuck in the wall. Most unthinkably, he had actually said "fuck you" during an argument with his mom, at which point his dad, an advertising executive, had come running out in just his boxers and T-shirt and chased him downstairs to whip him with a belt in the street. To Elliot they were like kings and queens, mad aristocrats reigning free in their palace.

Of course, it was Pedro's eggs they whipped at cars and his windows from which they launched the toilet paper bombs. And certainly, it was Pedro who had, in a moment of inspiration, run into the kitchen and come back with the U-Bet chocolate syrup. They squirted it on wadded toilet paper and dropped it on a guy in a suit. In a panic, the man ripped his jacket off and sprinted down the street. Elliot remembered laughing till he rolled on the floor, choking on happiness while the dog licked the tears from his face. It was the freest he'd ever felt, like an angel farting on a cloud.

"Speaking of old times," Elliot asked, feeling his way, "didn't I see Christine with you at that awful party?"

"The one where I accidentally pissed on you in that bush? Sorry about that by the way."

"Not on me. Just my shoes. And they were soaked already."

Pedro waved that off. "Still I feel like I owe you one."

"But you and Christine," Elliot pressed. "You still close? She around?"

He shrugged. "Maybe you heard she's with Chet Hunter now."

"I saw something in the paper."

"Well, then, you know how it is. She's with him, doing the film festival circuit. Not as much time for old pals anymore. Too busy walking red carpets." His face clouded for a moment, but then he grinned. "Not like me. I'm always ready to help a friend in need. How've you been, anyway? You look like shit."

"Thanks. How did you find me?"

He pulled out his wallet, a slim Louis Vuitton number, and carefully removed Elliot's warped and faded card. "I'd been meaning to look you up, but when I called they said you were gone. What happened?"

Elliot told him about how he'd been fired. He even told him about Farah and the jacket and the dead talent manager from the party. He wasn't sure why. He supposed he was lonely.

"Same old Elliot." Pedro shook his head. "Well, don't worry, we've got an opening. Lucky for you I saw your name on the list from the agency. You can work for me."

"Doing what exactly?"

Pedro pulled out a huge, matted wad of bills and began peeling off hundreds, while the other patrons watched impassively. "I'll fill in the details later. Take this as an advance for now." He folded the bills into Elliot's palm. There had to be a thousand dollars.

"I don't know," Elliot said, though it sure felt good in his hand. He could catch up on rent and even throw a bone to the student loan dogs.

"There's one condition," Pedro added. "That you settle things with Vic."

"His bodyguard punched me in the guts. I think that settles it."

"That's not what I meant."

"Then what?"

"Elliot, you're my oldest friend. I know I can help you. But I can't work with someone who doesn't even respect himself. I have to know that I can count on you. That you're the same person you were then. Now . . ." He leaned forward conspiratorially. "Do you still have the security codes for the doors?"

And so, that night, Elliot returned to fortress *Raunchy*. He was worried he'd be recognized, but Pedro had made him wait in the car while he ran into his apartment in an upscale West Hollywood duplex and came back with janitors' uniforms and caps.

"You just happen to have these?" Elliot asked as Pedro changed.

"They come in handy, as you see." He pulled a fake mustache, like a furry black caterpillar, out of his pocket. "Here, put this on."

It took more coaxing and pushing, but somehow, Elliot found himself entering the code for the basement door—feeling half-bullied, half-charmed and somehow flattered to be chosen for this caper, just like when they were kids. Plus there were those fresh bills making a nice thick lump in his pocket. They took the elevator to Elliot's floor. The place was deserted, and Pedro darted happily into the art department, sitting at a random desk. He stuck a disc in the computer and in seconds the screen read *Password Cracked*. Pedro quickly located the server and began opening files. Here were the corrected proofs of all Vic's magazines, the final files ready to be digitally transmitted to the printer. Pedro cut the copy for a nude photo spread, then jumped to a file for *Design Today* and pasted it in. He pulled a caption from *You* and switched it back into *Raunchy*. He went back and forth, cackling to himself, while Elliot looked on nervously.

A sleek Italian coffeemaker was now described as having "full sensual lips and an unquenchable thirst for warm jizz," while a bent-over brunette called herself "an amply cushioned two-person love seat with added lumbar support." In a *You* magazine profile, the caption under a photo of Laura Bush identified her as "Trish the raging hosemonster," and a blonde slattern wielding a dildo longed to "touch American families deep inside."

"You know," Pedro said, reviewing his work. "I don't think anyone's even going to notice the changes."

It wasn't until they were back downstairs and heading for the car that Elliot began to notice how peculiar he felt. He wanted to worry, but he couldn't stop smiling, and he realized what this odd sensation he was experiencing was: He was having fun. He was happy.

"So," Pedro asked him as they got back into the car. "Still want to hear about the job? How do you feel now?"

"Actually," Elliot admitted, "I feel great."

Pedro laughed, hair blowing as he raced a yellow light. "Just like old times," he said, clapping Elliot on the knee. And it was.

14

Melody Bright was a former hippie, failed singer-songwriter, and washed-up party girl until her awakening, when she began channeling the spirit of an otherworldly, thousand-year-old entity known as Zona, who educated Melody about the true nature of reality, the existence of angels, the fate of the spirit after death, and so on. She began preaching, lecturing for free to whomever would listen, at first mainly the desperate, ministering to AIDS and cancer patients, recovering drug addicts, and molestation victims, then slowly drawing a wider following of highly strung wannabe actors; depressed, unemployed screenwriters; and a few kooky celebrities, all of whom displayed a willing, even eager, suspension of disbelief. One of them happened to be dating a powerful agent and he got her a book deal. The week that the book came out, Oprah bought five hundred copies and had Melody on the show. The next week five million other people bought the book, and Melody bought a mansion. It was not known what Zona received.

Now Melody traveled the country giving workshops and interviews, and continued her free lectures in LA whenever she was home, though now they were packed houses, with VIPs filling the front row, like a fashion show. Pedro arranged for the lectures to be recorded and marketed the results from the small office where he, and now Elliot, produced and distributed Melody's tapes. The front room was Melody's office, although Pedro reassured Elliot that she had never and would never set foot in it, preferring to check in by phone or summon her employees for occasional meetings at her chateau in the hills above Sunset. Instead it was the roost of Pam, Melody's assistant, a one-time theater arts major who had served as an assistant under a series of agents, including Melody's. She shuttled back and forth from the house to the office, handling Melody's phone calls and correspondence and standing guard over Pedro, zealously recording what time he showed up in the morning and when he left for lunch, complaining that the coffee was too strong, the music too loud, even that there was too much laughter emerging from the back room. The faded blonde Janice, an acting school washout who'd started volunteering at Melody's lectures, was her helper, and the idea that Pedro, too, had hired an assistant infuriated Pam. Nevertheless, Pedro kept prodding Elliot to make a play for Pam, insisting that only rough sex could restore her human warmth and "exterminate the bug up her ass."

At first Elliot was rather unsettled by all this. He never would have guessed that his thoroughly profane childhood friend would be mixed up with some religious loony, but he was quickly reassured: Pedro seemed to have only the vaguest idea of what Melody was talking about and the copy of her book, *Wisdom of Zona*, that Elliot found, inscribed lovingly to Pedro and forgotten next to the toilet, had page three folded down. In fact, by hiring freelancers to take care of the recording and editing, and relying on their brief descriptions to inspire titles, Pedro managed to never even listen to most of what he sold, although he always seemed ready to suggest a helpful tape to others and to rave about his favorites whenever he spoke to Melody. His remaining duties were to run the dubbing decks on which the tapes were reproduced, take orders, and ship them out. All this was immediately delegated to Elliot, who found that, with minimal effort, he could easily stay on top of it.

Elliot and Pedro quickly fell into a daily routine. Elliot would show up first, make the coffee, and hide from Pam in the back office. Pedro would roll in around tenish, blithely ignore Pam's dirty look, and, over coffee, regale Elliot with exactingly detailed accounts of his prior evening's sexual exploits. Elliot was surprised to learn that Pedro was gay, although he insisted that he would "fuck any hole with a pulse." After that, Pedro retreated to the bathroom, where he often remained for an hour. The first time this happened, Elliot panicked, knocking, then pounding on the door, thinking that maybe Pedro was dead in there, like Farah. Finally he'd opened the door and found his boss curled up in the tub, happily snoozing with a blanket and pillow he kept hidden in the linen closet.

After his nap, Pedro called his friends and shuffled uninterestedly through the important papers that Elliot kept adding to the mountain on his desk. (Eventually Elliot devised his own filing system: he would add new papers to the top of the pile, then once a week he would remove the bottom three inches and throw them out.) Then it was time for lunch.

Lunch was an important affair. Every day, Pedro insisted on treating Elliot to an elaborate meal in a fancy restaurant. Once a week or so, he would run out of dough and borrow back from Elliot much of the money he'd squandered on him, then suddenly reimburse him later from another wad of cash. After a leisurely repast, they would often do a couple of errands, such as pick up Pedro's dry cleaning or shop for new towels. Elliot's suggestion that maybe he should be dropped off at the office to catch up on work was greeted with incredulity and hurt feelings, as if Elliot were trying to shirk his true job, which was keeping Pedro company, riding with him in the BMW that Melody's company leased for him while blasting punk rock and listening to his endless monologues. He loved reminiscing about their childhood adventures, though when Elliot tried, once or twice, to bring Christine up again, he brushed the topic aside, with a shrug.

Things slowed down a bit in the afternoons. Elliot made tapes and answered the phone while Pedro stared philosophically out the window, which commanded a view of a narrow alley and the identical building next door. Then they would have a coffee break or, if it was sunny out, they'd walk the few blocks to Thrifty's drugstore, where Pedro would fill his many prescriptions and then treat Elliot to an ice cream. It was on one of these occasions that Elliot saw a flash, in Pedro, of the violent temper he recalled from childhood. Pedro was feeling particularly flush that day and had grabbed an assortment of candy and toys as they cruised the aisles: two troll dolls, a jar of slime, fake tattoos. Then, after they ordered their cones, he announced, with a wave of his arms, that he was treating everyone there to ice cream.

"Ice cream for everybody, on me," he called, receiving cheers from the small collection of children and senior citizens. But one red-faced older guy in a shabby sports coat refused Pedro's largesse.

"That's okay," he told the countergirl, "I'll buy my own."

"It's on me," Pedro said, waving his money. "I insist."

"I don't want nothing from you," the man said, taking his cone and putting his dollar on the counter. "I pay my own way."

"What do you think, you're too good?" Pedro asked, snatching up the man's money and facing him down. "Just cause I'm happy and want to share it with the world?" The other patrons watched with interest, absently licking their free cones. Elliot shifted uneasily.

"I know your kind," the man said. "And I don't want nothing from you."

"What the fuck does that mean?" Pedro asked, closing in.

"What do you think?" the man muttered, trying to push by Pedro, who shoved him back. The man pushed Pedro again and Pedro pounced, slapping the strawberry cone out of his hand. They grappled briefly and Pedro had him on the ground, panting as he pinned the man's arms with his legs, and trapping his neck under his crotch. While the man squirmed, he took the disputed dollar and stuffed it into his mouth.

"Suck on this, asshole."

While the crowd laughed, an elderly security guard approached. "Hey now, fellas, what's the fuss over here?"

"Officer, this man's sick," Pedro told him. "He needs help." He stood up, crushing the man's hand with his shoe. The man sat up, coughing and gagging, pointing desperately at his throat. He turned a deep shade of blue. The security guard bent down and peered at him.

"I think he's choking on something." The man's eyes bulged and he gagged louder.

"I think you're right," Pedro said. "Quick, get him up."

The security guard helped Pedro pull the man to his feet, and Pedro got behind him, positioning himself for a Heimlich maneuver. "One, two, three," he shouted, pumping the man's diaphragm and thrusting into his rear a bit deeper than necessary with each stroke. "One, two, three!" The crumpled dollar shot out, and the man began gasping for breath. The crowd applauded and the security guard shook his hand.

"Thanks, everybody!" Pedro modestly waved them off. "I'm just happy to be of help."

The injured man, still breathless, pointed at Pedro accusingly.

"Don't mention it, brother," Pedro said, and slapped him on the back. "Well, it's back to work for us. Come on, Elliot." Waving to the crowd, he exited the store to more applause while Elliot trailed along behind. Back at the office, Pedro slipped the candy and toys into Jan's bag.

"Pedro!" she scolded when she found it. "I told the kids I am limiting their intake of sugar. I can't contradict myself. It sends an unclear parenting message."

He shrugged. "Just put it someplace and let them magically find it."

"Well . . . who will I say it's from?"

"Their favorite fairy," he declared, grandly, then glanced at Elliot. "And his elf."

❖

Elliot began spending a lot of his free time with Pedro as well, and soon discovered that his nightlife was even more complicated and outrageous than his day job. When Elliot thought about the child he had known so well, Pedro seemed like one of those wild kids, saddled with a bunch of terms, from *hyper* to *delinquent* to *incorrigible*, who shot off like a comet, too fast and too far, doomed to flare out and crash before the gravity of adulthood could, as with most of us, pull him into a regular terrestrial orbit, circling the mundane planet each day like the rest of humanity. He would not have been surprised to hear that he was dead.

But the pressure of life had instead transformed him. Not only physically—he was tall, dark, handsome, with white teeth set in a raffish grin, broad shoulders, strong arms—but also he was charismatic, charming and charmed. True, he was still a hustler, but he'd arrived in a world where hustling was the only real career, and he'd risen quickly through the ranks. And even his most useless and self-destructive tendency—his defiance and impish rebellion, his refusal to grow up or bow down to the grown-ups—had blossomed into something more. He had become, in his own weird way, political. He had found, at last, an outlet for his frantic energy, the burden of joy that he'd been hauling through life, and it had made him a kind of artist.

A typical Tuesday evening found Elliot at home, sitting on his milk crate, watching a cat step along the fence, shaking its butt and infuriating the dogs, when the frenzied call came through.

"The fuckers," Pedro began, with no greeting. "They put a camera up on La Ceinega."

The cameras, installed to catch traffic offenders, were up all over town, but apparently Pedro had been too busy to watch the news. Now that he knew, something had to be done, immediately. That night he stole a car and drove through the red light again and again, letting the flash hit him. Each time, he wore a different disguise: Abe Lincoln, Marilyn Monroe, Castro, an ape suit. Every day, like Zorro, he was fighting for the people. He shoplifted designer clothes and gave them to beggars. He followed a parking meter reader around and every time she stopped, he raced ahead of her and pumped coins into the meters, leaving a note on each windshield: "You have been given the gift of one hour. Spend it wisely." He picked random people from the phone book and had flowers or singing love telegrams sent to them by other random strangers. On Janice's daughter's birthday he snuck in with a dollhouse and set up an elaborate scenario, with a note from "Your Favorite Fairy."

No longer mindless pranks, he now referred to his capers as "actions" or, when in a theoretical frame of mind, as "interventions." He swapped posters advertising movies or politicians for ones demanding AIDs funding, renamed streets for Chicano labor leaders, and slipped HONK IF YOU HATE PIGS bumper stickers onto police cars. He flushed powdered concrete down McDonald's toilets and gave the counterpeople twenty-dollar tips with devil horns or giant Afros drawn on the presidents' heads. He purposely farted in fancy boutiques. He danced down the street, singing at the top of his lungs, shaking hands with the mailman and twirling delighted old ladies.

Elliot knew, of course, that Pedro was probably crazy, and that none of this was leading anywhere good. But still, with each new day, he found himself more cheerful, more eager even, to see what adventure would unfold, and he had to admit that somehow, although he'd never been so down and out, things were looking up.

15

Elliot worked for Melody Bright for a few weeks before he finally met her. He and Pedro were sitting around the office, having their midmorning coffee break, when the call came. Pedro, talkative after his nap, was describing his date of the previous night.

"So I get his pants off, and he's got his butt waxed, you know, like girls do their bikinis, right? Like this . . ." He picked the last glazed donut from the box and held it to his mouth, wiggling his pink tongue at Elliot through the hole. The phone rang and Pedro grabbed it. Elliot glanced in the donut box. Of course, Pedro had left him nothing but jelly, which he hated.

"Okay, this is it," Pedro announced, banging the phone down. "It's go time." Melody was back from a speaking tour, and an appearance she'd taped on the *Sandi!* talk show was airing that morning. She'd ordered all the employees up to watch it. Pedro tossed the violated donut back in the box, pacing around and hitching his pants like a SWAT commander mobilizing his team. A ring of frosting glistened on his lips. "Don't worry. Just follow my lead and you'll be fine."

"Wipe your mouth," Elliot said.

The house was in the hills beyond Sunset Plaza, the curdled heart of Eurotrash LA, where custom Harleys driven by marauding gangs of middle-aged music executives in leather jackets cruised past oil-rich Arabs in Bentleys scouting Swedish Amazons in Day-Glo gym shorts. It was apocalyptic. Roman. You couldn't imagine that this would be allowed to go on much longer.

Melody's house was like the Palazzo Vecchio, only bigger: a cobblestone courtyard, fountains and balconies, seraphim and cherubim, all snuggled on the hillside between her neighbors, a fine Tudor manor dating from the 1980s and an homage to the Taj Mahal, except for the satellite dish and huge air-conditioning units. It was like miniature golf of the gods. Elliot had an uncanny moment when he saw, poking its nose from the garage, a midnight-blue Lexus, a match for the one that had collected the payment for the congressman's video, or the one he'd seen at Farah's. But it meant no more or less than seeing a dream object in daylight, a premonition, good or ill.

"Whose car is that?" he asked Pedro.

"Melody's," Pedro said, as he opened the front door. "But she hardly ever drives." Inside, her home reminded Elliot of an expensive but not very good restaurant, full of sumptuous archways, soaring couches, marble and faux patinated walls. Melody appeared, five-foot-nothing in a bathrobe, flanked by Pam and Janice.

"Hi, honey," she cried, flinging her arms open. Pedro went in for a kiss on the lips. "How are you, sweetheart? Listen, could you help me please? I'd be so grateful. I want to see how these paintings look."

"No problem," Pedro said. "This is Elliot."

Melody turned to him with a look of delighted amazement. "Elliot, Elliot." He took a deep breath and stepped forward, hand extended.

"Hi," he said. "It's nice to meet you." She clutched his hand in both of hers. "Thank you, Elliot," she breathed.

"Sure."

"I mean it. Thank you." She stared deeply into his eyes and squeezed his hand harder. "I want you to know that I honor and acknowledge the help you provide."

"Well thanks . . ."

"I really mean it." Melody kept gushing. "I want you to really get how grateful I am. Do you?"

"Yes," he said, a little frightened. "Absolutely. Thank you very much."

"You're so very welcome." She smiled and released his sweating hand. "See," she continued, turning to address the others in the room. "That's how you treat an employee."

"Yes," her assistant Pam declared passionately.

"It really is," her assistant's assistant, Janice, added.

"Jan . . ." Pam turned to her assistant and took her hand. "I want you to know how much I honor you."

"Me too," Janice said.

"Wonderful." Melody beamed at them. "I really felt the respect there."

"I'd like to honor Elliot," Pedro announced. He leaned into Elliot's ear. "With a rim job," he whispered.

"Why don't the big corporations get it?" Melody mused aloud. "That's what their workers need, to be honored and respected. To feel like their bosses truly *get* them, you know? Respect is so much more important than money."

"So much," Janice concurred. Janice, Elliot knew, made a dollar more an hour than he did, but she was a single mother with two children to support and lived in public housing. Pedro and Pam made the same amount as each other, which drove Pam crazy.

Melody hopped onto the massive couch and tucked her legs beneath her. "Pam, honey, could you get my coffee? And get some for yourself, too, okay? Thank you so much."

Pam turned to Janice. "Jan, please get us some coffee. And get some for yourself." Janice hurried off.

"Pedro, honey?" Melody purred. "Would you and Eric get those paintings? And ask Ramon if he'll come help. And after this I need you boys to pick me up some books. You know, nice leather ones. I'm having people over tonight and I want the shelves full."

"No problem," Pedro said. "We'll get you some first editions. Elliot has a master's degree in English."

Melody looked at Elliot soulfully. "Then you really get me."

"We sure do," Pedro said.

Pam called the gardener, who came in smiling shyly, wiping his feet and mopping the sweat from his sunburned face.

"Hola, Ramon," Melody called. "Gracias!"

There were two framed canvases, each six by eight, abstracts in pastel hues. Elliot and Pedro hoisted one while Ramon got the other. Janice hurried in with the coffee and held it out to Melody.

"Thank you, just put it down, honey." She began arranging the paintings. "Over there. And honey, you over there, by that wall. No. Yes, there. Higher. A little higher. What do you think?"

Pam scrutinized them. "Hmm."

"I think the other way around maybe," Melody said.

"Yeah, the other way," Pam agreed.

They switched positions, backing around each other carefully. Elliot chipped his shin on the coffee table. Pain ran up his leg.

"There. Good. Higher," Melody declared, waving her arms. "Bueno. No, Ramon, to the right. My right. By the credenza. El credenza. Isn't *credenza* Spanish? Pedro, can you switch with that mirror?"

While Pedro went to remove the huge gilt mirror from above the fireplace, Elliot sweated, straining to hold the giant painting on his own. The phone rang. Pam picked it up and murmured.

"Yes, this is Melody's assistant . . . One moment, I'll see." She covered the receiver and turned to Melody. "It's Hank's assistant. Are you in for him?"

"Of course."

"Yes, she's here. Put him through."

Melody took the phone. "Hi, honey, how are you?" She began pacing around the house, padding on small bare feet. It was shocking to realize how tiny she was; she took up so much space. Sweat began to bead on Elliot's forehead. His scalp itched. A tremor shot through his arms and he tried to brace himself by levering his elbows into his sides. Across the room, he saw Ramon breathing heavily and grimacing in concentration. The tendons popped under his skin. Pedro grunted, shifting the grand mirror. He turned to Elliot and mouthed the word "agent," as Melody burbled and cooed into the phone. "Love you too, so much," she said and made kissing sounds, then dropped the phone onto the couch, where Pam retrieved it.

"Where was I?" Melody asked, picking up her cup. "Oh yes, let's get these paintings up." She took a thoughtful sip of coffee and then abruptly spit it back into her cup. "Jesus Christ," she shouted. "Pam, this coffee is like ice."

Pam twitched, jerking her head like she'd been slapped. Melody cornered her.

"How hard could it be? All I asked for was a simple cup of coffee." Her voice grew ragged and screechy as it climbed in pitch. "Is that too much to ask? Tell me, because I want to know. Really. Is it too fucking much?"

Trembling like a trapped rodent, Pam guessed, "No?"

"Jesus. Fuck it." They all stared in awe as Melody stormed off into the bathroom and slammed the door.

"What is wrong with you?" Pam hissed, turning suddenly on Janice. "I asked you to get a simple coffee. Can't you even do that right?"

Janice began to weep softly. "I need this job . . ."

Melody came flying back into the room, waving a roll of toilet paper. "Consuela! Consuela," she howled, jumping on the couch, toilet paper flying like a banner.

"Consuela!" Pam screamed.

"I'll get her," Janice spat and raced off, dragging back a terrified round Mexican woman.

"Look at this, look at this!" Melody screamed, jumping up and down. Her robe opened and a breast flopped out. Consuela gaped at the maniac.

"How many times have I told you? Put the toilet paper on with the paper in front! You had it backward! And it's almost empty. There's like two fucking sheets left. Dos! Dos! I'm having guests tonight. Mucho guestos. And that is the *guest* bathroom."

"That's the guest bathroom, Consuela," Pam said, joining in. "Banyo. Los banyo, Consuela."

Janice ganged up on her, too. "And the coffee was cold, Consuela. Mucho frio. What's wrong with you?"

Consuela began to cry while Elliot and Ramon watched in horror. Pedro seemed resigned. All were now visibly sagging under their loads. Dizzy, Elliot lurched forward and then leaned against a chair. Melody hurled the roll of toilet paper across the room.

"Cancer!" she shouted. "You're all trying to give me cancer. Why are you trying to kill me? Why?" She staggered around on top of the couch, railing against fate, while her assistants grieved like a Greek chorus. "You're all sucking my blood. You're living off my talent, my work. It's all on me, me, me!"

There was a sudden thump. Consuela screamed. They all looked over to where Ramon had fainted. Melody stared in amazement at his crumpled form under the painting.

"My God, what's wrong with him? Is he sick?"

An hour later, they were all upstairs in the bedroom, gathered in front of the TV. Melody and Pam cuddled on the bed while Pedro and Elliot sat with pillows on the carpet.

"Come on, it's starting," Melody called.

"Come on, Jan, it's starting," Pam added.

Janice came running in with a giant bowl of popcorn and hopped on the bed.

"Oh goody, lots of butter," Melody said.

"I love popcorn with butter," Pam added.

"Me too," Janice said. "I told Consuela, lots of butter."

"Shush, it's starting," Melody said. "Turn it up."

"Quick, Pedro, turn it up," Pam ordered.

"Righto," Pedro said, pressing the remote control. *Sandi!* was a talk show devoted to discussions with celebrities and other experts about healing and loving yourself. It had an immense audience and the brand had expanded to include a magazine and a publishing imprint. Elliot had never actually seen the show, but you couldn't walk on this hemisphere and not know who Sandi was.

"Eddie, you went to Columbia, correct?" Melody asked him.

"Yes, that's right," Elliot said.

"Then you've probably already read Sandi's book club selection for this month. It's incredible. *The Salt Gatherer's Stepdaughter* by Luna Hart Chambers."

"It's wonderful," Pam opined. "At least that's my opinion."

"I love it," Janice said. "So far, I mean. I just started reading it."

"I don't think I know it," Elliot said. Pedro kicked him.

"Oh my God," Melody shouted, turning to Elliot. Everyone tensed. "You are so lucky. Isn't he?"

The women smiled nervously, unsure where this was going.

"Because," Melody explained, "now it's like you get to discover her for the first time. Isn't that great?"

Pam beamed at him. "It's so true. You're so lucky."

"Thank you," Elliot said.

"I'm jealous," Melody said.

"Me too," Janice added. "I wish I hadn't started reading it."

"Shush, she's on," Melody said.

Sandi was bouncing through the audience, hugging and kissing. She turned to the camera, eyes and lips wet with dew.

"So who here loved *The Salt Gatherer's Stepdaughter*?" she asked. The audience went wild. "Didn't you love it? I loved it. For those of you who haven't read it yet, it's the story of a young woman from a family of salt gatherers who gather salt from the sea. It's her journey of self-discovery, after she falls in love with a young British officer but then discovers she has to be true to herself and love herself and the sea most of all."

"I love those descriptions of the sea and the salt," Melody said.

"It's so poetic," Pam said.

"Sea salt is the best kind for you," Melody said.

"It's more natural than regular," Pam explained.

"I never use regular," Janice said.

"Ooh, child, do we have a good show today," Sandi cooed. The audience cheered.

"I love how she says that," Melody said.

"She's got so much soul," Pam observed.

"I wish I did," Janice said.

"You do," Pam said. "Doesn't she, Melody?"

Melody thought it over. They all waited for her decision. "Yes, but in African Americans, it's deepened because of their suffering under racism."

"That is so true," Pam said. "I've noticed that."

"I hate racism," Janice said, her voice choking with emotion. She looked around defiantly, ready to take on anyone who spoke up for it. After a commercial, Sandi introduced Melody and they all sank to new depths of sycophancy.

"That dress looks great."

"I love your haircut."

Pedro tried to give Elliot an opening, nudging the other brown-nosers away. "She looks hot, doesn't she, Elliot?"

All eyes turned to him. He squirmed. It wasn't that he thought he was above it. He just couldn't believe Melody actually fell for this crap. She stared at him innocently.

"Great," he managed. "You look really great."

Everyone smiled in relief. Melody batted her eyelashes at him. "Thank you so much," she exhaled. Pedro patted his arm reassuringly.

"Now, in your wonderful new book," Sandi was saying to Melody on TV, "called *Love Is All, All Is Love: More Wisdom of Zona . . .*" Janice and Pam squealed. Melody shushed them. "You talk about how there are ghosts . . ."

"Spirits, Sandi," Melody corrected her.

"Sorry, spirits are all around us."

"That's right, Sandi," Melody said to the camera.

"Well, I have got to tell you, girlfriend, that spooky stuff gives me the creeps!" The audience howled at this, as did Janice and Pam and Melody, who shook the bed with laughter.

"That's so funny," Pam shouted.

"You go, girlfriend," Janice called at the TV.

On TV, Melody also laughed. "But seriously, Sandi. There's nothing to be scared of. Zona teaches that in reality there is no difference between life and death, any more than there is any real separation between you and I right now, they're just different planes of being. That's just an illusion of the mind. All there really is, is love."

"That is so true," Sandi said.

"So when Zona speaks through me," Melody went on, "it's like any one of us letting our higher self open up. It's really just love speaking to love."

"I love that," Sandi said. "Don't you love that?" The audience roared.

"It's like in the ancient Indian tradition," Melody explained. "The chakras open."

"They worshipped the Great Spirit and the Mother Earth," Sandi added.

"Exactly," Melody said. "Except that we've lost touch with our deeper selves."

"So then it's really the wisdom of the heart, isn't it, Melody?"

"Yes, that is so true, Sandi."

"Well then, let me ask you. Is Zona here with us now?"

"Yes, she is, Sandi."

"Then after this break, we'll see if she won't come out and speak to some audience members. We'll be right back!"

In the next segment, audience members came on stage and talked about their problems. One wanted to know if her dead sister was "all right." How could she not be? Another had shingles. A third was a single mom of three, struggling financially. After each contestant had described her plight, Melody went into a trance. She shut her eyes, pressed her fingertips together, and spoke in a different, deeper voice.

"I am Zona," she said. "I bring you the wisdom of love."

❖

Elliot was a little dazed driving home after that, and it took him a second, as he parked and got out, to register the giant white limo pulling up behind him in his driveway.

"Oh God . . ." he murmured aloud. He considered turning and running, but to where? Instead he waved tentatively as Moishe climbed out. "Hi. What's up?"

Moishe just nodded toward the open door and, when Elliot gingerly stuck his head inside, shoved him over and climbed in beside him.

Vic was stone-faced, sitting like an idol. "Let's not waste time," he said. "You know why we're here."

That stupid prank, Elliot thought. Pedro and his brilliant ideas. Just like that damned candy store. "Listen," he said, "I'm so sorry. It was foolish, I know . . ."

"What are you blathering about?" Vic asked, pulling a cigar from his pocket. Moishe lit it, eyes still on Elliot, as if ready for a sudden move.

"Me?" Elliot tried to pivot. "Nothing. Just blathering, you know . . . about the jacket! I feel so bad, not appreciating the lovely gesture . . ."

Vic brushed it aside. "Fuck the jacket. Ancient history. I hear you got a new job now."

"I had to. But it's not, you know, literary, so there's no conflict . . ."

"That's why I'm here. To give you some valuable advice." He looked deep into Elliot's eyes. "It might even save your life someday."

Elliot swallowed. "Okay," he said, softly.

"Crystal. Stay the fuck away from her."

"Crystal?" That was the last name Elliot expected to hear. "You mean Christine?"

"You know who I mean. Whatever else happened between me and her, I do not want her bothered by anyone, especially you, understand?"

Elliot nodded energetically. "No. I mean yes. Completely. But I haven't even seen her. I have no idea where she is." It was, unfortunately, the truth, he added to himself. He had given up even asking.

"Good. Keep it that way. And, Gross . . . listen closely . . ."

"Yes, sir." He leaned forward, at attention.

"About that tape? That missing video?"

"Yes, sir?"

"Forget you ever heard of it."

"I did. Totally. I mean, until you just reminded me . . ."

"Well, forget again! And this time keep it forgotten!"

"Yes, sir. Thank you. That's very wise."

Vic dismissed him with a wave, and Moishe helped him out with a shove. As they backed away, Elliot lit a cigarette. The match shook in his hand.

16

"Jan!" Pam squealed in the outer office the next morning, and Elliot felt the hairs on the back of his neck rise. Not only did Pam's voice grate his nerve endings, but, like a wary dog, he'd learned to recognize that specific frequency as trouble, and trouble always made its way back to them. They'd been having a quiet day so far, each with his own thoughts. With all four duping decks going and a pile of empty tape cases to label and fill, Elliot was brooding on Vic's visit. It shook him up, yet inevitably, being warned not to think about Christine or the mysterious missing tape ensured that he would. He glanced over at Pedro, who oddly enough was leaning back in his desk chair, feet up, resting comfortably on his pile of paperwork, and gazing out the window with the phone to his ear. This was odd because there was nothing to gaze at out there but a narrow alley and the wall of the next building. Also, he wasn't talking to anyone on the phone. More screeching and yelling came from out front and then, inevitably, an even louder, higher call, like a siren: "Pedro! Elliot! Get in here!"

With a dramatic sigh, Pedro hung up the phone and got to his feet. "What now?" he muttered, and led the way. Elliot followed reluctantly, standing behind him.

"Look," Pam said, pale with indignation, waving a small metal box with an open lid. Janice was weeping.

"What's that?" Pedro asked, helping himself to one of the oranges in a bowl on her desk.

"You know very well what it is," Pam said, as if cross-examining a suspect.

Pedro shrugged, unwinding orange peel. "It's the petty cash box."

"It's the empty petty cash box!" Pam waved it upside down, triumphantly. A receipt for toilet paper fluttered out and a few coins rained onto the floor, rolling crazily. "Someone stole the money. There was $108.42 in here yesterday!"

"I didn't take it, I swear!" Janice declared, beseechingly, wringing her hands.

"Someone did!" Pam insisted.

Elliot, to hide his extreme discomfort, knelt and gathered the coins. Pedro calmly took them. "Well," he said. "Here is the forty-two cents at least." He leaned over and dropped them in the box.

"At least! Is that all you have to say?" She waved a finger over them. "There is a thief among us. I'm calling Melody."

Janice began to whimper. Pedro shrugged and began eating his orange, offering a section to Elliot, who shook his head. Melody was in the car and demanded to be put on speaker.

"All right, everybody," her disembodied voice declared. "Family meeting. When was the last time you checked the petty cash, Pam?"

Pam sat up straight. "Yesterday afternoon, when I sent Elliot to get toilet paper."

"Objection!" Pedro yelled. "Elliot works with me, he shouldn't be sent on these errands. We have tons of orders to get out today. We should be working right now. Janice is supposed to get the toilet paper."

Janice, who had been weeping softly into a tissue, jerked like a rabbit. "I didn't even know it was out, I swear. There were three full rolls on Tuesday."

"Really?" Pedro said, thoughtfully. "That's interesting. Maybe the thief took them too. Pam, how many sheets did you use the last time you wiped?"

Pam scowled, but before she could respond, Melody's voice scolded: "Focus, people! Let's follow the timeline. Late afternoon. Did anyone else come by?"

"UPS," Elliot said.

"What? Who's that?"

"The UPS guy came," Pedro said. "But he's here every day."

"And how would he know where to look?" Pam added.

"Anything else? Anything at all unusual?" Melody asked. Jan raised a trembling hand.

"She can't see you, Jan," Pam said. "Go ahead."

"What? What does she see?" Melody's voice blared.

Janice tried to focus. "I was in the kitchen, washing my hands, when I thought I heard something like a child laughing, but when I came out, no one was here."

"Why would a child be here?" Pam asked.

"Was the door open or shut?" Elliot asked, trying to help her along.

"It was shut!" Janice sat up now, more confident. "I remember because I was a little you know, disturbed, and so I checked. And also, I felt like a chill or something, like a chilly breeze, but the window was closed, which seemed, like Melody said . . . unusual. I kind of thought, it might be, you know . . ." Here she looked around, as if worried she was being overheard. "A ghost."

There was silence. Elliot stared, incredulous. Pam seemed confused, as if her moment of glory was taking a weird turn. Pedro finished his orange. Melody spoke.

"You're right. That is unusual. Pedro, you're a sensitive. What do you think?"

"Well, Melody," he said, leaning into the phone, "there was that other time we felt a presence here, remember? The handprint on the glass door?"

Now Pam objected. "That was when we paid a crew to clean and there was a smudge on the glass right after. Remember, Melody? You said it was totally disrespectful."

"Yes," Pedro added, raising a finger, "but we realized the print was too small and too low to be a normal human hand. It had to be a child."

Pam glared at him, but Janice followed intently, with a rapt expression.

"There's one way to find out for sure," Melody declared, all business now. "I will make a call and be down there later. No one is to leave or go home until I arrive. Got it?"

"What about lunch?" Pedro asked. "It's almost eleven thirty."

"Order in," Melody said.

"But there's no petty cash to pay," Pam said.

"Jesus fucking Christ, do I have to think of everything?" Melody barked, her temper rising.

"I can cover it with tape funds," Pedro said.

"Thank you Pedro, now that is proactive problem solving."

After ordering Middle Eastern food from Ziva's Oasis, Elliot and Pedro retreated to their lair to work. Pedro leaned back in his chair and lifted the phone.

"What the hell are you doing over there anyway?" Elliot asked, removing the warm tapes from the decks and putting in another batch.

"Posing."

"Posing? As what? Someone who does their job?"

Pedro nodded out the window. "The old lady across the alley. She's been painting a picture of me for a few weeks. I like to give her my good side, but she's gone now."

Elliot leaned over Pedro's desk and peered out. Sure enough, right across the way was an open window, and behind a lacy curtain, he could see an easel and a coffee can of brushes.

"You should be naked when she comes back tomorrow," he suggested. "Holding a sword."

The doorbell rang.

"Food's here!" Pam yelled.

"Food's here," Janice echoed. "Bring the money!"

Pedro pulled a huge roll of bills from his pants. "Here," he said and peeled off a few twenties. "Give him a good tip."

❖

It was just before five that Melody finally arrived, bringing with her a friend who was even shorter than Melody, but round where Melody was sharp. She wore a flowing white blouse and skirt, a necklace festooned with a large pink crystal, a white straw hat with an immense round brim, a pink shawl, and Elliot couldn't help but notice, white sandals on her extremely rugged feet, the overgrown nails thrusting out like horns.

"Gather round, people," Melody declared, sitting cross-legged on an armchair. "This is Sharon. She drove in from Santa Monica."

"Greetings," Sharon said with a gracious smile. "Out at the beach, they call me a white witch."

"I think she misheard that," Pedro muttered into Elliot's ear as they reluctantly joined the others.

"Should I make tea?" Janice asked.

"Good idea," Pam said. "We have leftover grape leaves, too, and some hummus."

"And pita chips!" Janice chirped, walking toward the kitchen.

"Maybe after," Sharon said, sitting before the coffee table.

"After," Melody ordered. "Everybody sit down."

"After," Pam yelled at Jan, who jumped. "We don't want any tea right now."

Janice scurried over to join Pam and Sharon on the couch and Elliot and Pedro took the love seat. Sharon pulled a folded Ouija board from her huge woven purse and opened it on the table. "Now then," she said, removing the planchette. "Let's light a candle and get to work."

❖

By the light of a single candle, they all gathered close, with two fingers each on the planchette.

"Are you there, kind spirit?" Sharon intoned. "Please, we mean you no harm."

"It's moving!" Janice cried, happy and scared.

"Shhh . . . focus . . ." Melody snapped.

"Focus, Jan," Pam said, then, "It says *Yes*!"

"What is your name?"

Again the planchette rolled, over the letter *P*, seemingly of its own power, though Pedro peered at Pam suspiciously from the corner of his eye.

"*P* . . ." Sharon said and waited. It seemed to waver, jerking toward E and then A, then suddenly veering to *O*.

"*O* . . ." Sharon said.

It slid away, firmly to *O* again and then back to *P*.

"*P. O. O. P.* Is that your name?"

Yes.

"Maybe it's initials?" Jan asked.

The planchette jerked. *No.*

"Okay, that's fine," Sharon said soothingly. She lowered her voice confidingly. "Definitely dealing with a child spirit. They play games." Then, loudly, she addressed the ceiling. "Poop, how old are you?"

The planchette rolled to the number six.

"You're six? And, we are just asking now, you are not in any trouble, but did you perhaps take some money that was in the box in the drawer yesterday?"

There was a moment of hesitation, while all present held their breath, then . . .

Yes.

"Oh, thank God," Janice exhaled.

"Shhh . . ." Sharon went on. "And why did you take it, Poop? Did you need anything?"

The planchette moved: *C . . . A . . . N . . . D . . . Y.*

After that they held hands and said a prayer over burning sage. Then, while sipping tea and nibbling pita chips, Sharon suggested that, in the future, they keep bowls of candy out to appease the hungry spirit. Elliot was given cash and sent to Thrifty's, with special instructions from Pedro to get Reese's Pieces, black licorice (not red), and fun-size Snickers, which just happened to be his favorites.

17

There were two distinct classes of customer for whatever it was Melody sold: rich/famous people and common rabble. Of course, it was the rabble who provided the bucks, but it was the all-important celebrities that made Zona's wisdom seem wise. After all, there were already enough religions out there showing you how to be a loser, to suffer with dignity and learn to deserve your punishment. Bright's customers weren't buying any of that. They wanted "abundance." Melody taught her rich clients to forgive themselves and just accept that they deserved to be rich. Poor customers had only to realize that they, too, deserved abundance and it would effortlessly come, preferably in the form of sitcom roles and record deals, two of the blessings that Elliot heard them praying for. If it didn't come, well then, they just weren't forgiving themselves hard enough. Either way, filthy rich or stinking poor, they all wanted the same thing: to know that it wasn't their fault.

Although the wisdom was the same, it was doled out to rich and poor differently. The rich got one-on-one or, rather, two-on-one sessions with Melody and Zona. They got prime seats at the lectures and autographed books. They got patched through to the car phone. The poor got Elliot, who tried to sell them tapes. A woman whose unemployed husband beat her complained that her roof was leaking and there was no food for her kids. She prayed and prayed but no luck. Was she praying the wrong way? A man whose legs had been crushed by a drunk driver wanted to know why he'd chosen that fate for himself. Could Elliot explain the lesson? One after another, these endlessly beseeching voices came, haranguing him over the line. Many were surprised Melody herself wasn't there answering the phone. Some got angry and demanded to speak to her, others were certain if he'd just pass along the message she would definitely call back. Within the soft tissue of their brains, a face seen one too many times on daytime TV and a voice heard too many hours in the car became someone they knew, and if they knew you, then you had to know them, and owe them something besides. That was the problem with the needy: they were just so damned needy. Elliot could feel them trying to suck the life out of him right through the phone wire. What did they want from him? What could he do for anyone? In the end, he sent a free tape, any tape. At least they felt better. And who knows. Maybe there really were angels swimming in their cornflakes.

That was how Elliot finally met the real Vivian De Fay, when Melody sent him over to deliver some tapes. She and her husband, the studio boss Jerry Sumack, were acolytes of Zona, apparently, and Melody was cultivating their interest, counseling the couple through their issues. He drove up to Mulholland, checking the five-digit addresses, (signaling seven-figure homes?) and found it, a glass mountain in the hills. He stopped in front of the gate and pressed the intercom. A camera zoomed in. He looked up and smiled as a gruff voice asked "Yes?"

"Hi. I'm Elliot from Melody Bright's. She sent me with these tapes." He held up the bag.

"Pick up or drop off?" the voice asked.

"Uh, drop off. Dropping off these tapes." He waved the bag again.

There was silence for a moment and then the gate folded back. Climbing the steep driveway, he saw that the house was even bigger than it had seemed from the road, with wings and towers stacked along the hill. It was like a modern art museum, a multiplex of sprawling, gleaming cubes, growing like crystals along the ridge of the rock, surrounded by courtyards and reflecting pools and gigantic abstract sculptures. It was a public space. Elliot couldn't imagine walking around it naked or getting up at night for a glass of water without setting off an alarm and triggering steel gates. Surprised there was no valet offering tickets, he parked his own car, and proceeded to the entrance, ringing again. Elliot expected a maid or the guard from behind the camera, but Vivian De Fay herself opened the door.

"Hi," she said, holding out her hand, "I'm Vivian."

It was the kind of gesture, answering her own door, shaking his hand, introducing herself as if he didn't already know her name, that Elliot knew was calculated to make her seem humble, a real person just like him, and that, of course, always worked. He was hugely flattered and fell for her immediately.

"Hi," he said, "I'm Elliot."

"Please come in," she said, turning to lead the way. She was dressed in jeans and a sleeveless white T-shirt and was, like everybody famous, shorter than he expected. She was also younger. When he first saw her films he'd been, let's say, twelve, and she was an adult, playing the femme fatale roles that would make her famous. She'd seemed utterly beyond him, already at home in a complex, glamorous world of grown-up sex and pain. Now, years later, she seemed like she was still the same age, or even seemed younger in some ways as she bounced along in sneakers. It was as if time moved at a separate rate for each of them. While she led him through vast rooms, pointing out this or that modern art masterpiece, he tried to place what was so strange about her, something vaguely off.

"This is the study, where we usually watch movies and things," she said, waving at the leather armchairs, plush couches, and the billboard-sized screen, as if he were considering buying the place. The most striking thing to Elliot was the art. There were framed posters of her movies on the walls, but the space was dominated by four huge black-and-white prints, framed in silver and several feet high, each an extreme close-up of her famous face. It induced a kind of vertigo in Elliot, dizziness brought on by exposure to this height of fame. He even thought, staring at the photos, *That's Vivian De Fay!* You had to sort of rebalance to keep the real person in focus at the same time. Perhaps this was what it meant to be a real star—to have your persona float above you, bigger and higher, at all times, like a swollen shadow. Still, how could she bear it? Elliot could barely stand to look in the mirror each morning, holding a razor to his own throat. Living in a room with his own face as the wallpaper sounded like a recipe for insanity.

"Nice," was what he said.

She pointed at a set of built-in shelves. Tapes and DVDs, mostly, he noticed, also featuring herself, were stacked beside the players. "I think those go over there," she said. "I'm so bad at technical things."

"Me too," Elliot said, putting the tapes down. Her weird eyes blinked at him.

"But I thought you made those tapes?"

"Right." Elliot searched for an explanation. The phone rang.

"Excuse me for a moment," she said and picked up a wall phone. "Hello? Yes, this is she. What? When? Oh my God." Vivian De Fay moaned loudly, and sagged against the wall. Elliot was trapped. He felt acutely uncomfortable overhearing this, but there was no way to leave the room without her moving aside. He turned his back and stared at one of her giant photos, pretending to be too absorbed to notice her wailing. An eternity later, he heard her set the phone down and turned around. She was sitting on the couch, crying. She'd forgotten about him altogether. Finally, she blinked and focused on him. The weirdness he'd felt before. It was in her eyes.

"My mother's dead," she said.

"Oh my God. I'm so sorry," Elliot said, moving immediately toward the door. She reached out and grabbed his hand.

"Can you take me to the airport?"

❖

Elliot drove down the back side of the hill into the Valley, and took the freeway toward the Santa Monica Airport while Vivian De Fay made funeral plans on her phone, aiming the antenna out the window to try to get a signal. He was painfully aware of the shoddiness of his car compared to hers, a vintage Mercedes two-seater he'd spotted, sleeping like a cat on the warm driveway, polished to a glowing red. His car, on the other hand, was an ashtray on wheels, with a six-inch layer of trash on the floor and a landfill's worth of newspapers, cans, and bottles in the back seat. Maybe, he thought, he should casually mention his commitment to recycling.

This was the closest he had ever been to a truly famous person, a star he himself had admired from below in the darkness of a crowded theater, and yet, seeing Vivian De Fay like this, grief-stricken, caught up in real life, did not make her seem any more human. He did not think, *Hey, we all have mothers, we all lose loved ones, she's not so different.* On the contrary she seemed more glamorous, more like a movie character than ever. She had even dressed for the part, rushing upstairs to change into a black dress and headscarf before stepping daintily into his car and crossing her stockinged legs as he shut the door for her. Now she stared at the traffic through her huge round sunglasses and sighed. Perhaps, Elliot wondered, Vivian De Fay's real-life drama didn't seem real to him because it was at times like this that we all felt special: getting that shocking phone call, racing to catch a red-eye, we feel that our own lives are like a movie and that, at last, we are stars.

"Do you have a cigarette?" Vivian De Fay asked.

"Yes, of course." He handed her one, and when the traffic slowed, he turned to give her a light.

"Thanks," she said, blowing a stream of smoke between her pursed lips. "Jerry hates smoking. He'd kill me if he knew, but hey, fuck, my mother's dead, right?"

"Right." He glanced over at her, nervously. "Again, I'm very sorry. I know this must be even harder for you, I mean, to be with a total stranger at a time like this."

She smiled. "No. You've been wonderful." She patted his leg and a surge of lightning went through him. He gripped the wheel. "Besides," she shrugged. "It's rather appropriate, I think. My mother was a stranger to me. We didn't speak. I hated her guts for years."

"Oh."

"I left home at fifteen, took a bus cross-country to Hollywood." She chuckled ruefully. "That's how clueless I was, asked the guy for a ticket to Hollywood, one way. It dumped me in downtown LA. And I never went back. She tried to get in touch when she saw me on screen, of course. I sent some money, mostly to keep her away. But we never spoke again."

Elliot didn't know how to respond to this. He felt like he was in a movie, but he didn't know his lines. "I see," he said, trying to sound wise.

"You're wondering why I'm crying then."

"Not at all. It's normal to . . ."

"It's a good question. I don't know myself. Perhaps," she said, "I'm crying for my own lost childhood."

Elliot nodded. "Sure, I know what you mean." He had no clue what she meant. He put a cigarette in his mouth and pushed in the lighter.

"You see," she continued. "My stepfather molested me for years, and she never did anything. Just acted like she didn't know. But she knew. She knew."

Spending so much time with showfolk, Elliot was used to a certain amount of self-dramatization, to people who turned their own lives into a performance, if only for an audience of one, or maybe even alone, just for themselves. But Vivian De Fay was different; she was, after all, a great actress. True, he had never heard anyone talk like this, but it was exactly the kind of thing that happened in her films and that everyone admired for being so powerfully real. It was a role she was born to play.

The lighter popped. Elliot didn't dare reach for it. Vivian De Fay blew smoke against the windshield and it curled, drifting along the dashboard, rising between his fingers on the wheel. Her voice grew more gravelly as she spoke, taking on a slight Texas twang.

"I'd be out in the yard, reading in the sun," she went on. "Just lying on a towel in my bikini. I must have been thirteen. And he'd come out with a bottle of lotion and say I was going to get a burn. I'd say I could put the lotion on myself, but he'd insist I couldn't reach all the tenderest places that would burn the worst. That's what he called them, *tender.* I looked over at my Mom for help, she was taking down the washing, but she just went inside. I can still hear that screen door slamming behind her, like a whip cracking, as he knelt down, all fat and smelly and squirted that . . . that lotion onto my back and all down my legs."

Elliot stared at the car in front of him like he was trying to memorize its license plate. It was a Volkswagen with one of those Jesus fish on it. He hated those. Even worse, it had a bumper sticker reading MY BOSS IS A JEWISH CARPENTER. *So was my great-uncle*, he thought. *Big deal.*

"He'd rub it into my shoulders and down my back. I could hear him breathing and it was all I could do not to scream. Then he'd move up my thighs, working in that lotion. He'd rub it over my ass and then, he'd slip his hand under my pink bikini bottom and find those tender places."

She leaned back and took a deep breath of smoke. From the corner of his eye, Elliot peeked at her. She adjusted her dress, uncrossing and recrossing her legs, and he glimpsed the lace tops of her stockings. There was a sheen of perspiration on her forehead and her cheeks were flushed. He felt the left side of his own face baking in the sun through the window while she smoked on his right. She took another drag and stamped her cigarette out in the ashtray. He smelled perfume and fire. Why couldn't he have gotten his air-conditioning fixed? He honked his horn angrily at the Jesus fish.

"Come on, let's go." He caught himself and glanced at Vivian De Fay. "Sorry."

"My father," she said, breaking the silence, "I mean James Duffy, my real father, not that bastard. He was much older than my mother. The town hero. He was in the war, the Battle of the Bulge, and I guess he never really got over it. Couldn't stand cold weather. One time, I remember, I came running into his study after school, I was a daddy's girl and I was just dying to show him what I'd learned on baton team, I must've been eleven or twelve, and I just barged right on in without knocking. And there he was, sitting in his chair with his service pistol inside his mouth. And his finger on the trigger. Well! He just took it out, smiled, and put the gun down, like nothing had ever happened. So I guess I did the same. He even had me go ahead and show him my twirling, right there with that gun on the table. I never saw him hold it again. But I knew where he kept it in the bottom drawer. He died while I was away at summer camp."

"He shot himself?"

"No. He drank himself to death. Same thing." She leaned back and uncoiled her legs, revealing them almost to the tops of the stockings. Her breasts rose and fell with her breath.

Suddenly, Elliot blurted out, "My father was in a concentration camp." He had no idea why he'd said this. As far as he could recall, he'd never discussed it with anyone. Perhaps it was only to dispel the weird tension that was filling the car or perhaps, horribly, he was trying to impress her in some unforgivable way. But the strange, unreal atmosphere, the sense that her own stories, however factual they might be, nevertheless seemed like scenes from one of her movies, made him feel free, as if nothing said in this car could possibly matter. Still, he regretted it, and blushed as soon as it was out. This was her moment, and he'd stepped on her toes, tried to upstage the star. She was, however, enthralled.

"Really?" She turned sideways to face him, folding her legs beneath her. "How did he survive?"

"I don't know. He was just a kid, he was lucky." The truth was, his father had always refused to discuss it. But when he glanced over and saw her rapt expression, he plunged ahead, repeating the story his mother told. "When the Americans liberated the camp and saw all the dead bodies, and the condition that the prisoners were in, some of them freaked out. This one soldier, he spoke German and asked my father what had happened to him. He told him and the American got so angry, he gave his gun to my dad. Then he pointed at the German soldiers they had captured and told him to go ahead and shoot them."

"What happened?"

"He shot. I mean, these people had tortured him, killed his whole family. The kickback almost knocked him right over, he was so weak, but then he braced himself and started shooting until one of the other American officers came running up and stopped him. This officer was furious at the other soldiers, of course. It could have been a huge scandal. So they just rushed my dad over to the people who were looking after the kids and got him out of there. He never saw any of them again."

Elliot glanced over at Vivian De Fay, who was staring at him.

"Everett?" she asked, softly.

"Uh, yeah?"

"Will you fuck me?"

He did a double take. "What?"

"Fuck me. I'm numb." She reached over and put her hand between his legs. "I need to feel alive."

"Let me find someplace to park. There's an exit coming up."

"No," she said. "There's no time." She reached under her skirt and peeled off her panties. Elliot could hear her breathing, but otherwise she remained expressionless behind her slightly crooked sunglasses. Her panties were sheer and black. Elliot felt like he was dreaming. He felt so unreal, it was all he could do not to laugh. She unzipped his fly and squeezed him. In a spastic reflex, Elliot's leg jumped out, hitting the accelerator, and the car lunged ahead, ramming the Jesus fish. Vivian De Fay bounced forward, banging her head on the windshield. The Jesus fish driver and his several passengers got out, all shouting, and started toward them.

"Sorry, sorry," he said to Vivian De Fay. "Are you okay? Are you bleeding?"

"My panties," she hissed. "Find my panties."

He spotted them on the dashboard and handed them over.

"And you better zip up," she added.

As he hurriedly, and painfully, bent himself back into his fly, he saw that her own purse had spilled into the footwell. Along with a wallet that was open to a license made out to Vanessa Duffy, there was a fantastic amount of cosmetics—lipsticks, compact, brush, liner, potions—and an even more impressive amount of pills, several bottles, at least one of which had popped open, vomiting a candy-rainbow over the floor. But most riveting was the humblest item, a ratty old sock, from which there stuck a blackened spoon and, to his amazement, a syringe.

"What about your bag?" he asked, nodding his chin, and she gasped slightly, then bent to scoop up her valuables. Elliot examined her with new eyes, as if the character he'd been with seconds before had vanished in the crash. This new Vivian was slick with sweat and tears, and he saw, where her makeup had run, tiny wrinkles by the mouth, slightly off-color patches by the ears and along the neck. She'd even been wearing expertly applied concealer on her arms. He noticed a fresh bruise in the crook of her elbow. And when she removed her giant shades, just for a minute, to dab her bleeding eyeliner with a hanky, he finally understood about the eyes: they were pinned, the pupils pinpricks, a sure sign of opiates. Vivian De Fay was high as fuck, which helped explain her surreal performance. And he had seen those eyes before. It had not been an imposter, a wannabe, at Dr. K's. She was the imposter, going under the knife, who knew how many times, because she wanted to be herself, and keep playing the role of Vivian De Fay.

Compared to the other patients he'd met, her work had fooled him completely. But while it was too subtle and expertly crafted to be immediately obvious, it was not exactly right to say it was invisible either. The difference, he supposed, was that while others paid in cash and blood to look like an imaginary "better" version of whom they hoped to be, she endeavored only to keep looking like herself. Yet that original Vivian had been an illusion to begin with, brilliantly conceived by Vanessa Duffy and executed by teams of artists and technicians. She was like one of the famous artworks she had casually shown off in her living room: a priceless masterpiece, expertly restored, perpetually present and renewed.

❖

The aftermath was chaotic, with cops and tow trucks, but no one was seriously hurt and when they found out that there was a movie star involved, Elliot's victims became friendly, even grateful, and ended up shaking Vivian De Fay's hand and thanking her. She explained to a cop about her mother and they received a police escort. Elliot didn't dare take a hand off the wheel or an eye off the police car in front of them. Now the bumper sticker dared him to keep kids off drugs and he panicked, on the inside, about the huge motherlode of contraband in the bag she held on her lap. In silence, they sailed through traffic to the small airport, where a Learjet was waiting beside a hangar. Vivian De Fay smoothed her skirt and checked her face in the rearview mirror.

"Um . . ." he said. "You might want to, you know . . ." He nodded at her bag. "Tidy up a bit before you go through airport security."

She frowned at him, then realized what he meant and laughed. "Don't worry about that," she said, pointing to the jet. "Just pull right up to the plane, please."

He drove over and stopped. Then he turned to her, feeling like he should say something, but immediately people emerged from the hangar and began running over. He started fumbling for an apology, but she leaned over and kissed his cheek.

"Don't be sorry. I'm not. We shared a special moment. Thanks so much for being there," she said. "As soon as I land, I'm going to call Melody and tell her what an angel you are."

Then she got out and, escorted by the staff, hurried up the stairs into the jet, black scarf blowing in the wind. Elliot sat staring for a moment, lost in a daze, then noticed one of the staff signaling for him to clear out. The plane was powering up. He put his car in reverse and backed away.

18

"Hey, what happened to you?" Pedro asked Elliot as he slunk into the office the next day, second in for the first morning ever, and slumped in his chair. "You never came back yesterday. I was all alone and the phone kept ringing."

"Her mother died," Elliot said. "I got stuck driving her to the airport."

"Bummer," Pedro said, dipping a cruller in his coffee.

Elliot shut the door and lowered his voice to a whisper. "She came on to me in the car."

"What happened?"

"I got into an accident."

While Pedro laughed and recovered from choking, Elliot told him the events of the day before.

Pedro snapped his fingers. "Doesn't that part about the stepdad sound familiar from somewhere?"

Elliot shrugged. "Maybe I wrote it for *Raunchy*?"

"No. It was in her first movie. Whatchamacallit. *The Last Song of Summer*! She plays a young farm girl. Except it's a boarder not the stepdad."

"You think she could mix up her real life and her movie? Can anyone be that high?" Elliot wondered. "Or maybe she used her own experience for her character. Like for inspiration? And now that is coloring her memories?"

Pedro reached for another pastry. "All of the above. With actresses anything is possible."

Elliot slumped. "I sometimes feel like I fell asleep and woke up in the wrong life," he told his coffee. Although he hadn't been drinking, he felt hungover and on the verge of a deep revelation. "Do you ever feel that way? I mean, when we were kids, is this what you imagined life would be like?"

"Pretty much," Pedro said.

"Not me," Elliot said. "I used to feel like I had a special connection to things, and life was going to be this adventure. Like I was in on a big secret."

"So what happened?"

"I guess I forgot it. Or I was wrong all along." Elliot gulped his coffee, so moved by his own tragedy that he felt close to tears.

Pedro laughed. "You just need to get laid. Maybe take another whack at comforting the grieving daughter."

"I think I blew that when I rear-ended those Jesus fish people. Plus she's married to the most powerful guy in town and best friends with our boss. I don't think that sounds like a smart move, do you?"

"That's why you have the wrong life. Maybe you should make the dumb move once in a while. Remember, all the greatest adventures start with a single wrong step." He took a big bite of frosted grease. "Observe me. I do everything all wrong and look at my life."

Elliot observed him for a moment.

"Frankly, it doesn't look so good. You're sitting in this crappy little room making tapes with me."

"Exactly." He punctuated his point with the cruller. "But I got laid last night. Think about it."

❖

When he got home that evening, there was a message from Margie, inviting him for a drink at a new spot called Supply. There was someone she wanted him to meet. Was she setting him up on a date? Considering the state of his social life, he had little to lose, and the lounge, one of those trendy places that came and went so fast he didn't even notice, was close by. So he wandered in, just a few minutes late, and there was Margie, fetching as ever in a tartan skirt and black angora sweater, waving him over. The place, a former plumbing supply shop, featured raw concrete floors and walls, and extremely uncomfortable benches and tables made of iron. Sitting beside her, presumably waiting to be matched with Elliot, was a man in his early thirties. He was completely bald, his skull as round and white as an egg, and smooth-shaven, with chunky black-framed glasses that looked both nerdy and expensive and a chunky black watch that was either retro or futuristic, Elliot couldn't tell. Also clearly expensive were his purple fleece jacket, green track pants, and bright blue sneakers that looked like they came with rocket boosters.

"Elliot, over here," Margie called, rising to kiss his cheek. "Glad you could come." She gestured to her pal, who half rose too, extending his slim soft hand. "Elliot Gross, Armond Laxo. A real meeting of the minds."

"It's a pleasure," Armond said. "I've heard a lot about you."

"Same," Elliot said, looking at Margie, who shrugged.

"So, Elliot," he said, "What does your great mind tell you about the future? What's coming next?"

Elliot pressed his fingers to his temples as he saw the waitress approaching with a tray. "I see strange drinks," he said, as she set down two beakers of what looked like blue and orange goo. Margie laughed and Armond jumped in with a chuckle. The waitress, a moody beauty in a cap and a plumber's coverall that said SUPPLY on the back, and JAQUI on the name patch, sighed as she handed Elliot a small menu card. Supply served only juices, all healthy, weird, and expensive. He was about to order the Still Water with Lemon Essence and Hand-Chipped Ice when Armond said: "This is on me, of course," so he switched to Lemon-Ginger-Kale with Wheatgrass-Infused Beet Foam.

"All kidding aside," Armond said. "Do you surf the web much, Elliot?"

"Not as much as I'd like to, Armond. I'm just too busy." In fact there was one dial-up account for the household and the line was constantly ringing for his housemates, not to mention the scripts they were faxed for auditions.

"Well, you need to get out there and explore. There's hundreds of sites and more coming every day. I'd love to pick your brain. Hear any thoughts you have."

"About the net?"

He nodded and Margie nodded along encouragingly.

"Well, there is one thought that has occurred to me."

The waitress reappeared and set his drink down: it looked like a tube of foamy blood. "Thanks, Jaqui," he said and she scowled. He toasted his hosts and took a sip. It was sour with a bitter aftertaste. "Hmm, interesting." He wiped his puckered lips. "It's about that WWW thing. You know, the front part of the web address?"

"Yes." Armond nodded. "It stands for 'World Wide Web.'"

"Exactly. That's my point. The whole purpose of using initials is that it's shorter. That's why we say LAPD. Or NYC. Or KCRW. No, that's different, but you get my meaning. But . . ." He counted on his fingers. "double-you, double-you, double-you is actually, what . . . nine syllables, and 'World Wide Web,' the thing it stands for, is only three. It's ridiculous. So when announcing or promoting a website, just say *World Wide Web*, not *double-you, double-you, double-you, dot whatever.* It's annoying."

"Huh," Armond said, thoughtfully stroking his baby-smooth chin as if there were a beard there. "I never thought of it that way."

"Me neither," Margie added, rolling her eyes at Elliot. "I wonder why not?"

"I will certainly pass that along to my team," Armond promised. "But can I be honest?"

"I hope so." Elliot took another sip, it burned.

"It's true I'm a finance guy, lame banking stuff. And I'm a tech guy with a master's degree from Caltech. All boring to you I'm sure."

"Not at all," Margie said charmingly. "Sounds fascinating."

Elliot coughed, trying to clear his throat. "And confusing."

"But really, what me and my people are doing in Seattle, it's not that different from what you do down here in Hollywood. I fund the future, mobilizing money to turn dreams into reality. Isn't that what we all want?"

Elliot and Margie nodded eagerly.

"But there are many possible futures. All existing out there in a state of potential, like parallel universes."

"Like string theory, right?" Elliot guessed.

"Yes. Well, sort of. VC."

Elliot searched his mind. He knew it couldn't be Viet Cong.

"Venture capital," Margie explained.

"Exactly." Armond fluttered a hand. "So self-centered of me to assume everyone knows. But my point is, in several of these possible futures, there is a high probability that we might have a need for a resource you are uniquely qualified to provide."

"Really?" Elliot said, genuinely interested for the first time. He wiped his mouth with his napkin. "You mean writing?"

"Sure. The web will be a gold mine for writers. Think of all the readers you'll reach. But more specifically, right at this early stage, I was referring to gossip."

"Gossip?" Elliot looked at Margie, who raised her eyebrows.

Armond grinned. "You know, celebrity dish. People love it. We think it's one of the best ways to get folks to visit our websites. And you, Elliot, are in the perfect position to provide the juicy tidbits. For example, I know that your employer, Melody Bright, is spiritual advisor to Vivian De Fay and her husband, Jerry Sumack."

"Uh-huh," Elliot said.

"Well, I read that her mother just died. Is Melody counseling her on that?"

Elliot shrugged, sipped his drink, and coughed politely.

"Or . . ." Armond added, leaning forward and speaking low, ". . . what about Sumack's new movie with Chet Hunter? Is it true it went so far over budget Sumack's career is at stake?"

Elliot shook his head. "Sorry, Armond. I don't know anything about anything. I just make tapes."

"Interesting," Armond said, still crouched forward, and looking Elliot in the eye. "That you would mention tapes. I've actually heard that you might have access to a certain, let us say, scandalous tape I'd be very eager to acquire."

Elliot's stomach clenched as if feeling Moishe's fist. But he kept his grin on and held Armond's gaze. "You've been misinformed, I'm afraid. These tapes all just contain wisdom and spiritual love. I'd be happy to send you some."

Armond smiled. "My mistake then." His watch beeped. "Darn, it's time for my cardio." He waved his credit card and Jaqui magically appeared. "It was a pleasure meeting you, Elliot," he said and they re-shook. "Margie, we'll talk later." He pressed her hand between his. Then, after signing the credit slip, he took Elliot's napkin and scribbled on it. "And if you do happen to run across that tape, here's what it's worth to me." Then he hopped up and jogged out.

Elliot exhaled. "Jesus, Margie, what the hell was that?"

"Sorry, Ellie," she said. "I honestly thought it was going to be a nice normal porn job."

"And Victor just came and threatened me on Wednesday. The last thing I need is more trouble with him. He almost took my head off."

"Last Wednesday? Well of course he was in a dark mood. That was his wedding day. It would have been their eleventh anniversary."

"Really? I had no idea."

Margie shook her head. "Of course not. You only passed that painting a hundred times." She stood, smoothing her skirt. "I've got to dash. Sorry this didn't work out. Good intentions."

Elliot nodded. "Thanks, Margie." He watched her go. Then he peeked at the napkin. The first number was a five, but the moisture from his drink had smeared the rest and he couldn't tell how many zeros there were.

❖

As if in a kind of underground resistance to Vic's injunctions and Melody's secrecy, Elliot had begun to dream of Christine, and he supposed, of Crystal, his sleeping mind running together vague childhood memories with anxious images from *Raunchy*. Again and again, they fled through the snow, ending up hiding in the magazine office at night, whispering together, and always he failed to hear what she told him, always he lost her just before the kiss. He hid behind his desk, or at one point under Miriam's desk, terrified of the sound of wheels, of Miriam's heels clicking, of Moishe's breathing and the smell of smoke, desperately peering at the melted wad of wet toilet paper where Margie had written the secret that would let him escape before midnight, when the painting of Vic's dead wife in her wedding gown came to life. Frantic, he pulled open the vault, which seemed to be an escape hatch, and stepped in. There, to his horror, was Farah, hanging from her shower pipe, eyes popping, tongue protruding, while beside her, the little dog's little tongue lapped bloody water. He looked down at the sodden paper in his hand. It had transformed into Farah's suicide note: *So sorry! I had to go!* He woke up gasping. He guzzled water from the sink and went outside into the cool of night to light a smoke.

Then he smiled. At least his sleeping mind had cracked the combo. Of course. The closer the truth was, the more directly in front of your face, the harder it was to see.

19

The third (and next to last) time Elliot met Vivian De Fay was at Hollywood Cares, a star-studded fundraiser at which Melody Bright was performing a healing ceremony, to be held at the glass palace on Mulholland, in a tent on the grounds. Sandi was receiving a special award for her lifetime of caring. In the weeks preceding it, the mood in the office, high-pitched to begin with, seemed to approach liftoff, losing touch with reality altogether and soaring on mad, flapping wings. When rich people become hysterical, who slaps them? Everything just spins faster and faster. Security consultants—ex-detectives and Secret Service agents gone Hollywood, their bulky cop biceps and neck rolls covered in a lacquer of tan skin and hair gel—came by the office to interview them and obtain their "security clearance." They were issued code names and laminated IDs. Melody, to her delight, was Archangel. Pedro was Angel One. Elliot was Junior Angel. There were debates over what they would wear—jackets with STAFF emblazoned on the back, tuxedos, morning suits. Following a golf vacation, Vivian De Fay caught a sudden fancy for kilts, but mercifully it passed. In the end they decided on something classic: white tunics and turbans. A costume designer stopped in to measure their heads.

The morning of the event was foggy. The world beyond the closest hill was a white void in which the shapes of mountains shifted vaguely, like whales on the bottom of the sea. The view didn't matter today, though. The ceremony had to be held under a tent, rain or shine, out of fear of paparazzi helicopters buzzing the affair. Elliot had joked to the security consultant that they could have F-16s shoot them down. The unsmiling agent explained that although they were coordinating with law enforcement, they could not guarantee "integrity" and a total lack of "perimeter penetration."

Then, when they were driving up to the familiar gate, Pedro at the wheel with Elliot beside him and Jan and Pam in back, a sudden whining sound filled the car and Jan yelled, "Look out!" Elliot turned to see a motorbike pull up to his window, driven by a bearded guy pointing something black and sinister. Horrified, he ducked, then realized, as security rushed over, shouting and waving, that it was a camera, not a gun. Seeing that he was nobody, the biker shrugged and peeled off. Then the gates parted and the guards waved them through.

An army of caterers set to work, lighting tins of blue Sterno, polishing chafing dishes, folding napkin angels. White linen tablecloths unfurled like heaven's flags. Elliot's turban itched like crazy, and every time he tried to filch an hors d'oeuvre, the billowing sleeve of his tunic would clear the tray. The photographer sent him into the house for an extension cord. He got lost, of course, wandering through a series of gargantuan sitting rooms, each so big it contained its own smaller sitting areas with couches and chairs and tables. In the short time since his prior visit, the house had been redecorated and was now full of Moroccan antiques, low tables, pillows, and priceless carpets. Turning a corner, Elliot bumped into a balding middle-aged fellow, who was rushing down the corridor, looking lost himself in a tuxedo shirt, boxer shorts, black socks, and shoes. He looked familiar.

"Oh, I'm sorry, sir," Elliot said.

"Are you my dresser?" the man asked.

"No," Elliot replied, unsure what that meant. To him a dresser had drawers and was made of wood. "I work for Ms. Bright."

"I see. I'm Jerry," he said holding out a hand, and leaning in as they shook, he asked, "Do you know how to tie a bow tie?" That's when

Elliot remembered: This was the man he'd seen in Dr. K's hallway, being greeted like royalty. No wonder. Jerry Sumack produced blockbusters, which made him like a god, except he actually got shit done.

"No, sorry," Elliot admitted. "I can't even tie a regular tie."

"I can't get the damn thing." He tugged at the hanging ends. "My wife always does it. Hey." He tapped Elliot's breast pocket. "Are those cigarettes?"

"I'm afraid so." He knew this was a strictly smoke-free zone. "But I assure . . ."

"Got an extra one?"

"Oh . . . yeah, sure." Elliot reached for his pack, but Sumack stopped him.

"Not here. Jesus. My wife would kill me. Come with me." He opened a door and they were in the study. Elliot gave Sumack a cigarette and a light.

"Thanks." He took a tiny drag. "I quit four years ago, but today . . ."

"Who could blame you?"

"Are you Gross?" he asked, eyeing Elliot thoughtfully. Elliot quaked. Could he know about Elliot's near miss with his Mrs. in the car?

"Yes, sir, Elliot Gross."

"Vivian told me about you."

Elliot tried hard to keep smiling. He imagined Sumack hitting a button and the security team storming in, or maybe just a trapdoor opening beneath his feet, dropping him into oblivion.

"Oh?"

"Yeah, she told me how you were there for her when her mom died. I want to thank you." He held out his hand.

"No problem," Elliot said, shaking his hand with relief. "I'm glad I could help."

"And she told me that story you told her," Sumack added. "About your father."

"Oh yeah, right."

"He's really something."

"He sure is."

"You know, on a day like this..." Sumack leaned against the desk, puffing thoughtfully. "It makes you think. What truly matters? All of this. This house. The cars. My other house in Aspen. The one in Hawaii and the loft in Tribeca. What does it all mean? Nothing. It's just a way of keeping score, right? That's what they say. But what's the game?" He shrugged. "And who really wins in the end? I know you already understand this. I mean, you've devoted your life to spiritual things. Sikh, right?"

"Seek what?" Elliot asked.

Sumack gestured at Elliot's white tunic, already stained with food grease, and his slightly crooked turban.

"Right," he said quickly. "Well, we kind of learn from all . . . paths."

"And with your dad a great man like that. What you learned from just growing up around him, my God. Obviously, you know money can't buy happiness. I admire you. I admit it. But I'm caught up in all this bullshit."

"Well, we all have our things to work through I guess," Elliot offered.

"The money and all. The fame. Private jets. It's great, don't get me wrong, but to be honest, I've thought about just giving it all up. You know, donate everything to charity and go live like a monk, like you. But then I thought, no, that's too easy."

"Right," Elliot said.

Sumack looked him in the eye. "I'm going to tell you something now that I haven't told anyone else. Not even Vivian. I don't know why, Elliot, but I trust you."

Please don't, Elliot thought, bracing himself for an awful revelation. "Thanks, Jerry, I appreciate that."

"Did you ever have a moment when you knew, in your gut, this is it, I have to take the risk and just go for it?"

"Yes." Elliot had experienced such a moment only an hour ago, when he stole a roasted Cornish game hen while the caterers weren't looking and ate it in the bathroom. Sumack took another drag and thoughtfully blew out the smoke.

"I'm taking a vow. I'm going to make films that have a personal meaning to me. I'm through telling people what they want to hear. I mean, of course we need to make the big-tent pictures we do so well, to please the bean counters and stockholders. Like *Eliminator III*. There's a lot of jobs riding on that."

"Of course."

"But I'm also going to tell people stories that they need to hear, stories that need to be told. I'm going to make chicken soup that feeds the soul as well as the wallet."

So that was it, Elliot thought, the art bug. Of course. Universal adoration and respect weren't enough for this guy. Apparently, one had to have self-respect, too. But that was a luxury Elliot couldn't afford.

"If you have to, you have to," Elliot told Sumack. "You're an artist. That's your path." Sumack looked at him with something like real gratitude. Elliot held the look. Was this the moment to hit him up for a job? There was a knock at the door.

"Oh shit, take this," Jerry said, passing Elliot his cigarette. "One second," he yelled.

Sumack answered the door as Elliot flicked the butt out the window, holding his breath as it dropped into the guests milling below, then ducking back when one looked up, startled and rubbing his neck, as if stung by a bee. In walked Vivian De Fay.

"Do I smell smoke?" she asked, sniffing the room. She looked perfect.

Sumack sniffed, too, moving his head around as if tracking it. "I don't think so."

"It was me," Elliot said. "Sorry. I was dying and your husband kindly let me sneak one in here."

"Everett!" She exclaimed, happily. She ran over and kissed his cheek. "What a scamp you are."

They all laughed. "Now then," she said, hands on hips. "I heard a rumor that someone is having trouble with their bow tie."

At that moment, just when Elliot thought his acute sense of awkwardness would force him to leap from the balcony, a voice of deliverance reached out. It was Pedro, squawking over the walkie-talkie he'd shoved in a tunic pocket and forgotten.

"Attention, Little Angel, this is Angel Team Alpha, come in."

Elliot jumped. "Excuse me." He pulled out his walkie. "Hey, Pedro, it's me."

"Angel Boy, go directly to the kitchen and then report to the tent. Archangel needs more iced tea, pronto." There were murmurs in the background. "Correction! Archangel needs hot tea to add to the iced tea she already has. It's too cold. Repeat, iced tea too cold. Over."

Sumack smiled as Vivian tied his tie. "Sounds like break's over for us both."

"Right." He waved the walkie. "Sorry, but I've got to go." He hesitated at the door.

Vivian De Fay laughed. "Kitchen is right and then left, down the stairs and then the first door on your right." She playfully swiped Sumack. "And you . . . hold still. Or you'll be totally crooked."

Elliot dashed out, more eager to escape than to carry out his task, and quickly became disoriented again. "On my way!" He called into the walkie, which screeched back.

"That is green tea, Office Boy. Repeat. Archangel needs hot green tea."

Elliot was trying to turn the volume down when he turned a corner and found himself in a room that seemed like it was being used as a VIP lounge. There were a stylish sofa and chairs around a table with a huge display of flowers and a big bowl of fruit. A makeup and dressing table were off to the side as well as a counter stocked with various beverages and a microwave. A slender woman with long straight blonde hair stood with her back to him, in a red dress with spaghetti straps, staring out the window. Spotting a can of green tea, he headed over, but a thug in a black suit grabbed him.

"Hold it there, buddy," he barked, jerking Elliot back and around and putting him against the wall, his arm twisted painfully between his shoulder blades. Another guy began to frisk him and removed his cigarettes and walkie.

"What's this? You're in a no-smoking zone, bud," the second guy said, then started playing with Elliot's walkie.

"What do you want here?" Thug One asked.

"Nothing." He pointed at the counter. "Green tea."

The walkie blared. "Hot tea, Baby Angel. Confirm. It has to be hot."

The blonde in the window turned to see what was going on. She smiled. "Hello, Elliot," she said. "Remember me?"

"I've been wondering when we'd meet. Pedro told me you were working with him now." Christine smiled. They were sitting next to each other on the couch. As soon as she had smiled and spoken his name, like a magic spell, the two thugs had melted away, even shutting the door respectfully. "From up close you look just the same," she said. "Same eyes." She laughed. "Same messy hair. I'd recognize you anywhere."

"I wouldn't," Elliot said. *I didn't*, he almost said, but held that back. "You look a lot more grown up than I recall." She laughed. "Except for your laugh, and your smile," he added. "That's the same. Though I think you fixed your teeth."

She brushed her hair back and sat up straight, as if a little nervous, but her eyes narrowed coyly. "Well, I'm glad you didn't forget me completely," she said. "You were my first kiss, you know."

"I'd never forget that," Elliot said, though truthfully he pretty much had, for years, until seeing her photos had somehow brought it all back. "You were my first crush after all," he added. And she blushed.

This is going great, Elliot thought to himself. Then he heard a door open and steam rolled out. "Hey, babe, where's my suit?" a deep voice asked, and Elliot looked up to see a world-famous leading man in a towel, his muscles still glowing from the shower, his hair boyishly towel-tousled and damp.

"Elliot, have you met my fiancé, Chet?"

Elliot jumped to his feet as if he were the one caught nude, but Chet was supremely at ease and gave him a hearty handshake. "A pleasure."

"Elliot and I grew up together. He was my first kiss."

"Really!" Chet grinned. "I bet she was a cutie even then. Well, you had your chance." He kissed the top of her head. "She's all mine now."

"Congratulations. On your engagement." He nodded at the huge diamond on her finger.

"Thanks, bro," Chet said, then snapped his fingers. "Dude! You've got to come to the wedding. Melody's performing the ceremony, of course. You can be an usher. Chrissy doesn't really have a lot of family or old friends, besides Pedro. But I guess you know that."

"Honey," Christine intervened. "The ceremony is about to start. Unless you are planning to wear a towel, your suit bag is over there." She pointed and Elliot took his cue.

"I'll let you dress, I was just looking for . . ."

"No, stay! Sit!" Chet yelled, and Elliot sat on command. Chet grabbed a garment bag and headed back to the bathroom. "This will just take a minute."

Elliot smiled nervously. The magic spell was broken. "So . . ." he said, searchingly. "How did you two lovebirds meet?"

Christine told him how she'd come to LA with Pedro, seeking her fortune as an actress, with little luck, and finding her way, out of loneliness, into Melody's circle. "We actually met at one of her lectures. She's been our spiritual guide through the whole process."

"Amazing," Elliot said, "that's like a fairy-tale story," and he meant it, since he knew that there were some major plot twists missing.

Chet came out, looking close-up ready in a tan suit, blue shirt, and cream slip-on loafers. His hair was whipped into perfection, like a chestnut meringue. "Shall we, my love?" he asked, bowing to Christine. Christine stood and curtsied and took his arm.

Elliot's walkie squawked. "Baby Boy, we need that hot tea, stat!"

"I'm right behind you," he told the golden couple. Then he grabbed a can of iced green tea, poured it into a paper cup, and popped it in the microwave.

"Hot tea coming in fifty-five, correction, fifty-three seconds precisely," he told Pedro.

❖

The party wrapped, and Elliot was unwrapping, back at the office with Pedro, removing his turban, when he finally got to confront him alone.

"What the fuck! Why didn't you tell me Christine Smith was around?"

Pedro shrugged it off. "Why would I? We've been friends all along. You're the one who vanished for fifteen years." He laughed. "Since that candy store thing. When we all got busted. Remember?"

"Vaguely," Elliot said.

"Whatever," Pedro said. "We came out here together to become stars, of course. And now it looks like Chrissy might really make it. Or at least marry into it. Which is even better if you ask me."

"So she knows I've been working here all this time?"

"Of course. But she wanted to wait and talk to you herself, when she was ready. You know what girls are like." He shrugged. "Anyway, you should. You're the one who sleeps with them, not me."

He pulled off his tunic and sniffed his own armpit thoughtfully. He grabbed a bottle of cologne and sprayed a cloud about himself, then raised his arms and let it settle. "I've got big plans tonight and no time to go home," he explained, then pulled his waistband out and sprayed into his jeans. "Want some?"

"That's okay," Elliot said, "I haven't got any plans."

"Oh yes you do."

20

The club was somewhere on Santa Monica Boulevard, a typical stretch that, while smack in the middle of town, felt like the middle of nowhere, which might be one way to describe LA's particular lonesomeness, a kind of cowboy sadness, distinct from the melancholy of the dark and cold Eastern cities or even the foggy Frisco hills. That is the sadness behind the sunny smile, the deeper blue on the far edge of the ocean, the desert dust riding the back of the wind and settling in the back of your throat.

Elliot had asked, of course, where and why they were going, but of course Pedro had deflected the questions, so he sat back and rode along, till they arrived at a big cinderblock box with only a blinking red neon heart to mark it and, closer up, a sign above the door that read EL SUR. They valeted, but before climbing out, Pedro reached in back and pulled out two cowboy hats and two bandannas. He popped a black Stetson on his head and offered Elliot a ten-gallon of brown leather with a chin strap.

"Uh . . . no thanks," Elliot said.

Pedro shrugged and tossed it in back. "You'll be sorry."

"I just feel weird. I'm from New York after all. So are you."

Pedro spun the red bandanna into a narrow band and tied it around his own neck. "Yeah, but I'm Latino, don't forget. It's in my blood. I even habla español."

"Were there cowboys in Puerto Rico?" Elliot asked.

"Maybe not, but there were Indians. Gracias," he told the valet as he got out and accepted the ticket. Elliot followed, cautiously, as if into a possible ambush, but the woman selling tickets called out "Hi, Pedro" and waved.

"Howdy, ma'am," Pedro said, tipping his hat and slipping a couple of audiocassettes from his back pocket. "Just made these special for you," he said.

Actually Elliot had made them—two of Melody's newest, one called "Love Is Everywhere" and the other "Death Is Just the Beginning."

"Thank you so much," the woman gushed.

"More Zona-lovers," Pedro whispered to Elliot as she waved them through for free.

❖

Inside, the club was cavernous, with a high ceiling crossed with beams. There were tables around the edges, a very long bar worked by multiple bartenders, and a large stage above an even larger dance space, which was set lower into the floor. Country music with a Mexican flourish was indeed playing and to Elliot's amazement, everyone was line dancing, shuffling and kicking and turning and clapping, dressed in Old West gear. As he followed Pedro to a table, and a waitress in cutoff jean shorts and a Daisy Duke halter top set down a pitcher of beer, Elliot was even more mystified as to why Pedro had brought him here, but it was too loud to ask.

Then, looking closer at the dancers, he realized, while the dudes in the line sported handlebar staches and trimmed beards along with tight jeans, boots, hats, leather vests, and sleeveless flannels along with the occasional chaps, the gals were mostly in drag, shaved smooth and dressed in calico dresses, tight Levi's, snakeskin boots, and wigs. There was a strong lesbian presence, too, femmes in frills and heels and lipstick, their escorts dressed in cowboy butch, black leather, denim vests, wallet chains, neatly buzzed hair under their hats, and in some cases, fake mustaches and beards. It was a gay rodeo.

"Yeehaw," Pedro yelled, waving his hat. "Should we dance or have a beer first?"

"Beer."

Pedro shrugged and poured. Elliot sipped and started planning his exit strategy—a trip to the restroom as cover and then another long walk home—when the lights shifted, focusing on the stage, the music changed, with that old favorite "Proud Mary" starting up, and a drag show commenced. Elliot sat back and relaxed. This was more like it.

The ladies stepped out into the spotlights, and one after another, they sang a signature song, with Tina Turner up first, of course, followed by Cher, Barbra, Marilyn, Donna, and Liza. Some had a country flair, with Cher in buckskin singing "Half-Breed" and Marilyn dressed circa *The Misfits*, singing "Diamonds Are a Girl's Best Friend," but most were just full glam, in their iconic looks and poses. The crowd hooted and hollered, tossing their hats in the air, and the proceedings grew chaotic as more divas crowded the stage—Rita Hayworth, Jayne Mansfield, Veronica Lake—with some climbing from the audience onto the bar, all vamping and voguing at once. Then, off to the side of the stage, crowded in next to Madonna and Billie Holiday, he saw Vivian De Fay, wearing the black backless, strapless, almost frontless dress from *Wartorn*. As the colored lights shimmered along her sequins, and haloed the long blonde wig, Elliot strained his eyes to try and decide: was this a performer dressed as Vivian or Vivian herself, in disguise as herself from an earlier era? She did the slow, snaky dance she had done in that film, in the scene set in another club, dark and smoky, with Nazis sitting at tables sipping champagne, and though it was completely out of time with the pounding disco pop sounds, she seemed lost in her own dimension, eyes shut, gloved hands fluttering together like two black doves, the long gloves elegantly drawing out her arms, but also, perhaps, hiding the needle bites.

"Is that . . ." he asked, tapping Pedro's shoulder. He was watching the cancan line that had formed on the bar.

"What?" Pedro yelled.

"Is that Vivian?" he yelled back and pointed. But she was gone. Craning his head like a periscope over the crowd, he caught a glimpse of Vivian or "Vivian" being hustled out the door by two men in suits who looked like the security dudes from her house. Elliot stood and began to follow, but he was fighting the flow of the crowd, who were giving the performers an enormous standing, jumping, and yelling ovation, and she was gone before he made it halfway across the floor.

"Now, folks," the MC's voice boomed, "grab your partners and get ready to do-si-do as the square dance is fixing to start!" As the crowd obeyed, Elliot felt a hand grip his wrist. Figuring it was Pedro, he turned gruffly, repeating, "I think I saw . . ." but it was Christine.

"Saw what?" she asked. She was wearing cutoff jeans, a black Johnny Cash T-shirt, and red cowboy boots.

"Hi," he said, smiling involuntarily and letting his hand close in hers. "Fancy meeting you here."

"Nothing fancy about it," she said, grinning back. Now he understood why Pedro had brought him, but by then the MC had begun his routine—"Grab your partner, do-si-do . . ."—and Elliot found himself getting swirled from elbow to elbow.

"Saw what?" Christine yelled in his ear during their next twirl.

"Saw Vivian?"

"Sure, she loves this place. She goes to all the drag bars."

"Dressed as herself?" Elliot called as Christine danced away backward and Elliot found himself being twirled by a big fellow in a tall hat with no shirt but a sheriff's star on his vest. "Howdy, friend," the hirsute dancer said, and sent him spinning back.

"Always," Christine yelled in his ear. "She says it's the only time she can relax out in public without being recognized."

"But I saw some big dudes taking her out," Elliot yelled back as they heeled and toed.

"Well . . ." Christine shrugged sadly. "She also sees it as a chance to party without risk of the paparazzi catching on, and I don't think Jerry's a fan, so he sends people to keep an eye out. It's kind of codependent, I know. But at least he really loves her."

Just then he felt another, stronger arm grab him and spin him hard, so that he stumbled out of orbit. He looked back to see Pedro with Christine. The two began hoedowning at a much higher level, and he backed off to observe from their table. Clearly, they were longtime partners, dancing with abandon, with real freedom and grace. She caught his hat when he tossed it, he twirled her high off the ground. But then, as folks gathered to watch, Pedro took off, reaching heights that even Christine couldn't climb, and she watched and clapped while he went at it, shuffling and sliding, jumping and kicking, then dropping to the ground and flipping over backward, moving between acrobatic feats and a kind of roiling spasm not unlike a seizure.

"What the hell's he doing?" Elliot yelled as she joined him.

She laughed. "It's kind of like country-break dance-thrash, I guess. They love it."

And indeed the crowd was cheering hard, closing in, and obscuring Pedro from view. Christine lifted the pitcher of beer and drank deeply. She wiped her mouth and burped, pushing back a loose strand of hair.

"Want a ride home?" she asked. "Pedro will be leaving with some new friend for sure. Happens every time."

"You know, I had a dream about you."

They were sitting in traffic, of course, that nightly LA purgatory, vaguely hellish as the exhaust from a thousand cooking cars rose in the glow of the brake lights. But they had the windows down and there was even a hint of fresh breeze coming through from the darkness beyond the streetlights, like the promise of paradise, and he was smoking and it was nice to be rolling slowly along and chatting, like taking a late-night stroll. Elliot regarded her profile in surprise as she slyly eyed him.

"What?" she asked innocently. "I did."

"A dream? About me? What happened?"

She took his cigarette from his mouth, dragged on it, holding it awkwardly like a nonsmoker, blew out a cloud, and then handed it back with a frown. "We were running from someone, hiding in this basement. It was snowing outside, remember?"

Elliot nodded. "I do. I actually had a dream about that too. Sort of."

She smiled. "When I woke up I was shivering from the AC, even though it was like a hundred degrees out. I was in Palm Springs but when I got up and looked out the window, at the desert in the moonlight, it seemed like I was seeing drifts of snow."

Elliot considered this. "Weird," he said, taking a drag, ashing out the window. "Maybe we were psychically connected. Meeting up in our sleep."

She reached out two open fingers, like a peace sign, and he put the cigarette between them. "I like that idea. Like a secret life, where we are still kids, playing, even all these years later, living our grown-up lives far apart." She took a tiny puff. "It's a lovely thought, isn't it? That we are still connected somehow?"

"Sure. If you believe in that sort of thing."

"I do. It's what Melody teaches after all. No boundaries, no limits in time or space, only love is real and eternal. But you know that, you work for her. Don't you believe it?"

"Only when I'm getting paid to."

"Cynic." Pouting, she put the cigarette back in his mouth. He spoke with it dangling from his lips.

"Now that you mention it, I did have another dream about you."

She faced forward, the car easing ahead. Lights changed. "Oh yeah?"

"Except you were all grown up with red hair. And blue eyes. Weird."

She glanced over. "That is weird. What do you think it meant?"

"I don't know. Maybe just something I ate."

"Or smoked."

He took a last drag and dropped the butt to the pavement. "Or smoked."

Finally, she made a right turn and they were rolling down Western, still busy but not clogged like the crosstown boulevards. She shot him a sly grin.

"You know, I got you that job at *Raunchy*."

That made him sit up. "You did? What do you mean? I didn't even know you were around. Right here," he added, and she turned onto Beverly.

"Well, not literally," she said. "I was, as you obviously know, with Vic back then, and there were these résumés scattered everywhere in the study and I recognized your name. I just told him you looked smart and interesting. So anyway, I helped you get in. Though by that point I was already looking for a way out."

Elliot remembered. But he kept it to himself. "Right turn," he said at the light. Now it was quiet. They cruised sleeping residential streets. "That's me on the right."

She pulled to the curb and they sat, both facing forward, as if at a drive-in movie, while she narrated her tale. She'd come to LA with Pedro, and they'd bummed around at first, working in clubs and bars, waiting tables or working the door. "That's when we first met Melody. You know that's her real name? She was a singer then, not a very good one, but better than you'd think. She did, like, the piano lounge scene, worked some of the same bars. We'd hang out after hours, do coke at her place. When she first had her Zona experience, well, we both thought it was just some kind of passing episode. Like a bad acid trip or something. But when she started working with AIDS patients, holding people's hands while they were dying, Pedro signed on. I know he is super skeptical about the spiritual hoo-ha, but he did believe in her cause, back then. Still does deep down, I think. As for me, I had drifted into stripping for the money. Then I met Vic. At first we were sort of dating, I guess. I mean, I know I was like a kept woman or sugar baby or whatever, but sexually, he is very limited, you know. So I didn't really have to do much besides, like, cuddle and you know, receive . . ."

"Head?" he asked.

She blushed, looking at him quickly then away. "Yeah, right. Thanks for the help, editor. Head. That's basically all he could do, and he was very good at it. And very good to me honestly. Kind of sweet in his own way. Protective. Generous. I needed that. Then he started suggesting I model. He said with his help I could make a small fortune in just a few years and be independent, pursue acting without financial worry. And I was tempted. But then in the meantime, I was still talking to Pedro all the time and in touch with Melody, and she introduced me to Chet. And we fell in love."

Absurdly, Elliot felt a small twinge of jealousy. So this was why she'd been telling him all that. Probably the reason for the whole night, too, the dancing, the flirting, the dream business, heating up those childhood leftovers. All to keep him from ruining her perfect match with charming Prince Chet. He gave her a big grin. "Well, thanks for telling me your fairy-tale story. I love happy endings. But there was no need. I'm not going to mess anything up. I can keep my mouth shut. And if you need to uninvite me from the wedding, I understand."

It was dark inside the car, with only a streetlight's glow, but he saw hurt flash in her eyes. "That's not what I meant," she said. "I was just trying to be honest. I thought you'd understand, as an old friend."

"Okay," he said, shrugging. "My mistake. I apologize. And I do understand. Old friend."

A car drove by and for some reason they both fell silent and waited as its headlights raked over them, pulling their shadows along. She turned in her seat and looked him in the eye as darkness returned.

"Elliot?"

"Yes?" he asked.

"Did you really dream about me?" she asked.

"Yes."

She touched the back of his hand, just with the tips of her fingers. "Are you going to ask if I really dreamed about you?"

"No," he said. "I believe you." And if I don't, he thought, then asking won't make any difference.

"Elliot?" she asked again, softly, as if she were on the phone from far off, late at night, checking the line.

"Yes?"

"That night, in the basement, the one I dreamed about . . ."

"Yes?"

"Remember when you kissed me and I ran away?"

That wasn't quite how Elliot remembered it. But he nodded in the dark. She moved in closer.

"If you were to kiss me again now, I wouldn't run."

❖

In the morning, she was gone, not even a note left behind to prove it had really happened. But that night, as he lay back, watching an old movie and digesting his spicy noodles, he heard the telltale clop of shoes on the path and her peculiarly soft knock, like a cat scratching at the door.

"I thought we should talk," she said.

He held the door open and stopped the movie, but she preferred to sit outside. He gave her the chair and took the crate.

"About last night . . ." she began, then laughed. "Ugh, I hoped never to use that line."

"Look," Elliot broke in. "I understand. I think. Or even if I don't, it's okay. It just happened."

"I'm glad it happened. Seeing you again, being with you, it made me feel like myself for the first time in a long time. It made me happy."

He smiled now, relieved. "Me, too."

"But I don't want to lie to you either. I love Chet. I'm not going to wreck my future for . . ." She hesitated.

For me, he thought. For nothing? He shrugged. "Sure. I get it. It was just one of those things."

"Still friends?" she asked, her eyes big, and took his hand. This, he felt, was genuine, and it melted his hurt pride. He smiled.

"Of course. I don't want to lose my old pal again."

She smiled now. "Do you still want to write books? I remember those poems you used to write. I was so impressed. I thought you were a genius."

Elliot had to smile too. "My genius has kind of been in decline since fifth grade."

She laughed. "Well, I believe in you. And who knows, a month from now, I might be a very influential friend to have."

Elliot's smile cracked a little and she frowned.

"Ugh, sorry again," she said. "I'm not very good at these things. The complications of grown-up life."

"Right, we're grown-ups now," Elliot said, lighting a smoke and trying to ask himself, what would Humphrey Bogart do, since that was the only convincing grown-up he could readily picture. "Don't worry about it, kid," he said. "Let's just pretend it was a beautiful dream we had about each other. Besides, I want you to be happy."

She squeezed his hand. "Thank you," she said, softly. "It means a lot to hear you say that." She took his cigarette from between his lips and took a puff. Then: "You know what else you said, about us, it just being one of those things?"

"I remember. It wasn't that long ago."

She smiled now, a sharper grin. "What if we make it two?"

21

Though once again Christine slipped away in the early hours, Elliot woke up happy and well rested for the first time he could recall, ready to greet the sun, even whistling while he strolled, enrobed, to the kitchen for coffee and back, pausing to pet the dogs, who were equally joyous, scarfing down their breakfast. Back in his room, he was deciding if he should risk his good mood by calling his parents, when, for the second day running, there came a knock at his door. Delighted, Elliot laughed.

"Just can't keep away from me can you?" he laughed, pulling open the door. It was Detective Santos. She did not look delighted.

"Guess not," she said. "Let's go. Anderson wants to see you." She looked him over, then added: "In pants."

"Tell us about your relationship with Florence Houseworth."

Elliot shrugged. He was back in the interrogation room, sitting across from Sergeant Anderson, who wore a blue cotton suit, white shirt, and loose navy tie, his hat set back on his head. Santos was beside him, and on the table was a file and a portable tape player.

"I have no idea who that is," Elliot told him.

"Are you sure?" Anderson asked, flipping the folder open. "Let's see if this jogs your memory." He pulled out a full-sized print: It was Farah, in a sparkling G-string and some kind of feathered Vegas headdress, pasties covering her nipples, rising from a cake that said "Happy Retirement," no doubt the least revealing photo they could find. "Or this," he added, pulling out a photo of her dead, slumped in the shower, belt around her throat. "I have more . . ."

Elliot shook his head, looking away as a mix of nausea and sadness ran through him. "Yes, I know her. Knew her. As Farah."

"We know you did." Anderson sat back, hitching his trousers as he crossed his legs, revealing tan dress socks. "I've got to give Santos the credit on this one. She's up on the latest computer stuff. I'm old-school." He wriggled his fingers. "Two-finger typist."

"Thanks, Sarge," Santos said, proudly. "It's all because I flagged you in our system as a person of interest. You see, when Ms. Houseworth's body was discovered, investigators followed procedure and her death was ruled a suicide. But when the file was inputted into the system, a number popped. Yours. A number of her last calls were made or received from your number, though she'd erased all the messages from her machine. Then I heard this." She hit the play button on the tape recorder. Elliot heard his own voice, though it was so shaky and raw it hardly seemed like him. "Please, send help. Someone needs assistance . . ."

He sat back, nodding. Santos stopped the tape.

"So we ask you again," Anderson said, "what is the nature of your relationship?"

"It was work. From *Raunchy*. We were colleagues, I guess. And friends. I liked her. And when I found her like that I freaked out. I'm sorry."

"Well, if you really are her friend," Anderson continued, "you'll help us out now at least. Besides yours, her last calls, other than liquor and deli delivery, were with a mobile phone registered to this man, Hank Sterner. Know him?"

Elliot shook his head. Anderson took another photo from the file. This was a glossy, professional shot of a stout man with a tanned lined face and swept-back gray hair, dressed in an expensively casual suit and standing before a sleek, expensive house with a gorgeous yellow Ferrari glowing beside him.

"He's an agent," Anderson said. "A big one."

"Boutique," Santos piped in. "Only handles a few top clients."

"He's also known as a fixer, makes trouble disappear for his clients. Or appear for their enemies. And we believe he's been mixed up with your old boss Vic Kingman for years. Burying dirt or digging it up. See?" He tapped the photos again. "It always comes back to Vic. And to you."

"I'm sorry," Elliot said. "I'd help if I could, But I don't know anything. I'm just a nobody."

Anderson chuckled. "Hell, we know that. But if you're a smart nobody, you'll let us know what you hear." He waved him off. "Now you can go. Somehow, you still haven't committed an actual crime."

Santos eyed him. "But you are a person of interest. And we got you flagged."

Anderson nodded. "Remember, nobodies are expendable, and they end up like poor Farah."

Santos shook her head. "Another fallen angel."

Meanwhile, like a secret angel all his own, Christine kept miraculously appearing to Elliot. Always, she came late at night, often with a quick call before, asking if he was alone—he always answered yes—and if she could come over—also, always, yes. Then there were her steps on the driveway, the small, shy knock, as if she were afraid of disturbing him, even when she knew he was waiting. Often he'd been waiting a long time when she came in late, in sweatpants and flip-flops, hair in a ponytail, as if direct from her bed to his. Other times she was glamorously dressed, trailing a cloud of perfume, no doubt fresh from some A-list event, sneaking in the back way for fear of paparazzi, and once she even asked him to fetch her around the corner from a screening she'd attended with Chet, a private peek at his new blockbuster, which she'd seen a dozen times, so she ducked out and snuck into his car, crouching on the filthy floor. It made him feel both vaguely paranoid and vaguely important, looking for fans and photographers, in what felt like a distinctively LA mix of anxiety and ego—dreading exposure yet hoping someone cared.

Then there was the night when he walked her to her car around the corner, only to see a white limo pulling into the driveway as he returned. He hid in the bushes, his ears ringing with Vic's warning—*Stay the fuck away from her!*—his mind full of visions of Moishe hauling him to Dr. K for punishment. Then his roommates hopped out, and he realized it was not Vic's Mega Hummer, just an ordinary stretch, but he had to admit, he had his own reasons for keeping things under the covers.

Sometimes she took so long to arrive that he fell asleep. And then it was like she really was visiting his dreams, especially when he'd purposely left the door unlocked, and she'd tiptoe in, disrobe in darkness, and slide, smooth and cool, between his warm sheets and into his arms.

It's not like they didn't talk. They talked for hours, long conversations in the dark, cuddled up together, or lying side by side staring up at his ceiling, passing a cigarette back and forth, the red tip aglow. But he never asked the question that he asked himself the most—Why? Why come to him when she had Chet? Or could have anyone? Maybe he was afraid to hear the answer. Maybe he was her secret vice, like the cigarettes she sneaked only with him, a dirty little habit she would have to kick eventually for her future well-being. Instead they talked about the past, their childhoods, the time that had passed since, the books they loved, their favorite movies. She loved horror and old Hollywood. The great actresses of the golden age, bigger than life. They talked about their families and about Pedro.

Or maybe he didn't ask because he knew the answer. This was the first crush they'd never had, arriving late but still passionate and pure as puppy love, and like all childhood romances, doomed to be outgrown when real life began, in this case, her wedding, which was as real as it got. He was, he knew, her last fling, her extended bachelorette party, and honestly, he was fine with that. More than fine, he was thrilled, flattered, grateful. He knew a crash was coming, but as he saw it, the worst he could expect was ending up back where he was the day before they'd remet. So what was there to lose?

Perhaps he didn't ask for the same reason they only met at night: to keep their little dream alive as long as possible, the fragile web of fantasy and desire that they had woven, that held them together, and that he was afraid would crumble if they took it out into the sunshine or even looked at it too hard. Like a ghost you really wanted to believe in. And sometimes, when he woke in the night, she was there, sleeping, in his bed, snoring gently or drooling slightly into his pillow. Sometimes she mumbled, and it woke him and then she curled into his arms. Then he just lay there, silently, in the dark, staring at her closed eyes, and hoping she was dreaming about him.

Elliot tried to avoid attending Melody's live lectures, since, he quickly realized, he would not be paid for the time spent sitting in the audience. He just agreed with Pam, or Jan, or whoever else asked, that she had been great. Pedro, however, used the opportunity to line up prospects for a side business he had going. It seemed that an unusual number of Melody's fans, especially the wealthy ones, lived in haunted houses. As with reincarnation, where everyone was a king or queen in their former lives and no one a slave, everyone also wanted to believe that they were extraordinarily perceptive, sensitive souls, in touch with otherworldly beings. Pedro fed this desire, while feeding off it, by videotaping the spirits in their homes, a science he called Spectergraphy.

"It comes from *specter*, meaning ghost or spirit," he explained, "and *graphy*, meaning like graphic or a graph."

"Yeah, I get it," Elliot said. "But what's the trick?"

In one sense the trick was simple, as Elliot learned when he became Pedro's assistant. First, Pedro would connect with a wealthy, needy person and get them to invite him over to check out the ghost situation. That evening, he drove them up into Nichols Canyon, and parked on the concrete slab outside a low, modernist box, with a Ferrari, a Mercedes convertible coupe, and a Volvo SUV already angled outside. The house's outer layer was wood and stone, with inner glass walls staring into a central pool. Not Elliot's idea of a creepy, haunted house. Perhaps Frank Lloyd Wright appeared, demanding credit. Pedro loaded him up with the equipment he had briefly explained to Elliot and knocked confidently on the door, and Elliot had his own psychic event, a shuddering déjà vu, when it was opened by Misty, Dr. K's star patient. Though it made sense, he supposed—whether shopping for the physical or metaphysical, she could afford the best. But this time her earthly form, as expertly curved as the cars out front, was demurely draped in a black tunic.

"Pedro!" she cried and gave him a big hug. "Thank God you're here."

"Shhh . . ." Pedro soothed her, rubbing her back. "Everything is going to be all right."

She laughed in embarrassment. "Sorry! The emanations are just so strong."

"We understand, don't we?" Pedro said, gesturing to Elliot. "This is my assistant psycho-technician, Elliot."

Smiling, Elliot put his hand out, and was about to say, we met, when he realized from her dull stare that she had no idea who he was. "Thank you for coming," she said, squeezing his hand. "You're so lucky to be working with a genius like Pedro. I think of him as like a doctor." So Elliot just smiled and nodded.

Pedro promptly went into genius mode, listening and breathing in the atmosphere, feeling for vibes, Elliot supposed, by slowly weaving his fingers in the air, and moving through a series of modern dance poses as he, and not Misty, led them through the house, sniffing like a dog on the trail of a hamburger. Each room was exquisite and severe: leather couches, Danish chairs, glass and steel tables, a huge stone fireplace. The pool was lit from within and glowed like an apparition itself, a blue-green ectoplasm pulsing beyond the glass doors.

"You're a little psychic yourself, aren't you?" Pedro asked Misty, as he did with every single client and a lot of random folk he encountered. Sometimes he said "artistic" instead. They always agreed.

Misty blushed. "Well I'm just a nice small-town girl from Canada," she cautioned, "but I do feel something cold here. Like a presence. Especially alone at night. Like something is watching."

"Yes, I knew it." Pedro waved his arms under the cut glass chandelier, which tinkled obligingly. "This space is definitely a special power portal or sacred site. Make this Zone One," he told Elliot, who then had to take readings with a light meter and a barometer, which registered the mysterious atmospheric changes caused by ghosts or possibly drafts.

Now, prior to the visit, Pedro always questioned the client extensively about what sort of spirit he or she wanted. Children and celebrities were most popular but murder victims and the occasional old miser also had to be provided. Misty had requested a tragic beauty. Now Pedro shut his eyes, murmuring softly. "You are right," he told Misty when he awoke. "There is a female spirit here. A woman."

"I knew it."

"She is very beautiful. But with a profound sadness deep inside."

"Yes!" Misty clutched her expensive chest.

"I think we will set up in the bedroom," he told Elliot. "That's where the presence is strongest."

Elliot set up the tripod and camera, pointing toward the closet, which was where Misty had sensed the visitor hiding, then connected a monitor and VCR.

"Elliot," Pedro muttered, shaking out the bag. "Did you forget to put a fresh tape in?"

"Shit, Pedro, sorry. I thought you did."

He shook his head at Misty. "I'm so sorry. He's still training. Do you have a videocassette we can use?"

This was a key part of the con. If she said no, he'd suddenly remember having one in the car, but it was always more convincing when the sucker provided their own.

"I think my husband has one," she said. "For taping the game." Her husband was out at a business dinner. He didn't believe in ghosts. Elliot unwrapped the tape and made sure Misty witnessed him putting it in the recorder, while Pedro did some more vibing and focused the camera on the closet. Then they started to record. Pedro stood beside the camera, as if directing. Elliot sat on the edge of the bed, pretending to monitor the equipment. "Remember to watch the screen," he told Misty, who sat and leaned forward, focused on the feed of her own closet.

"Gentle spirit," Pedro intoned. "We have heard your call. We are here to help. Please appear to us now."

The image on the screen began to waver and fill with static. The sound hissed and popped. Softly at first, then more clearly, a moan came over the speaker, high and thin.

"Oh my God, I hear something . . ." Misty whispered. "It's working."

The staticky image cleared and there she was, the ghost. It was a woman, silhouetted in dark tones, long black hair, bare white shoulders, a tattered gown clinging to her form. She floated, semitransparent, over the image of the closet, in uncanny contrast to the empty room before them. Misty gasped and grabbed Elliot's hand tightly. He squeezed back. The spectral image rotated, turning to the viewer, her face a pale shade, with only the dark eyes and lips legible. The moan rose. She reached out an arm, beseechingly, and Misty reflexively reached back, touching the screen. And then, abruptly, the static flickered back, and the ghost was gone. All the screen showed was this dull dimension, an open closet full of designer clothes. Misty sighed. Elliot stopped the tape. Pedro slumped, face in his hands, exhausted by his psychic labors.

Now that he had confirmed there was indeed a spirit present, he performed a cleansing ritual, intended to help the lost soul find her way out of Misty's closet and into the next dimension. He scattered dried rose petals across the floor to a window he insisted be left open all night.

"And no screen. That can catch and confuse the spirit." He also burned sage, waving it around and getting ash on her white fur throw, and lit some candles he'd picked up at a botanica.

It was while Misty and Pedro were settling the bill that Elliot, packing the equipment, had time to glance at the family photos on the mantelpiece. And there it was, in a silver frame: a photo of a stout gray-haired man in an expensively casual suit posed in front of a modernist home with a Ferrari beside him. Hank Sterner, he thought, spotting him in other photos with Misty – at the beach, sharing a moped in Europe somewhere, in a tux at their wedding.

"Elliot!" Pedro called out, as he and Misty entered, arm in arm. Elliot started, as if he'd been caught peeking into a secret, though he didn't know what it was. Had Misty's hubby been one of Farah's more intimate fans and supporters? Or did it, as the cops thought, have something to do with Vic?

"Yes? Sorry? What?" he stammered out.

"Her tape?"

"Right," Elliot said, ejecting it. "Here you go, Ms. Sterner."

She beamed at him. "Misty please," and insisted on playing the tape immediately. But just as Pedro promised, it showed nothing but the closet. If anything she was even more amazed, thanking them profusely and sending them off with hugs and a promise to tell all her friends.

Elliot was impressed, too. Of course, he already knew the gimmick. Pedro would take a snip of video that suited the fantasy, often just something taped off an old *Outer Limits* rerun. He'd manipulate and degrade the image until it was suitably vague and load it onto the video player hidden in the monitor. Then, on the visit, he always made a point of forgetting a videotape and asking to borrow one. He'd pop it in, tape the bedroom or basement, and voilà, there on the monitor was the ghost, superimposed on the room's image. The finishing touch, of course, was the tape, which when played back showed only a normal den or pool house. While Spectergraphy could pick up emanations, they could not be captured.

The real mystery to Elliot was not why they fell for it. After all, Pedro was just telling them what they were paying to hear. It was why they wanted to believe it so badly. Was it just a question of real estate values, the California version of "Washington slept here"? A clue came when Pedro explained why he didn't just give them a tape of the ghost, a souvenir they would no doubt pay a great deal for.

"The more someone watches something over and over, and shows it to their friends, the more they'll start questioning it. But something that we only see once just keeps getting more real." We doubt and devalue our reality. A fantasy is true forever.

22

Glimmers of reality began to seep through the cracks in Elliot's own fantasy when he visited Christine at home for the first time. She had always come to his place, for reasons of discretion of course, but perhaps, too, because it was easier to pretend the outside world didn't exist while alone together in the small square of his garage, which she'd even jokingly referred to as her "happy place," though she did bring a gift of new sheets. He took the hint and bought towels and swept the place out, changed a burnt-out light bulb. She brought sunflowers, which he put in a coffee can.

Elliot even managed to forget the inevitable wedding was coming, though he found himself avoiding Sunset Boulevard, where a giant billboard now hyped Chet's new movie. He didn't like those glinty eyes staring down at him from that ruggedly handsome face, flanked by small versions of his sidekick and leading lady, another blonde, more athletic than Christine. The four corners of the billboard showed a plane, a speedboat, a black sports car, and a red motorcycle, all flying or crashing, and a giant fireball erupted behind him, like a peek into the gates of hell. Elliot just took Fountain instead, which was better for traffic anyway.

But then, one evening as work wound down, Pedro told Elliot—not whispering but quietly, discreetly, which was highly uncharacteristic—that Christine needed to see him, urgently, at her place. He pressed a folded sheet of directions into his hand and, again uncharacteristically, offered to close up the office. Asking no questions, Elliot climbed in his car and headed up Crescent Heights as dusk settled in, gathering under trees and dripping through the canyons, the last of the sun burning out behind the hills.

Pushing his old engine, wheezing and complaining, he climbed Laurel Canyon, the most bohemian of the canyonlands, combining luxe living with a hippie-chic demeanor codified in the '70s, and now calcified in million-dollar tree houses and designer shacks. Still, the magic lingered, and Elliot did feel, as night fell, that he was on a country road, albeit one with stop-and-go traffic. He drove one-handed, trying to follow Pedro's scrawl as he turned off the main pass, and rose into real darkness and silence, empty lanes, leaning trees, the scent of eucalyptus rather than exhaust on the air. This was really something worth buying, if you could afford it.

Truth was, he was always one wrong turn away from lost in the Hills. They were like a maze that he might enter or exit in a hundred ways but never really solve, and even if he followed all the signs, clutching his directions like a guiding thread, he never quite learned what lay at the heart of the labyrinth, be it monster, or princess, or just the blank spot in the center, waiting like an empty tomb. Slowing to a crawl, and hitting his high beams, he turned left at a cluster of mailboxes such as you expected to see on a rural highway, rolled down a dusty narrow lane, then finally stopped at a high gate of redwood planks, like a rolling paneled wall. The Hunter residence—Mr. and future Mrs.

For a megastar, Chet Hunter had less security than Elliot expected, but living in an impossible-to-find corner was a big help, along with the cameras that he noticed as soon as the motion-detector lights came on. If the other tycoons of Elliot's acquaintance had purchased prominence and attention in their showcase homes, then this genuinely famous person, the only one who probably couldn't ever just go to Whole Foods for a wheatgrass juice, had bought privacy and discretion.

Elliot got out—it was chilly up here, as if the rich somehow got fresher air, too—and pressed the buzzer on the small intercom beside the gate. Christine answered.

"Hey," she said. "Come on up."

The gate drew back, almost soundlessly. He drove in, slowly, and stopped in the driveway, which was just dirt, parking behind a Volvo wagon. The house was big and gorgeous, of course, but sedate by LA standards, a shingled two-story cabin with a vaguely Japanese air: bamboo and dwarf maples in the garden, smooth stone paths, paper-looking lanterns, exposed beams. He parked and got out. Immediately the door opened and there was Christine, in jeans and a sweatshirt, her hair down and backlit, like a saint in the golden box of the door. She hugged him tight, but it was needy, not hungry.

"Thanks for coming," she said. "I'm afraid to be seen out right now."

"Why? What's wrong?"

"I'm in trouble."

They were in the living room. A fire was crackling in the massive stone hearth, which was clearly hand-formed and rose above them to the ceiling. The decor was High Western: comfortable leather furniture covered in woven rugs, plaster walls, wooden floors. No servants, bodyguards, or fiancés were in sight. Just a cat spread like a rug before the fire. Christine had insisted on making them mint tea and now she sat cross-legged on the couch, holding her cup in both hands, as if it were a littler hearth that warmed her better than the roaring fire.

"Remember the last time we saw each other?" She was smiling now, seeing it in her head. "When we robbed that candy store?"

Elliot nodded. "I haven't thought about it in years."

"I was today. I'm not sure why." She shrugged. "I guess because everything changed after that. For me at least."

"Come on, Christine," Elliot said. "You didn't bring me up here to reminisce. What's really going on?"

"To be honest, I don't want to tell you," she told the tea. "I keep putting it off. I'm ashamed I guess." She looked up. "But now I feel like you might be the only one who can help me."

Elliot felt mingled dread and pride. "Tell me."

She took a deep breath. "It's about Vic."

He felt a stab of fear. Had Vic finally learned about them? But he just nodded. "Okay, well, you told me about that already."

She laughed, harshly. "I wish that was the end of the story. You see, Vic had a dark side, too, which probably doesn't surprise you. He was controlling, jealous, obsessive. And when I told him I wanted out, he took it badly. Like a big baby, I suppose, but a very powerful and dangerous baby. That's when I saw the gangster side."

She paused, looking down, and Elliot braced himself. "Go on," he said, voice calm. He nodded encouragement.

"You see, he had this video and he was holding it over me." She looked up at him, searchingly.

"Oh," Elliot said. His head was spinning. "Really?"

"Yeah. Stupid of me, I know, but there it is. I confided in Pedro, who brought me to Melody and she reached out to Sumack, who is even more powerful than Vic. And then Vic said I could go. He agreed to destroy everything, to just drop it and it would be like we never met. But he also said, and at the time he made it sound kind of fatherly, that I'd be sorry. Then, after the engagement, I started getting letters, threats. Blackmail I guess. Someone saying they had that tape. It was Vic."

"I see," Elliot said, the pieces dropping into place. "He can't be the only one who knew about it."

"Sure, other people knew. But how would they have the proof? I sure as hell destroyed my copy." She shook her head. "It was Vic. Making sure I would be sorry."

"So what did you do?"

"I paid. Pedro made the drop-offs. But the threats keep coming and what I really dread is that he's waiting for his big moment, like right before the wedding or something, to release it and ruin my life."

Elliot grimaced, involuntarily, like he was downing a shot of vinegar. He swallowed hard. "You wouldn't want that," he said from behind a tight jaw.

"I know, I'm sorry, it's wrong to come to you with this. But who else could I ask? You and Pedro are my best friends, sad as that might be."

"But what about Chet? Wouldn't he stick by you? What does he say?"

"He doesn't know. He can't. I mean . . . he's a sweetheart, and I know he loves me. But people like him, who have been famous since they were twenty, they live in a bubble that shields them from the world. This would shatter him. Shatter the bubble. I know he plays tough guys on screen but really he is naive. I don't think he could forgive me."

Elliot nodded. His tea, he realized, had gone cold. He put it on the coffee table. "I'm sorry to hear all of this, really. It sucks. But what can I do?"

She put her tea down and leaned into him. "Pedro told me about sneaking into *Raunchy*, the prank. He says that if you help him . . ." She grabbed his hands and hers were ice cold despite the tea, and up close the look in her eyes was desperate. A tear ran out. "I want you to get what he has. I want you to break into the vault."

Elliot didn't know what to say. He was staggered, like he'd been kicked in the gut, but he understood that he had to be careful how he reacted. He reached for his cold tea and gulped it.

"I know it's a lot to ask," she said, wringing her hands. "Believe me, I know. I feel terrible even mentioning it, but I like to think we are friends above all. And look, I won't insult you by offering money, but yes, if things work out I will be in a position to help you a lot, to get you on your way wherever you want to go. Writing, whatever. It's for Pedro too. He can't work for Melody forever."

Elliot nodded. "Sure, maybe I can be your houseboy."

She flinched, as if he'd slapped her, but spoke calmly. "I deserve that," she said. "But I'm frantic. It's my last hope. I had to ask. But I understand how you feel. I won't mention it again."

"What's he got anyway?" he asked. "What's so bad?"

She gave him a sad but loving gaze. A dignified gaze. "Do you really want to know? Isn't it better to remember me like you know me now?" She shrugged. "If you get it you will have the choice to look or not. You'll decide."

"Look, this is a lot to digest. Let me think it over," he said, feeling bad now, knowing that he did not want to do this, though not sure how he could refuse. He started to stand, but, as if she could read his mind, she put a hand on his wrist, to keep him from slipping away.

"You know," she said. "I wasn't completely honest before."

"What do you mean?"

"I was afraid to tell you everything." She smiled, though her eyes were teary, like a little rainbow on a gloomy day. "I didn't want you to know that I'm not that innocent little Catholic schoolgirl anymore, who ran away when you kissed her. But back when I was, you know, stripping, I slept with men, not a lot but I did it, for favors or for money."

Elliot shrugged. "I understand. That's life. We all have to hustle."

"I knew you'd understand, more than anyone, but Vic, he knows all that too. And I'm so afraid he will tell the world, my family, everyone." She began to weep now, really crying, her face turning red and the tears and snot streaming. Instinctively, he patted her back and she buried her face in his shoulder, gripping him tight. His arms folded around her.

"Shh . . . it'll be okay . . ." he said, stroking her back, though not really knowing if it would. "Don't worry."

Somehow her mouth found his. He tasted her salty tears and the sweetness of her lips. She kissed him harder, teeth grinding, and he tasted blood. "You'll help me?" she asked, her voice a raw whisper in his ear. He pulled away.

"You don't have to hop on my lap to get a favor," he said. "I'm not one of those men." She jumped back, like a furious cat, eyeing him wildly from the other end of the couch. He almost expected her to hiss. He stood, wanting to say something else, something better, but it was too late. "Good luck" was all he could think of.

Elliot crossed to the door and made his exit, and he did not look back, though some part of him was reaching, waiting, hoping she would stop him or call out. She did not. He walked out and shut the door behind him. He got in his car and pulled out and the wooden gate swung shut. He drove home, his mind racing far ahead of the headlights, replaying everything Christine had just said, her every look and gesture. And then his mind ran further, back to the old memories she had stirred up, memories that were sweet, like a tearstained kiss, until you bit down and tasted blood.

Knocking over the candy store was a three-person job. First, Elliot and Pedro started perusing the comics. Then, a minute later, Christine wandered in with an empty backpack on, acting like she didn't know them. Pedro gave Elliot a shove.

"Shut up, fucksnot," he shouted, loud enough for the whole store to hear. Elliot shoved him back.

"Fuck you, assbreath." They began grappling and fell to the floor, using the stunt fighting techniques they'd rehearsed back in Pedro's room. While the old man behind the counter rushed over, and the few other customers gathered to watch, Christine went into action, dumping candy from the shelves into the bag. Snickers, Pop Rocks, peanut M&M's, whole boxes of Bazooka disappeared while everyone was distracted by the performance. The old man's wife came out with a broom and started trying furiously to sweep them out the door. Finally, the old man and another customer pulled them apart.

"Let me go," Pedro shouted, imitating something he saw in a late movie. "I'll kill the bastard!"

Christine slipped out unnoticed, and as soon as she was clear, Elliot and Pedro just stopped fighting and stood up. Then, as everyone watched, they did something Pedro suggested, just to freak out the marks, as he called them. They kissed, full on the mouth. The old man's wife gasped and crossed herself. The men just gaped. Smiling, Pedro and Elliot took a deep bow and walked calmly out, while the marks stared in stunned silence. They didn't even know they'd been taken.

At first.

Then the owner's wife noticed the empty shelves. Her eyes boggling, she rushed to the door and spotted Christine lurking across the street. She was supposed to split with the loot and meet up later, but she couldn't help lingering to watch the show.

"Thief!" the owner's wife screamed, pointing. "Call the police!"

But Christine, too far to really hear over the constant dull roar of Queens, understood too late that she was in danger. The old man was on her, yanking her arm, shouting for the cops. The wife was on the move, too, wielding her broom like a vengeful witch. And as luck would have it, right down the block, stuck in traffic, was a cop car.

Elliot was frozen in terror. Even worse, a kind of fatalism descended, like those animals that just give up and relax when they feel the jaw of the wolf. Pedro however, was already in motion. He snatched the broom from the witch's hands. Dashing across the street, he began whacking the old shopkeeper in the butt with it, and when he turned, shocked, to see what the hell was going on, Christine slipped loose.

"Run!" Pedro yelled as the cops, stopping traffic, reluctantly climbed out, hitching their pants. Pedro went into kung-fu mode, twirling and swiping the broom under his arms and over his head, while the cops and the shopkeeper and his wife all watched curiously. Christine ran for her life, long hair streaming, and as the cops, with a sigh, grabbed Pedro and tossed him in the back of their car, Elliot finally snapped out of it. He hurried down the street, trying to look inconspicuous and sticking close to the walls like a rat. At the corner, he was forced to pause for a light, and there, rolling past him, was the cop car. Pedro looked out, making eye contact. He smiled warmly, like a hero on the way to the gallows, and was borne away to jail, as Elliot, already burning with shame and self-disgust, pretended not to see. He rushed home to dinner. He couldn't be late. It was meatloaf night.

Pedro was home in a few hours as well, after his parents agreed to pay the shopkeeper twenty dollars for the candy. But he was shipped off to a shrink for counseling and shifted into a "special" school. Christine, scared straight, transferred to a Catholic girls school, though it was never known what became of the candy. Elliot carried on as before, reading, writing, brooding. He was placed in the "gifted" classes, where if he didn't make friends as deep as Pedro and Christine, he was at least bullied only at chess. Then finally he got into Stuyvesant High School, answering his parents' prayers and guaranteeing himself a brilliant future. He never saw Pedro or Christine again.

When he heard the knocking, Elliot knew who it was. He'd been lying in bed, smoking, in the darkness. He was still fully dressed, as if waiting. He leaped up. And as soon as the door was open, Christine was in his arms, and her mouth was on his, saying sorry, sorry, and as they fell, together, onto the bed, he, too, was apologizing, though he couldn't have said what for.

23

So once again, Elliot and Pedro put on their janitorial disguises, though this time they wore full beards and glasses, just in case. Something about Pedro's face in that getup disturbed Elliot—the lips protruding pinkly from the black bush, the eyes enlarged like tropical fish behind the lenses—while his own skin itched relentlessly from his synthetic, ludicrously red beard. There was a lot about this caper that disturbed him. But the sleeping building was indifferent. A guard snoozed peacefully at the front desk. Cleaners came and went minding their own business; few spoke English or knew much about what went on in the offices whose trash they emptied and whose toilets they scrubbed. Actually, aside from the floors dedicated to *Raunchy* and to Victor's other holdings, Elliot himself had only a vague idea: a firm of fabric importers, some patent lawyers, the Ecuadorian consul. He keyed them into the employee entrance and they rode up to the top floor.

The imperial suite was in darkness, which erased the lines between the plate glass windows and the surrounding floor and walls, so that you felt like you were stepping onto the deck of a starship, floating over the galaxy of city lights that streamed and blinked into infinity, as if the vast Persian carpet really were magic and about to soar into the night. Pedro clicked on a small Maglite and handed him one as well. Again, it was unlikely anyone out there would notice the lights in this window come on, but the thought of that exposure, in a glass booth atop Beverly

Hills, made Elliot nervous. He tiptoed to the vault. He'd told Pedro that he was pretty sure he knew the combination, without mentioning that it had come to him in a dream. He checked the painting, which looked a bit haunted-house in the spotlight of his Mag, then entered the date inscribed on the frame into the safe's keypad. Nothing.

For a moment, he was relieved. Now they could go back to Christine and say *Sorry, we tried.* But then a key turned in his mind, a tumbler clicked: Margie had said the *clue* was right there in front of him. The painting was commemorating Vic's tenth anniversary. So Elliot subtracted ten from the year and tried again. They heard the lock open. Now Elliot felt a jolt go through him, as if a demon were about to be released, and in that moment, he was certain they should bail, forget this whole thing, and just go home. But Pedro reached over to turn the handle and pulled back the door.

"Hold this open," he said, handing Elliot a black plastic trash bag. Reluctantly, he unfolded it while Pedro, flashlight clenched in his teeth, began to dig. From what Elliot could see, most of the shelf space was taken up with the familiar plastic folders containing photo sets along with their matching paperwork. A bottom shelf held what looked like legal documents, certificates of various kinds, and some wrapped stacks of fresh cash, which Pedro nobly ignored, like a crack jewel thief who disdains the flashy baubles as he searches for the uncut gems. And there, on the top shelf, in a sort of deep drawer, like a lettuce crisper, he found the booty, at least judging by his gleeful cackle.

"Amazing," he muttered in admiration as he dropped a stack of prints into the bag. Elliot looked down; they featured the owner and founder of a premier news network getting pegged by his wife. Next came the editor of a rival nudie magazine, one with far more mainstream success, completely nude himself, and not very impressive, except for a top hat and tie. Next was a senator, a real hard-line traditionalist, here dressed in a diaper and sucking a bottle, then a famous televangelist, tied naked to a bed. A pop singer who led a campaign to keep kids off drugs was captured in a Polaroid hoovering up white powder. A staunch Southern minister was wearing makeup and a dress. And so on—a governor, a publishing titan, more congressmen, the hostess of a morning talk show. He tossed in videocassettes as well, which Elliot peered at with keen interest, each marked with a well-known name or names. It seemed to Elliot like everyone was represented, with one glaring exception.

"Where's Christine?" he whispered.

"Not here," Pedro said, replacing the empty drawer. "Come on, let's go."

"But we don't need any of this . . ." Elliot started to argue, but Pedro abruptly shut the door to the safe.

"I need it," he said, grabbing the bag from Elliot, and before Elliot could respond, the lights flicked on, bright as day. A small, stout woman pushing a cleaning cart stared at them in amazement. They stared back.

"Janitors!" Pedro said finally. "We're here to fix . . ." He looked around, as if for something broken.

"The lights," Elliot suggested, then added, "they're working again!"

Pedro frowned at him but then nodded and smiled at her. "Yes, all fixed," he said, as he began edging toward the door. "We have to go now."

Elliot smiled and nodded too. "Have a wonderful evening."

It was just as they moved past her and sidled into the hall that she let out a bloodcurdling scream.

"Run!" Pedro commanded, though Elliot had already thought of that, dashing down the corridor to the elevator. He frantically pressed the button.

"Stairs!" Pedro yelled, passing him, and he followed, shouting as he clattered after him down each flight of stairs.

"Why!"

"Did!"

"You!"

"Take!"

"That!"

"Stuff?"

But by then he was gasping, so he gave up and just staggered along, choking on hair, his beard starting to slip as his sweat dissolved the glue. They reached the basement and paused.

"Why . . ."

"Shhh . . ." Pedro put a finger to his lips and peeked out the stairwell door. All was silent. No alarms. No cops. He tiptoed out, with Elliot close behind, back to the employee exit and they left. The warm, dry night air felt cool and refreshing on Elliot's sweat-drenched skin. They hustled down the block to Pedro's car and were cruising around the corner and onto Beverly Boulevard before he got his breath back and spoke again, asking the central question.

"What the fuck?"

⁂

As they drove, Pedro peeled his beard and glasses off and tossed them in the back. Elliot spit out hair and tried to rub off the glue.

"What the fuck?" he sputtered. "The mission failed, so why take all that other stuff?"

"Leverage," Pedro said with a shrug. "Maybe she can use it to force Vic to return her pictures."

Elliot shook his head. "Or maybe you were wrong to blame him."

"Maybe so." Pedro nodded. "But I'm still going to publish that stuff and expose all those bastards once and for all."

"Jesus, Pedro. Why?"

"Why?" He waved a hand, unconsciously accelerating, then braking hard at a light. "Look around. There's a war on. The bodies are piling up. America finally found a way to kill off its gays. And I'm going to be one of them, but at least I can fight back."

A silence opened between them, filling the car. It was the first time either of them had acknowledged the truth—Pedro was sick, possibly dying, even now as they drove and argued. For a moment Elliot heard only their mingled breath, and his own still pounding heart, then Pedro went on as before:

"It will expose their hypocrisy once and for all," he said. "Air all the dirty laundry on one big washday. And who knows?" He hit the gas again and turned down Elliot's block. "Maybe it will work. Maybe instead of another scandal, this time, everyone will finally look at each other and say . . . who the fuck cares? So what if you like to be spanked or wear a tutu? Maybe everyone will finally just admit that sucking a dick now and then is no big deal. And we can all just live our lives as best we can, for as long as we've got." He stopped in front of Elliot's house, then turned and grinned. "Or maybe it will just be hilarious."

"Where would you even publish all this? These people control everything. Except *Raunchy*."

"They don't control the internet. That's the future of democracy. I just put it all on the web for free and everyone can see it."

Elliot laughed. "The internet? Now I know you're joking." He looked at his watch. It was after three. "And what are you going to tell Christine?"

"I can't call her now. Chet will be there. I'll talk to her tomorrow."

"Okay, good," Elliot said, grasping at this. "So you won't do anything till then, right? Let's talk again in the morning."

"Sure." He patted Elliot's leg. "We'll have coffee and donuts."

"Okay, good, that's a start," Elliot repeated, as if trying to talk down a jumper or maybe just convince himself. "Sleep on it."

"Oh, I will," Pedro said with a grin, patting the bag that nestled on his lap. "This baby is going right under my pillow."

❖

But Elliot did not sleep on it. He tried, but after a couple of hours of thrashing about, he gave up. Instead, he sat outside and smoked. From some backyard somewhere, a rooster crowed. Then the dogs came out, shit, pissed, and lay down at his feet. He petted them. Finally, he put his shoes on and walked to the car wash for a breakfast burrito. He got back, brushed his teeth, and decided to just lie down, fully dressed, for five minutes before leaving for work. And, of course, fell deeply asleep.

The ringing phone woke him. He sat up with a lurch, and as he reached for the phone he realized he was late. It was Pedro, no doubt, outraged to find Elliot later than him for once. "Yeah, I'm on my way," he said, rubbing his eyes.

"On your way where?" It was Christine.

"Oh. Hi. To work. I thought you were Pedro."

"You haven't heard from him either?" Christine asked. "He's not at work or at home. I've been waiting all night." She took a breath. "Did you get it?"

"He didn't call you?" Elliot hesitated. "No. But he took a whole lot of stuff. I . . ."

She cut him off. "I'll meet you there."

"Where?"

"Pedro's."

What about work? he was about to say, but she hung up.

He found a spot down the block. He had passed Christine's convertible already resting in an illegal spot right in front, then, as he approached the corner, saw a big red motorcycle departing in his rearview and seized the moment to back up along the empty street and angle into the space it had left by the corner. He thought of Miriam for a moment, but of course this rider was on the way out. He hurried along the brick path, ducking between the swarming bougainvillea, into the courtyard and across to Pedro's wooden door, which popped open when Elliot pushed it. He was picturing Pedro in there in his bikini briefs, the phone unanswered because he was online, listening to the whine of the dial-up connection as he loaded his dynamite onto the web.

"Hey . . ." he said as he entered, seeing Christine standing in the living room, but freezing when he saw she was frozen, or rather, petrified. She was staring into space and trembling. "Christine?" he asked.

She just pointed into the empty room, seemingly at nothing. Elliot took a step in that direction. And then he saw him, stretched out on the rug behind the couch, just as he had been when Elliot first caught him that time, taking a nap. But he was not sleeping. Even Elliot could see that. There was a red hole in his chest, from which blood had gushed out to puddle beside him. There was another red hole, this one bloodless and precise, in his forehead. His brown eyes stared up at heaven, or the ceiling. Or nothing.

PART III

24

Elliot called Sergeant Anderson. But he was not their first call, and they did not use Pedro's phone. As soon as he was able to move, Elliot had grabbed Christine and pulled her out. She followed like an automaton, obedient but mute and seemingly insensible. Then they drove till they saw a pay phone outside a liquor store, the first morning clients shambling in. Elliot dug the cop's card from his wallet, but at that point Christine snapped out of it enough to grab the receiver.

"Let me call my lawyer first," she said, by which she meant Chet's lawyer, Morgan Jeffers. He told them he'd meet them at the police station. Then Elliot called Anderson's direct number. At first someone else answered and said he wasn't available and what was it regarding, but when Elliot said "Murder," they put him right through.

❖

In the parking lot, before going in, Jeffers bought them coffees from a cart and sat them on a bench to hear them out. A tall, charismatic, and commanding Black man in a gorgeous three-piece pin-striped navy suit with a matching light-blue tie and pocket square, he seemed to Elliot very much like the manager of a championship ball team that, as a lawyer known for winning trials for superstars, he sort of was. He agreed that there was no choice but to admit the break-in and blackmail, but that he would do the talking and, it seemed to Elliot, copyediting, as he went on about "controlling the narrative": Elliot was only along for the ride, and only out of concern for Christine; it was Pedro who took everything; and just to keep things simple, they had discovered Pedro together that morning, when again, out of concern, they went to his place.

Neither Elliot nor Christine interrupted, though Elliot felt her take his hand, not romantically, but in a childlike way, as if they were schoolkids again, caught stealing candy and getting a stern talking-to. Jeffers appeared not to notice, but he did step between them as they entered the station, where they were all ushered into a much nicer version of the room Elliot had been in before: this one had carpet, drawn venetian blinds, and a wood-veneer table instead of Formica. And they were offered more coffee, which their attorney declined on their behalf. They waited in a tense silence till Anderson and Santos arrived, direct from the crime scene.

"Good to see you, Jeffers," Anderson said, shaking his hand. "Nice suit." He too was nattily dressed, if a bit more louche, in an unstructured linen suit, white shirt, and pale tan tie, like the hero of a Graham Greene novel. Santos was in a polyester pantsuit, red, with a white blouse and a small red-ribbon tie that Elliot thought was a mistake and contrasted oddly with her sensible orthopedic black shoes. Christine, in a white T-shirt and dark-blue jeans and big dark sunglasses, looked both glamorous and suitably mournful. Elliot, unshaven in a creased black button-down and black jeans, looked, and felt, both guilty and traumatized, criminal and victim in one.

"Miss Smith," Anderson continued. "Thank you for coming in. I know this must be very difficult." Santos, who stood as if at a ceremony, hands behind her back, nodded solemnly. "And Elliot," he finished. "Why am I not surprised to see you again?"

Santos shook her head sadly.

"Well, let's sit down and begin."

Smiling, Jeffers unbuttoned his jacket as he sat, and slid a yellow legal pad (it was the first time Elliot had seen one fulfilling its name) from his briefcase. "My clients," he began, "have asked me to read a statement."

After Jeffers finished, Anderson asked a couple of follow-up questions. Did Christine have any proof that Vic was the blackmailer, or indeed behind Pedro's death?

"I'll field that one, Sergeant," Jeffers said. "In short, the answer is no. As stated, Victor Kingman is the only person who, to my client's knowledge, might be in possession of the . . . sensitive materials. Pedro, a close friend since childhood, volunteered to try retrieving them and Mr. Gross here, also my client, and also a lifelong pal, agreed to act as lookout, purely out of concern for Ms. Smith and his best friend's safety."

"I can speak for the DA," Anderson said, "when I say we will waive any charges in return for cooperation. You are being treated as witnesses here. Nothing more. And we do thank you very much, Ms. Smith, for coming forward."

At this point Santos, who'd been standing, arms crossed, glanced out the window and goggled, peeking out the blinds. "Oh my God, it's him!" she called out, pointing excitedly out at the parking lot. "Boss, it's Chet Hunter. I mean, Mr. Hunter is here. I mean . . ." she looked at Christine. "Your fiancé is here, Miss. Ma'am."

Anderson scowled at her. "Okay, Santos, let's take it easy."

Everyone stood and looked, except for Christine, who remained seated, legs crossed, toe tapping. Indeed, Chet was approaching the building, guided now by some kind of handler, a woman in a gorgeously tailored dark suit and heels, two bodyguards, and a couple of uniformed cops, with an assortment of reporters trailing behind shouting excitedly and aiming cameras. More cops appeared and held back the press, who immediately began to jostle and yell, transforming the parade into an instant circus. The mood was more joyous than anything else.

"He insisted on coming and supporting Ms. Smith," Jeffers explained. "But I want to make it clear, he's purely here as support and to escort her home, not as a witness."

"Understood," said Anderson.

With that, the door opened and Chet swept in, flanked by the cops, guards, and PR flack. "Darling!" he called, and Christine threw herself in his arms, tears flowing.

"Thank you, Chet," she sighed. "Thank you for coming." She looked up at him. "I love you."

"I love you, too, baby," he said. Everyone beamed at them. Chet cleared his throat and spoke, one arm still hugging her shoulders. "Gentlemen, ladies . . . Elliot . . ." He leaned over and shook Elliot's hand heartily, then addressed the room. "I want to make it clear, I am not speaking as a witness or even as an actor, but purely as a man, supporting the woman he loves."

Santos clutched her hands in delight, while the cops and guards murmured their approval.

"That's so beautiful," the PR lady gushed.

Chet turned humbly to Anderson. "And now, sir, if you don't mind, I'd like to take my lady home."

"Of course." Anderson concurred, twirling his hand a bit like a courtier. "I won't keep you. But I would like another word with Elliot."

Jeffers hesitated. "Off the record?"

Anderson shrugged. "Sure."

"I will escort Ms. Smith to her car and come back." He turned to Elliot. "And not one word in the meantime."

"Take your time," Anderson said. "We'll grab coffee."

Elliot sat back down, reluctantly. Jeffers patted his shoulder and Christine glanced back as Chet led her out, accompanied by his retinue. Santos began to follow, but Anderson barked, "Santos, shut the door," and as soon as she did, he reached under the table and pulled out a stack of *Raunchy*s.

"Well, Elliot," he said. "We meet again."

Santos nodded. "We said you were a person of interest."

Anderson patted the magazines. "Since we last met, I've had a chance to peruse some of your work." He flipped open an issue to a Post-it–tagged page. "I especially like this one, 'Legend of the Pussy Bandit.' Remember?" Elliot remembered. It was about a young woman with extraordinary control of her vaginal muscles who was able to smuggle jewels and even pull the rings off the fingers of unsuspecting Hasidic diamond merchants. Her tragedy, however, was that her physical condition prevented her from ever enjoying penetrative sex. "Can't say I've ever run across a case like this, have you, Santos?"

Shaking her head, she turned her chair around backward and sat, legs apart. "No, Sarge, I have not," she said. "And I hope to Christ I never do."

"You've got imagination, I'll give you that," Anderson said. "This scene is my favorite." He showed Elliot the picture, which featured the petite white model handcuffed in an obviously fake jail cell and coupling ecstatically with a Black detective wearing only a fedora and a suit-vest adorned with a gold badge. "Where she finally gets her comeuppance, thanks to, how did you put it?" He peered through his reading glasses. "Oh yeah . . . a big Black dick named Johnson."

In the final image Detective Johnson stood boldly, fists on hips, a fake diamond necklace dangling from his stiff baton. Anderson pushed the magazine away as if in distaste. Santos shook her head.

"What a waste of talent," she said.

"Hey," Elliot said. "I quit, like you said. Got out of that life. Went to work for a spiritual healer. And now look what happened."

Anderson nodded. "True. Out of the slimy frying pan and into the spiritual fire. Right, Santos?"

"Exactly. You might have gone to college, Elliot, but you've got a lot to learn about real life. Artists!" She shook her head again, this time more in bemusement than anger. "Right, Sarge?"

"What are you saying?" Elliot asked.

Anderson shrugged. "Think about it at your leisure. When you're meditating with your new pals."

Santos leaned in. "Meanwhile, Victor Kingman. You think he's capable of murder? Based on your personal knowledge of the man."

Elliot shrugged. "I don't really possess that kind of knowledge. I worked for him in an office. He definitely scared me. But he has to be the main suspect, right? I mean, who else would have a motive?"

"Easy now," Anderson said. "This ain't the case of the pussy bandit. Leave the detective work to us. We'll be talking to him today. Him and his high-priced lawyer."

Santos chuckled knowingly. "Guess speech ain't so free after all."

The door opened and Jeffers was back. "Sorry," he said, stepping in. "We had to run a gauntlet. Now where were we?"

"We were just about to let your client go and thank him for his cooperation," Anderson said, standing and smoothing his pleated suit pants.

Surprised but eager, Elliot stood too.

"Well . . ." Jeffers said, "all right then," and held the door for him.

"Keep your nose clean," Santos called out. "If it ain't too late."

25

Elliot did not run the press gauntlet. The circus had packed and left, no doubt right after Chet and Christine. And Jeffers did not escort him to his car, but shook his hand and reminded him not to talk to cops or reporters or really anyone without him. Then he hurried off and got into his own ride, a Bentley. Elliot looked around, squinting in the sun. Remembering he had not eaten in a long time, he drove to a dollar taco place and ate three: one carne asada, one al pastor, and one carnitas, each served on a small paper plate with a slice of radish, a little cup of pickled carrots and a lime, then went back for another al pastor, washing it all down with horchata. Feeling, if not better exactly, at least a little more substantial, he got back in his car, put on his seatbelt and realized had no idea where to go next. So he went to work.

"Oh hi," Pam said when Elliot walked in, looking up from her desk and trying for sarcasm. "How nice of you to stop by." She turned to Janice who was busy stuffing envelopes. "Isn't it nice of Elliot to stop by before we close for the day? Especially since Pedro didn't even bother to come in at all today?"

"Totally." Janice looked up, tossing her hair. "I'm sure Pedro is too busy doing whatever to stop by himself. Even though he supposedly works here."

"Pedro is dead," Elliot said. "Sorry I'm late but I was at the police station."

"Yeah, right." Pam laughed hollowly. "And tomorrow you'll both be busy at his funeral. Maybe if we're lucky we'll get a break to go. Maybe I did it, just to get some peace and quiet and a day off."

"Yeah," Janice added, giggling. "Maybe I stabbed him to death because he drank all the coffee and never puts any money in the can. Hahaha. Better tell the police, right, Pam?"

Elliot shrugged and walked into the back office. He sat at his desk, regarding Pedro's empty chair, and on his desk, the now abandoned piles of paper that Elliot had hopefully sorted into unopened mail, unanswered messages, unfilled orders, and unpaid invoices. He stared across the alley and wondered if he should tell the old lady that she would have to finish her portrait from memory. Or perhaps it could be displayed at the memorial, if there was one. In the meantime, he was still here, with rent to pay and a gas tank to fill. So he reached for an order and began to gather the tapes while the phones continued to ring. It was getting dark outside the window when he heard a wail from out front. A second cry joined in and as the sound of sobbing crested, he opened the door and peeked out.

"Oh my God!" Pam screeched at him, her face streaked with tears. "It's true. He's dead. Melody just called." She stood, arms out and, seeing no alternative, Elliot reluctantly let her hug him. "Poor Pedro. I'm going to miss him so much. We fought like brother and sister, but you know how much we loved each other."

Janice ran over and joined, wrapping her arms around them both. "It's true, Pam. You're so right. He was like family. I talk about stabbing my family to death all the time, but you don't mean it. I'd never stab anyone."

"Except the person who hurt Pedro," Pam noted.

"Yes, I'd stab him through the heart."

Despite his awkward detachment—still in shock, no doubt, he felt like he was observing this scene from above, and even imagined laughing with Pedro about it later—Elliot did not doubt the truth of their grief. Theirs had indeed been a dysfunctional family dynamic, and Pedro had played an essential part. The loss was real and so was the toxic love. Just because a feeling was shallow and self-serving did not make it any less true. Hadn't Elliot himself first reconnected with Pedro only because he was broke and lonely? Perhaps the one really authentic person he knew, the only one fully himself at all times, was brutally honest Pedro. Though Elliot would also have to describe him as a cunning manipulator and congenital, even joyful, liar.

"What am I going to tell my kids?" Janice suddenly wailed, clutching her shoulders, as if giving herself a hug.

Pam grabbed a box of tissues, and pulled some for herself then handed it to Janice. Elliot, dry-eyed, declined. "Melody wants us all up at the house right away," she said, wiping her runny nose and eyes and then replacing her glasses. "She says we need to help his soul transmogrify or he might be trapped on this plane."

Janice nodded eagerly. "It's so true. Pedro would hate to be stuck between dimensions."

❖

Elliot drove his own car up to Melody's—the thought of being trapped, in a car or on this plane, with Pam and Janice was too much to bear—and parked behind them in the courtyard. Sharon, the white witch, stood at the door, wearing a long white tunic that brushed the ground, her bare toes oddly emphasized where they jutted like horns from under the hem, and of course, a large white hat, like a straw sombrero. She held a stack of folded garments in her hand.

"Greetings, friends," she said, with a sad smile. "Welcome to our house of mourning." She waved them in. "Please put these on. Ladies, please change in the guest room. Elliot, you can use the study." Janice and Pam went off with the white robes Sharon gave them. Elliot got a yellow robe.

"Why is mine yellow?" he asked.

"You represent the male principle." She pointed at a door that he had always assumed was a closet. "Join us in the chamber when you're ready." Then she turned and went, tunic fluttering.

Elliot went into the study and began to undress. *If your wallet is stolen, nobody better say a ghost did it*, he heard Pedro's spirit say. He smiled. *Wherever you are, pal, you better at least be enjoying this.*

❖

Elliot descended into darkness. He felt his way, one hand on the wall, and caught flickers of light as well as faint humming or moaning sounds. He reached the bottom step and came around the corner. There they were.

It was a wine cellar. There were racks partially full of bottles on one wall and what looked like a freezer in a dark corner. The ceiling was low but vaulted, with the walls built up out of brick and stone covered in rough plaster. In the center of the floor was a white cloth with five sputtering candles around it. Janice, Pam, and Sharon, all in white, were kneeling around the side, while Melody herself, in a hooded red robe, knelt at the head, leading the others in a low chanting, like a hum emanating from their chests. Oddest of all were a row of shadowy figures sitting against the wall behind her, so motionless that Elliot didn't even notice them until his eyes adjusted. They were black robed, with their faces hidden under their hoods and they were also chanting, adding volume to the sound that reverberated in the chamber. Were there six or eight of them? Elliot peered into the shadows, but Sharon pointed to his spot, before the fifth candle, so he knelt. Melody began to talk.

"Oh, we mourn our loss today, our sorrow for the departure of our dear Brother Pedro." The women nodded and Janice wept softly. "But!

Cry not!" she called, raising her arms, and Janice stopped. "For we also celebrate his ascension to the higher realm!"

"Yes!" Pam said, clapping, and the others joined in, though not the black shadows.

"For remember," Melody went on, "there is no separation between life and death, self and other, or male and female when all is love. There is only love loving love!"

"All is love! All is love!" the women chanted and Elliot mumbled along, wondering when they had rehearsed this and why.

"Oh, Mistress Zona," Melody went on, "holy one, be our guiding spirit! Help us reach our dear brother, if it be thy will." She pointed at the sheet and Sharon leaned forward and yanked it clear, careful to avoid the candles. There was a Ouija board, in the center of a star that had been chalked on the concrete floor. It was five-pointed, with Melody at the head and Elliot at the lower right. He leaned toward Janice on his left.

"Isn't that . . . ?" But before he could speak, Melody pointed at him.

"Brother Elliot, as the writer in our family, you will act as scribe."

He felt a tug on his right sleeve, and realized Sharon was handing him a notebook and pen. He accepted them, not sure what he should say, or even how he should address Melody. Surely not as *Mother*? *Older Sister*? *Aunt*?

"Um . . . okay." He uncapped the pen, but realized he couldn't see well enough to write, and shifted to move the candle closer. For a moment, the jumping flame cast a light onto the row of silent shadows, and Elliot realized, with a start, that they were all masked in black as well, a bit like Raunchy Raccoon.

"Zona," Melody intoned now, raising her arms and voice. "I beg you, speak through me. I offer myself as your channel. I am your humble vessel, nothing more."

There was a long moment of silence as Melody slumped, head down, and everyone waited breathlessly. Then she sprang forward, pushing her hood back. Now Elliot saw she was heavily made up, with black-lined eyes, green eye shadow, red lips, and a sparkly costume gem stuck to her forehead. She began to chirp and screech and all the while her hands grasped the planchette, the small, cursor-shaped wooden pointer, and moved it rapidly from letter to letter. Elliot scribbled it down frantically, but it made no more sense than the gibberish she was mumbling. Then, just as suddenly, she blew out her candle and collapsed, sprawling forward into the star. Sharon spoke.

"Zona has left us. The ceremony is concluded. May you all be blessed and cleansed." With that, she, Janice, and Pam each lifted their candle and, at a nudge from Janice, Elliot followed suit. As they proceeded to the stairs, they blew out their flames. He glanced back and saw that the black figures had finally arisen, and were now gathered around Melody, seeming to lift her up, but it was already too dark to be sure.

Back in the study, he scanned his notes and could make nothing of them. But still, out of curiosity, or some intuitive suspicion, he went to the small copier/fax machine and made a copy. Then he called Christine, bracing himself to hang up if Chet answered, but she was there alone and told him to come right up. There was a knock on the door.

"Join us in the living room as soon as you're changed," Sharon called. "And don't forget to give me that notebook."

"One minute!" Elliot dressed quickly and folded the copy into his pocket. His wallet and watch were where he'd left them.

In the living room, Janice and Pam were on the couch sipping tea. Sharon beamed at him. "I'll take that notebook. Thank you so much for your service and positive energy."

"Yes, thank you for your energy, Brother Elliot," Pam said.

"We really needed the yellow male principal to balance us out," Janice added.

"Who were those other people in the black robes?" Elliot asked, handing over the book.

Pam and Janice stared at him blankly and for a moment he felt that maybe only he had seen them. Sharon smiled.

"Just friendly visitors who came to pay their respects. Elder spirits."

"Spirits?" Elliot asked.

"We are all spirit under our robes of flesh," Sharon said.

Pam and Jan nodded vigorously.

"And wasn't that star," Elliot pressed, "a pentagram? That's a satanic symbol, right?"

All three women laughed. Sharon shook her head. "Elliot, Elliot, that's so yellow of you."

"Exactly," Pam agreed. "So heteronormal."

"Typical dude," Janice chimed in, scolding.

He shrugged. "Well, I am the male principle."

Sharon schooled him. "It's a star, which focuses power and summons universal energy from five cardinal points. Calling it satanic is just the hierarchical patriarchal view of a capitalist society trying to demonize and repress these deep pre-Christian beliefs. But once all people worshipped the Earth Mother. It's only later that white Christian men imposed these ideas of"—she made quotes in the air—"devil worship or dark magic." She chuckled ruefully. "Next thing you'll be burning witches."

The women shook their heads disapprovingly.

"You're not even Christian, are you, Elliot?" Pam inquired. "You're a Jew. They would have burned you too."

"Don't be so masculine," Janice told him.

"Sorry," Elliot said. "I'll try."

Sharon patted his hand. "There's nothing to be afraid of really. It's just the hysterical—and I spell that *h-i-s*-terical—male fear of female power and uncontrollable sexual desire, the source of all life on earth."

"That's so true," Pam said. "We are incredibly powerful and fertile."

"I am full of uncontrollable desire," Janice announced, nodding vigorously.

"You're not afraid of that," Sharon asked. "Are you, Elliot?"

"A little," he said, and chuckled. They joined in. "But also really tired. So if you don't mind." He stood. All three jumped up and hugged him. Then Sharon gave him a little bow.

"Namaste," she said.

26

They needed to talk, but they did not talk. As soon as she opened the door, she took his hand and pulled him in. He stumbled, struggling to untie his shoes and add them to the pile near the door.

"Fuck the shoes," she said and led him urgently across the living room and up the broad floating stairs, pulling him into the bedroom. It was very sparse, very clean, vaguely Japanese. There was a low wide mattress on a wooden platform, dark wood floors with woven rugs over the wide planks, an orchid in a blue vase. Of course, he slept on the floor in a bare room, too, but in squalor, because it was all he could afford. This kind of simplicity and space was very expensive indeed. Even the clear moon in the skylight seemed deliberately chosen and perfectly framed, as Christine stepped into the silver shaft, like chiaroscuro lighting in a black-and-white movie, and was suddenly, perfectly, there, in his arms.

He was, as they say, hungrier than he had realized. As starved for human contact as the most foolish or confused of his pervy readers, as desperate for spiritual consolation as the neediest of Melody's saps. And so, it seemed, was she, reaching out to lay her two palms on his cheeks, her eyes shining right into his, and drawing his head down, lips parted, as though to drink from hers.

They did not speak until after. They made love—that is what it felt like to Elliot anyway—then lay in silence, holding each other, slick with sweat, eyes closed, and he drifted off. He awoke sometime later—the moon had shifted behind a branch—and saw Christine sitting cross-legged, still nude under the skylight, smoking one of Elliot's cigarettes and reading a folded page. Their clothes were scattered in a trail leading back to the doorway.

"Can I have one?" he asked, sitting up. She picked up the pack and matches and brought them to him, then slid under the blanket while he lit up.

"What is this?" she asked, showing him the page. It was the copy of the notes he'd taken at the séance.

"Did you get that from my pocket?"

She took a drag. "Sorry. It fell out when I was stealing your cigarettes."

"It's just gibberish," he said and told her the story. Laying her cigarette in a saucer, she turned on a bedside lamp and went back to staring at it while he stared at her.

"I don't think it is," she said finally.

"What do you mean?"

She got up and went to the dresser and returned with a pen. "I think it's backward writing. I mean, it's scrambled up because you were going so fast but look . . ." She circled a cluster of letters. "'Tirps' could be *spirit*. Over here, 'lives' could be *evil*. And these letters that keep getting repeated in different ways, 'Orped,' 'Oderp,' this is *Pedro* for sure." She was right. He leaned over as she went through, spotting and circling words like in a jumble.

"Help Pedro. He here with me. He was (something?) by evil spirits. He needs your prayers. Pray for Pedro. Help him (something?) peace. Pedro lost in darkness. Help dear brother Pedro (?) the light. Send love to Pedro. We forgive you. We love you. We are with you. All is love."

Elliot lay back and blew smoke at the ceiling. "That's fucking crazy," he said. "Why would she go to all that trouble? Say all that stuff backward? For who?"

Christine shrugged. "For you maybe. For those people watching in the masks. I mean, word is out right? She wants her community, the new age people, to know she was not in on all this with Pedro."

"But why would she be?"

"Because she was, for a while. I mean, not breaking into Vic's, of course, but . . ." She stole a look at him but then, with a sigh, she turned and spoke into the shadows, as if reciting a soliloquy. "Like I told you, Pedro and I both met her back when we first moved out here. Melody was playing piano and singing at this lame cocktail lounge where Pedro tended bar for a minute and I served drinks. He helped her cook the whole Zona thing up. They just went through the books she had and cobbled it together. I helped a little too." She took a final drag and ground her butt out. "It was a grift. But at the same time, you know, she really did seem to comfort people and she really did go and visit AIDS hospices when no one else did, for free, and pray with those poor people and I don't know, help them feel loved, feel like there was someone who cared and something waiting on the other side. She helped the dying. And if that helped them con money out of the rich folks, Pedro figured, why not? Who cares if it was bullshit? It's all bullshit, right? I mean, isn't all religion just a false comfort? A fairy story? So why not this story, about angels and love instead of the church telling people they were going to hell? And I mean, she really did raise all that money for charity." She smiled now, at a private memory, then: "But . . . as she got more famous, more selfish, and piled up more dough for herself, Pedro started to resent her. While she seemed to, I don't know, take herself more and more seriously, he got more and more cynical and, I guess, felt justified in taking more money."

"How?" Elliot thought about the petty cash. He had sort of assumed it was Pedro, but it had only been a hundred bucks.

"From the tape sales," she said. "Melody had no real idea how many they sold, plus she gave them away all the time. So he just started pocketing most of the cash sales. A lot. I'm sure it was thousands every month. Maybe she finally figured it out. Or suspected at least. And now, with the possible scandal, I mean, there's a very good chance some of her famous friends are in that pile of stuff that he took. She wants it to all be his fault."

Elliot nodded. "So she creates an elaborate con and uses me, as Pedro's friend, to back it up. Now she can wait for her guests or whoever to decode the message, and if there is any fallout, she has an alibi from beyond." He shrugged. "Maybe."

"There is another possibility," Christine said.

"What?"

"Well, Pedro also felt, like, maybe Melody was starting to believe it. You know? He said she was smoking her own shit, getting high on her own supply."

"Like falling for her own con?"

"Like I said, her magic worked, kind of. People do feel better, having a community, having faith, and once in a while someone does get better even, and who's to say the prayers don't help? How do you prove something isn't a miracle? And then, with all that power and money flowing in, it's like, she must really be the chosen one, right?"

"But she'd have to be crazy."

She nodded. "That's what Pedro said. He worried she was going crazy. Like a cult leader, he said. Like they'd created a monster."

Elliot shook his head. "I guess it's time to look for a new job."

Christine smiled and stroked his chest, snuggling in. "I could still talk to Chet. I mean, he has a whole company. You could work at the office, write some kind of PR stuff or something."

"Yeah, that sounds much healthier and less creepy." He stood and began collecting his clothes. "Speaking of PR, I better go. I think we've all had enough scandal for one night."

Christine shrugged. "Actually Chet's agent Hank called and he thinks it's actually giving him a boost. The public is fascinated."

Elliot paused, sock in hand. "Hank, did you say? Hank Sterner?"

She nodded. "Yeah, he discovered Chet, been with him from the beginning. Why? You know him?"

"No . . ." Elliot shook his head. "It's nothing, just . . . he works with Melody too. If that means anything."

"It means they're all rich and famous," she said, watching as he pulled on his pants and shirt. Then she stood, wrapping the blanket around herself.

"Will you call me tomorrow?" she asked. "Or maybe I better call you. Chet will be back."

He winced, as though stung. "Why?"

"Because I want to. If you want me to."

"Of course I do, but what's the point of this really? What are we doing? It's not like you're going to call off your wedding, leave your handsome movie star husband for me, are you?"

She shrugged. "You haven't asked me to."

He smiled at that. He stepped back onto the mattress and squared up, looking her in the eye. "Will you call off the wedding and leave your movie star husband for me?"

She gazed back. "Probably not."

He laughed. "Okay then, good night."

He turned and as he walked out she called after, again: "Will you call me anyway?"

"Maybe," he called back, waving a hand over his shoulder. "Probably. Yes."

Elliot drove home. It was late and he was tired, and he got a little lost on the twists heading out of the Hills—though as long as he kept going downhill he eventually spilled back out onto Crescent Heights and down onto Sunset. By the time he parked and walked back to his garage, he was beginning to think he might really sleep tonight. Then he opened his door.

The place was trashed. Not that it wasn't fairly trashy to start with, but all his clothes were dumped out, the sheets were stripped, and there were books and papers everywhere. Then, before he could take in the whole disaster, he glimpsed movement on his right, felt a sudden, sharp pain in his head, and the lights went out.

27

Elliot woke up with a throbbing headache. He was tied to his only chair with his only necktie, the belt he'd been wearing, and a scarf his mom had knitted. A thin man in cool glasses and an artfully loose black suit and white shirt was glaring down at him while two others, younger and in slightly less fashionable suits, continued to ransack his room.

"Where's the tape?" Cool Glasses barked, breathing coffee in Elliot's face.

"What tape?"

"Don't bullshit us. The tape you and that shitstain stole from the *Raunchy* office."

"Look," Elliot tried reason. "Tell Vic I'm sorry, but whatever we got, Pedro had it. I was only there to help Christine. I didn't know he was going to take anything else."

Cool Glasses slapped him hard across the face. His head snapped right and his cheek stung so sharply it brought tears to his eyes. He blinked rapidly, refusing to cry.

"I don't know what the hell you're talking about," Cool Glasses said. "Just give us the damned tape and tell Vic yourself."

Elliot shook his head. "Vic already fired me. And I don't have anything."

"Quit stonewalling! We hold all the cards here. We got you by the balls." He slapped him again, from the other side. Elliot glimpsed a wedding ring and a Rolex on his wrist.

One of the younger men, in a dark-blue slouchy suit and white shirt buttoned to the neck, David Byrne–style, came over with Vic's gun. "Look what I found, sir."

"Holy shit," said the other young guy, in a gray suit over a black shirt. "That's a Sig 9. Gangster special."

"Get over yourself, Larry." Slouchy Blue sneered at him. "Just cause you do coverage on action properties doesn't make you an expert."

"I was at the range last week, asswipe."

Cool Glasses, clearly the boss, grabbed the gun and waved it in Elliot's face.

"What the hell is this for?" he asked.

"It's not mine." Elliot flinched, trying to remember if the safety was on. "It was a gift."

"A gift?" he asked, brandishing it but also seeming to admire it a little. "From who?"

"Vic!"

"Wait a second," Slouchy Blue demanded, pointing a finger at Elliot's chest. "You just said he fired you. You just contradicted your previous statement, dumbass."

Gray Suit scoffed. "What are you, a lawyer now? You going to sue him, jerkoff?"

"At least I did pre-law, dickweed. At Princeton. What did you major in, dickweeding?"

"Cinema studies, bitch."

"This is going nowhere," Cool Glasses said, and tossed the gun onto the bed. "Let's just take him and go."

"What? Wait. No . . ." Elliot, imagining some torture chamber or maybe concrete boots and a pier, began to struggle frantically, but only succeeded in tipping over the chair and knocking himself to the floor. The two underlings fought to untie the bounds while he squirmed.

"Shit," Gray Suit muttered. "Why did you tie this so tight?"

"To keep him prisoner, moron," Blue Suit said, pulling Elliot's right wrist free. "I got mine undone."

"It's silk. That's easier."

"Just cut it," Cool Glasses said. "Who's got a knife?"

"My mom made that . . ." Elliot told the carpet, while the two underlings patted their pockets.

"Sorry," said Blue Suit. "You never said to bring one."

"Got it," Gray Suit said, pulling the scarf loose. The two junior suits grabbed him while Glasses opened the door. As they dragged him out into the yard, and the dogs inside began barking, Elliot's handlers shifted their grip. Seeing his chance, Elliot broke loose and kicked Blue Suit in the shin.

"Ow! Shit!" he moaned, hopping on one foot and clutching his wounded leg.

Elliot bolted, dashing across the lawn. "Help!" he yelled, hoping to alert his housemates, but of course they were all out on dates or at parties. The dogs barked back. Gray Suit tried to block him, like in football, and Elliot swerved around, pushing him aside, but by then Glasses was jumping on his back and he fell forward, grabbing at Gray Suit's shirt, which tore under his hand. He had some kind of ID clipped to his shirt pocket which had been hidden by the jacket before. It came loose in Elliot's hand as he was tackled and dumped face-first in the familiar dog shit smell.

"Grab him," Glasses ordered, kneeling on Elliot's back. Elliot shoved the ID in his pocket as the two men seized him, tightly this time, and began to drag him, stumbling, along. At least when the cops found his body, there'd be a clue.

"He tore my goddamn shirt," Gray Suit muttered.

"Quit whining," Blue Suit mocked, as they hauled him into the driveway. Elliot was surprised to see a huge Range Rover waiting.

"It was brand new," Gray Suit complained. "From Fred Segal."

"From the sale," Blue Suit countered. "Half off."

"Get him in," Glasses demanded, opening the back door, but as they began to muscle him in, another car, this one a white BMW convertible, pulled up onto the curb, headlights blasting the scene. Two hugely buff boys, one white, one Black, both in their early twenties, leaped out, one from the passenger seat, one from the back. The white boy had long blond surfer hair, with a skintight white muscle T-shirt encasing his massive chest, very tight white shorts, and sneakers. The Black kid was even more immensely built, in a black T-shirt so tight it was slit for his biceps, and equally tight black shorts. His hair was buzzed close. The suits gawked. A smaller, older white guy hopped out of the driver's side. He was in a rainbow tie-dyed T-shirt and purple short-shorts.

"Hold it right there!" the driver yelled. "Leave that man alone!"

"Help!" Elliot shouted. "Call the police! I'm being kidnapped!"

The driver yelled, "Get them, boys!" and as the two weight lifters headed over, Gray Suit and Blue Suit immediately dropped Elliot in panic. Meanwhile their boss had already started the engine and put his Range Rover in reverse.

"Wait! Wait!" They scrambled into the back seat. As the big boys jogged over, the Range Rover backed up and screeched away.

Elliot ran into the arms of his rescuers. "Oh my God, thank you so much," he gushed. "You'll never believe what happened. These gangsters had me tied up."

"Gangsters," the driver scoffed. "Agents more likely. Junior agents."

"Agents?" Elliot asked. "You mean like CIA? Or FBI?" Did they have junior agents? He pulled the ID from his pocket: Larry Dingler—Mail Room. The logo read THE STERNER AGENCY.

"Holy shit, you're right," Elliot said. "He works for Hank Sterner. How did you guess?"

But the driver didn't reply. He was opening the trunk. "Let's go, boys," he ordered and the two giants grabbed Elliot, lifting him like a doll. He dropped the ID in the street. The driver fitted a burlap sack over his head and the sensation of being unable to see triggered immediate panic.

"Hey! Hey! Help!" Elliot yelled again, kicking helplessly, like a child throwing a tantrum, as they tucked him in. Someone fixed the sack with tape and wrapped his arms to his side, like a package. Then the trunk slammed shut.

❖

In the trunk, which was surprisingly spacious, Elliot got to thinking. It had not even occurred to him that anyone other than Vic and his crew could be involved, but why would he send off-duty talent agents rather than his usual thugs? And then what about these new characters, who, as far as Elliot could guess, seemed to be gym rats from Boystown? What did they want from him, he wondered, rolling nauseatingly from side to side as the car swerved and braked through traffic. Based on the movies he'd seen about kidnappers being tracked down with headphones and maps, he tried to count the turns and listen for a factory whistle or train crossing—not that he'd ever heard those things in LA. He just heard honking and the music blasting from other cars. At last they jerked to a halt and Elliot pitched forward and then bounced back against the rear of the trunk. He heard the lid pop open and felt a sudden volume of fresher air. Again, strong arms lifted him, gently but firmly, and this time, hobbled by blindness, he simply slumped like a sack of potatoes as they carried him who knows where. He floated somewhere cool, an air-conditioned space where their steps echoed, a corridor most likely, and then again there was heat and silence. They lay him down and cut the tape. Then, after a bit more whispering and positioning of his limbs, the sack came off.

He was staring at a wooden ceiling. The two hunks stared down at him, seeming even bigger from this angle, like looming colossi. He was, he quickly realized, spread on a massage table, quite comfortably, with a white sheet under him and the little padded pillow under his head. The space was tight—wooden walls, benches, tile floor. A sauna.

"Where am I?" Elliot asked. "A spa?" Were they going to try and steam it out of him?

"That's right, smarty-pants." The hippie driver leaned over him, his bearded and bespectacled face appearing upside down over Elliot's view while the musclemen held him pinned on each side. "You're sealed tight in the sauna room, where no one can hear you scream."

With that, the white guy squeezed something—a nerve, an artery—in Elliot's neck and pain shot through him like electricity, lighting up his whole right side. The Black guy pressed something in his thigh and his sciatic nerve jumped and burned like a broken wire. He screamed. And as promised, nobody heard or came. Or cared. Elliot shut his eyes and when he reopened them, the upside-down face was blurry with his tears.

"Enough," the face said and the pain stopped immediately. The fingers even rubbed him soothingly. These guys had to either be CIA-trained torture experts or professional massage therapists.

"Now then," the bearded face leaned in, speaking, as it were, right into Elliot's own mouth. "Where is the tape?"

"Jesus . . . I don't have it," Elliot pled, desperation and fear mixing with annoyance. "I mean, don't you think I would have given it up by now? Or else that last crew would have found it." He tried to sit up but was pushed back down by heavy hands. "Look, someone fucking killed my friend. For all I know, maybe you. I'm no hero. If I had something, anything, I'd give it up."

The upside-down face stepped back, with a deep sigh, and the torture-therapists let go, too. Swiveling his head, Elliot could see them all take seats on the benches, slumped and glum. Carefully, he sat up, legs dangling off the table.

"We would never harm Pedro," the driver said. Right side up, his face, which had seemed like a brutal inspector from a Russian novel, just looked gentle and sad. And tired. The two giants nodded in agreement. "He was our friend," the Black guy said, in a surprisingly soft voice. His white partner patted his back.

"He never mentioned anything to me," Elliot said.

The three exchanged another quick round of looks and nods. "We're in Act Out," the driver said. "We fight for gay rights and justice for AIDS victims. We specialize in civil disobedience and direct action."

Elliot nodded. "I remember. You threw blood on that senator. He nearly shit himself."

The driver grinned. "It was cherry syrup."

"It was Pedro's idea," the white giant said, proudly. "Me and Evan here splattered him."

"That does sound like Pedro," Elliot admitted.

"The stuff you stole from *Raunchy*," the driver explained now, "he was going to deliver it to us. We were going to distribute it, make copies, be sure it all got out. Evan even knows how to put it on the internet. It would have gone global."

Evan nodded enthusiastically. "The World Wide Web will change everything. All those hypocrites and liars would be exposed. They might control the newspapers and TV. They even control the government. But on the web information is free. True democracy is coming."

"And you think whoever killed him did it to stop that?" Elliot asked. "The cops seem to think it was Victor Kingman."

The driver shrugged. "What do you think? You know him better than us."

Elliot considered this. "I don't know what to think. He's kind of a gangster. But now that I really think about it, I have a hard time seeing him as a killer. At least over this. I mean, he might break some fingers. But murder?"

"We think it's the same people who have been terrified of Vic all this time," the hippie said. "All the ruling-elite assholes he was able to fuck with by keeping them in check with his stash. Everyone knew or at least feared that Vic had dirt on them. It made him untouchable."

"So then what's so important about this tape?" Elliot asked.

"We're not sure," Evan said. "Pedro told me and Tony it was pure dynamite, but that he was holding it back from the rest of the material, which he was going to pass off to us the next day."

Tony nodded sadly. "He said he had to talk to some people first. Including you."

"But why don't you think it was taken when they killed Pedro?" Elliot asked. "They got everything else."

Evan shrugged. "Because they're still coming after you."

"We've got no beef with *Raunchy*, or with you," Tony said. "We support the First Amendment. But we're fighting for our lives here."

Evan nodded. "And the truth is our only weapon."

Elliot took a breath. "So what happens now?"

The old hippie gestured at the door. "Now you can go. Unless you want to stay and take a sauna. Might help loosen you up, after that ride in the trunk."

"No, thanks," Elliot said, standing. "It's been a hell of a day."

Evan opened the door for him. "Sorry about the roughness."

"And you might want to get some bodywork done," Tony called after him. "I sensed that you hold a lot of tension in your shoulders."

28

Elliot stepped out into the night. Where was he? A wide roadway with squat blank buildings, a rush of swiftly passing traffic and no humans in sight, the landscape felt remote but was quickly revealed to be good old Santa Monica Boulevard. He was somewhere in far West Hollywood, and could make out a large and now closed pet supply shop, a lush pan-Asian restaurant and, down a ways, the nightclub El Sur, which he recognized from the neon heart, throbbing redly like a cartoon lover. He hadn't recognized anything at first, since he had only ever glimpsed this landscape in passing from a moving car. LA, the vertiginous, decentered city of the future, was beautiful in motion, circulating on its freeways or boulevards, when the whole system was able to spin and blur. It was walking that made you carsick, dizzy and lost and possibly nauseous, depending on the neighborhood. It was, after all, the city of dreams, and dreams disintegrate when seen with open eyes.

Reoriented, Elliot turned east, glancing at the traffic on his left. There was no chance of a taxi just cruising by, and he had no idea what bus to take, so it looked like he was walking home again. He realized, as he hit his stride, that his headache was gone. Even his calves felt looser as he warmed up. Those revolutionary massage therapists had done a good job after all. He lit a cigarette and began to ruminate, stepping over the long bony shadows of the palm trees that towered above him, nodding their shaggy heads in the slow breeze. Their outlines lay like hurdles that the streetlights threw across his path. He noticed his own shadow, extended before him, like a puddle, so that he was following it, shadowing his own shade, rather than the other way, stepping on its heels, as it were. It was because he was backlit, he realized, and it was coming from a headlight on the boulevard, but as he glanced back over his shoulder, into the sharp glare, he saw that it was not passing but keeping pace, cruising along five or ten feet behind him. And it was a single bright lamp, like a spotlight exposing him on an empty stage: a motorcycle, engine growing louder as it drew closer, like a mosquito in his ear. He looked back again, and in a streetlight, he saw a red bike and a black-clad rider in a helmet whose visor glared right back at him. He made the connection. He had seen this biker before.

"Miriam?" he called, shielding his eyes, trying to remember the color of her bike and gear. "Is that you?"

But the biker showed no reaction; like a cyborg it only came at him. He dropped his cigarette and ran, instantly realizing the foolishness of that reaction. For now, the biker knew that he knew he was being followed, and of course, was much faster than Elliot, who sprinted past closed shops and sleeping offices as the bike streaked alongside, the engine roar now filling his mind. Expertly steering with one hand, the rider drew a gun, which seemed three feet long.

"Holy shit," Elliot yelled, to no one, a prayer of sorts, as he dove forward, and the bullets hit a closed beauty parlor's window behind him. The glass fell with a tinkle, like ringing bells. He jumped up and ran, scurrying forward while bent over double, like Groucho Marx, hiding behind parked cars, heart pounding so hard it seemed to leap into his throat. The biker, clearly frustrated at trying to aim between the passing obstacles, suddenly sped up. Elliot caught his breath, relieved for a moment, but then seized by another wave of panic. The biker had raced to the corner and was now coming right at him, zooming down the sidewalk, gun braced on the handlebars, headlight pinning Elliot like a rabbit. He turned and ran again, back the other way, as he heard what had to be another shot cracking and whistling over his head.

Elliot knew it was over. He was doomed. Of course, the bike would outrun him, and the biker, clearly a skilled shot, would aim better next time. As the microseconds passed, and the bike's roar rose, and he felt it gaining on him like a cougar about to bring down a dumb, slow beast cut off from the herd, he had perhaps his first smart idea in recent memory—he ran into traffic. He jerked right, pivoting like a matador as the bike brushed passed him, a blur of leather and chrome, then scampered between two tightly parked cars, their bumpers nearly kissing, and stumbled into the roadway, causing the cruising vehicles to swerve and honk and stomp their screaming brakes. Waving and shouting *sorry, sorry*, Elliot darted across the median and then the opposing lanes, arriving safely on the other sidewalk, drenched in sweat and gasping like a survivor tossed up onto a shore.

The biker skidded to a halt, back end sliding sideways. There was no way to cross the four lanes of traffic without going back to the corner. Meanwhile, Elliot ran toward the nightclub, the flashing heart now a beacon promising safe harbor. His own heart ready to burst, he joined the line of people waiting to pay admission.

But the crowd was different, no one was in cowboy gear, for one thing, and now that he was up close, he saw that the sign no longer read El Sur. This was now Club Clitorious. Still, he pushed fearlessly to the front, where a coolly beautiful, pale young woman, very Bowie-esque in a white suit, black shirt, and greased-back, iron-red hair, was taking money and stamping hands.

"One, please," he said, still out of breath, digging in his pocket for money.

She regarded him with more boredom than contempt. "You see the sign?" She pointed at the symbol on the door: a pink oval, vertically halved with a pink line. "No shoes, no shirt, no clit, no service."

"Please," Elliot said, waving a damp, wrinkled twenty. "Somebody's following me. I need sanctuary." He tried to make eye contact. "I'm scared, to be honest. Please help me."

She laughed in his face. "I said you have to have a clit to get in, no balls doesn't count." She jerked a thumb. "Take a walk, scrote."

"Excuse us." The couple behind Elliot, an older Latina, black hair high, makeup severe, dressed in designer rags, was arm in arm with a young Asian girl made up like a pinup. Bowie turned to them, but Elliot pressed in.

"You know what?" he said, raising his voice. "I'm not leaving. Sorry to create a disturbance. You can go ahead and call the cops. Call Homicide, ask for Detective Santos," he added, thinking that she might even know this place.

"We don't need cops," Bowie said and snapped her fingers. Two women stepped over from where they'd been checking IDs. They were as tall as the massage therapists, but thicker and less sharply defined, in loose jeans, motorcycle boots, and chain wallets. One wore a plaid flannel shirt, the other a sleeveless T with the club's symbol.

"What's your problem, breeder?" Plaid Shirt asked, getting right in his face.

"No problem, ma'am," Elliot said, backing away. "My mistake."

"You said it," she said, glaring, but her partner in the sleeveless T was staring at him curiously. Then she smiled.

"Hey, you work for Melody Bright, don't you? What's your name again?"

"Yes! I make the tapes! I'm Elliot."

"Right. You were Pedro's friend." She turned to her partner. "I think we can make an exception just this once."

Silently, like a door opening, Plaid Shirt stepped aside. Sleeveless T grabbed his arm and steered him, not into the noisy club itself, but past the coat check and into a small side room where employees were changing and taking breaks.

"Thanks so much," Elliot gushed, amazed at how grateful he was for this indulgence. "If you can just call me a cab."

"Sure, sure. Have a seat," she told him. "Sorry, but I can't let you into the bar. It's not your night."

"No, that's fine. Just the cab is all. I appreciate it."

"No problem," she said, turning to the two women at the table, who were primping and fixing their makeup in mirrors. One had her shaggy black hair chopped and layered, the other a bleach-blonde buzz cut. "This is Elliot. He works for Melody Bright."

"Cool," Shag said. "I listen to her tapes all the time."

"Are you all right?" Buzz asked, frowning at him. "I think you better sit down."

"Yeah, you're really sweaty," Shag added.

"Sorry. No, I'm good. Just a bad night." He took a seat and tried to stop sweating. And shaking.

"I know how that goes," Shag told him. Buzz nodded. Then they ignored him and went back to their labors, preparing to serve drinks or dance. He couldn't help notice that, haircuts and color choices aside, they didn't look all that different from the strippers he met working for *Raunchy*: glitter and hairspray, lace and leather. And just like most of those girls, or Melody and her acolytes, or even Christine for that matter, these two were no doubt aspiring actors or singers. In the end, they were all in showbiz somehow. Elliot included. That is to say, they were liars, practiced at deception, even if no one believed it but themselves.

Sleeveless came back, balancing four shots on a tray. "Here we go girls . . . and boy." Lowering the tray, she carefully set a glass before each of them. "The cab will be a few, busy night, but you looked like you could use a drink."

"I know I can," Shag said, laughing and reaching for her glass.

"It's tequila too," Buzz said, grabbing hers. "My fave."

"Yeah, the good stuff," Sleeveless said, laughing. "I helped myself."

"I don't know," Elliot said. "I don't feel that great."

"Come on," Sleeveless said. "Have a drink with us." She lifted a toast. "To Pedro."

The two girls raised their glasses and stared. With a shrug, Elliot lifted his.

"To Pedro," he said, and drank.

The liquor burned going down, and tasted like medicine, but on the whole it was no worse than the juice he'd had with Margie and way more effective. A calmness spread immediately from his belly through his limbs and then to his mind, which seemed to unclench for the first time since the break-in.

"I'll go check on that taxi," Sleeveless said, retrieving the empty shot glasses, and walked away. Elliot sat back and sighed deeply. Shag lit a cigarette, then leaned into her mirror, tracing on dark eyeliner while she talked to Buzz.

"So I told my agent, I mean, I'm really more of a film actor. But I wouldn't say no to a series."

"Totally," Buzz agreed. She was applying lipstick. "Like my true passion is the stage. That immediate connection to the audience. And the material. But I'd consider TV."

As their voices droned on, Elliot felt his eyes drooping shut. *Where's that damned cab?* he thought to himself. *I better go outside. Get some fresh air.* But as he tried to stand he felt his legs were numb and he slipped back into darkness.

"I mean, cable only, of course," he heard Shag say as he passed out.

"Of course. It's so much more artistic."

It took Elliot a moment to realize he was naked.

Through a mist of drugged sleep, he saw flames leaping before his blurry eyes. He heard a drum, low and steady, like the throb of his blood, with pipes dancing above it and a jangle of voices chanting an unknown tongue. As if through a prism, he saw dark figures, the same robed strangers from Melody's basement, hooded and masked, but now with their robes open to reveal their naked flesh. Men and women, old and young, thin and fat, they danced in a circle around him, their shadows jumping in the light of flaming torches set in the ground. Beyond that, he saw trees, branches etched against sky, the moon. And somewhere above him, silhouetted in the firelight, he saw a woman in a red robe. Was that Melody? He tried to sit up and found he was bound hand and foot.

Straining forward, he realized he was nude, or almost; he still had his socks. And even more disturbing, he was pinned in the center of a circle of white sand with a pentagram marked in red across his chest. Noticing his drugged movements, like he was a dreamer fighting a nightmare, a short, round woman, who seemed older as well, based on her long-tanned and wrinkled skin, and the gray braid that snaked down her back, raised up a wooden staff decorated like a maypole with colored ribbon. She wore a horned devil mask.

"Silence," she yelled through her mask and the dancing and music ceased. "It is awake."

Her voice sounded familiar, as was the pendant that hung between her enormous breasts—a diamond-shaped pink crystal, it reminded him of Vic's, as well as the symbol above Clitorious. He felt certain she was the white witch from Santa Monica. Were these all Melody's followers? Her tribe of desperate and deluded Actors Studio rejects? In a panicked delirium, he recalled what Anderson and Santos had said about death cults, and what Christine had told him about Melody's growing belief in her own powers.

"Sharon? That you?" he mumbled, peering at her but seeing double. He couldn't get both eyes to agree and his own voice sounded far off. "Melody?" he called out, head craning. "You there?"

Sharon poked him with the staff. "Silence, knave! Speak only when commanded." She waved her arms. "Bring the dagger and chalice."

Two other women appeared above him, both with blank white masks. One pressed a bone-handled dagger to his throat, while the other held an ornate, silverish chalice. Now Elliot lay very still, as if in a barber's chair getting a close shave. Sharon pulled out his crumpled copy of the Zona script—no doubt found when they undressed him—and held it in his face.

"What means this? Speak, knave!"

Elliot spoke slowly and carefully, his tongue thick, his own words echoing in his head. "Is . . . backward. You can see . . . where words . . . are circled."

"Very good, knave. You deciphered the message of Zona. And have you told anyone of the truth contained therein?"

"No." He shook his head. "Promise."

She stamped the staff. "Fool! What good is a messenger who doesn't deliver? You were chosen to carry this knowledge from a higher realm. The world needs to know that the cruel murder of our spiritual brother Pedro was committed by the evil minions of an oppressive and misogynistic patriarchy. That is your task. Understood?"

He nodded.

"Let's sacrifice him, Priestess!" This was the woman with the dagger. He'd heard her voice before somewhere. "He failed us! He is unworthy to carry the word. Let me feed his blood to Mother Earth."

Elliot shook his head, blinking as if trying to wake himself up.

"I think we should keep him," the chalice bearer said. "At least he's youngish and sort of cute." Elliot felt like he knew her as well, and he peered up to where she clutched the chalice between her perfectly round, signature breasts. He'd know them anywhere. She was Dr. K's prize patient, Pedro's ghost client, Ms. Sterner.

"Misty?" he asked. "It's me . . . Elliot. Help . . . please."

"Shut up, pig," the dagger holder said. She pressed the dagger point against Elliot's pulsing throat, looking into his eyes. "It's what he deserves after all the suffering he caused in the flesh trade."

Flesh trade. Two synapses crossed the swirling darkness of Elliot's skull and he realized that some of her body markings were familiar tattoos.

"Krystal Kanyon! Remember me?" he pled. "Two *y*s...and two *K*s!"

"Krystal is dead. I am Isis now, for the goddess of healing and magic. With two *I*s and two *s*s. And you were a cog in the objectification machine, a lackey serving the patriarchy. You may have been feeding at the bottom of the trough but you're just as guilty as the rest of them."

He shook his head, gasping for words. "But . . . you said it was . . . your choice."

"In a culture where I have no freedom, there is no free choice." He felt the dagger press his flesh, and a single drop of blood formed like a tear at its point. Feebly, he tried to struggle, but his eyes shut against his will. Too exhausted to fight, he surrendered to oblivion, which seemed to swallow him whole. Then, a moment or a century later, he heard a voice in the darkness.

"Elliot? Can you hear me?"

He opened his eyes. Images swam before him, bending as if underwater. Melody was sitting over him in her red robe, stroking his brow, her outline haloed in firelight. She spoke in soothing tones.

"Elliot, don't be afraid. You are safe now. I bring you good news. I've heard from Pedro, your dear friend."

"Pedro?" Elliot rasped. His brain was hopelessly foggy but he seemed to remember Pedro was dead.

"Yes. He says he's sorry that he got you involved. That it was wrong what he did. But that the men who killed him will pay for it, in this realm or the next. He wants you to know that he is watching over you, and he loves you. He's here now. Can you feel his presence? His love?"

She gazed down at him, eyes shining, and for a moment he thought he did feel something. His eyes filled with tears. "Pedro?"

"Yes, Pedro is here now, speaking through me. But he says he needs your help, Elliot. To carry on his mission, our mission, to help love defeat hate, and light overcome darkness. Don't you want to help?"

Elliot nodded eagerly. He felt a surge of emotion.

"Good. He wants you to give us the tape. The one you helped him steal."

"Tape?" Elliot was confused.

"Yes, the tape, Elliot. Where is it?"

He shook his head. Pedro had it wrong. "No tape," he mumbled. "Pedro knows. No tape."

A flicker of annoyance crossed Melody's face and she turned away. Misty was there, holding what looked like Elliot's clothing. She shook her head.

"God fucking damn it . . ." Melody muttered, then gazed back down at him, smiling beatifically. "Rest now, Elliot. And don't fear. Love is all. All is love." She stroked his forehead gently as the others took up the chant.

"Remember, children," he could hear Melody preaching as he seemed to drift away. "In the year 2000, when the new millennium begins, and the systems of oppression collapse in the Y2K apocalypse, and banks, governments, even the World Wide Web are all wiped out, the Age of the Goddess will dawn."

Everyone cheered.

"But what if that doesn't happen?" Misty asked, quietly.

Melody smiled sadly. "Then Mother Earth will have her vengeance—floods, fires, droughts, plagues. Don't worry. Mankind will pay for his foolishness and greed, one way or the other. Now come, beloveds, it's time for the invocation."

The drum rattled again and a slower, more dirgelike chant went up. Elliot tried to focus, but his eyes were too heavy. He sank back into nothingness.

29

He woke up on his front lawn. That is to say, the fresh air and stale grass brought him around and, as he heard the sound of an engine pulling away, he sat up to find himself more or less safely at home, dropped off like a lazy delivery, slightly dented. Elliot was dressed, thankfully, but quickly realized his shoes were untied, his pants unzipped, and his underwear backward. Peeking under his shirt, he saw the rubbed-out traces of marker. So definitely not a hallucination then. Almost definitely.

He stood carefully and brushed himself off. His first thought was to go to his room and call the cops, but considering the hour, it was unlikely that Anderson or Santos was on duty, and even less likely that a regular patrol officer would make much of his tale, so he decided the best thing was to try to get some sleep and call in the morning. But was it even safe to sleep? Would yet another gang stop by? Then he remembered the gun. He'd fetch it and let himself into the main house and crash on the couch, then explain it all to his roomies when they woke up, if they were even there.

But as he turned toward the house, something odd caught his eye. Like a Hollywood miracle, or a piece left from his drugged delirium, a yellow Ferrari lay in the driveway like a dragon at rest. No one was in it, but the trunk was ajar and light was leaking out, as if a glow beckoned from within. Curious, he lifted the lid. And there was a stout man in an expensively casual suit he recognized as Hank Sterner. Except now he had a bullet hole in his forehead and a bloom of drying blood spreading from behind. He looked up at Elliot with empty, wide-open eyes.

Instinctively, Elliot slammed the lid back down, plunging the scene into darkness. But as if on cue from an unseen director, he was caught in a beam of light. A headlight. He froze like a deer on the road, peering into the glare. Then he heard it. A motorcycle.

There it was, caught in a streetlight up the block, the red bike, roaring into life, with the unknown rider, once again heading his way, like a scene from a nightmare, like the mythic horse for which nightmares are named, galloping out of the darkness to snatch his soul. But this time he had something to run toward at least, the gun. He took off like a sprinter and bolted down the driveway toward his garage.

He raced alongside the parked cars, giving him a slight lead, since the biker had to slow down to squeeze through, and came around the corner of the house at a run. That was his next surprise: his roommates were not only home but in the hot tub, which was now miraculously revived, bubbling and steaming. The screenwriter from Joe's party and his model wife were with them, along with the bro in the fanciful mustache, enjoying some beers, while the dogs napped nearby.

"Hey, bro," mustache said as he appeared in the backyard. "Got a cig?"

"Hi," Sequoia called. "Check it out. Derrick fixed . . ."

But their dialogue was cut short as the bike arrived, right on Elliot's tail as it regained full speed. He dodged and weaved, jumping clear of the bike, but as it passed him and then skidded around, tail sliding sideways, it cut him off from his door, and from the gun. With the hot-tubbers watching in silent amazement, the bike revved up and came straight at him, chasing him in a frantic circle before catching him from behind like the horns of a charging bull. Fortunately, his pants were undone and he didn't have his belt. The bike's front wheel went between his legs and the handlebars caught him, but only by the jeans, which pulled loose. He was lifted and thrown clear, tumbling across the grass with his pants around his ankles. The bike circled again and made another pass, this time on target to crush him as he fumbled, rolling on the ground and yanking up his trousers.

That's when the dogs joined in. Barking, perhaps joyously, perhaps ferociously, the pack came flying into the game, heading right for Elliot, who shut his eyes in terror. But the dogs leaped over him, making a beeline for the bike, and Blue, the Rottweiler, sank his teeth in the rider's ankle. The bike wobbled and slid while the rider struggled. The boot prevented serious damage, but still, it gave Elliot a chance. He got to his feet and ran in the opposite direction, now making straight for the neighbor's yard. He heard the righted bike behind him, and the dog now barking behind that. Summoning whatever strength and agility he had left, and firing on full adrenaline, he jumped onto a rusty lawn chair, grabbed the top of the fence, and hoisted himself over, a feat that might have been impressive except that the decrepit fence collapsed under his weight, leaving him totally exposed. The yard, he was amazed to see, contained a ramshackle chicken coop, which explained the rooster crowing as well as some mystifying smells. The falling fence had smashed in the roof of the coop, awakening the furious birds.

The sound of the bike was now deafening as he scrambled, scattering chickens, who clucked in fury. The approaching biker rose up into a standing position, leaning forward, pointing the pistol with one hand, taking careful aim. Then, like a mystical vision, Elliot saw it, faintly, just slightly brushed in moonlight—the clothesline, hung at chest height between metal poles. With his last drop of flagging energy, he made for it, the bike nuzzling his ass, and like a hitter rounding third, he slid under. The biker tripped the line, which caught right across the neck.

The line was heavy-gauge wire, stiff enough to hold wet clothes without drooping, with the insulated coating providing some protection against weather and time. It let out a twang as it snapped, catching and lifting the rider, who seemed to float free for a moment, caught by the throat, before being flung backward like an arrow from a bow. The body landed with a thump as the bike shot away, running riderless through the chickens, and then, as the handlebars turned, flopping harmlessly onto the dirt. The back wheel whined a bit then stopped. The rider, too, had stopped moving, now a pile of limbs covered in leather. As Elliot limped over, he saw how the helmet was turned, three-quarters clockwise, as if trying to see what was coming up from behind. A small patch of exposed pale neck was twisted rudely and scored with the wire. Still, he had to be sure, so he gingerly reached down, using just the tips of his fingers, and pulled the helmet free. His housemates and their guests, all clad in swimsuits, gathered to watch, Derrick still holding a beer.

It was not Miriam, but a total stranger he had never seen before. That was the first surprise. The next surprise was her coloring: she was ghostly pale, white as baby powder, with bright red hair. And when the screenwriter produced a lighter, her dead eyes stared out, stark red and veined, bulging from her nearly backward head. The girls gasped. The dogs barked. The chicken feathers floated about.

"Who the hell is that, bro?" Derrick asked, which was a good question, but no one answered.

❖

"She's a professional stuntwoman," Sergeant Anderson said. They were back in the shabbier, windowless room. Clearly, despite becoming a regular, Elliot was no VIP. "Name's Casey Bucks. We'll have to confirm, but her ID matches and there is only one female with albinism registered with the guild. And the slug we found in Sterner matches her gun."

"Which explains a lot," Santos added. "Why she was so good on the bike. Shooting a pistol while in motion is extremely difficult. Also explains why she never took off her helmet. Can't handle the sun."

"It doesn't explain why she was trying to kill me," Elliot pointed out.

"True." Santos nodded. "That we may never know." Anderson scowled at this and she quickly backtracked. "I mean, we will crack it eventually, of course, we never give up but you know . . . she's not talking. Not with her head almost snapped clean off."

Anderson cleared his throat and she fell silent. "We checked out that gym you told us about, in Boystown," he said. "But it was closed at the time you were there and, based on your description, the kidnappers could be anyone. As for the, um . . . lesbians, they say you showed up seeming drunk and disoriented. They called your employer, Melody Bright, and she says they picked you up and performed a, quote, 'healing ceremony,' then dropped you off at home."

Santos shrugged. "Honestly, if they really wanted to sacrifice you, they'd take you out into the desert. We'd never find your remains."

"Maybe just your bones," Anderson said. "Eventually."

"Anyway," she went on. "That should ease your mind somewhat."

"Not really," Elliot said. "What about giving me some protection?"

They grinned. "What is this, the FBI?" Anderson asked. "Look around."

"Get a dog," Santos put in.

"You know, kid," Anderson leaned forward. "Usually at this point in an ongoing investigation, I tell the witness not to leave town, but in your case I'm going to suggest you get the hell out, for all of our sakes."

Santos nodded sagely. "ASAP," she said, lingering over the syllables. "A . . . SAP."

Two uniforms dropped him back home, which looked, in the glare of day, to be almost back to normal, except for the scraps of crime scene tape still hanging like party leftovers and the fresh bits of plywood patching the fence. Elliot had been thinking the whole time about what the detectives had said about leaving town. And, of course, about Christine. He even drifted into a fantasy of them running off together. But that was exhaustion talking to him in his own befuddled head. Where would they go? When he finally got back into his room, the light on his answering machine was blinking and there was a message from his sister. His father had suffered a mild stroke and was in the hospital. He had to go home.

Elliot called and confirmed he'd be on the flight they'd booked, which left later that day. His father was critical, if stable, and unconscious. He reserved the airport shuttle van. Next, he left a message for Christine. Then, to be cagey, he called the office and told Janice, who promised to pray and send good vibes. He showered and changed and only then, as he was folding T-shirts and underwear, did it occur to him to wonder about the weather. He called his mother back; it was freezing in New York with more snow expected that night. So he hopped in his car and drove to an army surplus shop where a curt Armenian fellow with a cigar stub rolling moistly in his mouth sold him a used but very warm and cheap infantry parka, drab green with a fake fur-lined hood, an itchy olive wool hat and scarf, and a khaki duffel, since he realized he also lacked a suitcase. Then he went home and packed and finally sat on the front steps smoking and waiting for his ride. About fifteen minutes before the van was due, a black limo pulled up and a uniformed driver got out, doffing his cap.

"Mr. Gross?"

Elliot stood, confused, and pointed at himself, as if he wasn't sure. "Yes?"

"I'm here to take you to the airport, sir," he said, and opened the door.

Elliot hesitated. A prickle of fear moved up the back of his neck. His recent rides with strangers had not gone well. Hoisting his duffel, he made his way slowly toward the car.

"Please allow me," the driver said, popping the trunk. Elliot stepped back. He'd developed a trunk phobia. Smiling, the driver reached out a hand.

"I think there's a mistake," Elliot said, clutching his bag. "I didn't order a limo."

"There's no mistake, sir," the driver said. "It was ordered on the account of Chet Hunter, on your behalf." Now he reached out and grasped the strap of Elliot's duffel, tugging gently. Reluctantly, Elliot let go, then ducked to peer into the rear seat, as if checking for booby traps. Christine sat smiling in a white shift, its thin straps bright across her tan shoulders, her bare legs crossed.

"I got your message," she said. "I'm so sorry about your father. I thought you could use a ride." She smiled shyly. "And I wanted to see you before you go."

Sighing with relief, Elliot slid onto the seat and, as the driver shut the door, he leaned in for a kiss. But Christine pulled away, shaking her head no and pointing at the front seat as the driver got back in. So Elliot sat back, keeping to his side, and while the limo pulled away, he told her about his night since they parted.

"Jesus Christ," she said. "You've really been through it. And you have no idea who's behind it all?"

"It can't just be Vic can it?" he said. "Even if he killed Pedro or had him killed, maybe by that stuntwoman, why keep sending her after me? He has to know I don't have anything. The activists are looking for the goods Pedro was going to give them, from Vic's safe. And maybe, just maybe, that agent was worried about that, too, protecting his clients? But why are Melody's people after it?" He shook his head. "Whatever it is, I wish I did have it. Just so I could get rid of it."

"And you're sure," she asked, "there's no way Pedro could have had anything else that you didn't see, or that wasn't in that bag? Something he found and hid somewhere, at his place or at the office or anything?"

Elliot shrugged. "I don't see how, but then how would even I know?"

"Think. Just try. Maybe shut your eyes and think hard."

Elliot shook his head. "I'm sorry. If I shut my eyes, I'm going to pass out. And now I've got my dad to worry about."

"Of course, of course, I'm sorry. That's so thoughtless of me." She patted his hand. "Why don't you just relax till we get to the airport?"

So Elliot leaned back, and stared out the window at the traffic. A minute later, he felt something, a small warm touch on his pinky, and he glanced down. Christine's hand was spread beside his on the seat, her little finger kissing his. She smiled at the back of the driver's head. So did he. And when the limo stopped at the curb before the terminal, and the driver hopped out, during the few seconds it took him to pull Elliot's bag from the trunk and open the door, she leaned over and kissed him hard. Then she pulled away.

30

It was cold in Queens and the cabbie's radio was predicting snow. You could sense it in the air. It had that clarity. The black streets, the cracks in the sidewalks, the distant skyscrapers, everything was in tight focus. In LA the streets had less garbage and there was plenty of elbow room, but everything seemed coated in a sky that was sometimes more like a gravy. New York was dirty and crowded, there were mountains of trash on the streets, but the air tasted clean as ice.

In the hospital, nurses and doctors padded around in their scrubs and clogs, some wearing institutional green, others in maroon or blue. They expressed their individuality with eccentric shower caps. Patients shuffled along in robes. The sight of so many people in what looked like pajamas, combined with the stifling heat, gave Elliot a feeling of childhood, of a nursery or playpen. At the same time, the medicinal smells and the suffering and fear on the faces of the sick reminded him that death ruled this house, even if he was, hopefully, only visiting. He imagined that for ages, even up to his parents' youth, people sickened and died at home and wars were fought in the front yard while animals were slaughtered in the back; so perhaps death, however terrible, once seemed natural and connected to life. These days, it all happened off-screen and out of mind, Elliot thought, as he rode the elevator and wandered the long hallway, following the arrowed room number signs.

It didn't seem normal, dying. We are shocked when a steak bleeds and worry about overexposure to fake death on TV and in the movies.

But now the secret was out: His father would die. Not yet—according to his mother, the attack was not life-threatening—but that inconceivable event would happen, and in an unknown but finite number of days. Then after another dark number turned, his mother would die. The image of her alone without his father stabbed Elliot deeper than the image of her death, and for a moment he debated, as if it were his choice, which of them would be more helpless, more lost, without the other, but he couldn't sustain the thought. It was too much.

When he found the room, both of his parents were asleep. Elliot's father was in a bed by the window, hooked up to a pile of machines. Elliot couldn't recall ever watching him asleep before. His face sagged, and his eyes moved beneath their lids. Elliot pictured an old movie playing in there, silent flickers rising and falling back. Already middle-aged when Elliot was born, he had always seemed old, ancient even, in a mythic and all-powerful way; but now, for the first time, he looked fragile, with his threadbare strands of hair matted to his skull. His mother was asleep in a chair with her coat on, but as soon as Elliot looked at her she opened her eyes and smiled, as if some motherly alarm clock had gone off. And then, as if she remembered why he was there, she began to cry. Elliot knelt by the chair and hugged her, dropping his bag on the floor. This is it, he thought, everything has changed: now I am holding her.

After much debate and protracted negotiations, he convinced his sleep-deprived mother to go home to his sister, who had flown up the day before, and after a long shift at the bedside, had finally gone back to the apartment to shower and prepare food. Elliot took up her post in the chair. An hour later, his father opened his eyes and smiled, which gladdened Elliot at first, but scared him when he saw no recognition in his father's gaze. Facing this smiling stranger was far worse than the taciturn man he knew. Later, the doctor came by and explained, as his mother had, that his father had not yet regained full consciousness or begun to communicate. He was in and out. At the doctor's suggestion, Elliot tried talking to him for a while, reminding him of familiar things. His father stared at him blankly, without a trace of interest. Nothing unusual there. It was hard to say if he was brain damaged or just bored. A nurse came to check his dad's vitals and he decided to slip out for a smoke.

Outside, Elliot lit up and exhaled warm smoke into the freezing air, his foggy breath rising in tatters like a baby ghost. The street was quiet and when he stepped away from the door, which kept automatically parting and shutting, sensing his presence, it was dark too. Then he felt it, tiny pricks of cold on his neck and hands like white embers. Snow. He hadn't seen snow in a long time, since he usually avoided the worst of winter on his increasingly infrequent visits. He stared up and saw it in the halo of the streetlamp, the delicate flakes fluttering like moths around the light, then spiraling down. It clung to his shoulders and eyebrows, dusting the sidewalk and gathering in corners, swept by the wind, as if a million tiny flowers had suddenly dropped their petals, as if heaven had invaded the earth. He tossed his butt, which burned into the snow, the ash bleeding black, as he remembered the blizzards of his childhood, the snowball wars and Christine in her white hat. Head back, he opened his mouth wide, to let a perfect flake land on his tongue. It melted, cold and fresh in the warm aftertaste of smoke, and suddenly he remembered his dad. He, too, had a childhood winter story: his arrival in the camps, it was freezing cold but still he was eager to climb off the cramped, filthy, stinking train, and scared as he was, the sight of snow, spiraling down from above, seemed like a momentary reprieve, a little slice of normal life for the child he was. And he was thirsty too. His throat dry as paper. So he opened his mouth wide and caught a big fat snowflake on his tongue. And he retched. It was ash. Smoke and ash from the crematoriums that he would come to know so well, like a cloud of death, the fate that hung over them all.

Elliot thought of that child's story, and of how it had formed the man who lay in the bed upstairs, hardened him, twisted him even, but never broke him. He thought of his moment of glory, when on another cold day, that American captain, horrified and disgusted with what he'd found when entering the camp, had thrust an automatic pistol into the young boy's hands–"Here you go, kid"—had held his shoulders steady while he raised the gun with two hands and fired until the gun was empty.

Who was he, Elliot asked the sky, to judge a life like that? Let him live, he begged the same sky, which only sent more white crystals, like confetti, down in reply. His hands were getting numb—he'd forgotten to buy gloves at the army store, and he went back in, rode the elevator up to the room. This time, although the lights were down, he could see that his father was awake. He lay on the pillow, tubes in his arms, hair sticking up like a newborn chick, staring out the window, wide-eyed, at the snow.

"Dad?" Elliot said.

His father looked over and gasped. Seeing Elliot there, in his army coat, his shoulders and olive hat covered in snow, and lit from behind in the doorway, he began to whimper. "Ich kann nicht. Entschuldigung. Ich kann nicht."

"What? Dad?" Elliot came forward, trying to remember the German. "Sorry for what?"

"Please," his father pleaded, looking up at him, his accent somehow thicker, his voice younger, childish. "Please, Hauptmann, I cannot. I am sorry. Please don't make me." His eyes were pooling, tears ran down his cheeks. "I cannot shoot. I am too scared. Please. I am sorry. I am sorry. I cannot." He reached out, grasping at Elliot's hands and, afraid he would pull his tubes out, Elliot sat on the side of the bed, patting his hands.

"It's okay," he said, stroking his head. "Don't worry. You were just a child. It's okay." It was only when he heard his own voice that Elliot choked up and, tasting salt, realized that the droplets crossing his own cheeks were not melting snowflakes. They were tears.

❖

His father had begun to improve rapidly since Elliot's arrival, eating, talking, berating the nurses. His mother, too, had snapped back into her normal self, arguing with his father, fussing and nagging Elliot over his hair, his clothes, his smoking. The new and terrifying reality Elliot had glimpsed that first morning in the hospital had turned out to just be a hiatus, a commercial break in the now resumed rerun of their long-running family comedy. His sister, always a little smarter, had retreated to Miami, where she had her own family to look after. When Elliot asked his father about their conversation on the night he arrived, he claimed to have no memory of it, and insisted it had been a dream of Elliot's. Later, at home, he asked his mother.

"You know Dad's story, about when the camp was liberated? Has he talked about that lately?"

"Lately?" She shook her head as she took rye bread from the fridge. "Only to Jerry."

"Who the hell's Jerry?"

"You know, Jerry. Jerry what's his name? Sumack."

"What?" Elliot blurted. "What do you mean?"

"What're you so surprised about?" his mother asked. "When he called, he said it was you that gave him the tip. At first we didn't believe it. A big-time movie producer? But he showed up in a limo with a Junior's cheesecake . . ."

"What tip?" Elliot demanded. "What are you talking about?"

"Your father. He bought your father's whole story."

"Which story?"

"Which story, he wants to know!" She shook her clenched hands at him. "Only the story of your own people's survival."

"Jesus, what did he tell him?"

"Everything. The whole gedilla."

"How come you didn't call me about this?"

"It happened so fast. And Jerry said you knew all about it. He said it was your idea. Anyway, I can't talk details, okay? We signed a paper not to discuss the property with any third parties."

"I'm a third party?"

She shrugged noncommittally. Elliot pressed his temples together with his fists. "A property, you're calling it now? I can't believe this."

She waved a knife and began spreading mustard. "You should be happy. With this money, we can finally move to Florida and get away from this cold. Your father's hospital, the best doctors, it's all paid for."

"Of course, I'm happy, Ma. Congratulations." He took a breath and tried to keep his voice steady. "I'm just shocked. He never mentioned anything to me."

"So call him up," she said, folding slices of turkey onto the bread. "Maybe he'll give you a job. Maybe for once you'll write something your mother can read." She pointed the knife at the desk set in a corner of the living room. "Have you seen your mail?"

"Mail? For me?"

Random junk still showed up for him now and then. Usually he had his mother open and trash it over the phone. "I forgot to tell you, when everything happened with your father."

Elliot reached for a small stack. A couple of catalogs from clothing brands he had purchased once years ago but that hounded him forever. A calendar from a Manhattan cinema, out of date. Bills from the student loan people, escalating in anger and bold type. And then a manila envelope, folded and taped into a small, flat package. There was no return address, but the postmark read WEST HOLLYWOOD, CA. He ripped it open, heart racing. It was a videotape. The only identification was a repurposed produce sticker: a little cartoon pineapple with a smiley face and the motto FRESH FROM PARADISE!

"Mom," Elliot said, rushing to the TV. "Where's your VCR?"

"My what?" She came in from the kitchen, holding a jar of pickles.

"VCR. For playing movies."

"It broke. So we got rid of it. Your dad said who needs it when there are plenty of free movies just as bad on TV."

"Right," Elliot said. "Good point."

She handed him the jar. "Here. Open this for me." She turned to go back into the kitchen. Elliot remained staring at the tape. "You want coleslaw on your sandwich?" she called, and he looked up.

"Yeah," he said, shaking the jar to unseal the vacuum and then cranking the lid with all his might. It opened with a pop.

❖

Although still weak and in need of treatment, Elliot's father was expected to make a full recovery. He came home with a cane and with his suitcase full of booty he'd stolen from the hospital: a huge box of cotton balls, a bedpan, a gross of rubber gloves he'd no doubt force Elliot's mother to use when doing the dishes. He still seemed to have no recollection of speaking in German to Elliot or crying, nor did he mention the Sumack affair. Finally, on the morning of his departure, Elliot stared into the bathroom mirror and told himself that today, over breakfast, he would bring it up. But when he came into the kitchen with his luggage, his father already had his head in the trash. His mother stood beside him, fists on her hips, tapping her foot in fury.

"Look at your father," his mother said, pointing at him. "He's digging for gold. Lunatic!" she shouted.

"Aha," his father yelled, raising his head. He was smiling triumphantly, leaning on his cane and waving a hunk of cheese around like it was a recovered murder weapon.

"What's this? What's this?" he demanded.

"Cheese. So what?" she said.

"A whole thing of cheese you threw out? What, did we win the lottery?" He pointed at Elliot. "You can make the boy cheese sandwiches for the trip."

"It's no good. It's moldy."

"They have food on the plane," Elliot tried to interject, but they ignored him.

"No good?" his father roared. "In France they pay extra for that."

"The French! What do they know?"

"Cheese," his father said. "They know about cheese. No? Who knows then, Americans, with their little orange slices wrapped in plastic?"

"Don't give me the French," his mother said, shaking her fist. "Where were they when the Nazis were loading you onto the trains? Huh? I'll tell you. Cheering. The French. What did they ever do for the Jews? And now you want to eat their cheese."

"I'm going," Elliot said, picking his duffle bag up. "I've got to go."

He kissed his parents and left.

❖

They flew west, keeping up with the night, the rounded earth outside the porthole fading through a thousand shades of orange and blue. There was no true sense of speed. The plane seemed to be cruising at a stately pace over the vast range of clouds. To Elliot, the clouds appeared not to be objects suspended in air but the air itself become visible, like a wave in a frozen sea, like the wind would look resting or the rain standing still. Here and there, through thin patches, the ground could be glimpsed as if over the side of a boat. The earth was tan and black and white, laid out in rumpled squares like an old quilt. A long trail of vapor hung beside them, under the right wing, a thin milky river running backward into the night.

Then, approaching LA, he saw those countless city lights, tiny beads of yellow, gold, silver, and white, strung along the finest line, like jewels threaded onto a spider's web, some lights dim but warm, like embers, others sharp as pinpricks, and the cars and trains and buses darting back and forth. He was always breathless in the face of these great works of unconscious art, this embroidery on darkness, the one masterpiece that we all, each carrying our little light, have together unknowingly formed.

31

Elliot had called Margie from his parents' place, without telling them he was making a long-distance call, and asked her if he could come by the office after hours. He took a taxi straight from the airport. He knew he was being paranoid but now he really did have a tape, possibly even *the* tape. They really were after him, whoever "they" were.

Margie was leaning against the wall beside the back entrance, looking bored. She did look perfectly cast for a spy flick, though, Elliot thought, but then she always did: belted raincoat, red lips, red nails, that Veronica Lake curl in her gleaming black hair, fishnets, and heels.

"So, what's the caper this time?" she asked, dubiously.

"Hi," he said, and then, "Sorry. I didn't think it would all go so wrong."

"You didn't think about a lot of things. And you only call when you need a favor."

"Sorry," Elliot said again. He felt himself burn with shame and defensiveness, but he knew she was right. "I've been really busy."

"So I gather."

"I hope it didn't come back on you."

"No. But it could have. But then you didn't think about that either. You know, lover . . ." she said, in her best tough chick voice. "You might need to seriously consider the possibility that you're not as good a guy as you think you are."

"This is the last time, I promise."

"I know it is," she said, and unlocked the door. "That's why I came. I wanted to say goodbye."

"Goodbye?" He followed her into the building and down the hall toward the elevators. "Where are you going?"

"Seattle," she said, pressing the button. The elevator opened and they got on. "I gave my notice last week, packed my stuff, even had my going-away party, all of which you would have known if you'd called me."

"Why Seattle? Just because you have such a cool raincoat?"

"That and I took Armond's job offer. I'm going to help him launch an internet porn site."

"Jesus, that dude? He's just some rich douchebag."

"In case you haven't noticed, they're all rich douchebags. Who do you think owns this place?"

"Yeah, but I mean . . ." The doors opened and they walked into the art department. He swept a hand over the empty desks. "At least this is still real publishing, sort of. The internet? That's a joke."

"Maybe. But it's an expensive joke. The douchebag doubled my salary. And I don't know . . . I've got a hunch this web thing is going to be big. It's the next porn frontier. You should consider it. He actually liked you. Remember, in porn, being a dick is no impediment."

He laughed. "True enough. Always plenty of room for assholes and pussies too. But I'm out of the game, remember?"

She pointed at the package in his hand. "So then what's this?"

He took a deep breath. "Good question. Let's find out."

They sat at the same desk where they'd watched the yacht tape, alone in the office that night, with the same chairs pulled up, though this time without the snacks or giggles. They were silent in their one island of light in the dark office as Margie loaded the tape and powered up the monitor. Static roared on and she lowered the volume. A soup of blurry color appeared through a dizzy, swerving camera. Then abruptly, the image came into focus: a hotel room, warmly lit, seen, it seemed, from the balcony. Furnished in browns and grays—a wide flat bed, the blankets kicked off, one of those console desks, wall-to-wall gray carpet. Two bare bodies on the bed. Beautiful bodies, but neither was Christine. This was two men kissing, hands running over each other. It was all very ordinary, and for a moment Elliot felt profoundly disappointed. This had to be some kind of mistake. Or one of Pedro's jokes fallen flat. There was nothing here anyone would pay, much less kill for. It was harmless. Sweet. Then it zoomed in and suddenly, Elliot gasped and Margie leaned forward, peering through her glasses.

"Is that?" she asked.

"It is," Elliot answered.

It was Pedro. And with him was Chet Hunter.

After that, neither said anything; they watched them make love, and it did seem loving. Elliot couldn't help but feel moved. Then, at one point, Pedro rolled on top of Chet and there was a good look at a dark marking on Pedro's tanned and muscled back.

"Freeze!" he yelled, like a TV cop. Margie jumped and hit a button.

"Jeez, you scared me."

"Sorry. Can you get that clearer? His back?"

She made some adjustments. And there on his back was a tattoo, a winged skull between the blades. Elliot sighed.

"Okay, let it play."

Afterward, the lovers lay in each other's arms. Then while Chet lit a cigarette, Pedro got up and approached the camera. He pulled a bottle of champagne from a fridge and then grabbed a curtain that hung just out of frame and drew it closed. But just before the view from the balcony was obscured, and with his back to Chet, he quickly but most definitely winked right at the camera. Elliot almost felt as if it were meant for him but, of course, that was impossible. Then Pedro shut the curtain, cutting off the light. The screen went dark and the video ended, switching back to static.

Elliot and Margie sat motionless, watching the snow on the screen and for a moment he flashed back to his dad. He felt lost in the cloud of secrets. But there was something there, too, a flicker of understanding in all the distortion. Then Margie spoke.

"Damn," she said. "That was hot."

"Can we go back?" he asked.

"Want to run it again?" she asked. "Me, too."

"No, just the end."

She leaned forward and reversed it. The curtains parted, Pedro walked backward.

"Stop," Elliot said. "Now go forward."

"Yes, sir."

"Slowly . . . please."

She clicked forward, frame by frame. Pedro, like one of the fake ghosts in his own bogus videos, inched forward, a messenger from beyond. He winked.

"He's definitely winking at us," Margie said, freezing it.

"Yeah, so he knows the camera is there. And maybe Chet doesn't?" Elliot said. "Now go super slow."

The curtains stuttered shut. And then, as the internal light was cut, for a frame or two, a fraction of a second, another dim, translucent image appeared.

"See? That's it. Stop," Elliot said, leaning forward. "What's that?"

"It's a reflection," Margie said, tapping the screen with a nail. "They must have been shooting through the sliding glass door."

"Right," Elliot said, seeing it now. "It's the camera."

"And the cameraman," Margie added.

So it was, the reflection of a video camera and a silhouette behind it.

"Can you enlarge that?" he asked.

She got to work, nails clattering, as she zoomed in and opened up. Finally a figure appeared, slightly smeared, as if seen through dirty glass, but nevertheless he knew. It was a young woman with long straight blonde hair. It was Christine.

They stared together at the frozen, blurry image.

"Is that . . . ?" Margie asked, staring close. After all, she had spent hours laboring over her pictures.

"Crystal Waters, back to her original self. Her real name is Christine Smith."

"And you think she was the reason for all of this trouble?" Margie asked. She sounded impressed.

"More than the reason," Elliot said. Then, as if to shut off the conversation, he reached out and ejected the tape.

"So what will you do now?" she asked, standing and smoothing her skirt and hair as she saw her own reflection in the now-dead screen.

He stood, too, and stared at the tape in his hand for a moment, lost in thought. He drew a cigarette from the pack in his shirt pocket and put it in his mouth.

"What I'd really like to do is smoke," he said. Then he picked up the phone, hitting 9 for an outside line. He dialed, letting the unlit cigarette dangle from his lip. "Hey, Christine, it's me. I'm back . . . Yeah, he's okay, thanks. Back to his old self, for better or worse. But listen . . . I've got the tape." He paused, as Margie watched him, the two of them together in the empty office. "We need to talk," he said. "I'll come to you, give me an hour or so. Don't worry. It's someplace very safe." He hung up and looked at Margie, holding up the tape. "Can you think of anyplace close by and very safe?"

In the elevator, going back down, Margie eyed him suspiciously. "I don't like your plan. It's risky. Actually it's borderline stupid."

"I'm safe as long as I have the tape," he said, the unlit smoke still jiggling on his mouth. "And in twenty-four hours, it won't matter anyway."

"Well, if you do survive, and you ever make it up to Seattle, look me up."

"I will," Elliot said.

"No, you won't," she said, "but it's probably for the best. I'm really getting the message now that you are terrible boyfriend material."

"I kind of thought you were gay."

"I kind of am, usually." She shrugged. "People are complex."

"I'm learning that."

"And most men are creeps. You're mixed-up and clueless and inconsiderate and emotionally stunted, but not a creep."

"Thanks, I think." The elevator landed with a ding.

"And you're cute, in a lovable loser kind of way."

"Really?" Elliot smiled for the first time in a while as he followed her out. "You think I'm cute?"

She laughed, and when they got outside, she took the cigarette from his mouth and, out of nowhere, reached up and kissed him, hard. He stared back, stunned.

"That was for good luck," she said, her lipstick smeared. She lit the cigarette, cupping it against the wind. Then she slid it back between his red-stained lips. She turned and went, waving a few fingers. "So long, loser."

"Bye-bye, winner," he called after her, taking a deep drag and letting out the smoke.

32

Elliot had the taxi drop him around the block and snuck into his yard through the back yet again, then peeked in his own window before going inside. The place was undisturbed, or only as disturbed as he'd left it. He went straight for the gun. There it was, sleeping safely in his clean underwear, a pair of which he changed into after a quick shower—though he felt both silly and exposed trooping back and forth to the house with the weapon in his robe. Still, he wanted to be clean and correct for his big scene. Then he drove up to Christine's.

She buzzed him through the gate and he parked, then walked up toward the house. She was waiting on the deck, cantilevered out over a steep, densely grown hillside and revealing the glittering city below. She wore her white silk slip dress, her hair was loose, and her feet were bare. The picture of innocence. She rushed up, grabbing his hands in hers.

"How's your father? Is he really okay?"

Elliot nodded. "He's fine, like I said. Thank you."

"Do you have the tape?"

"Not with me."

"But you watched it," she said, not a question, a statement, and when he nodded again, she dropped his hands. "It's not what you think . . ." she said, and he laughed.

"That's for sure."

She scowled. "At least let me explain."

"That's why I'm here," he said.

She took a deep breath and looked out at the dark landscape.

"I'm waiting."

"That was back when Pedro and I were roommates. I was stripping, dating Vic, and Pedro was working with Melody. Well, we both were."

"You were his camera assistant then, instead of me."

She shrugged. "We switched off. As Melody met new prospects or people came to her ministry, we'd find ways to get to know them, party, or hook up, or whatever, and then feed their info back to Melody to use in her sessions. Tape it if we could. Some just got drunk and confessed private things, stuff from childhood or whatever. Some had drug issues. And some, we, you know . . ."

"Had sex with."

She nodded. "I'm not proud of it."

He laughed. "Why would you be?"

"Pedro was, in a way. He thought it was all a lark, one of his pranks, you know? Just like when we were kids, remember?" She started to get misty, and Elliot picked up the thread.

"So Melody would have Zona suddenly reveal these secrets, which made the suckers into believers," he suggested. "But also gave her some nifty blackmail just in case."

Christine nodded. "She was subtle about it, of course, but the more successful the client was, the more they had to lose if their secret was exposed so the more generous they were with donations and helping build the hype."

"Not to mention what you were getting on the side, from selling Vic the copies you made."

"No, that was Pedro."

"Please. How? Pedro didn't know Vic. You were his girlfriend."

"Never. But okay. Yeah. After I met Vic, at the club, I started selling him copies of just a few of the clients. It couldn't be anything that would blow up Melody's thing, so he didn't expose them, but just used them for leverage with people, or sometimes, when a scandal broke, he'd be first with the news."

"Like with the congressman," Elliot said.

"Yeah. That should have been a clue that Pedro was getting more political about it. But Vic was after the guy, and offered a big bounty, so . . ." She shrugged. "It was a hustle, and we were hustlers. But we were just small-time. Not hurting anyone, or at least not anyone who wasn't a raging asshole. Not really. Until . . ."

"Until Chet came along."

She nodded. "He was different. Really fell for Pedro. So his people convinced him to seek spiritual counseling and Melody came up with a suggestion."

"That she find a nice girl for him to marry. A beard."

"Right. Someone from the ministry, you know, from within the community."

"It was your golden opportunity, wasn't it? The part of a lifetime. And a real step up for Melody too. That was all part of the deal, right? She'd perform the wedding, Chet and his pals would endorse her books and lectures and even the stupid tapes I was duping back in the tape mine. And behind closed doors, Chet could still be with Pedro. Happily ever after for everybody."

Christine threw her hands up. "Why not? My acting career was going nowhere, Chet was sweet, we all helped each other out."

"But now you had to get away from Vic. You couldn't be Chet's wife if you were still Crystal. You had to be Christine again, the girl next door."

She turned to him. "I was afraid of him. Afraid of what he'd do if I left."

"I don't think so." Elliot shook his head. "I think he fell for you. I think he saw you as a replacement for his wife, his new partner in crime and love. I think you had him wrapped around your little finger and he'd never use anything against you. Even after you dumped him, he was still looking out for you, trying to protect you. Even from me. He knew you were the one who had the tape all along. I think he really gave back or destroyed whatever he had, and you believed him. Until the blackmail threats showed up, targeting Chet, and you decided he must have betrayed you. That's where I came in." Now Elliot smiled. "That was lucky, wasn't it? An old friend working there? Except it wasn't luck. You told Vic to hire me."

"I wanted to help you. I told you, I always had feelings for you."

"Sure, maybe. Or maybe you were just playing the long game. Seeing how useful it could be to have another potential sucker on the inside. But you didn't realize it was Pedro all along. He was the loose cannon. The one you couldn't control."

"He was jealous. He thought of us as three-way partners, Melody, him, and me. But as she got bigger and I got Chet . . ."

"He saw you both making millions, ascending into royalty, while he got the tapes and the same old scams and a secret part-time relationship. So what happened, he started milking you? Letting you think it was Vic?"

She nodded. "He was clever. I told Chet about the blackmail, I had to, but we both thought it was Vic, taking revenge. And, of course, Pedro was the one I sent to deliver the payoff money I got from Chet. But he was also the one person who could tell Chet I had been in on it, so I had to keep him happy too. Finally he suggested using you, and we set up the break-in."

"But that was all just part of Pedro's plan. Because he didn't really care about money anymore, did he? He wasn't going to live to spend it."

She nodded. "He called me after you two broke into the safe. He told me he'd taken all Vic's files and that he was going to publish it all, including the tape with him and Chet. He said that we'd be okay, we'd still be rich no matter what, but that there was a bigger cause, justice for all the lives being ruined or lost. Hope for the future. He said it was too late for him, but that he was okay with it. He said that was a cause worth dying for."

"But you couldn't wait for him to die from AIDS. You had to kill him that night."

"What?" She shuddered, jolting upright. She backed away from him, staring in horror. "What do you mean? Vic killed him. You know that. You know what he's like."

"Yeah, I do. He's a pig. And a gangster. And a rich asshole. But I just don't figure him as a killer. Not over this. It's true, Vic sees himself as an outlaw, but he's sentimental about it. Like a pirate king." Elliot had to laugh. "He's a romantic, in his own totally depraved way. An idealist. Actually he's a lot like Pedro." He pointed a finger at Christine. "But not you. You are a stone-cold realist, aren't you? You had to be. You do what you need to do to survive. Lie, cheat, manipulate. Seduce who you need to. Or make them feel sorry for you. Or kill them. That's why you got me here tonight. To kill me for the tape." Elliot pulled the gun from the back of his waistband. "But this time you're the one taking the fall."

Christine gaped at him, her eyes wide on the gun and genuine fear on her face. "I . . . no . . . kill you? That's crazy. I was going to . . . here. Look." She turned toward the house but he waved the pistol.

"Careful!"

She put her hands up. "Please. Just let me . . ." She pressed an intercom on the wall and spoke into it. "Chet, honey? Could you step out here . . ." She looked at Elliot and then added "Very carefully."

The curtains over the dark interior parted and Chet came out, hands up, holding a chunky manila envelope. He was in white jeans and a black T-shirt, white espadrilles, a Rolex, and a gold cross. He set the envelope down on the table.

"Here," he said, clearly petrified, and stepped back.

"I . . ." Christine began. "We . . . were going to offer you this."

Elliot opened the envelope and dumped it with one hand, keeping the gun on them. A huge lump of cash plopped out, bundled with rubber bands. Elliot took the bands off and rifled through. It was all hundreds.

"That's fifty thousand," Chet said. "It's just a down payment. We can arrange a job, writing maybe, or doing PR."

Elliot grabbed the money and threw it, as hard as he could, into the darkness. He saw the bills flutter away. They gasped.

"You think I'd take blood money?" he shouted now. "Make myself an accessory to murder? How many now? At least three?"

"Murder?" Chet yelled, too loud, then swallowed hard, looking around. His eyes were big.

"Three?" Christine yelled, seeming genuinely startled, and for the first time, Elliot felt a twinge of doubt about his plan. "What three?"

"Of course," he sneered. "How much of a fool do you think I am? I know Farah didn't kill herself. Why would she? She was happy. All she wanted was money. That's why she wrote me that note, canceling our meeting. Because she thought you were paying her off."

"We did pay her off," Christine said. "Chet had Hank do it."

"But you had to be sure," Elliot said. "So you had her killed." He waved the gun for emphasis and they squirmed, bending in place. "I saw the biker outside! And then Joe. He was killed because he had my jacket on. That was supposed to be me."

"What jacket?" Chet asked now, seeming to lose the thread, addressing Christine and letting his hands droop to his sides.

"What biker?" she responded.

"Casey Bucks," Elliot said. "The stuntwoman you two hired."

"Casey Bucks!" Chet blurted. "Wait. I know Casey." He nodded, explaining to them both. "Sure. She doubled for my costar in *The Eliminator* and *Eliminator III—Hard Justice*. She wasn't in *II* because my costar in that one, Nancy Newsome, was Black, but I never personally hired her to do anything." He looked at Elliot. "I swear."

Elliot stared, as a terrible feeling crept into his belly. He believed him. His total distress and confusion were genuine. He wasn't that good of an actor. No one was. Then he heard a movement from behind, but it was too late. He felt something hard and cold in his back.

"He's right," Jerry Sumack said, pressing a gun between Elliot's shoulder blades. "I hired her. I hire everyone. I'm the boss. Now give me the gun."

33

They took Sumack's car. Christine drove, with Chet sitting beside her, safety belt tight and staring into the rearview mirror at Elliot and Jerry, who casually pressed his own gun into Elliot's stomach, while holding Elliot's in his left.

"Drive carefully," he told Christine. "No sudden moves. One bump in the road and my gun could accidentally discharge."

Elliot said nothing. He was afraid of moving, speaking, even breathing. He had one card left, but he didn't know how to play it. Jerry sighed.

"It's too bad you're such a damned idiot," he told Elliot. "Everything could have worked out fine. Farah was a misstep, I admit. Casey turned out to be a bit over the top. She was just supposed to scare her. But she squeezed too hard, and Farah choked to death, so she made it look like a hanging." He shrugged. "But still, everyone bought the tragic suicide of a fallen porn starlet. It's classic Hollywood. And Dejavu's people were happy. Thanks to Joe getting shot, Dejavu's a gangster-rap hero. His sales went through the roof. I should know, my company owns his label. There is already a new album in the works. It's called *My Name on Your Bullet*. Pretty good, right? What do you think will happen if it comes out that a very white woman shot him by mistake?"

"What about Hank?" Elliot asked.

Sumack nodded ruefully and gestured at Chet and Christine. "That was these two, sticking their noses in, getting Hank involved. Figures, a frightened actor runs to his agent for help, not to me. And once Hank was connected to all the parties, it was inevitable he'd figure it out. You don't get cars and houses and wives like that without a nose for a deal.

"As for your savior, Vic." He stared close into Elliot's eyes. "You think Vic cared about being the prime suspect? He's got the smartest lawyers in town. He knew the cops were never going to prove he killed anyone. There was zero evidence. But the rumors? They'd only increase his power. Think how scared anyone will be to cross him now. He's sitting pretty in that golden wheelchair. Even your own parents were going to win big."

"You were never going to make that movie," Elliot said. "It was just a way to control me. Buy me off."

"I might have. Why not? It's a good story. The world needs heroes, like your father. That's what I am."

"A hero?"

"A father. Protecting my family. My children. Like Chet." He looked up into Chet's eyes in the rearview. "No offense, you know I love you, but you're a movie star, kid. You can't even do your own grocery shopping, much less plan a murder." He turned back to Elliot. "So, he's a child, but he's a golden child. Worth a billion dollars. A whole industry, hundreds of jobs. *Eliminator III* is projected to be the biggest opening weekend ever. You think I'm going to let anything or anyone destroy that?"

They had arrived at Sumack Manor just before dawn. The gate opened, but this time no servants appeared, not even security. "Drive up to the house," he told Christine, who nodded stiffly. "I gave everyone the night off," he told Elliot. "Keeps things simpler, fewer people to pay off or scare. Though it does mean disposing of your corpse myself. I think the fire pit will do nicely. Finally have a reason to use that thing. Now let's get out."

"Jerry, please . . ." Christine said, parking in front of the main house. Chet twisted his head around, frantically. Sumack prodded Elliot, who opened the door.

"Take it nice and slow."

Elliot got out very carefully, hands up. Chet and Christine followed, watching in amazed horror.

"Sorry, kids," Jerry said. "I know you'd prefer not to know about any of this. But I guess you have to grow up some time. This is what it takes to keep all this safe. But don't blame me. It's Elliot's own fault." Sumack shook his head, genuinely annoyed. "Why couldn't you just drop it?"

"Because you killed my friend."

"He was going to die anyway, sooner or later."

"So are we all."

"Yes, well, you just joined the sooner club. Much sooner." He prodded them along the path into the garden. The sound of birdsong filled the space around them and the dark air seemed charged with particles of light, trees and shrubs and flowers emerging from the shadows though no sun was visible yet. They stood on the open patio where the auction had been held. "I think this is a good spot, don't you?" he asked, pointing with his gun and holding Elliot's in his left. "I can hose off the blood. Or maybe it's better on the grass."

"Wait," Elliot said, trying to keep his voice from cracking. "What about the tape? Don't you want to know what happened to it?"

"If you want to tell me."

Elliot played his last card. He even managed a defiant grin, though it came out crooked, more of a bitter grimace. "I put it in Vic's safe."

Christine and Chet gasped, but Sumack stayed stony.

"By morning, they'll find it," Elliot told him. "And the world will know. Including the cops. It's over, Sumack. The whole story will come out now."

Sumack sighed irritably. He yelled over his shoulder into the house. "Viv? Viv, honey?" There was a gap of silence. Christine and Chet both looked from Sumack to Elliot, who looked from them to the gun, all of their eyes rolling desperately in silent conversation. "Hey, Viv!" Sumack shouted.

"Yes?" finally came a faint reply.

"Bring me that package? The one on my desk."

There was a tense moment while they waited, Sumack tapping his foot. Then the curtains parted and Vivian emerged. She was in a green silk dressing gown, barefoot, her hair undone. She looked ghostly. Smooth and perfect and cold as marble, except for the dark puffy circles under her eyes. She held a manila envelope. "Is this it?"

"Thanks, my love," he said, backing over and taking it. Carefully, he lay Elliot's gun down on the glass dining table, making sure it was behind him and out of Elliot's reach, then opened the clasp on the envelope and pulled out the tape. "Here we go," he said, holding it up. "Is this the tape you were referring to?"

It was. Something in Elliot sank, as if his spirit were collapsing. He was going to die. He thought about begging, but knew it would never work. He thought about running, dashing across the lawn and trying to outrace a bullet. He thought about rushing the gun and glared beseechingly at Chet, hoping for some action hero moves. Chet stared back, looking stricken. Not even a clever catchphrase.

"So much trouble over this stupid tape," Sumack said, turning it in his hand. "Then out of nowhere, someone dropped it off in the middle of the night. The sound of the car engine woke us up. Anyway, it woke me. Viv was awake already, weren't you? Watching TV." He glanced over, but she was impassive, staring into space. "Viv watches a lot of late night TV. Especially when her own movies are on, don't you, babe?" He snarled at Elliot, pointing the gun. "I know you fucked her by the way."

Elliot shook his head. "I didn't."

"Almost," he spat out, moving in on Elliot. "You wanted to. She told me. She tells me everything, eventually, when she's high enough. Not that I mind her fucking someone, mind you, but I decide. I tell her who to fuck and when." Elliot was staring into the mouth of the muzzle now, watching it tremble in Sumack's hand. Behind him the first rays of dawn were beaming over the hills. "If I wanted to I could make you two fuck right now, here on the lawn, before I put you down like a stray mutt. She'll do it if I say." He smiled sadly. "Not that you're missing much to be honest. She just lies there like a corpse. I don't think she has any feelings left." He glanced over at her. "Do you, babe?" There was no reaction. "Never mind then." He tossed the tape at Elliot's feet. "Here. I'll burn it with your body and sprinkle the ashes in the ocean. Maybe have Melody say a prayer." He grinned, pointing the gun at Elliot's head. "Don't worry though, there is no such thing as death, is there? You should know that better than any of us by now. Death is an illusion. All is love."

Elliot shut his eyes and, feeling the gun press against his forehead, something in his mind opened, as if the gun muzzle had released it, turning the lock: a fragile hope went up, like one of the million tiny chattering birds all around him, and reached toward the sun rising beyond his lids, a slight, slender, silly, stupid hope that maybe that was true after all, maybe love went on forever and death was just a blink, a flash, a jump cut, and on the other side, there we'd be, made whole again, with everything lost or forsaken restored, with all mysteries solved and all suffering at an end. It was, he supposed, a prayer. His first and last, spoken wordlessly into silence, from nothing to nothing, as he prepared to return to the nothing from which he'd come. Then he heard a shot.

He jumped, hearing the blast, and stumbled back, even thinking, for a mad moment, that he'd been shot, that he was actually dead or dying. Then his eyes popped open and there was Vivian, holding his gun, and standing over Sumack, who was bleeding out into the lawn.

"Vivian . . ." Elliot said, surprised at his own voice, which was a ragged whisper.

She pointed the gun at him, and his hands went up.

"Run," she said. She swept the gun toward Christine and Chet, who were staring in shock. "Run!" she told them. "All of you, run and keep running. Don't look back."

"Vivian, please," Christine said, stepping forward, hand out. "Let me . . ." But Vivian swung the pistol up and fired a shot into the air.

"Run!" she screamed, waving the gun wildly. "Run and don't look back."

So they ran. All three took off, though Chet had the presence of mind to scoop up the tape as they passed by. And as they darted frantically through the trees, Elliot couldn't help but notice Christine and Chet were holding hands, instinctively grasping each other, like Hansel and Gretel.

Christine drove fast, as if they were still being chased, while Chet called the lawyer, who met them at their house, and helped them all get their story straight before taking them to the police one last time. Before they left, Chet burned the tape in the barbecue. Elliot saw his lips moving, as if in silent prayer, and tears spilling over his cheeks. Then again it might have been the acrid fumes from the burning plastic stinging his eyes.

34

Sergeant Anderson was in a black suit, which fitted his somber tone. Detective Santos stood, nodding respectfully, in a white suit, her hands clasped at her waist, as Elliot, Chet, and Christine found themselves back in the VIP interview room, accompanied, of course, by Jeffers.

"It is," Anderson said, "my sad duty to inform you that, after the call that you made to 911 this morning, officers arrived on the scene to find Mr. Sumack dead by gunshot and Ms. De Fay also dead, of an apparent overdose."

"Oh my gosh . . ." Chet rasped. Christine started to weep and he put his arms around her. Elliot stared, blankly.

"Murder-suicide," Santos said, pushing a box of tissues across the table.

"From the condition of the body," Anderson told them, "it looks like she was a chronic drug user and, we suspect, the victim of long-term abuse."

Santos sighed. "Tragic."

Anderson nodded. "Yes. You have our sympathies. She was a great talent."

Santos reached for a tissue. "A true goddess," she said and wiped her eyes. Anderson reached over and patted her on the back.

It was not until Jeffers dropped them off back at the house in Laurel Canyon that he and Christine had a chance to speak alone. She walked him to his car, while Chet and Jeffers discreetly went inside, no doubt to continue dealing with the fallout, which they'd been discussing on the ride home—agents and publicists had to be called, a press release prepared. The studio had been in touch, of course. The board of directors of the giant multinational corporation that owned it had held an emergency meeting and, as if a head of state had died, an acting CEO had been appointed. He called with his condolences and assured Chet that the movie would premier as planned. That's what Sumack would have wanted, after all. He even hinted, tactfully, that the added publicity would push them into the stratosphere.

It had only been hours since that last confrontation on her deck, but immediately, Elliot could feel, standing with Christine in the driveway, everything was different between them. They were no longer lovers. Christine now stood, hands at her sides, and looked him frankly in the eye.

"I could say I'm sorry," she told him. "If that will help any."

Elliot shook his head. "It won't."

"What about thank you?"

Elliot shrugged.

"You know, you really did save me," she said. "Even if it was by accident and it was all lies."

Elliot nodded. "You're welcome," he said, and turned to go.

"Wait," she said. He looked back. "I wanted to tell you that, the things I said, you know, some of it was true. The feelings, about you, about us. They were true." Her hand fluttered as if trying to grasp something fleeting, or like a bird trying to escape a trap, but she stayed put. "I just wanted you to know that."

"I believe you," Elliot said, and he did.

"And I really did love Pedro. He was my best and oldest . . . well, really, my only friend. Except for you." She took a big breath, swallowing her rising emotions. There were tears in her eyes. "And he really was so happy to find you again. He told me, more than once. He loved you. A lot."

Now Elliot smiled. "Yes. I know. But thanks for telling me."

"Chrissy!" It was Chet, calling from the door. "Sorry, but Jeffers needs us both." Christine shrugged at Elliot, who waved and got in his car, and she stood still and watched, finally blowing a kiss as he backed out, but by then his head was turned away.

Elliot reversed out of the driveway, and as the gate automatically closed behind him, he shifted into drive and started down the hill. Around the first turn, he saw, on his right, the steep overgrown hillside overlooked by the deck where he and Christine had been arguing the night before. Abruptly, he pulled over, and parked on the dirt beside the road. He got out and made his way carefully up the hill, fighting brambles and tripping over roots, sliding in the loose dirt and scrambling for hand- and footholds as he searched for the money he had thrown into the darkness. Why did he need to be so fucking dramatic? Well, it had felt right at the time. Now he was unemployed and broke again. But after an hour of searching, he'd managed to locate only half a single bill, torn and hanging from a thorn on what looked like a wild rosebush, fluttering slightly in the breeze. The rest had flown away. Or been gathered by other travelers. Or been stolen by birds and woven into their nests.

Exhausted, he arrived home, only to be waylaid by his roomies, who stepped out of the door as if they'd been waiting, as soon as he parked.

"There you are," Sequoia called, bouncing over. She hugged him tightly, which caused him to awkwardly freeze. They'd never had any physical contact. She smelled like priceless shampoo. "We were so worried."

"Worried?"

Area rubbed his back. "All that murder stuff. It's so scary. And you were gone all night."

Feather smiled. "We saw it on the news. Did Vivian De Fay really shoot Jerry Sumack execution-style right in front of you? Then light his body on fire?"

"We heard he kept her drugged up and made her sleep in a cage," Area added.

"You guys," Sequoia scolded. "He can't discuss it. He might have to testify in open court, right?"

"Not really," Elliot said, frowning. "I hope not."

"Chet and his fiancée looked so sweet together," Area said. "Remember Joe's party in the Hills? She was there!"

"There's no picture of me, is there?" Elliot asked, concerned.

"No. You're just named as their close associate."

"You know," Area said, brightening, "our friend Madrid just bought the cutest house in Nichols Canyon. She's having a housewarming tonight. You should come."

"She's so talented," Feather chimed in. "A model and actress. And a sheet metal sculptor. You'd love her."

"Totally," Sequoia agreed. "It's just casual so maybe pick up some flowers. Or a nice bottle of wine."

Behind her, the Hummer limo pulled in, long as the yard. The front passenger door opened and Moishe stepped out. He stared at Elliot for a moment, then opened the rear door, and just stood there, waiting.

"Sure, some wine," Elliot agreed, dismissing the idea immediately. He loped across the lawn, as Moishe nodded once then stepped aside. Elliot took a breath and climbed in.

"Hey, kid," Vic growled as Elliot settled in on the seat beside him, really more like a big leather couch. Moishe climbed aboard and shut the door, sitting on the seat across from them. Vic smiled. "I noticed you stopped by the office."

Elliot nodded. "I have to say I was shocked that you returned my gift. I thought for sure you'd be the one guy brave enough to publish it."

Vic shrugged. "I don't know about brave. It's true, I make a lot of money stirring up trouble. And as a patriot, I'm not afraid to open my mouth and speak up." He pointed a fat jeweled finger. "But I survive by knowing when to keep my mouth shut." He sighed, dropping his hand like an unused weapon. "That Sumack business, it sorted itself out in the end. And certain people, the right certain people, they know I did the right thing. There's no reason to hurt anyone else."

"And Christine?" Elliot asked.

He sighed again, deeper. "True," he nodded, "I let a girl make a schmuck out of me. So did you. But everybody is a schmuck sometime. That's love." He tapped his vagina pendant. "That's why I wear this, to remind me. People think we're foolish, filling magazines with pussies and cocks, but that's what makes the world go round, isn't it, one way or the other? Every story, including this one. There's always a pussy or a cock behind it all. You should have learned that much, working for me."

"So you let it go. A wedding gift for her and Chet."

Now Vic grinned. "God bless them. Anyway, my mother warned me not to fall for a shiksa. Didn't yours?"

Elliot laughed at this. Moishe grunted gently. Vic said, "Give him the envelope," and Moishe reached into his inner jacket pocket for an unsealed envelope embossed with the *Raunchy* logo. Elliot looked inside.

"That is a business-class ticket to New York," Vic said. "One-way."

"Is this my punishment or my reward?" Elliot asked.

"A little of both," Vic said. "Let's just say, there's no hard feelings, but maybe, by general consent, your sojourn in LA is at an end. Face it. You were always just a visitor here, a tourist passing through. Now it's time to go home. Let this trip to Hollywood be a pleasant memory that you keep to yourself and quickly forget. "

Elliot nodded. "Thanks."

"You're not a bad writer, though, I'll give you that. If you need a job in New York, I can put a call in to Al Goldstein at *Screw*. He's always looking for talent."

"That's okay," Elliot said. "I think I've done my time in porn."

"Maybe so," Vic said. "But remember, it's cold and lonely at the top. There's always room at the bottom. And it's warmer too."

On cue, Moishe opened the door and got out, holding it for Elliot, who took the hint and climbed down into the street. But before getting back in, the giant leaned down and held out a massive hand. Elliot shook it, or rather laid his hand across a palm that was like a baseball mitt. The handshake was shockingly gentle.

"It's a nice day, isn't it?" Elliot asked. "You can smell spring in the air."

"All I smell is dog shit," Elliot's father declared as they made their way to a bench. They were in a playground, mostly concrete and iron fencing and broken glass, but there were kids climbing and screeching on the monkey bars and soft green buds swelling the tips of the branches on the few spindly trees. "They got a law now, you got to pick up after your dog, but no one cares. Let the children play in it. You know, if I was mayor, I'd give them a choice when they get caught, ten-thousand-dollar fine or eat it, live on TV. Then it would be a hit show too."

"You got my vote, Dad," Elliot said. "Watch your step." He rested a hand on his father's arm, not really helping him, just there.

"You know, back in Germany, before the war," he went on, "the streets were spotless. You could eat lunch off the sidewalk."

"Oh yeah? Remind me. How did that work out again?"

His dad half grumbled, half chuckled as they settled on the bench. The cries of the kids carried on the breeze. A few pigeons pecked around. His Dad stared murderously at a young woman with a poodle until she compliantly pulled out a plastic bag and picked up its tiny turd.

"So your mother says you're applying to Columbia for grad school. To be an English professor."

Elliot nodded. "Yeah, I'm applying to a few places. We'll see what happens."

"I think it's a smart move."

"Really?" Elliot was shocked. He didn't recall his father ever approving any decision of his, much less calling it smart.

"Look, I'm no prude like those crazy book-burning freaks, but let's face it. The porn thing was a dead end. How much money are people honestly going to spend just looking at naked pictures? Or movies of sex?" He waved it off. "You seen one, you seen them all. There's no future in it." He raised a finger. "But an English professor? Teaching in a college? There will always be a demand for that. Go ahead. Get a PhD. Borrow more if you have to. You'll never have any trouble finding a job."

"Thanks, Dad," Elliot said, brightening.

His dad grunted.

"You know," Elliot said, "I'm sorry that movie about you and your life in the war never happened." Elliot flashed back to his father in the hospital bed, suddenly grasping him with the eyes of a child and letting Elliot see the terrified child he had once been.

"With that meshuggener producer whose own wife blew his head off?" His father shrugged. "Okay, that new movie he made, with the motorcycle jumping over the fire? That was pretty good, and your mother loves Chet Hunter, but we're better off not doing business with a nut like that." He brushed it off like a crumb. "It was good luck it didn't happen. Anyway, who cares about fame?"

"Mom does. She's still upset about it. She says the world should know you were a hero."

"Hero, shmero. All that matters is that you and I both know the truth, right?" And now, his father smiled, almost shyly, showing a few gold and brown teeth.

"That's right," Elliot said, smiling back. "We know the truth."

ACKNOWLEDGEMENTS

I would like to express my deep gratitude to my editor and mentor Otto Penzler for our long collaboration and to everyone at Mysterious Press, especially to Luisa Smith for her devoted and invaluable work on this book, to Charles Perry for believing in this project and for an awesome cover, and to Will Luckman and Julia O'Connell for all their tireless efforts. I would also like to thank my wonderful agent and friend Doug Stewart for all his help and support over these years and for everyone at Sterling Lord Literistic, especially Danielle Bukowski, Silvia Molnar, and Tyler Monson. I want to extend a special thanks to the friends who read and in some cases re-read this book during its long incubation, particularly William Fitch, Gregg Horowitz, Aaron Peck and Eng Sengsavang. As always I am grateful to my family for all of their infinite love, constant support, and mysterious faith in me. And I would like to send out my love, prayers, and solidarity to everyone in my former home of Los Angeles. This book is for you.